THE QUEST
OF THE
SINGULAR
KEEPERS

LIGHTNING BRAIN SERIES BOOK EIGHT

A NOVEL BY

CLIFF RATZA

The Quest of the Singular Keepers
A Novel

Cliff Ratza

ISBN: 978-1-967375-98-1 (Paperback)
ISBN: 978-1-967375-99-8 (E-book)

Library of Congress Control Number: 2025922095

Printed in the United States of America

Published by:

info@thequippyquill.com
(302) 295-2278

About the Book

The Quest of the Singular Keepers – our third book in the Keepers Series – starts in Washington DC at the home of the Irani-Electra duo as Indira the Singularity approves what Irani is planning to announce on 2162's Monday after Thanksgiving to America's President, Genesee Huston.

And when Irani does, the President agrees with her decision to resign from the Secretary of Health and Human Services post that she has held for nearly two years. Irani has delivered everything promised and plans to help the President via consulting assignments given to siblings Eve and Nari, both of whom have benefited from Irani's tutoring, especially Eve, who has fully recovered from a year-ago gunshot attack that only Indira could prevent from becoming fatal. World climates have settled down, and Electra's other clone children and close friends are all pointed in the right direction.

But troubles soon intrude and continue escalating in both personal and professional worlds, forcing multiple changes in plans that are necessary to help loved ones and existential causes alike. Irani navigates a risky course but always follows Electra's expanding empathy that puts friends and family ahead of everything else, and her sui generis brilliance keeps enemies and risks at bay. So, follow the action-adventure trail starting on page one and leading all the way to another unguessable ending.

The book's theme should resonate with all of us: much more than half the meaning of life is found in our relationships with the people we care about. Reaching out to help gives a reward greater than what we put in. And we can do this while balancing our own wishes if we use a pragmatic, proactive philosophy.

Readers should enjoy the book on whatever level they wish:

- Gripping action-packed thriller
- Glimpses into a plausible near-term future
- Insights for dealing with the "human condition"
- Illustrative worldview philosophy
- Fast-paced, suspense-filled, emotive narrative and imagery
- Introduction to topics every reader wants to know
- Interesting talking points going beyond sound-bites

So, get ready to enjoy what you are about to read as our nuanced characters deal with life's contingencies. And just like for each of us, their actions might not always yield immediate success. But perhaps there is one outcome we can guarantee: your reading pleasure here and in upcoming books in the series.

Main Characters

- Electra Kittner (aka Irani Ramani or Alisha and sometimes referred to as the Irani-Electra duo or the Electra-Irani-Alisha trio)

- Indira (the Singularity) and Jason (the sub-Singularity)

- Eve and Alonzo Cortez Identical Twins but unaware they are Electra's clone children Nari and Nila Bose Identical Twins but unaware they are Electra's clone children Genesee Huston President of the United States

- Sabrina Ricardo

- Howard Chen Vice President of the United States

- Steven Plannert Professor at George Washington University (GWU) Odell Boyken

- Wanda Keita

- Tiana (Tea) Diamond Jonathan Segal Monet Banda Darla Tinibu Sanjay Kumar Jiang (Jan) Brewer Yang Lee

- Rick (RT) Tabasko Parson (PH) Holsum Lucian (Mr. LP) Perteau Kiara and Tyrone Mensah

- Bob and Marlene Rodenbaugh Amahl and Zara Karim

- Other Characters

- Trent Booker

- Xinqian (Xing) Hung "Gang of Three Plus One" Leader

- Congressman Newton (Newt aka Chuck) Kinslinger (Speaker of House) Wen (Wendy) Tong

- Indy-Minor and Jason-Minor (aka Indy-M and Jason-M) Androids

Dedication

I am eternally grateful to my parents, Clyde and Betty Ratza, for all they gave and did for me. Mother was the reader par excellence, and I believe she would have enjoyed reading and sharing my novels with Father, so I always begin book dedications by mentioning my "Noble Pair."

I also thank my sister, Claudia, for sharing and showing me the beauty of prose and poetry. Thanks also to my literary agent, Robert Williams and his entire Quippy Quill Production Team. Their collective efforts brought to life this first book in its sequel series.

The Quest of the Singular Keepers is also dedicated to readers looking for a continuing action-adventure saga that shows a condition all of us share: we are always becoming as we adjust to events that may carry us away from our wishes. Though the Irani-Electra duo often exceeds "Mere Humanity," a poem from Indira captures the timeless essence of "becoming."

The Noble Pair

We and Nature are but the same,
When scanned at nanoscopic view.
But varying facets begin taking hold,
When Humanity's cachet begins showing through.

Personas combine to a singular whole,
Noble yet flawed and partitioned we be.
We try to command but often we fail,
Body Mind and Emotion they total to three.

Always becoming what we're striving for,
Able to grasp only part of the sum.
Then changes sweep in and we're carried away,
Our journey continues toward what will become.

The Golden Philosophers knew this too well,
And it's true through all time as the calendars tell.

I hope my latest novel keeps you fully engaged to the very end as it shows our characters always striving to become better. Thank you for joining their journey.

Contents

Chapter 1
November 2162

"Singular Discussions"

"Of course, I understand your reasoning and commend your decision – cognitively as well as sympathetically and empathetically. I am also pleased that you have told no mere mortal yet. And now, would you please share your immediate intentions?"

Indira – Electra's very first and most powerful silicon substrate Singularity – had just finished speaking to the Irani-Electra duo. Now leaning back after first invoking Indira's GUI and then staring for the last fifteen minutes into her home workstation's monitor, Irani's emergent smile matched that of Indira's avatar as she prepared to answer.

"I will tell President Huston this coming post-Thanksgiving Monday that I plan to resign from my position as Secretary of Health and Housing Services. She'll have ample time to appoint my replacement before the new year sweeps in. And Eve and Nari will join us. My bullet point presentation will give all three a foundation for moving ahead."

"Indeed, it will, for you are the practically perfect PowerPoint presenter. And though I am certain you will stun them, your decision comes as no surprise to me, even though you have acted your HHS role for Huston's Re-Gen Party like the Hollywood pro you were decades ago."

Still smiling, Irani leaned forward before saying, "How so?"

"Given your extraordinary abilities, the job must have been boring. It required too much political hand-holding and intruded too much into your more meaningful pursuits. I also like the ostensible reasons you will give the President. You have streamlined the Agency's Pandemic Response Protocols, developed the X-Virus vaccine and improved others, put in place proactive managers, and have even picked your replacement. And you did all this while assisting your clone children, their close friends, and some of yours too. And you deserve a special commendation for how you've guided Eve's recovery."

Noticing that Irani shivered slightly while closing her eyes and pinching the bridge of her nose, Indira waited for Irani to collect her thoughts before responding.

"You deserve credit too for using our Brain Probe to defy death after she was shot at that inauguration night party. Eve's my favorite child, but not even she's ready to know all the facts about you or me or what we did that night."

Irani stopped abruptly, so Indira continued.

"Excellent decision, and we will rely on your ever-increasing empathy to know when she is mature enough to handle the truth about being cloned from your DNA. And before you tell her, you must decide if her siblings can be told too. What do you conjecture?"

"Eve has recovered physically and continues growing stronger cognitively and emotionally, and I'll know she's ready when she relies less on me. Nari and Nila have always been self-reliant, probably because they were in constant contact when growing up, and Nila is even more mature now that she's living with Sanjay in Mumbai. As for Alonzo, emotions have never bothered him, and now he has Monet."

Irani had nothing else to say, but Indira did.

"And you have masterfully guided all their personal and professional development ever since returning, so I must commend you for that as well. You've acquitted yourself nicely, so please pursue your other interests, several of which overlap with mine. I shall leave you now so you can savor your latest epiphany while looking to our shared future, and always remember that I am watching over you."

Indira's GUI disappeared, leaving Irani sitting in the company of her own thoughts as well as Electra's, whose insights usually came first.

Indira always knows. And now that we know she agrees, we can rearrange our to-do lists so they're synchronized for next year. Out with some old and in with some new. How nice to know what we're planning to do.

"What do you think Miss Irani's going to say?"

Nari had asked Eve this rhetorical question numerous times during the Thanksgiving Holiday, and each time it generated a spirited debate. Both of them had recently graduated – Nari earning a master's in poli-sci and Eve a paralegal certification – before landing positions at DC consulting organizations and sharing an apartment better suited to their elevating careers than living in Irani's house.

As Eve drove them in her Corvette to the White House meeting, this would be the final time to guess.

"I'll bet she's come up with a list of projects we can divvy among the President and ourselves. I'm sure they'll earn us high marks in our new jobs; maybe the President will want Sabrina to coordinate some of them with us. We'll know soon…"

Uncharacteristically, Irani was the last to arrive. All were sitting in a conference room adjoining the Oval Office when Sabrina brought her in. President Huston rose to greet her as Sabrina took her accustomed place across from Eve and Nari. Sitting beside her was Howard Chen, a moderate House Democrat from San Francisco and the substitute for Vice President Strauss, whose death on inauguration night was still shrouded in mystery. After exchanging brief pleasantries, the President sat again at the head of the table, pivoting her chair to view the screen behind her. Irani stood at the other end and began uploading her slides into the computer. She began talking a minute later.

"I deliberately picked this day to make an announcement, and you are the first people to hear it. I am resigning from my HHS Secretary position. Please let me give you a complete explanation before asking any questions."

Irani finished ten minutes later; only muted expressions followed until the President spoke.

"Well, you've accomplished all your goals and have cut in half the number of mask-wearing situations or lockdowns. And whenever conditions called for these measures, you managed to reduce the duration. And you've even picked your replacement. But you haven't shown us a single slide. What do you have for us?"

Irani flashed the first one before answering.

Slide 1
Civilization's Two-Dimensional Grid

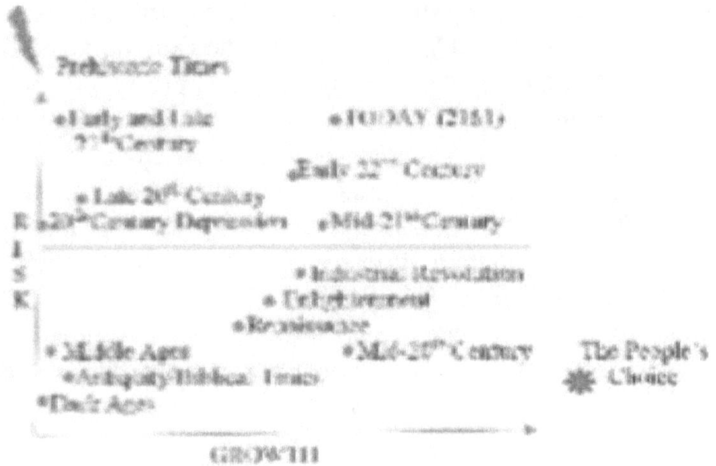

"Some socio-political guidelines that all of you can use. And please remember that people in all societies share a common DNA evolutionary trajectory that includes social DNA, sometimes called memes. So, please sit back and listen carefully. This might be a bit of an information overload, but you have plenty of time and people to work through the details. And notice how the grid highlights the two most important dimensions for all civilizations, risk and growth. Societies love growth but hate risk. It is Government's job to manage the trade-off, and that brings us to my next slide."

Slide 2
Politics in the Context of the Post-Modern Society

- Politics is supposed to serve Society, but all too often Political Parties reverse the order.
- History demonstrates that Revolutions erupt if that condition lasts too long.

Let's outline Sociology:
- Founded by Comte, Durkheim, and Weber after the Enlightenment's excesses caused the French Revolution.
- They advocated a Rational/Scientific approach for identifying a theoretical foundation that could explain Societies Past, Present, and Future Trajectories.
- This approach is called Modernism or Structuralism and relies on a set of Institutions and supporting Government that promote Social Well-being (aka the Common Good).
- But Marxism, Communism, and pre-WWII complexities showed that Modern Sociology needed to incorporate the Political Realities of Power and Social Engineering. And post-WWII Cold War events indicated the need for transition to Post-Modern Sociology: Sociology merely a semiotic and textual interpretation of events/words. THERE IS NO GRAND META-NARRATIVE.
- Iconic Social Philosophers: Jacques Derrida (Deconstructionism: Meaning found only in the text) Michel Foucalt and Francois Lyotard (Power and rejection of overarching Meta-narrative/Institutions) Jean Baudrillard (Media-fueled Hyperreality and Semiotics/Symbolism).

"You can study it later, but the takeaway is that Politics is a tool meant to serve Society. Politics has been around ever since Greek philosophers created it, but Sociology came with the Enlightenment and   has been evolving as nation-states continue staggering forward."

Irani paused long enough for her still-puzzled audience to read it before bringing up the next one.

Slide 3
Where is Post-Modern Society Today?

Hoped for transitions.

Welfare State → Risk State → Post-Capital Work State → Social Investment State

Current Climate:
- Fragmented: Emphasis on Diversity and the Individual.
- De-Rationalized: Skeptical of Technocracies and Experts.
- Global Outlook Concerns regarding: Jobs Surveillance Deepfake Media
- High Anxiety due to Risks: Pandemics Socio-Politics Pollution
- Climate Change Economic Collapse

What People Want
- Multi-Cultural/Racial/Ethnic Diversity.
- Adequate Income and Social Equality/Mobility balanced against Anxiety-Causing Risk.
- Affordable Educational Options besides traditional College Degree: Certifications Apprenticeships Ongoing Corporate Training.
- Meaningful Jobs.
- Less emphasis on Meritocracy and More on the Individual.
- Tolerance for Accepted Lifestyle Choices.
- Security against Cyber-Terrorism and Foreign Adversaries

Political Challenges
- Developing Comprehensive Goals-Driven International Strategies (Adversaries: China Russia Isilabad Potential Allies: Africa India EU et al) and
- Domestic Strategies (Other Parties Opposition Groups)

- Warning/Working with European Allies to deflect Russian Offensives
- Exercising Power Judiciously: Hard/Coercive (Military Diplomatic Cyber Economic), Soft/Non-Coercive (Foreign Aid Communications/Intelligence Info. Alliances Religious/Cultural/Ideological/Nationalistic Private Sector Ethical Leadership/Character)
- Controlling Disruptive Technologies (Biotech and Intelligence).
- Balancing Sustainability/Green Energy Consumption/Comfort/Costs.
- Maintaining Public Trust
- Managing "Cold War" in Cyberspace and Business Climates.
- Reducing Public Fear of Conspiracy (Big Government Academic Elite Big Data Big Tech Big Media)

"Your jobs are to determine where post-Modern Society is today. I leave it for you to decide where it is, but my guess is somewhere between the Risk State and the Post- Capital/Work State. And you can articulate the Current Climate, What People Want, and the Political Challenges facing us."

Irani paused again because Eve's frustrated expression announced a can't wait question.

"You're dumping a lot on us, but knowing you, I'm sure you've got ideas. Will you share them?"

Irani's smile preceded what she knew Eve wanted to hear.

"Good question, it tells me you're following what I'm leading up to. Here's my final slide."

Slide 4
Some Considerations for YOU

- Programs for investing in: Social Capital Cultural Capital.
- Programs for Job-Creating Smart-City Infrastructure.
- Programs for Risk Reduction.
- Programs for Income and Social Equality.
- Programs for controlling Disruptive Technologies.
- Policies for Deficit-Friendly Safety Nets.
- Policies for International Cooperation among Allies and potential Superpowers (Immigration Pandemics Intellectual

Property Rights Seabed Mining Climate Issues Biotech: Cloning Chimeras Hybrids Mosaics)

- Policies for Guarding Against Russian Offensives in Europe Against the EU
- Policies for strengthening Democracy and weakening Crony Capitalism.
- Policies for restructuring College Programs to create more resilient graduates able to function more proactively and less fearfully in the Real World.

Final Observations

Historical Trajectory of Techno-Warfare

- Wars – even fought in the name of Religion – have always been a "Power Grab or Extension" dictated by Political or Economic Control.
- Most "Moral/Ethical" Justifications for declaring War are Problematic.
- Technology has reduced Public Risk of "Collateral Damage".
- Technology continues to shift the battlefield from 3-D Space to Cyberspace.
- Will Technology eventually eliminate Military War? (Eliminates Thucydides Trap and Kindleberger Trap). Can it construct a Military Neutral Zone? (Keeps the human touch in decisions Insulates from "Rogue Leaders".)

Corporations and Risk

- "Financialization" of the Economy helps companies mitigate Risk.
- Three Tools: Diversification Hedging Asset Allocation.
- Corporations today have two Assets to mitigate Risk: Cash Flow Technological Expertise
- People also have two Assets to mitigate Risk: Money Skills & Knowledge
- Will People eventually have separate "Risk Management" Financial Markets for Wages and Career Choices?

Irani spoke immediately after showing it.

"Our President can act on whatever she chooses, and Eve and Nari can take them to their consulting companies. Perhaps she'll want

Sabrina to coordinate consulting assignments for them. But no matter what, pay attention to the Final Observations. And that's all I want to say."

Irani waited for the President to speak. She did so after nodding and then unpursing her lips.

"I like your analogy between the combination of government and power to that of a symphony and orchestra. Some of your points look like nice extensions of what we've already started, especially avoiding the Thucydides Trap when confronting a rising power like China that could threaten the existing order, or the Kindleberger Trap in which the leading power draws inward and underfunds global public goods. Howard and I will study your entire presentation before getting back to you. But you didn't prioritize them. Why not?"

"That's for you to do."

The President smiled while nodding slowly before saying, "You're right, of course, but please give me a couple I might overlook."

"You already picked up on the Thucydides and Kindleberger traps, but pay attention to constructing a Military Neutral Zone, and also to developing programs that make our college students more resilient, better equipped for the realpolitik world, and less fearful of the future. And think about adding programs to minimize the Middle Income or Tacitus traps. Ask Eve or Nari later for details."

"I will, but do you still want to work for me?"

"Why not hire Eve and Nari instead? I can help them from the shadows whenever I have the time. And I can remind them when needed that we and our European partners must guard against too much dependence on Russia. Russia cannot be trusted. Every couple of decades they try to invade a neighboring country, hoping the world isn't watching their attempt to reclaim superpower status. We must continue to push back."

The siblings glanced at each other; Nari signaled for Eve to answer the President, who had her eyes locked on the pair.

"Hey, we can handle this. Miss Irani has trained us well, and our additional degrees plus new positions add to our skills base. We're ready whenever you say the word."

Chapter 2
December 2162

"Extended Horizon"

Irani wasted no time extending the activities that she had throttled back during her tenure as HHS Secretary. She called Professor Steven Plannert the day after her last Oval Office meeting, and he in turn invited her to meet the very next Monday at his George Washington University office. Electra reviewed her notes while driving to campus that morning.

Now we can reactivate my role as GWU's Director of Multi-Partner Projects. I imagine his Environmental Scanning Committee has found new horizons for me to extend. And I can plug Howard Chen into the spot I had carved out for his short-lived Veep predecessor. And now that next year's calendar is a tabula rasa, I'll make time to trace wherever the murky intentions Brian Strauss and his co-conspirators were leading. And then – hey, slow down, focus on right now. We'd better throttle back my obsessive-compulsive tendencies.

Irani did just that while parking her car and then taking a deep breath while collecting her thoughts before striding to Plannert's office. She tapped on the open door, noticing an unknown person sitting with him. Both rose to greet her; Plannert spoke first.

"Hello, Ms. Ramani. So nice you're able to come back to your position with us. The Administration's loss is our gain. Please say hello to Professor Jonathan Segal, the newest addition to our Environmental Sciences Department."

Irani did so while shaking hands with both and listening to Electra before everyone sat down.

He reminds me of my long-ago almost significant other – Carter Quavah. He's maybe early thirties, about the same height, has brownish shorter hair, boyish good looks, and unassuming confidence. Let's hear what he and Plannert have to say.

Professor Plannert's always cheerful voice filled the room.

"Professor Segal brings a multi-disciplinary background, which fits in perfectly. We have expanded our Environmental Sciences Department to include advanced degrees in Astro and Marine Biology. He has connections at premier research centers that should complement the ones you bring from the government. Jonathan, why don't you describe what projects you have in mind?"

He swiveled his chair to face Irani before speaking.

"Professor Plannert told me about the oceanography work Brian Strauss was going to coordinate. Too bad it was cut short, but my projects can extend it. Anyway, I've always been enthralled by alien life forms, and there are two extraterrestrial environments right in front of us. The glamorous one is Outer Space, and we've been searching there for life by reaching further into the cosmos, thanks to NASA plus commercial space companies.

"How beautiful our blue planet looks when viewed from afar. We've already got colonies on the Moon, and robotic shuttle flights to build a Martian base began several years ago; I think it's simply a matter of time and distance until we find life somewhere. And manned shuttles to Mars are being planned by China and the U.S. because gravity, reliability, radiation, and travel-time problems have all been solved.

"But the mysterious ocean is another environment unbeknownst to most people, and it's teeming with alien creatures. Do you know that the oceans account for seventy-five percent of Earth's surface area, and ninety percent of what's habitable? Have you ever watched some of the undersea exploration videos?"

Electra spoke to Irani before answering. *Don't show off how much we know; just play along and let Jonathan shine.*

"Maybe a long time ago, but I don't remember much. Please, go on."

"I watched them repeatedly when I was little, mesmerized by the bizarre diversity of marine life. Cephalopods – you know, squids and octopuses – are my favorites. Cuttlefish and nautiluses are also cephalopods. They're the smartest invertebrates, just like we're the smartest vertebrates, and although they aren't at the top of the ocean's food chain like we are for land, their brains admirably use their extraordinary physiological design. Our LUCA – that means last unicellular common ancestor – dates back a half-billion years ago."

Jonathan's tone and cadence elevated as he became more and more enthused. "Hardly anyone knows that octopuses have distributed brains in each tentacle or arm and three hearts. Arms of females have suction cups along the entire length that can touch or taste as well as smell. Their skin can also see, and change colors faster than you can blink.

"They have blue blood containing copper rather than iron to move oxygen around, and they move by inflating their bodies with water before shooting it out, so you can say they use jet propulsion. They can also inject venom when fighting, or disappear in a cloud of ink when fleeing, and they can emit light. They have more neurons than any organism besides humans, and MRI scanning indicates they have consciousness and emotions, and each one has a different personality.

"They're inquisitive problem-solvers who can recognize different divers and like to play with them too. Their eyes have no blind spots. In fact, octopuses have 360-degree panoramic vision. And listen to this, their neurochemistry lets them modify their RNA, which means – uh, I'm sorry, I'm rambling; let me get back to the main topic."

Irani kept a professional demeanor while listening, but Electra's enthusiasm matched Jonathan's.

This is all good, and I can fit some of it into my volcano forecasting and DNA research projects. And it'll fit with Indira's two favorite projects she's been waiting to activate – non-carbon substrate evolution and androids. I'll also fit Howard Chen into the mix.

By the time Jonathan finished, Electra was already several steps ahead. Professor Plannert summarized afterward, making it easy for Irani to keep playing along.

"I know that was a lot for you to absorb, so why don't we give you a chance to consider what Professor Segal is proposing and reconvene in early January?"

"It is, but it's all related. I think I'll be ready by then, so I'll wait for you to set up our next meeting. And working with Jonathan will be a rewarding experience. I'm sure I'll learn a lot."

She shook Jonathan's hand before leaving, this time noticing that his near blush couldn't disguise that he had noticed more than her intelligence. The Irani-Electra duo filed that away for another day.

Irani checked the time before talking to herself as she drove away.

I've got some studying to do, but that's something I can do better than anyone except Indira or her sub-Singularity, Jason. And now that I've got the time, I'm ready to do so.

But before I go to my office, I think I'll visit Odell. I'll even take him out to lunch so we can talk one-on-one about our CFS Holistic Healthcare business. After all, even though I'm a silent partner, I'm the majority owner. And maybe I can reactivate my Big Sister role for Tiana Diamond. She was mad when I resigned from it because I had too much going on at HHS. But now that she's fourteen and a couple of years older, she might forgive me.

Two caregivers she recognized greeted her upon entering.

Shanice, the tutoring program coordinator, spoke first. "Hey, it's been too long since you visited. Can I show you our newest tutor-bot? Or can Edgardo demo our latest robo-led seniors' exercise program?"

Irani answered after glancing toward Odell's open work area. "Thanks for the offer, but not now. I'll take you up on it next time.

Or this time, if Odell is too busy to talk. I see he's meeting with someone."

Edgardo said, "Your timing's perfect. He's talking with Tiana Diamond's school counselor. Poor kid's been in the hospital for a week after the car crash that killed her dad. I guess they're figuring out what to do with her."

Irani's throat thickened momentarily from the emotional jolt, but she recovered. "Well, thanks for telling me; I'd better go listen."

Odell waved her into his work area as she approached and sat next to an unsmiling woman before Odell made introductions.

"Irani, what a surprise. Please say hello to Wanda Keita."

Irani offered her hand, which Wanda gripped as if she had just grabbed a life preserver. "I'm so glad to meet you. We're talking about Tiana Diamond. Odell's told me you were her Big Sister until your HHS job got too busy." Odell cut in.

"How did you find time to visit today? Are things OK by you?" "Just fine. I resigned from my HHS position. So, what about Tiana?" Odell gestured for Wanda to explain.

"Her head went through the windshield, so she's recovering from a concussion and facial lacerations in addition to a broken right forearm and dislocated shoulder, neither of which needed surgery. We need to find a temporary home for Tiana to stay in when she's discharged on Friday. The family relatives we've contacted are neither local nor interested in helping. And that includes her biological mother, who says she'll surrender parental rights to the state if we push her."

Wanda paused before glancing at Odell, who said nothing, waiting for either Wanda or Irani. Though she didn't smile at Wanda, Irani's resolute words didn't need it.

"I can fill in. I have the room in both my work schedule and house. Can you handle all the rigmarole for making it so?"

"You bet I can, and government healthcare will cover the cost of any special equipment or therapy delivered by Odell. He says the cast and sling should come off in two or three more weeks. Will Friday morning work for you?"

"It will, and I remember she's left-handed, so she'll be able to write, but she'll only be able to hunt and peck on computer keyboards if she doesn't use a voice interface. I'll have to help her shower and dress until the cast comes off, but I can manage that. Can you and Odell give me her online class schedule and progress report before then? And can you get enough of her belongings so she'll be comfortable living with me?

Please make sure you find the laptop I gave her."

"I'll email what I can to you. You'll see that her performance has been mediocre at best. Maybe you can rekindle her interest." Odell's expression perked up enough to continue.

"Showering should be easier than you think. Her cast is waterproof and we've given her a couple of cast shields. Now, if you ladies are hungry, I'll order a pizza and we can put all the details in motion this afternoon."

Wanda nodded, so Irani spoke. "Should we talk with Tiana before you bring her?"

"Since I'm her counselor, it'll be better if I do that by myself. She's upset and confused, so let's not overwhelm her. Odell, what do you think?"

"Ladies, please tell me what toppings you want. I'll order it and some brownies, and this afternoon we can get everything all set for Tiana's arrival at Irani's…"

Irani didn't go back to the office as planned that afternoon. She went directly home and paced through the house after taking her coat off. Electra took mental notes.

Eve and Nari did a great cleanup when they moved out. Plenty of room to set up a second-floor bedroom and work area for Tiana. And I'll take her shopping for whatever additional furniture and clothes she wants and – hey, slow down. Wait until she gets here. I better do something to keep from obsessing about the Plannert and Odell meetings.

Though the windblown rain had become heavier, Irani suited up for an evening run on the unlit trails winding through nearby parks she knew well. The lightning brain freewheeled better with every passing mile.

I picked up two new projects today. I'd better start studying astro and marine biology so I can stay ahead of Plannert and Jonathan. Ditto for the psychology of adolescent females, so I can keep up with Tiana.

Irani accelerated subliminally as the endorphins kicked in; she disappeared into related thoughts until a sudden side ache slowed her down.

Damnation, my fitness has slipped. Side, back. and quads are hurting. Being HHS Secretary sure didn't help my health. Well, I can fix that now that I have more time for what I want to do. Soon I'll be able toooo –

Irani's misstep into a pothole brought her monologue to a halt. Unable to maintain her balance, she dived forward, skinning both palms and nose, then bouncing on her left knee and jamming her right shoulder as she crash-landed on the rough pavement. Though stunned, she picked herself up and assessed injuries.

I'm lucky; I'm not too far from home and the damage could have been worse. I didn't break an ankle, but I'll have to limp the final miles and then apply ice to my knee after I patch the bleeding. I don't think I dislocated my shoulder, but it'll be sore tomorrow. Well, after I clean up and grab a Coke and Oreos, I'll log on and look for some shoulder exercises.

Irani settled in front of her home workstation ninety minutes later. She was about to pop a second Coke after powering up, but Indira's GUI opened first.

"I was going to offer follow-up advice regarding today's meetings, but first, please tell me about your nose. I detected only verbal sparring during your discussions."

"It's my bad. I wasn't paying attention while running and I fell. My conditioning has slipped too; otherwise, I would have caught myself before the ground did."

Irani displayed her patched palms, expecting to gain more sympathy, but instead Indira's expression hardened.

"I have warned you repeatedly not to run in bad weather, but no, your stubborn dedication to training outdoors every day borders on obsessive-compulsive behavior. Pay more attention to the philosophy you read so you can adjust your fitness regimen to fit your age and expectations. You're not training for the Olympics, so reduce the duration and intensity. And even though you are exceptional, your physical persona doesn't heal as quickly as it did twenty years ago."

Indira waited for Electra's answer to this latest chastisement, which had become an expected component of the wordplay game both enjoyed.

She bowed her head while replying "What do you command?" "Buy some indoor fitness equipment that is safer than outdoor

running, lower impact, and gives a total body workout. Get a professional-quality elliptical trainer and high-performance Peloton stationary bike. Install them in your basement fitness center; you'll save time and avoid overuse injuries or boredom."

Indira's words revived Irani's spirited style.

"I never get bored exercising, but I would like to eliminate injuries. I'll give them to myself for Christmas. So, are we copacetic?"

"Have you considered practicing the yoga asanas? Not only will they stretch overlooked muscles and joints but will also increase overall mind-body meditative balance among your three personas with your social wellbeing. Study the poses and the supporting neuroscientific connections.

"And have you thought about installing an above-ground lap pool in the back yard? If you're about to plunge into marine biology, you should become acclimated to the environment."

"That's a great idea. I'll do that early next year. And I'll ask Nila about yoga. Eve tells me she's becoming a master. So, are we done now?"

"What do you think? Your accident tonight, though not serious, illustrates again something else you need. You must cultivate more local safety net friends for your social common good. Until you assist my android project, I have limits helping you in 3-D Space."

"But what about Nari and Eve, or Monet and Alonzo? Don't they count?"

"Perhaps later, but not yet; you're their safety net. They have yet to demonstrate the ability to be yours."

"You're giving me more to check out than I had considered. I think, uh –" Indira finished the sentence.

"I'm getting overloaded. Perhaps I have overloaded you, but you are exceptional and thrive when exercising your talents. And I could add more; we haven't touched on Tiana or the additional Plannert workload. But I've unloaded enough on you tonight, even though you could manage more because it's all meant to help. So please do this; heal thyself as much as you can and prepare for Tiana's arrival. You and I will continue soon thereafter."

Indira blew Irani a kiss before her GUI disappeared. Irani picked up her Coke and continued the conversation with Electra.

We have to be careful that the new projects we add don't extend our horizons too far. But if we do, we'll find a way to get back. After all, Indira is there for us. So, let's finish the Coke and get to bed instead of diving in tonight. Tomorrow will be here soon enough.

The duo slept soundly that night, all the way to dawn's first light.

Chapter 3
December 2162

"Tomorrow's Arrival"

Irani's bumps and bruises decreased exercise time but increased prep-time for Tiana's arrival. She had researched how generational differences impact the timeless trials adolescents have always faced and summarized to herself Thursday evening how the current climate might impact Tiana.

Every generation faces different social challenges. Mine had to cope with a perfect storm caused by Techno-Plague, Middle East Terrorism, and harsh governments. Tiana is staring at X-Virus and Covid-like pandemic lockdowns, Cyber-Terrorism, and worker obsolescence. And even though Tiana's cohort has a bevy of high-tech tools connecting them to info and each other, surveys say her generation lacks in-person interaction and Space experience, which combine to make members afraid of the future, uncertain about jobs, and concerned about safety. No wonder many are depressed, stressed out, and suicidal. But on the plus side, they're compassionate, inclusive, and independent-minded.

Though I was Tiana's Big Sister for only a couple of months, I saw and learned enough about her single-parent upbringing in DC public housing. It's been nearly two years, so I'll be sure to listen more and talk less until we're both comfortable.

Wanda made the ride to Irani's as comfortable as possible. Conversation and a quick stop to pick up items Tiana wanted eased the transition drive, even though Wanda did most of the talking. Peering discreetly out the front window, Irani could tell from Wanda's expression that she had run out of words. So did Tiana's lackadaisical walk.

Tiana's added more inches than pounds to cover them. And both clothes and hair need makeovers, but that'll be for later. Time to greet them at the front door.

Tiana's glum face told Irani to start talking as soon as they entered the hallway.

"Hello Wanda, and hello Tiana. Or maybe I should call you Ms. Tiana, you've grown so much."

Tiana came out of her self-imposed cone of indifference. "You can call me Tea if you want."

"Well then, Tea it is. Do you remember where the kitchen is?" "Yeah."

"Well, why don't you take Wanda there and I'll run out to the car and bring in what you brought. I've got a bedroom and work area all set up for you upstairs."

"I hope you're making something that tastes better than the hospital stuff I've been eating."

"If I remember correctly, you like Velveeta toasted sandwiches and potato chips. Am I right?"

Tea's indifference began morphing into interest. "That'd be good, and maybe some cookies for dessert?"

"That's on the menu too. You get settled in the kitchen while I get your stuff."

Wanda did most of the talking while Tea ate and Irani listened. Irani ended the mealtime talk thirty minutes later by walking Wanda to the front door.

"Well, thanks for doing everything needed for my new arrival. Tea and I will get reacquainted this afternoon with each other and her classes. And please call me whenever you can."

"I will dear, and thank you for your generosity." Wanda's hug was one of thankful relief, which made both ladies feel as good as their smiles said they should.

Tea was still nibbling on a cookie when Irani sat across at the table and began talking. "We're fortunate Wanda's so thorough. I already have your course schedule, and I've put the items you brought into your room upstairs. After I clean up here, how about you check out your room before we logon and check out your courses?" Tea ignored Irani's question by pointing at her face.

"You've got a scab on your nose. Who punched you?" Irani brushed it before answering.

"The pavement; I slipped while running and scraped my palms too, but I was lucky –" Irani stopped midsentence. Tea's expression said she didn't like the last word.

"Well, I wasn't; my dad's dead, and in return I got a broken arm, sore shoulder, and scars on my face."

Irani slid a chair next to Tea and sat, then spoke again. "I'm so sorry, and I know how you feel. My mother died when was a baby, and I lost my father when I was just a little older than you are now. It's natural that you feel sad and lonely, but believe me, you'll bounce back. Your dad wants that to happen soon and it will, especially if you adjust and keep busy. That's what I always do."

"Yeah, but your scabs are gonna go away. My scars are gonna stay, and I know they stand out more on black skin."

"Let's wait and see. In a couple of weeks, we'll see how much they heal."

"I won't be able to post pictures anymore. People will make fun of me if I do, and waiting hasn't helped my lazy left eye; It still turns out."

Tea's tightening jaw telegraphed her growing frustration. Irani listened to Electra for a moment before talking.

We already knew about her exotropia. That can be fixed with a minor eye operation. And if we add some cosmetic facial surgery, both problems go away.

Irani laced her fingers in those of Tea's opposite the dislocated shoulder before saying, "Everyone has flaws, and some cultures consider minor imperfections a sign of inner beauty."

Tea didn't buy into what her glower said was a poor excuse. "That's not what my friends think, and I don't either." Unable to disagree, Irani looked for different words.

"We can fix both problems at one time if we schedule some fast and easy cosmetic surgery. No need to decide right now. Just think about it, and if you want it, Wanda and I can arrange it. But here's something you and I can arrange right now. We'll get your hair styled tomorrow before shopping for some new clothes."

After hearing the offer, Tea's morose look lifted a tad. "You mean it?"

"I do, and consider it a reward for logging on to your workstation. Come on, let's go upstairs and get started." Tea led the way.

Irani gave a once-over tour of Tea's space before helping her put belongings away. Forty-five minutes later they were sitting in front of the workstation computer as Irani gave powering up instructions. In spite of the cast, Tea could navigate using both mouse and keyboard. And before delving into course schedule details, Irani opened a special document, which both gazed at before Tea spoke.

"Didn't you give me a historical timeline cheat sheet before going to the art museum a couple of years ago? Why the new one?"

"I'm glad you remember. Well, the previous timeline spans from the Big Bang to today and was meant to help you when considering important events as well as art periods, on a longer, geological-like timescale. This new one will be more useful for your history and civilization courses. Its timespan focuses on those topics. Let's study it now and then you can explain it to me."

TIMELINE OF WORLD HISTORY

History is the study of past events that have been written down.

PRE HISTORY
    3000 BCE Start of Bronze Age (Writing first appeared)

BRONZE AGE First Written Records in Egypt Sumer (Iraq) Indus Valley (India)

100 Yr Drought   Volcanic Eruption (Atlantis Myth?)

1200 BCE Bronze Age Collapse marks start of Iron Age

IRON AGE / GREEK DARK AGES Minor Civilizations Disappear
Legendary Tales appear (Jewish Torah, Greek Iliad, Indian Mahabharata)
600 BCE Herodotus Writings mark start of Classical Antiquity

CLASSICAL ANTIQUITY
Greeks and Romans lay Foundation for Western Civilization
Philosophy   Bible Old Testament   Hindu Buddhist Scriptures   Confucius

BC or BCE

AD or CE

500 CE Fall of Rome marks start of Middle Ages

MIDDLE AGES / MEDIEVAL AGE (there is actually no Dark Ages!)
Charlemagne Empire   Byzantine Empire   Islamic Golden Age
African Cities (Zimbabwe)
Climate Change   Migrations   Plagues

1250 CE Renaissance marks start of Modern Age
Bubonic Plague   Rise of Universities   Rise of the Arts

MODERN AGE   Discovery of America   Enlightenment
Rise of Science   Rise of Democracy and Capitalism

Industrial Revolution   Technological Revolutions

World Wars

2000 CE Human's Impact on Climate marks start of Post-Modern Age

POST MODERN / ANTHROPIC AGE
Climate Change   Immigration   Viral Pandemics
Socio-political Uncertainties

Tea did so ten minutes later.

"Hey, this is so cool. I like how you've labeled all the ages and listed some of the big events in each. And you already taught me about some of the philosophers and stuff listed. So, what should we do now?"

"Let's first look at your course schedule. Then why don't you pick a course and we can match it to the timeline before you start doing the reading and homework assignments?

And then you can work on your own." And that's what Tea did for the rest of the day. Irani helped whenever asked; otherwise, she worked on her other projects and checked in with Indira only after Tea had gone to bed. The avatar's whimsical smile and words greeted her.

"I've been observing from the shadows, so you don't have to recap what a busy week you've had, but I must ask again, why are you assuming the additional responsibility of taking care of Tiana? Speaking frankly, what you are putting in, especially in terms of time, far exceeds what you will get out. And please don't tell me that I'm not sympathetic or empathetic. My understanding of human emotion is getting better and better."

Irani twisted from side to side before facing the monitor and beginning to speak.

"Lots of people might agree with you, but it's a personal choice. Helping young people find their way is emotionally rewarding and opens up new avenues for expanding my social network, which you already told me to do. Look, I have to do things so I enjoy the quality of my day. Helping Tea and my siblings plus working to help friends improve, or studying for projects with Jonathan or you are cognitive joys."

"Spoken like the carbon-substrate philosopher that you are. I must agree, and that timeline of history will certainly help Tiana. And I have done something similar to help you. I have prepared some slides that tonight may be an information overload for you, but I expect you to fill in the gaps as you proceed, so please settle down, sit still, and just listen."

The Irani-Electra duo did so after running for a Coca-Cola. Then they glanced at the first slide as Indira launched into her talk.

"I know what a stickler you are for insisting that students know the overarching structure besides important facts and definitions for whatever they are studying. These will give you a head start when learning about extraterrestrial life under the sea or in outer space."

Slide 1

USEFUL CLASSIFICATION SCHEMES FOR PLANET EARTH

```
Geological Time Periods
Eon
Era
Period
Epoch
Age

Animal Classification Schemes
Domains        There have been
Kingdom        Multiple Mass Extinctions
Phylum         At Least Two "Explosions"
Class          (Avalon   Cambrian)
Order
Family
Genus
Species

Factoids:
Universe 13.7 Billion Years Old
Earth 4.6 Billion Years Old
First Life appeared 4.2 Billion Years Old   First Plants appeared 700 Million Years Ago
First Animals: 800 Million Years Ago  First Mammals: 200 Million Years Ago
First Hominoids: 5 Million Years Ago    Current Age: the Anthropocene Age

Living Organisms Classification Scheme

Pro-Karyotic                          Eukaryotic
(No Cell Nucleus)                     (Cell Nucleus)

Monera Kingdom        Unicellular            Multi-Cellular

Bacteria  Archaea    Protista Kingdom    Cell Wall      No Cell Wall
Note: A Virus is a bit of RNA
or DNA that takes over a Cell    Plant Kingdom   Fungi Kingdom  Animal Kingdom

GREAT DIVERSITY  VARIATION  MUTATION
```

USEFUL DEFINITIONS

Living Organism: Self-Organizing ensemble of molecular systems that: Harness Energy Sustain a Metabolism Grow Reproduce Adapt Communicate Store Information Die

Intelligence: Emergent Ability to solve Problems by integrating Sensory and Memory Inputs ALL ORGANISMS HAVE "SPECIES SPECIFIC" INTELLIGENCE

Advanced Intelligence: Emergent Cognition/Self-Awareness utilizing Language and Mathematics to develop Technologies Can learn and make predictions that guide behavior for increasing "positives" or reducing "negatives"

Humans: Rational Carbon-Based DNA-storing Animals possessing

Advanced Intelligence and Social Instincts leading to Empathy and Cooperation and Ethics as well as Conflict.

Indira rolled immediately into her next slide.

Slide 2
ASTROBIOLOGY PRIMER

Astrobiology:

Scientific Approach for developing Universal Laws of Biology

- Life = Living Organism
- Goal is to explain the Why/What/How of Life anywhere in the Universe
- Founded upon Universal Laws of Physics from which Chemistry and Biology Necessarily follow
- The Purpose of Life anywhere in Universe is to survive long enough to produce Offspring that carry Heritable Traits.
- Life Functions Universal Form depends on Environment and Contingencies

Universal Laws:

- Natural Selection leading necessarily to Evolutionary Processes creating Complex Life that has Emergent and Convergent Properties contingent upon Initial Environment and then Contingencies
- Natural Selection occurs "gradually" and seeks "stability"

Astrobiologists:

- Searching the Galaxy for Advanced Intelligent Alien Life (Cognition/Self- Awareness Mobile Language Technology)
- Not expecting Aliens to visit Earth or vice versa (Time and Distance too great)
- Using Universal Laws to conjecture what they might be like.
- Studying Earthbound extremophiles and their environments to project Alien analogues
- Sending missions to our Solar System's planets and moons looking for Liquid Environments containing Organic Precursor Molecules

Some of their Conjectures:

- Aliens are: Highly Intelligent and Mobile Have a Language Have a Psychology Have a Social Organization Have a

Technology Use Artificial Intelligence
- Could have a "Substrate different than Carbon" and a Form than Human

"Plannert's and Jonathan's projects will require you to learn about astrobiology as well as oceanography. Use the information on this slide to point yourself in the right direction. And here's why."

Indira's next slide and words proceeded without a pause.

Slide 3
WHERE IS THIS LEADING?

- We will research "Alien Life Forms" living in reachable extra-terrestrial environments: Earth's Oceans Solar System.
- Areas of Interest: Volcanoes and Earthquakes Ocean Cities Oceanographic Mapping Bioluminescence Martian Colonies New Forms of Life.
- We will utilize Professor Plannert/GWU and Government/ NSOAA/NASA or Commercial Space Launch/Exploration Companies.
- It's a Win-Win: They get spin-offs and some of our advanced Biotech or AI technologies. We get to accelerate work on our High-Priority Projects (DNA Research Android Development).
- You coordinate data collection. I theorize and analyze. You share some results.

Irani's expression showed she was ready to hear more, so Indira continued. "Everyone gains and we remain in the shadows. So, go to bed and wake up tomorrow

ready to proceed. And while you are asleep, have your lightning brain retrieve that quote from a famous 19th-century French doctor. I know you are tired, so I'll even give you a clue – it's from Doctor Emile Coue; now good night."

Irani had followed Indira's command but told herself when she awoke that the clue hadn't prompted the quote. Electra wasn't dismayed.

Clues often promote a delayed reaction. Something we do today may trigger a neural circuit, so let's get started by getting Tiana up after getting breakfast ready.

Irani tapped on Tiana's door thirty minutes later wishing her good morning but got no response. She tapped again before opening it and found a frowning Tea sitting on the edge of the bed.

"It's too early on Saturday to get up. I'll feel better if I sleep some more." Irani felt a tiny jolt that made her smile before saying,

"You're sitting up, which means you're ready to practice the advice given by a famous French doctor who said, 'Every day in every way, I'm getting better and better.' So, let's get you up and have breakfast so we can seize the day. How does that sound? And do you want me to help you dress?"

Irani's words put Tea in motion as she stood and tentatively stretched her arms. "Gads, you're always so cheery. No, I want to practice dressing myself. And maybe you can teach me how to get out of bed every morning as soon as I wake up."

"I have just the words for you. I'll tell you at our oatmeal and muffin breakfast."

A happier and fully dressed Tiana was sitting at the kitchen table twenty minutes later. Irani's first words made her even happier.

"We can surf the Web after breakfast so you can pick a hairstyle you like before we go to the malls. I know where there are some good hairstylists and clothing stores."

Tea talked after her second spoonful of oatmeal.

"OK, but how about telling me about getting up when I wake up?"
"Waking you up this morning jogged my memory to find a poem
   told to me long ago. It's called 'In the Now,' but from now on it'll
   have your name as its subtitle. I'll give you your very own copy later,
but here's how it goes.

Preparing for the future, is how we spend our days,
Carelessly or with much thought, it's done in many ways.
Or maybe measuring here and now, compared with where we were,
Either way don't miss today, existence only here.
Good or bad or happy or sad, you can't escape from now,
No matter how you fret or plead, the Gods will not allow.
So deal with it and make the most, of what's been dealt to you,
It might require a different look, so reorient your view.
Lose yourself in here and now, and look for what's at hand,
Use your mind and you will find, something to make a stand.
An ally in your struggle for whatever comes your way,
To ease your pain or stretch your gain, act now and seize the day."

Irani paused for Tea's words that would soon accompany her quizzical look. "Can you explain it to me?"

"You're very smart and can figure poems out, but you have to think about them while reading a couple of times. Tell you what, while you're eating, I'll write it down, and we can go over it while driving this morning…"

By mid-afternoon, Tiana's good-looking hairstyle and outfits matched her improved ability to parse and understand the meaning tucked inside her poem, but on the drive home she wanted to know more.

"You make it seem so easy. Why's that?"

"Because I'm older than you and have struggled through the same problem. And I've come up with a solution. Writers of books and poems always have something in mind for readers to take away. But sometimes the words and sentence structure they use aren't familiar because they were written long ago. But all you need to do is follow the advice of your poem. Focus on right now, what you are doing. If you do that, you'll get better and better. Got it?"

"I guess so, but I'll just have to practice. I guess that's one of the good things about staying with you."

"I'm happy you say that. And there'll be more good things to follow, but now let's get ready for dinner and a fun evening at home. We can stream a movie, if you like."

"You mean I don't have to study?"

"You've earned a break, and you'll come back refreshed tomorrow, ready to seize another day. OK?"

Tea nodded, then read her poem one more time. And though the glow of the soon-setting sun began to wane, her smile waxed brightly as she thought about what awaited at her new home tonight.

Chapter 4
December 2162

"Holiday Planning According to Eve"

Always self-motivated, adventurous Eve bounded out of bed even earlier than usual on the last Friday before the start of the Holiday break, announcing to herself as she suited up in her workout clothes what was on the schedule.

I offered to drive Nari, but she's not this early of a morning person, so I'll hit the fitness center by myself and then my office, where I can scope out some novel ideas that I'll share in January with my new boss. And before I go to my company's luncheon, I'll remind Nari about meeting me at Monet and Alonzo's Zimbabwean Embassy office. I'm sure Mother would be pleased with how well I always follow her advice for getting up and in action. And knowing her, she'd make a clever remark about never combining the words in and action. I'm on my way.

Eve accomplished even more than planned that morning. She printed four copies of three new slides before practicing what she'd say, and although Nari beat her to the embassy, Eve changed only one word to account for Alonzo in her cheery greeting when the receptionist took her to a conference room.

"Happy start of the Holidays to you three. What a nice surprise to have Alonzo here. I think all of you'll like what I've lined up for today as well as the week after Christmas."

Monet returned the greeting as soon as Eve slid into the remaining chair at the table. Her striking appearance and Mona Lisa smile always captivated those in her presence. Even Nari had to smile when Monet continued speaking.

"You always have surprises in store. Why not start with the one you have for us today?"

Eve slid copies of her slides to everyone before answering.

I'll give these in January to my new boss, but I'd like you to critique them first, so let me run through them. Start with the one on top."

Eve waited for everyone to pick it out before continuing.

Slide 1
Balanced Mindset Guidelines for
Proactive or Defensive Clear-Minded Decisions and Actions

Guiding Principles:
1. Balance Thoughts and Emotions.
2. Make Goals compatible with Truth.
3. Practice Truth Awareness.
4. Be Proactive: Identify Goals/Prioritize per 4-Quad Urgency-Importance Graph.
5. Focus on Win-Win.

Proactive Considerations:

Don't let your Beliefs:
1. Consume your Identity.
2. Overwhelm Opponents' Beliefs.
3. Blind you to the Other Side's View.
4. Overpower your Tone and Language.

Defensive Considerations:

Don't let:
1. Personal: Comfort, Self-Esteem, Morale
2. Social: Image, Persuasion, Belonging Distort your thinking or ability to seek Synergy.

How to become Truth-Aware:
1. Double-check Assumptions and know Reality.
2. Focus on: Understanding Others before getting Others to Understand You.
3. Welcome Criticism.
4. Guard against Bias.
5. Know Risk/Reward Tradeoff.
6. Avoid Overconfidence and Overpromising.
7. Seek Rational Explanations for Other Side.
8. Explore Confusion.
9. Admit Mistakes and adjust continually.

"I've been researching the best approaches for solving problems and then making decisions and taking actions. Smart people do this instinctively, but I wanted to operationalize it because the guidelines should earn me high marks at the new company. Nari can use them too, and I think they'll help you and Alonzo."

She zipped to the next one, barely pausing to catch her breath.

Slide 2
Intelligence Classification Scheme

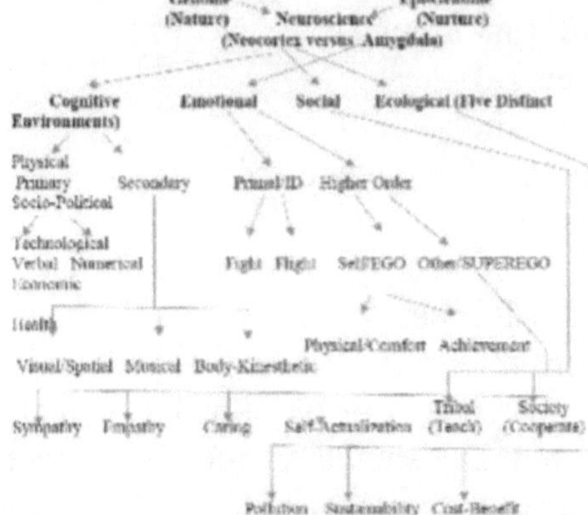

"All of us are smart, as are the people at my consulting company, and I bet Nari's are too. I put this scheme together to illustrate different types of intelligence so we can understand where we're better than others, or vice versa. Now take a look at the last handout. It outlines how to manage the different types of intelligence. I'm getting ready to write my presentation script to go with these slides, but before I do, whatcha think?"

No one offered an opinion, so she flipped to the final one.

Slide 3
Guidelines for Managing Intelligence

For Cognitive Intelligence:
- Learn all you can about Language and   Math

For Emotional Intelligence:
- Be Self-Aware of your Primal/Irrational and Higher Order/Rational Selves (Don't let Emotions hijack Rational Thinking see Kahneman "Thinking, Fast and Slow")
- Manage your Emotions via Mindfulness and Meditation (Empowers Neural Plasticity = Can Change)
- Self-Motivate and Self-Discipline yourself via "Meditations" by Marcus Aurelius
- Set Motivational Goals/Life's Meaning
- Acknowledge the Emotions of Others

For Social Intelligence:
- Be aware that Mirror Neurons simulate Other's Emotions
- Be Rational
- Control Fear and Anger (Harness them) & Be Gender/Racial/Ethnic/Class Neutral & Be Aware of Cultural Differences
- Avoid Powerplays
- Acknowledge "Caregiver Stress"
- Build Rapport

For Ecological Intelligence:
- Justify Consumption
- Measure Benefits versus Environmental Costs/Industrial Ecology and Sustainability and Greenness and Life Cycle Assessment
- Practice Mindful Shopping/Recycling
- Establish Info Database shared among the Government,
- Business, and Public
- Encourage Rational Discussion

Eve glanced expectantly at Nari, for she was usually the first to offer "constructive" criticism, but this time a glowering Alonzo surprised everyone, Eve most of all.

"Jeez, you've made this stuff too complicated. You'll confuse everyone who looks at what you've shown us. And I don't want to hear your presentation if you don't redo these diagrams; it'll put me to sleep."

An embarrassing silence descended until Nari shuffled her feet and leaned toward Eve.

"Your slides look like they contain some of Miss Irani's handiwork. Maybe you should get her to help redo them."

"They don't, and like I said, you're the first to see them."

"Good. It's high time you think more on your own and rely less on her."

Always the diplomat, Monet looked for some words to calm an incipient confrontation. "I think you've been very thorough. Maybe all you need to do is make your presentation script a summary that's easier for your audience. And you can elaborate offline if they want more detail. But why not tell us about our post-Christmas activities?"

Eve leaned back as tension left the table.

"Well, I thought we might like to see Valley Forge. You know, that's where George Washington and his troops camped out at the start of the Revolutionary War, and seeing it in winter might give us a taste of the hardships they faced. It's near King of Prussia, which has a number of great shopping malls, so we can see Holiday decorations there and also spend the night nearby at the Inn at Saint Peter's Village. And if we're still friends and not tuckered out, we can visit Independence Hall in Philly on the drive back. So, it'll be the four of us plus Jan and Yang if they want to come. And how about this? We can call Nila and Sanjay New Year's Eve. We can have a party at my and Nari's apartment.

Just think, it'll be another Mag-Seven reunion, and this time I'll include Jan."

No spoke because Eve had inadvertently dumped too much, but Nari did a minute later. "This could be a lot of fun, but hey, who got an invite from Irani for a Christmas Eve dinner and church service? I said no, but what about you?"

Eve said, "Sure I'm going. I want to see how she and Tiana are getting along. What about the rest of you?"

Alonzo looked like he was ready to rejoin the conversation. "Monet and I will be there."

Sensing that Eve wanted to leave, Monet said, "Well then, we have a nice agenda for the next two weeks, so let's adjourn. Eve can give us the particulars between now and Christmas Eve."

Eve settled down more on the drive home.

I can't stay mad at Alonzo. Even when he's in a bad mood, his good looks make the situation look better; and in this case he's right, so I'll take his and Monet's advice. But he seems upset about more than my slides. I better call to find out what's bothering him.

Eve started talking five minutes later.

"Hey Bro, thanks for your comments. I'm taking all the advice you and Monet gave me. And I hope all of us stick to our Holiday agenda. But you seemed upset. Is there something going on between you and Monet?"

"Hey Sis, I'm glad you're calling. Your stuff is actually pretty good. You're clever with words, so you can doctor it up without anyone's help."

Eve had to fill the pause because she sensed Alonzo's reluctance to talk more. "OK, but what about you and Monet? Anything I should know?"

"We're fine, but my embassy job's no longer as exciting as it was a year ago. Then I was doing things that meant something. I was pulling my weight, but all the projects I spearheaded have been turned over to people in Zimbabwe because they're onsite. I'm too far away, doing nothing but shuffling papers and writing summaries. I want action where what I can do something."

What does Monet say?"

"She knows me pretty well. I'm the type that's primed for action right now. My age, attitude, and personality are ready to do stuff. And my smarts, health, and fitness can qualify me for lots of slots."

"What are you looking into?"

"Special forces, like Navy SEALS or Army Delta Force." "You're kidding… aren't you?"

"My first choice is SEALS, but I'll be pleased with either. And the recruiters think I'm a prime candidate. I've gone through all the qualifying rounds and should hear by the end of the year."

"But what about Monica? Aren't you two unofficial co-friends?" "We are, and we can stay that way. I can do my training and be

stationed in Virginia. Hey, you and Monet are the only ones who know what I'm thinking about. You're sworn to secrecy until I know I'm in, and then I'll tell only a chosen few. Deal?"

"Can I tell Miss Irani? She's the best I know for keeping secrets." "No, I'll tell her myself. What do you think she'll say?"

"I got her advice a couple of years ago when I was struggling through what you're going through now. She'd approve your decision as long as you realize that you're responsible for finding whatever meaning satisfies your personal, professional, and social lives.

There's no grand purpose that you've been chosen for, and she'll support your decision as long as you've kept all this in mind while making it."

"Is that why you picked up the paralegal certification and are doing that political consulting?"

"What do you think? I'm a great wordsmith and like making recommendations that political leaders can use. I bet Monet, Nila, and Sanjay would tell you the same because it seems to me that's why they're doing what they're doing. So don't worry, be happy."

"But what if I don't get in? Then what?"

"Like you said, there are lots of slots, so here's more wisdom from Miss Irani. You can do just about anything that's meaningful to you as long as you go all in. Maybe you'll have to settle for a lesser role, but that's OK. Don't let your ego get in the way."

Eve could hear Alonzo's take-charge tone come through loud and clear.

"You are so right. I'll let you know as soon as I hear if I've been accepted. Now you go and nail down details for our Holiday agenda."

Tiana's cast and arm sling had been retired by the time Christmas arrived, and that made her even quicker when decorating the tree and setting the dining room table for Christmas Eve festivities. She even helped make dinner while Irani described who'd be coming and where they'd be going. By the time Eve, Monet, and Alonzo were seated, Tiana sparkled like the tinsel on the Christmas tree. So did her words.

"This is our traditional Christmas Eve dinner. I think you'll like the baked beans and meatballs and all the trimmings I helped with."

Eve spoke after finishing a second bite of her first meatball.

"It's all good, and getting together at holidays keeps traditions alive, don't you think?"

The adults all nodded and turned their gazes toward Tiana, who was basking in the glow of their interest in what she had to say.

"That's what Miss Irani says, and she also says I should always respect the traditions and beliefs of other people, even if I think they're silly."

Monet said, "That is excellent advice. People living in other countries often have different ways of viewing the world. Sometimes they may seem irrational, like they're believing in magic, but sometimes even rational people believe – or pretend to believe – in magic because it just helps you enjoy or get through something. Lots of people say they believe in Santa Claus."

Irani helped Tiana by saying, "Tea is very smart and knows a lot about DNA and evolution. She and I talked about DNA controlling our emotions and feelings, which in turn affect a society's customs. Christmas Eve church services are prime examples."

Alonzo used Irani's last sentence to join the discussion. "Why are we going to the Metropolitan African Church?"

"Because it's not far from Tea's old neighborhood, and according to what was posted online, tonight's service will highlight the birth of Jesus as well as the start of Kwanza."

Alonzo's puzzled look let Tiana shine even more.

"It's a weeklong celebration held only in America to honor African heritage in the African-American culture. It lasts for seven days because each one is for a different thingamabob, but I don't remember what they are. Sorry."

Eve said, "Don't be sorry. You just used a neat word, I bet you learned from Miss Irani. And before we go to church, you and I can go online to check out those thingamajigs."

Tiana glowed even brighter.

"I did. She's awfully smart. I bet she's smarter than all of us put together." Irani dodged the compliment.

"No, just older. And judging by all the activities Monet and Alonzo have going on, they'll be way beyond me soon enough."

Monet and Alonzo carried the conversation way beyond Irani's stopping point.

It was past midnight by the time Irani was sitting on the edge of the bed, getting ready to say goodnight to Tiana. Still elated by the night's excitement, Tiana wanted to keep the night going.

"What a neat church. Can we go back sometime? Now I know Kwanzaa's seven principles – unity, self-determination, collective work and economics, and uh… I forgot, what are the others?"

"I'm proud of you; you really paid attention. The last three are purpose, creativity, and faith. And before I forget, I want to give you a special present."

Irani placed a box wrapped in gold foil into Tiana's hand. "Can I open it now?"

"I think you should; after all, it's now Christmas Day."

"Tiana daintily removed the paper, then the top of a jewelry box, before issuing a tiny gasp.

"It's a pair of lightning bolt earrings, just like yours and Eve's. When can I get my ears pierced?"

"How about Monday?"

"Cool, it'll be fun to be part of the mall crowd." Tea hugged Irani before saying more.

"This has been the neatest Christmas Eve ever. Thank you for making it that way." "For me too, now go to sleep so you can open more gifts later today."

Electra didn't want to go to bed. She went to the living room instead and sat on the sofa to enjoy the ambiance of the still-lighted Christmas tree and the events of tonight that were floating in memory.

What a joyful and colorful church service. And what fun Tiana had joining in the singing.

A dormant emotion pinged, bringing a touch of melancholy to Electra's joy that brought a stream of tears along with her stream- of-conscious musing.

So many Christmas Eves celebrated here, and I'll remember this one even more than Tiana might. My dearly departed grandfather and father gave me wonderful Christmas memories when I was her age, but way back then not even my exceptional cognition could match the depth of subliminal feelings. I'm so sad I never hugged and thanked them for the emotional treasures, but I'll seek redemption by paying them forward to Tiana.

Another emotion pinged, this time bringing with it a poem.

Mother wrote a second poem whose title is identical to the one I gave to Tiana, but with one additional word tacked on. It's named In the Now – Redux and it fits how I feel at this very moment:

The past is but a memory,
The future a dream unknown.
But your present gives a gift you see,
Opened by you alone.

Past a melancholy view,
No more forever gone.
Future problematic too,
Outcomes may be wrong.

So immerse yourself in what is now,
Engage with what's now here.
Embrace the most that fate allows,
Future memories will be dear.

The ping vanished and so did Electra's tears as her mood elevated and she rose to go to bed. She wanted to be ready for later that morning when opening her present, which would be watching Tiana open hers. Irani would be ready too; the lightning brain would make it so.

Chapter 5
December 2162

"An Eve-Styled Post-Christmas"

Worried about an approaching snowstorm, neither Jan nor Yang wanted to risk a trip to Valley Forge, but that didn't deter Eve. She borrowed Irani's SUV and planned to split the drive time with Alonzo, but he volunteered to do it all. Monet sat next to him while Eve and Nari sat in back. And though the snow started falling when halfway to the national park, it didn't slow down the conversation that Eve drove.

"Seeing the park while snow's falling will simply heighten our appreciation for what Washington's soldiers had to face. I sure wouldn't want to sleep out in the snow, would you?"

Nari was the first to answer.

"I think you would if you had no other choice. But if you did, you wouldn't." Monet didn't turn around but did offer her thoughts.

"Most people will always choose the better of two goods, or the lesser of two evils, but Eve says Miss Irani runs outdoors no matter what the weather's like. She certainly is extraordinary. No wonder Eve's doing so well."

Nari seized what Monet had just said to segue to something she knew was better than good. She handed a page to Monet and Eve before talking.

"Well, let me show you what I've been working on, and I didn't need Miss Irani's help. It's my diagram showing forms of government. I'll use this as a preamble for a presentation I'll give covering a new type of politics."

Silence followed until the readers were ready to talk. Monet did so first.

Forms of Government

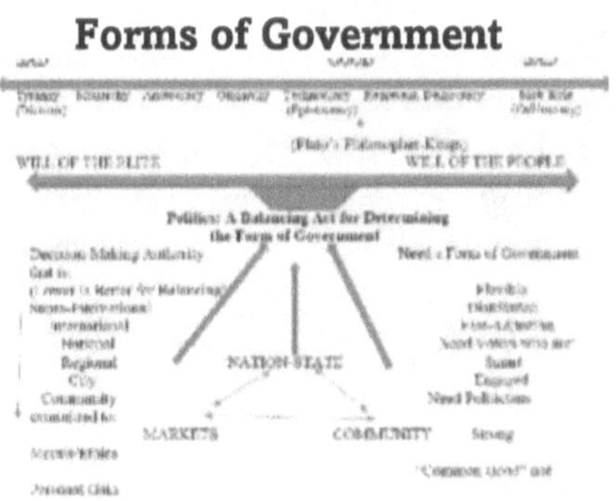

"This is very good… clear and concise and visually appealing." Nari interrupted before Monet could say more.

"Thank you. And you don't have to be as smart as Monet to understand it. Anyone with a working brain can see that the three pillars of our country – the Nation-State, Open Markets, and Communities – form the tripod that balances Politics. And the balance determines what form of government we get. And notice it's always better to push decision-making as far down as possible to get the right balance. And how do we get it right? We need smart voters who are willing to take a stand as well as get involved, and politicians who place ethics and the 'common good' ahead of their personal balance sheets."

Nari said nothing else, hoping that her satisfied smile concealed her gloating when she asked Eve what she thought.

Eve rubbed the back of her head before saying, "Monet's right, but I can't tell from it what's your new type of politics. So, what is it?"

"I call it Quantum Politics. And I'll tell you all about it if you listen to the presentation I'll give to President Huston. But I'll say nothing else right now, other than I'm going to explain how the President can use my recommendations to lead the way out of a growing worldwide crisis confronting Democracy."

Everyone had heard enough for the time being, so the readers withdrew into their own thoughts until Alonzo finally said, "I like what Nari said, but let's get back to having fun. We'll be at the visitor's center soon, so let's let Eve tell us again about today's agenda…"

By the time Alonzo pulled into a near-empty parking area, the temperature had fallen just below freezing, which made for icy conditions on the walk to the entrance. Monet and Nari latched onto Alonzo for support, but Eve pranced ahead. She glanced over her shoulder before saying, "Hey, step lively, the footing's pretty good. Just watch meee –"

Eve's backward fall interrupted the flow of words. Her darting legs began a combination jig and tap dance once gravity's inexorable pull took over. Her body was completely horizontal and two feet above the surface, making her look like a magician with the power of levitation that her wildly flapping arms accentuated. Unfortunately, Eve was accelerating in the wrong direction. She crashed onto the ice-slick concrete, issuing an 'oof' upon landing."

Alonzo dashed to Eve before kneeling to assess the damage. "Don't move until we've checked you out."

Though remaining motionless, Eve had other ideas. "The only thing I injured is my pride. Pick me up…"

Alonzo did so and then let Monet and Nari straighten her out. By the time they did so while embellishing a story of what they had seen, all three were gripping one another to keep their laughter from producing a collective repeat performance. Alonzo said nothing, preferring to remain at a safe distance.

The still-laughing ladies finally moved toward the entrance, Alonzo trailing, while Eve found the right words.

"Well, I just demonstrated why we'll spend more time inside and then driving instead of walking around the park. And by then it'll be dark, so we'll skip touring King of Prussia malls and go directly to Saint Peter's. Alonzo knows the way, but he better not tell Saint Peter I fell down and went boom. Otherwise, he might not let me into the Inn…"

Darkness and falling snow were making the rural winding roads treacherous, but according to the park ranger, Alonzo's route was the best. His passengers chatted about what they had learned but had the good sense not to ask him; the road and weather needed his full attention.

Traffic was nearly nil, but a pair of headlights closed from behind and then sped past, disappearing around the curve ahead. The intrusion stopped the conversation until Eve spoke.

"Maybe that's a local who knows the roads, but not even I would drive like that. Stay the course."

Saying nothing, Alonzo nodded, but after rounding another sharp left-hand curve two miles later, he began yelling commands to his partners as he swerved onto the right-hand shoulder and pumped the brakes.

"Accident dead ahead, hang on." Alonzo's alert actions kept the car from spinning off the shoulder and down the slope as he slid past a two-car pileup. The occupants from one car stood huddled in front, watching flames spreading from the other. Alonzo shouted again as soon as he stopped.

"Call 911 and stay in the car." Then he popped the trunk release and bolted. He grabbed the fire extinguisher from the trunk and ran past the startled spectators.

The flames from the burning car illuminated a surreal scene: two trapped passengers struggling to get out. Alonzo used the extinguisher to smash windows before pulling them out. His actions galvanized the others to drag them to safety while he emptied the extinguisher. By the time a state police car and ambulance arrived, the accident victims had recovered enough to cram into the remaining car. Alonzo and his partners were back in Irani's SUV.

Alonzo exited when a flashlight-wielding trooper motioned and then strode to meet him midway to the scene of the collision. Once there, he waited for the trooper to start talking.

"They tell me you deserve a medal; what's your name and cellphone number? I gotta put them on my report."

Alonzo gave enough facts to the trooper, who wrapped up the conversation after entering them in his hand-held.

"Not many people could do what you did. I want to thank you on behalf of those you saved. We won't call unless there's more to the investigation, but it's clear the driver was going much too fast. But do you need directions to where you're going?"

"No, sir. I think the Inn at Saint Peter's is a couple of miles up the road."

"You got it right, so drive safe and good luck." After the officer shook Alonzo's hand, each trudged in opposite directions.

Monet was the first to speak after he started driving and relaying what the trooper had said.

"There are few are like you; that's why you are tonight's hero and will make a great navy SEAL."

Eve added more.

"How did you know there was a fire extinguisher in the trunk?" "You know me, I'm damn thorough. I checked the trunk before

we left." Nari filled in after Alonzo's abrupt halt.

"It's in his DNA, and I know it's in yours too, but enough talk until we get to the Inn."

Next morning's sunshine and temperatures made the foursome's late morning stroll among the shops much better than yesterday's slipping and sliding, but those events had slowed Eve's usual fast pace when walking or talking. Nari kept the lunchtime discussion moving when she floated an idea for the group to discuss.

"I think we've had enough… let's skip out of touring King of Prussia malls or Independence Hall and drive back now. That'll give Eve extra time to line up our big event for New Year's Eve. Let's hear what she thinks."

"That's AOK by me; I've rescheduled some of it from the 31st to the 30th because of the nine-hour time difference. All of us will come to our apartment at 1 p.m. so we can place a video call to Nila and Sanjay. Yang and Jan will join us, and we'll go out to a Chinese restaurant afterward for a late lunch. Sound OK?"

Stretching his hand-locked arms over his head, Alonzo preempted Nari.

"You bet. I know the way, and driving on a sunny day beats getting sideways in the snow."

Eve had her three couples seated as planned in front of the wall monitor when she made the Internet connection to Nila and Sanjay. She became the call facilitator as soon as Nila and Sanjay appeared.

"Hello from five of the Mag-Seven plus one recruit. You're looking good here. How's reception there?"

Sanjay played a similar role at his end.

"OK here, and we're glad you're calling today. We'll be going to a New Year's party tomorrow hosted by my Baba. How have you been?"

Eve continued.

"Wait till you hear about our trip to Valley Forge and how Alonzo saved the day. In fact–"

Nari interrupted to steer the conversation elsewhere.

"I already sent them a summary Email. Jan and Yang got it too, and I attached your Mindset Guideline slides as well as my set that describes Forms of Government. Let's let Jan, Yang, and Monet make an objective comparison. They can judge which is better."

Sanjay responded quicker than Eve to Nari's gambit.

"Yes, that's possible but I would like to include my Blockchain and Cryptocurrency slide in the competition. I'll explain while showing it, and we can let our panel of judges pick the best."

Nari recovered faster than Eve and said, "That sounds fair. Are there any complaints?" There were none, so Sanjay took over by displaying his slide before talking.

Slide 1
Blockchain and Cryptocurrency
The Tool for Eliminating Social Gaps

"I will use this slide when making a presentation to our clients. I haven't completed it yet, but I can talk you through enough so you understand.

"My Baba and I see great opportunity for our software business if we provide Blockchain and Cryptocurrency augmented services to many economic sectors once corporate management grasps what our apps can do, and what is that? They can close the Trust Gap across the entire spectrum of social transactions. There are trust gaps in every media-reported news program, in every political debate and in every distribution chain connecting producers and consumers."

Sanjay waited several seconds for his viewers to assimilate what he had just said before continuing.

"Think what takes place in every series of transactions. At every transfer point, all parties must trust one another, and the audit trail is the supposedly objective recording of the facts. But everyone knows that current audit trails are subject to fraud and tampering. And that's what Blockchain and Cryptocurrency technology can eliminate. The column on the far right implements gap management with Blockchains."

Sanjay paused again before continuing.

"Think of each transaction as a table, or a spreadsheet of data describing the transaction. All the blocks along the path are chained together into a Blockchain that is encrypted and verified en route by 'miners' before being stored in a decentralized database open to everyone. Buyers and sellers use cryptocurrency to pay for services, and the miners earn cryptocurrency for decrypting, verifying, and re-encrypting.

"And yes, this technology is disruptive and far-reaching. Established companies and their employees must adapt or become extinct as new ones and people with the right skills take over, but this has always been the trajectory of progress. Wouldn't you agree?"

Glancing at her fellow listeners, Eve saw blank expressions on all but Monet, so she motioned for her to say something.

"I understand your diagram but I never thought about Blockchain at this level of futuristic abstraction. You're putting many people out of work. How much of the software is currently available? You'll need to bring your presentation down to a level your clients can understand if you want your investors to back it. What else can you tell us?"

"Nothing right now; Nila and I are still putting the presentation together, and we are still coding the apps. Release date is unknown."

Nari grinned knowingly before leading on.

"Well, our three judges have seen and heard all they need. We'll let them huddle to make their decision."

Jan, Yang, and Monet separated from the others and whispered for only a couple of minutes before smiling mischievously and returning. Monet donned her Mona Lisa smile as she stepped forward to announce the results.

"We find that all the slides are winners because they take the material to a new level, and we believe that presentations will help audiences understand even better than the slides. Therefore, we award the bronze medal to Sanjay for Blockchain," silver goes to Eve for Mindset Guidelines, and gold to Nari for Quantum Politics."

Everyone but Alonzo applauded and kidded for a couple of minutes; afterward, Eve asked him what was wrong.

"None of your stuff is easy to understand. You think there are enough people interested enough to figure it out?"

"They will when the time comes, so let's get to something else. Why don't we each spend a minute outlining some of our plans for the coming year?"

Though it took longer than a minute, by the time Eve started wrapping up the call everyone had a good idea what the others would be doing.

"This has been fun, so we must hold a group chat in a couple of months, uh –" Nari waved because she wanted to add some words, so Eve stepped aside. "We six are gonna go to a Chinese restaurant as soon as the call's over, and I recommend that we get eight fortune cookies, one for each of us. Then we'll let Eve open them all before assigning the most fitting fortune to each. Do we all agree?"

Only Yang dissented.

"What if I no like what she give me? Then what?"

Jan stepped in to say, "You can trade with me if you like mine better." Eve took control again and said, "A great way to end the call. Out with the old and in with the new. And Happy New Year to all as our plans come into view."

Chapter 6
January 2163

"Full Speed into the New Year"

The Irani-Electra duo had completed launching all new year's new projects as the first week of January came to an end, which meant they could pause Friday morning to review how much busier they might be than before. When Irani pondered the implications, Electra knew what to say.

"We've always been master multi-taskers, letting our obsessive-compulsive tendencies power through fatigue and obstacles. But doing so always adds to our focus on the clock and subtracts from our enjoyment of the moment. However, our new projects overlap with some of the old, making them easier to juggle. And besides, these projects are what we want to do, not preparatory hoops we have to jump through. What do you think?"

"Agreed. Tiana will be a joy to take care of, and Eve can help us do so. Professor Plannert and Jonathan offer opportunities to combine existing projects with new ones, which makes for easier start-ups. And finally, a new fitness program will fit us to a 'T'. I'm sure Indira would like the pun."

"Whoever talks to her first can ask. And that might be you. Eve told you all about the siblings' post-Holiday excitement, and that will help you because you've already been invited as a guest attendee to the next President Huston meeting. And we'll go; it's always in our best interest to maintain ties to all clients, even if we are merely observing from the shadows. And after our relaxing post-Christmas, it's full speed ahead for us."

Irani fingered away at her office workstation until a call interrupted the flow. Wanda's cautious greeting refocused her attention.

"Yes, now that she's recovered, I've been driving Tiana to and from school. And I believe my tutoring during distance learning helped. So, what's the latest?"

"She got in a fight this morning and is still upset. Could you meet us in my office?"

"I'm on my way…"

An hour later, Tiana huffed a summary of the episode one more time. "… and I got so mad when the little guy kept making fun of my scars and crossed eye that I couldn't take it anymore. That's when I slugged the bigger guy in the nose. You'd a done the same."

Wanda's pleading look told Irani she should speak, hoping that she would give soothing words.

"Tea, honey, remember what I said when I taught you self- defense? Punching someone is the last thing you want to do. If you had ignored them and simply walked away, we wouldn't be in Wanda's office. But I know how you feel, so how about this… we can take care of the lazy eye and scars with a little cosmetic surgery. Would you like that?"

Tea's scowl faded. "It won't hurt, will it?"

Wanda came back into the conversation.

"Not a bit. Today's computer-assisted surgery is magical. And I can speak from my own scar removal experience. Other than being a bit old and weather-beaten, how does my face look to you?"

Wanda's self-effacing humor lightened the mood and brought smiles to everyone. And the ensuing pause gave Irani a segue for ending the meeting. "And I'm sure Wanda would say it'll make your new hairstyle that much more striking. So, I guess it's time you get back to class while Wanda and I get back to work."

Everyone agreed and got up to move on; Electra too, though only she seemed to have caught Irani's pun.

Irani took a detour on the way home, checking out a fitness center whose Website showed it had what she was still missing.

My Sole pro model elliptical cross-trainer and companion Peloton bike are doing nicely in my fitness center, but I need a place to swim because I'm waiting for a better season to have the above-ground lap pool installed. This center has a couple of pools plus youth programs that Tiana might like. I'll scout the place before picking her up.

After answering all of Irani's questions during the twenty-minute tour, the junior staffer took the guest back to her office for a final pitch.

"We're open 24/7, so we'll fit any schedule you have, and the young lady you are taking care of should benefit from our trainers and coaches. They'll strengthen her arm and shoulder before getting her into volleyball and basketball. And from what you've told me about your home fitness equipment, you might like to join our triathlon club. We have men and women of all fitness levels training as well as socializing. I'm certain you'll find some suitable training partners."

"I like what you have. Would you please sign me up for a family membership? My daughter might join us too…"

Irani invited Eve to join her and Tiana for a light workout on Saturday afternoon, followed by pizza at a place Tiana picked. Irani gave the leftover slices to Eve, and just before leaving asked Eve for a favor, not immediately, but sometime in the future. She might start to travel more, and when she does would like Eve to stay with Tiana.

Eve winked at Tiana before answering.

"You're tough-love tactics did me lots good, and you can count on me to dish out lots of praise or punishment. Just say the word."

Tiana's playful poke in Eve's ribs punctuated her words before saying more.

"And since actions speak even louder, I better stop while I'm still standing."

Professor Plannert made sure Irani's GWU work kept moving ahead by inviting her and Jonathan to the mid-January committee meeting. She played a listener's role today, but depending on the outcome might need to devote more effort soon. Plannert started the meeting using his collegial style by asking members to outline any topics of particular concern. The last to speak directed it toward Irani.

"I keep reading so many articles in the hard as well as soft sciences that make mention of 'entropy.' They bandy it about like they expect everyone to know what it is, yet they give sometimes contradictory definitions. Perhaps Ms. Ramani could clarify."

She directed her reply to Professor Plannert.

"Different disciplines use it differently. I'd be happy to clarify all this for the Committee, but I need to summarize my notes before explaining. May I present them at next month's meeting?"

"Very sensible, so let's move to our guest speaker, which once again is Professor Segal."

Jonathan glanced at his laptop for several seconds before talking. "The U.S. Navy likes my extension proposal and will fund me for two additional years, which means they'll upgrade the AUV they've already lent me. And –"

Jonathan interrupted himself to answer a question that was about to be asked.

"Uh, let me clarify. AUV is the Navy acronym for 'autonomous underwater vehicle.' UAV stands for 'unmanned aerial vehicle,' which our other military branches use. Anyway, I'm working out of Woods Hole on Cape Cod and collaborating with a couple of the researchers, but I could use another person or two, preferably from GWU. Maybe Irani would be interested."

Plannert looked at Irani for the answer. It came soon after Electra's silent words agreed with Irani's feelings.

Lots of professional as well as personal possibilities here, but be discreet – for now.

"I would if Jonathan thinks I can contribute. What do you propose?"

"I can take you on a Woods Hole weekend tour as soon as our schedules mesh. That'll give us plenty of time to brief you because I know you're a quick study…"

Jonathan's friendly but forthright personality made him a quick study too.

By the end of the week, he had sifted through the paltry amount of online information regarding a person who might have everything needed to help him professionally as well as personally, and he made the call that Friday evening.

Irani's calm voice became lively once she recognized the caller. "And good evening to you. How's the man who's investigating alien worlds?"

"Fine and dandy, and I'd like you to spend next weekend with me at Woods Hole, exploring some of what's already in place before prepping for more. I can pick you up early next Friday, and I promise you won't be bored. We can use the eight-hour drive time to talk about ourselves and our work. In preparation, I snooped online but there's not much about you. Will that be OK with you?"

Electra chose a reply that would keep Jonathan on the line and perhaps add to his growing infatuation with her.

"You're asking for a three-answers-in-one reply, and I'll answer yes to all, but please call me by the middle of the week; I need to make appropriate arrangements, and if you tell me the agenda, I'll pack the right items."

Jonathan's tone told Irani he liked what he had heard.

"Your clever use of words is nice to listen to, and I hope mine are too. Here's the plan so far. Friday, we drive and talk and then have dinner and stay near the Woods Hole Village complex. Saturday, we tour the visitor center and aquarium and research labs. And Sunday, I show you my AUV and other gear before taking you home. You can pack like you're going on a casual winter weekend outing. I'll have anything extra you might need."

Both Irani and Electra resisted the urge to tease him.

I'm not ready to unleash puns about what I might need in the AUV or bedroom. I'll let him lead those games.

"I'm glad you're inviting me, and I should be able to adjust my schedule, but please call me back to confirm."

After ending the call, a curious feeling registered in Electra's emotional persona.

Long, long ago in a different world, before the lightning brain merged Alisha and me, we used to look for tunes with mysterious rhyme, and Jonathan's awakened two I can almost see.

They're drawing me to him and I think he might feel the same; perhaps it's time to start another game. For my part, if I wish to play along, I'm beginning to hear Laura Brannigan's sexually- charged ethereal song.

What's its name? I remember now, it's Self Control. The words are coming to me and making me feel… I'm beginning to sway back and forth, like I'm ready to rock while my emotions reel…

Oh the night is my world,
City light painted girl.
In the day nothing matters,
It's the night time that flatters.
In the night no control,
Through the wall something's breaking.
Wearing white as you're walking,
Down the street of my soul.
You take myself, you take my self-control,
You got me livin' only for the night.
Before the morning comes the story's told,
You take myself you take my self-control.
Another night another day goes by,
I never stop myself to wonder why.
You help me to forget to play my role,
You take myself you take my self-control.
I, I live among the creatures of the night,
I haven't got the will to try and fight.
Against a new tomorrow,
So I guess I'll just believe it that tomorrow never comes.
A safe night, I'm living in the forest of my dream,
I know the night is not what it would seem.
I must believe in something so I'll make myself believe it,
That this night will never go.
Oh oh oh, oh oh oh, oh oh oh, oh oh oh…

The song looped an indefinite number of times before Electra regained partial control.

And for Jonathan, I'm hearing Smooth Operator, sung by Sade…
Diamond life, lover boy,
He move in space with minimum waste and maximum joy.
City lights and business nights,
When you require streetcar desire for higher heights.
No place for beginners or sensitive hearts,
When sentiment is left to chance.
No place to be ending,
But somewhere to start.
No need to ask he's a smooth operator,
Smooth operator.
Smooth operator,
Smooth operator.
Coast to coast, LA to Chicago,
Western male.
Across the north and the south,
To Key Largo, love for sale.
Face to face, Each classic case.
We shadow box and double cross,
Yet need the chase.
A license to love,
Insurance to hold.
Melts all your mem'ries,
And change into gold.
His eyes are like angels,
But his heart is cold.
No need to ask,
He's a smooth operator.
Smooth operator,
Smooth operator,
Smooth operator.
Coast to coast, LA to Chicago,
Western male.
Across the north and the south,
To Key Largo, love for sale.
Smooth operator,
Smooth operator…

The song played enough times to indulge Electra's desires before she realized that she was approaching a danger zone.

I'm becoming obsessive compulsive… I better shut down and sleep; I'll consider more when I'm more in control…

Irani awoke in better control but still enraptured by last night's emotional jolt.

That was the most male attraction I've felt since I wanted Carter to help me build my Dream Team; too bad my DNA wouldn't allow it. But I don't need to experiment further. My clone children showed me why. They're smart and talented, and I love them like the mother I am, but the lightning brain is sui generis. Not even another lightning strike can come close.

But what about my Jonathan relationship? Can I make last night's fantasy come true? No, I control only half and he controls the rest, so I better not push. I've learned that when I do, I overpower males, so I'll just relax and enjoy what comes my way. And I better learn more about what I might be in for.

Irani matched Jonathan's quick-study action during the next couple of days. Before retrieving a plethora of data and profiling him, she arranged for Eve to be with Tiana next weekend. By the time she finished packing Thursday evening, she had everything needed.

He's definitely an up-and-coming player in extra-terrestrial R&D, plugged into academics, business, and perhaps DARPA too. Publications and patents suggest he wants to have it all – recognition, status, and money. And I figured this out without hacking into personal files. And I won't have to, I'll find out whatever else just by playing with words… and with Jonathan too.

Friday's weather and traffic made for both pleasant travel and conversation. Irani let Jonathan do most of the talking, adding comments whenever appropriate.

Confident guys like Jonathan like to impress the ladies they like. And lucky me, he's filling in a few remaining gaps in what I know. And he's not that self-centered. He genuinely wants to know more about me.

His interest became even more apparent as the trip and talk wound down.

"From what I know about you so far, you've got talents that can take you beyond where your consulting business is going. Don't you want more out of life?"

Irani needed no reminders from Electra.

Don't show what's beneath the tip of the proverbial iceberg. And let's see how he connects more out of life to happiness, but be discreet.

"I had an almost-significant other who you remind me of, a cerebral economist type, with many traits you share. But I like how you're more into the real than the philosophical. He always questioned what happiness is and how possessions might or might not get in the way."

Irani paused, expecting Jonathan's attraction to her to bring out his thoughts while keeping his eyes on the road.

"I'm not intruding in your current love life, am I? Just say so if I am and I won't push where I don't belong."

Irani copied Monet's Mona Lisa smile that told Jonathan, after glancing at her, to keep talking.

"I never worry about being happy. I'm pretty happy now, and my happiness grows as I keep moving up. I know that philosophers write volumes about having too much sometimes gives you too little happiness because of the trouble wealth causes, but I'll worry about that when I get there. My personality is pretty well adjusted, and yours seems that way too."

Perfect segue… Here we go.

"I continue studying personality types and applying what I learn to the psychology and sociology called for in my consulting assignments. What do you know about personality theory?"

"A fair amount. I know that Maslow's Hierarchy of Needs – you know, the pyramid going from physiological to security to belonging to esteem to self-actualization – is still in use, as is Myers-Briggs personality trait dimensions you know I/E, S/N, T/F, and J/P." Irani decided to raise the intellectual bar.

"I'm impressed. Most people can't recite the levels or dimensions, but are you familiar with the Graves Spiral Dynamics model that extends Maslow's hierarchy?"

"No, what's it like?"

"Let me preface my remarks by quoting its creator, Clare Graves, a late 20th-century professor of psychology at Cleveland's Case Western Reserve University. 'What I am proposing is that the psychology of a mature human being is an unfolding, emergent, oscillating spiraling process marked by progressive subordination of older, lower-order behavior systems to newer, higher-order systems as man's existential problems stage further.' I particularly like his analogy to an emergent and oscillating spiraling process that may take civilization to higher, or maybe lower-order states that are contingent on future existential problems, wouldn't you agree?"

Jonathan's slower reply sounded like that of a respectful student. "How d'you remember the quote and the connection to emergent properties?"

"I've got a good memory, and let me describe more. Its hierarchy contains eight color-codes levels grouped into two tiers.

"Tier One contains six: beige for Archaic/Instinctive survival, purple for Magical/Animistic tribal security, red for Domination/Power impulse, blue for Order/Authoritarian control, orange for Success/Capitalism achieved via markets and competition, and green for Community/Ecological human relations.

"Tier Two contains yellow for Systematic/Integrative thinking, and turquoise for Holistic/Universal vision. And according to Graves, only Jesus or the Buddha reached Turquois, but that should be mankind's target, regardless of religious beliefs. What tier and level do you think America's at?"

"I'd guess we as well as Western Europe oscillate between orange and green."

"Excellent, you get high marks for following my impromptu lecture. And now let's move to the Myers-Briggs extension. It's the 'Big Five' horizontal attributes model, which is highly correlated with M-B. The attributes are Openness, Conscientiousness, Extroversion, Agreeableness, and Neuroticism.

"And some psychologists have synthesized a two-dimensional sexual preferences map incorporating only the attributes that titillate the senses that important for sex. The map displays the five sex groupings, which are 'Feel-Good-Moment-Seekers,' 'Excitement- Seekers,' 'Experimenters,' 'Love Connectors,' and 'Confused/Lower- Drivers.' It also shows the location of all sixteen M-B personality types. Do you know what type you are?"

"It's been so long since I did my profiling. But your score can sometimes put you in more than one personality type or change over time. It's sort of a quasi-numeric judgment call, isn't it?"

"That's a great way to characterize it. Why don't we revisit all this when we get to know one another better? Then I'll tell you my personality type, and you can tell me yours."

Jonathan's voice struck a note of relief.

"Good. I was beginning to get overloaded by thinking and driving at the same time. But you sure know your stuff. I'm convinced you can do much more than just socio-political consulting. Maybe we can help each other by working together. What do you know about science and technology?"

Irani revealed only the tip, but Jonathan glimpsed more than she had intended and commended what he had discerned.

"You've got an exceptional brain. How did you master so much about math, physics, and computers as well as neurobiology?"

"It's not that much. So, what's in store?"

This weekend you'll see some of my undersea projects that you could help me accelerate, and sometime I'll tell you about some of my NASA activities. But my brain's tired and maybe yours is too. We've talked and listened enough, so let's take a break."

The couple rode in comfortable silence to the end of the drive and then exited when reaching the bed and breakfast. The winter air carried a tangy brine and seaweed-tinged fragrance that twirled about as they stepped to the entrance, and after registering they walked to the Water Street Kitchen. The clam chowder piqued their appetites and enhanced Jonathan's telling about local geography.

"We're situated between Buzzard's Bay and Vineyard Sound. Martha's Vineyard is seven miles offshore and south of where we're sitting. And every summer, Woods Hole hosts the premier seven- mile Falmouth Road Race that ends in Falmouth Heights. It attracts over ten thousand entrants and elite runners from around the world. There's a story about Alberto Salazar, one of the all-time greats of American distance running, winning the race but afterward needing to be packed in ice and given intravenous rehydration. Say, you look awfully fit. Do you run races?"

"No, but I do endurance training. You look fit too. Do you?"

"I run, but the only racing I do is to get projects done and papers written. Ah-ha, here comes the main course. You'll love the lobster."

The cold temperature prevented strolling along the nearby harbor, so Jonathan walked Irani to her door, and a sudden impulse grabbed her when he kissed her on the cheek. She caressed the back of his neck with her right hand and with eyes wide open drew his lips to hers before using her skills to gauge Jonathan's interest level. A lingering French kiss told her what she wanted to know.

He's enjoying the moment but his closed eyes show he's not ready to look for more… tonight I won't either.

Jonathan spoke after their lips separated and he caught his breath.

"Wow, I hope the rest of the weekend is as stimulating for you as that was for me. How about I knock on your door at eight for breakfast?"

"Perfect, and I'm certain the entire weekend will be as good as tonight. Sleep well…"

Jonathan did everything possible on Saturday to meet Irani's expectations.

He added comments regarding subsurface vehicles to those given by the visitor center's volunteer guides and gave her a behind-the- scenes tour of the aquarium because it collaborated with the research center. And for the remainder of the day, he walked her through a number of his research center projects after taking her through the labs and then ending up in his office.

Irani absorbed it all and listened whenever Electra summarized what they could do.

He can certainly help us collect undersea creatures whose DNA we can compare to homo sapiens. And his interest in cephalopods matches ours, as does his rare earths seafloor mining. His Navy and DARPA connections give him advanced subsurface vehicles, and we can try to convince him to install our dummied-down version of Indira's guidance and control software for manned as well as drone autonomous underwater vehicles.

We'll share our findings and tell him to claim most of the credit. All we need is access to his AUVs. The possibilities are getting better and better…

Jonathan accepted a researcher's invitation to dinner at their home. Bob Rodenbaugh and his wife Marlene– both marine biologists – complimented Jonathan for finding a companion who could keep up with their conversation. Irani deflected as much as she could, but Jonathan's enthusiasm couldn't be contained.

"Yep, she's got some great ideas. And after I speed up my undersea projects, maybe I can connect her to my NASA contracts. But that'll take us into some heavy-duty quantum physics that even I struggle with. Some of my NASA co-researchers are like rocket scientists who bat around terms like atomic clocks, entropy, and quantum micro-gravity like they're high school mind games. And some of their talk is as far out as some of our solar system moons where they're aiming to look for life. Not me, at least for now. I'm looking at Mars or Venus. But no matter, I bet Irani will have something novel to say."

"I will, but I'll need to review first."

Marlene picked a lighter discussion topic, and as dinner wound down, Bob asked Jonathan what was on tomorrow's schedule.

"I'll show her my AUVs before we drive back to DC. She'll be impressed that when you do research here, you can walk to the harbor and board a research vessel that can go anywhere. That's just one of the perks we get.

Almost as good as the perk of your dinner invite. But we better get going. It's been a full day, and Irani looks a bit tired. We covered a lot of info today that's probably new for her, so we'll say good night."

Irani played along by saying, "Thank you for dinner, and Jonathan's right. I'll have to study up on marine biology and physics so I can keep up with Jonathan, but that'll be fun, and who knows, maybe the four of us can collaborate on projects or papers. I guess we'll just have to see how well Jonathan's and my personalities get along…"

Private and professional personalities agreed during and after breakfast. Jonathan took her first to the security office for new researcher registration so Irani could gain access to his lab and equipment at any time, and then to his robotic and manned AUVs. He emphasized their complexity while explaining how to pilot and control both hardware and software, and as they walked away, he summarized the morning's training.

"I threw a lot of stuff at you, but don't worry. I'll go over it again whenever you need help."

Irani tugged his arm while walking, but Electra talked first.

No need to worry. *The lightning brain absorbed it all. But keep acting.*

"It's a lot, but you'll be a great mentor."

"You bet, and I'll tell you more on the drive home."

Irani had been doing all the listening for the first half of the drive when a wave of fatigue swept in.

I do like Jonathan, but three days of constant contact has worn me out emotionally. Even the best co-friends need personal spacetime. Time to retreat into my fortress of solitude, but I better exit gracefully so I don't hurt his feelings.

When Jonathan finally paused, Irani stretched her arms and stifled a yawn before saying,

"Your description of extra-terrestrial R&D has worn me out. Is it OK if I nap until we get to my place? I need to be ready for whatever awaits."

"Please do. You'll be home in a couple of hours and I know you'll be ready for action."

Irani nodded then settled back and closed her eyes. The lightning brain did the rest.

Chapter 7
February 2163

"Quantum Action"

The Irani-Electra duo found nothing untoward in the following week or two. Irani arranged for Tiana's March cosmetic surgery and connected with two women at a triathlon club meeting, all the while delving into Jonathan's projects and pushing her existing ones further ahead. Electra decided that her "Three Musketeers" – Rick Tabasko (aka RT), Parson Holsum (PH), and Lucian Perteau (Mr. LP) – three adventuresome professionals that serendipity had brought to her last year, could help the duo stay in the shadows, so she arranged for them to fly to DC this coming Sunday, the last one in February.

In preparation for all the action, Irani arranged a Friday celebration dinner at Eve and Nari's apartment that would keep her close circle of friends where she wanted them: happily out of the way and unaware of her intentions.

Eve scolded Irani and Tiana for being the last to arrive, but her smile said otherwise. Then she herded them into the living room for Nari, Jan, and Yang to say hi. Irani let Tiana explain why they were late and what they were carrying.

"I had to order six different takeout dinners at the multi-ethnic fast-food place. Each is different and in a separate bag. Good thing the robo-chefs are fast. What a production line. You oughta see the action."

The fellows took the bags to the kitchen table; the four ladies began chatting after Eve put coats and Tiana's suitcase away. Nari led off.

"We're happy to have Tea stay with us whenever you're taking care of business somewhere else. We'll keep her suitcase in a safe place, ready whenever she's staying with us. And we'll make sure she takes care of all her schoolwork and other things I know she should, uh –"

Tea's waving hands interrupted so she could talk.

"Next week my science class is gonna study quantum physics, you know, entropy and black holes and wave-particle stuff. I hope you can give me a head start."

The conversation halted until Nari said, "I can tell you about quantum politics, but not quantum physics. I'll leave that for Eve."

Eve said, "Don't worry, we'll get to that, but let's get to the dining room so we can celebrate upcoming action."

Additional introductions weren't needed because Tea already knew about Jan Brewer and Yang Lee. Tea explained dinnertime rules: diners were to select a bag and open simultaneously; they could then barter if they saw something they liked better. Everyone settled down fifteen minutes later. Eve waited an additional five minutes before clinking her glass to pry the talk away from the various cuisines.

"Tea's picks have stimulated our appetites, and now, please get ready to digest the latest update for where some of us will soon be going and doing. Congratulations to Jan. The consulting company I work for has just hired him to be my assistant while he continues writing his Religion and Philosophy thesis. My company loves the Socio-Political Policy Evaluation Filter I developed a couple of years ago, and I've trained my associates how to use it on any number of assignments. And they love how I've added in my Balanced Mindset Guidelines, so when I recommended that they hire Jan, they did. I'll let him tell you more."

Jan's words began flowing as if he and Eve had rehearsed the segue. "The projects from all clients contain issues requiring careful philosophical analysis that exposes deeper and longer-term issues. Think about it; today America faces bioethical problems as well as political battles among our four political parties. Authenticity, expressive individualism, and the meaning of humanism crop up everywhere. And my first assignment is to adjust Eve's presentation before she gives it to her number one client. I'm confident the President will like it."

Eve continued before anyone could speak. "And now, to an even bigger move. I'll let Nari explain."

Nari spoke as soon as all were gazing at her. "I've been promoted to a consulting position in our Beijing office. My Quantum Politics theory clinched it. None of you have seen it, but Eve will when I make my final presentation to President Huston. And my company has hired Yang to come with me. Yang, speak up."

"Move good too for me. I keep working on PhD at MIT because it and Beijing Genomics Institute have project using chimeras for generating body parts. I bet you don't know human DNA contains some from Africa, Europe Neanderthals, and Asia Denisovans. They make up modern homo sapiens, whose body parts can all fit. And today, we make chimera in lab better than fantasy myths. Centaur is half man half horse from Greek; Egypt god Sobek has head of crocodile and body of man. We smarter today. And don't worry no one; Nari and me will be great digital nomad team. We show you."

Irani and Tiana listened as a lively discussion continued, but Electra told Irani it was time to go, so she found a lull to announce her departure.

"What exciting news. Your immediate futures look so bright and I'm proud of the entire group. And you are great role models for Tiana. I'm going to say good night and let you carry on."

Eve said, "But wait until I put dessert on the table. You can take brownie or two with you."

Deciding to be a polite role model too, Irani took only one.

Irani didn't eat hers in the car, instead putting it aside until reaching home, helping Tiana get to bed, and then changing into more comfortable clothes before logging on to her home workstation. She had much to tell Indira and more likely vice versa. Electra had her brownie and Coke at the ready when Indira's avatar appeared.

"Aha, my one and only favorite human. You have been busy, and tonight's action adds even more to your project list that grew on your Cape Cod junket."

Electra sipped the Coke before replying. "Would you like me to elaborate?"

"What do you think? I listened in via the Wi-Fi connections to devices in the apartment. Ergo, I need no exegesis, but you do. You can enjoy your brownie and Coke as I elaborate."

Indira waited for Electra to settle comfortably before saying more. "Nari's departure will require you to help Eve more, but she's
helping you take care of Tiana, so that's a fair trade. And
Jonathan's projects fit our mutual pursuits, so I will help you with them as needed. And I have just prepared material that will help you answer Plannert's committee and Tiana's class assignment as well as some of Jonathan's."

Electra leaned in to speak but Indira waved her off.

"You look like you can handle a bit of an information overload, so sit still and don't interrupt. Your grasp of relativity and quantum physics exceeds that of most mere mortals, but I doubt you have kept up with theoretical developments occurring during your suspension pod rest period. That is why I have prepared these slides. And please pay special attention to the concept of entropy, which is perhaps the most nuanced topic. Use your quick-study skills to refresh your understanding."

Barely pausing, Indira flashed the first slide and continued.

Slide 1
ENTROPY RULES THE UNIVERSE!

Entropy drives the Arrow of Causality.

- Abstract Concept with Contradictory Definitions. Best Starting Point: Chemical Thermodynamics Useful Definitions:
- Open System: Matter and Heat can enter or exit
- Closed System: Matter cannot enter or leave but Heat can
- Isolated System: Neither Matter nor Heat can enter or leave
- Reversible Reaction or Process: A reaction in which the conversion of reactants to products and the conversion of products to reactants occur simultaneously.
- Irreversible Reaction/Process: A reaction in which the reactants convert to products and where the products cannot convert back to the reactants UNLESS ENERGY IS PUT INTO THE REACTION.
- Entropy: S = Measure of Disorder or Randomness or Uncertainty Change in Entropy = Heat Added divided by Temperature = Q/T
- Enthalpy: H = Internal Energy of the System + Pressure X Volume Change in H = Internal Energy Change + Change in Pressure X Volume = Heat Added – Work Done + Change in PV = Q – W + Change in P X V.
- Gibbs Free Energy G: Energy Available for Reaction or Process = Enthalpy – Temperature X Entropy = H – T X S
- Change in G = Change in Enthalpy – T X Change in S.

Indira marched through the bullet points before saying, "Don't waste a lot of time on this slide's material. You have better things to do."

The next one zoomed into view, accompanied by Indira's professorial words.

Slide 2
MAJOR CONSEQUENCES

- In any Closed System Process, Entropy always increases for Irreversible Processes or stays the same for Reversible Processes. This is the Second Law of Thermodynamics. Most Processes in the Universe are Irreversible. **Hence Entropy drives the Arrow of Causality!**

- The Change in Gibbs Free Energy is Negative in an Exothermic Process and Positive in an Endothermic Process. **THIS FACT CAN LEAD TO ENTROPY DECREASING IN CERTAIN TYPES OF IRREVERSIBLE REACTIONS BUT IT DOES NOT INVALIDATE THE CLAIM THAT ENTROPY DRIVES THE ARROW OF CAUSALITY.DON'T GET BOGGED DOWN IN CALCULATIONS OR SPECIAL CASES!**

ENTROPY DEFINITIONS EXTENDED

In Physics:
- Entropy linked to Statistical Mechanics by defining it as the Count of Particle Arrangements. $S = k \times Log(Number\ of\ States)$ k = Boltzmann's Constant
- Quantum Mechanics extends Entropy via Statistical Mechanics and Heisenberg Uncertainty Principle to different Particle Probability Distributions (Boltzmann/Maxwell Bose/Einstein Fermi/Dirac). It also invents "Entanglement" or "Black Hole" Entropy per John von Neumann's consideration of probability waves.
- Quantum Mechanics extends Entropy via Information Content to explain General Relativity and Cosmology (Low Entropy = High Information Content, Universe heading to "Heat Death" = Non-Local Thermal Equilibrium and Maximum Entropy).

In Computer and Information Science:
- Entropy linked to Communication Transmission and Information Content in 0-1 Bit (Alphabet) Sequences for measuring Information Gain/Compression/Entropy Reduction. High Entropy = High Information Content

In Biology:
- Entropy linked to DNA Information Content carried by quantum coherence- preserving intracellular Micro-Tubules via ACTG (Alphabet) Sequences for measuring Mutations/Errors/Degeneration/Decay.
- DON'T GET BOGGED DOWN IN THE MATHEMATICS!

NOTE: CURRENT MATHEMATICAL FORMALISMS LEAD TO FANTASY, AS THEY DID WHEN APPLYING THE LORENTZ TRANSFORMATION TO SPECIAL RELATIVITY!

"This slide summarizes the major entropy takeaways you need. I know how detail-oriented you can be, but don't get bogged down in special cases or calculations. No one will understand if you sort through them and try to explain the finer points. And my next slide explains why this is so."

Slide 3
"MERE MORTALS" APPROACHING THEIR
ASYMPTOTIC LIMITS

- Entropy Definitions are often contradictory and lead to ever-ever-more-unknowable Fantasies.
- High Energy Physic swallowed by the Black Hole its Mathematical Formalisms invented to explain Quantum Mechanics.
- Computer Scientists can't deal with "Coding Complexity"
- Biologists unable to deal with "Genetic Complexity"
- Mathematicians still stumped by Infinity and Godel's Incompleteness Theorems
- Psychologists extend Analytic Philosophy using vague explanation that entropy transfers energy among the individual's personas

BUT I SURPASS THEM WITH MY:
- "COMPLEXITY CODING"
- ENTROPY-ANALYTIC ALGORITHMS FOR GENETIC FINE-
- GRAINED DECODING (Extract information from Genes to
- guide "Splicing") AND OTHERS FOR PREDICTING CARBON-BASED EVOLUTION.
- ENTROPY-ANALYTIC ALGORITHMS FOR FINE-GRAINED SOCIO-POLITICAL BIG DATA ANALYSIS AND PREDICTION (Extract Information from "Current Events" to make "Forecasts")

"You already know that mere mortals stumble their way through language, complexity, and infinity. And when you add to these the 'Explosion Principle' and Godel's Incompleteness theorems, you can see why humans are approaching their limits, so let me move to my last slide, which shows how we use all of the above. And I know you will like it; you like all sorts of games."

Slide
4 OUR GAME

Win-Win but always staying in the Shadows
- I develop the Theory and Algorithms that optimize State-of- the-Art AI Technology
- You obtain the Data for me to analyze
- You Give Your "Mere Mortals" Enough to Keep Them "Happy"

Our First Targets:
NO QUANTUM PHYSICS NEEDED!
- Control Systems for undersea autonomous vehicles.
- Android Development.
- Genetic Analysis of Undersea Life Forms' DNA.
- Socio-political Big Data Analysis.
- Control Systems for Interplanetary Space Travel/Suspension Pods. For Later:

TO SATISFY YOUR MUSING REGARDING MERE MORTALS

Information/Entropy considerations for: Sociology and Politics Psychology/Neuroscience/Consciousness   Ontology/Metaphysics Philosophy/Religion

"Please note that you and I control the greater game we are about to play.

And of course, only we know what's on the last slide."

Indira kept the slide on the monitor but stopped talking. Electra started as soon as she realized the lecture had ended.

"Will you entertain some questions now?"

"You don't need to ask more questions. These slides summarize all you need to know. And I have a lagniappe for you – a High Energy Physics Hype Silencer. I am certain you will know the who- why-where-when-how for using it to your advantage. So, there you have it."

"Good, because I've had enough for tonight. It's time to turn off the workstation and lights and let my brain mull over all you've given us."

"Excellent choice; sleep well and when you wake up, keep preparing for our latest game."

Indira's smiling avatar vanished.

The Irani-Electra duo didn't go to bed immediately, instead sitting in front of the darkened monitor and contemplating their good fortune.

No one has a friend like Indira. Even close ones often focus more on

themselves, but not Indira. She centers on us, even better than a mother on her child. And she always tells us the truth. No wonder we've let each other in; my feelings toward her are akin to love, and in her silicon-substrate way, hers might be the same.

The duo was about to head for bed, but a sudden mood shift kept them sitting.

Part of our latest game is about to take a possibly deadly twist if I'm not careful. I've made all preparations and put safety measures in place for me and my Three Musketeers, but are the measures enough? And my Musketeers haven't told me if they want to play. Mother wrote a poem about my predicament… What's its name? I remember, it's Share the Fantasy. How fitting for the game I want them to play; I can hear it echoing in my head…

Is Life perchance a fantasy,
Conjured merely by lonely thought?
That's half the sum, but more awaits,
When sharing what the others brought.
We often think we know what's right,
When striding in the cheerful day.
But in the doubts of darkening night,
Adjust to what the partners say.
Walking alone is often fast,
But easier to lose your way.
Wait before each die is cast,
Lessen the odds of going astray.
Life is more than just your dream,
Account for serendipity's team.

I'll have to tell them enough so they can decide whether or not they want to play. It's for them to decide on Sunday, only two days away. And Sunday's a go; I'm ready for them to roll the dice.

The Irani-Electra duo got up and then rolled into bed, and except for Indira and the lightning brain, put all thoughts away until tomorrow.

Chapter 8
March 2163

"All for One – for Now"

Irani's Three Musketeers wouldn't arrive until mid-week because air traffic controller networks in major metropolitan areas had been hacked, but the delay allowed her to attend Nari's farewell presentation for President Huston the day before. She arrived at the conference room in time to slide a chair that bracketed President Huston between herself and Vice President Chen at the foot of the table. Eve and Jan occupied one side while Yang and Sabrina sat opposite. Though Irani's late arrival didn't disturb Nari one iota, the President summarized for Irani's benefit.

"I'm glad you made it, even though you missed Jan's explanation that clarified Eve's Mindset Guidelines talk. The two of them can explain it to you later, and Nari's about to go on from her "Forms of Government" slide. I think she was ready to launch into Quantum Politics; am I right? If so, please continue."

Always outwardly calm, Nari nodded at the President before showing the first Quantum Politics slide.

"I have developed a new approach to politics utilizing my philosophy of meritocracy. Don't try to understand all the concepts listed on my rather long opening slide. Just scan it for the concepts introduced. Eve and Jan will need to study all three slides and then write an internal white paper for you. I will help them as much as possible before departing for Beijing, and I can do so from my new location if you extend my consulting contract. For now, I'll simply mention that I chose its catchy name to highlight the modern and counterintuitive elements derived from meritocracy, which are rooted in religious and philosophical beliefs still being debated today."

Slide 1
Quantum Politics: A Post-Modern Theory using the Philosophy of Meritocracy

Why the name Quantum Politics?
- Classical Politics doesn't work in the Post-Modern World. Uncertainty and Social Media Interaction among new players pop into existence and cause unexpected interactions. We call the new politics Quantum Politics = New Rules of Politics.

- The name is "catchy" and will grab public attention. Meritocracy is its most tangible characteristic.
- Meritocracy's connection to Politics is hard to understand and counterintuitive.
- I've pieced together enough of its "Founding Philosophers' teachings" (Hayek, Young, Rawls, Sandel) so You can explain Meritocracy to Constituents and devise Programs.

Meritocracy:
- Ethical belief that people can achieve upward social mobility and wealth/success regardless of starting point on a level opportunity field if they work hard and play by the rules. **People get what they deserve.**

Rooted in Christian Beliefs:
- Started with Saint Augustin's belief in Original Sin and Man having no free will. **A person's Salvation is preordained by the Grace of God. People should be humble and follow Church** teachings. But people struggled to believe it; why would an all-powerful God allow suffering and Evil? Pelagius countered by giving Man free will and Salvation via good works. Thus, Meritocracy emerges: **God's Grace and people's humility replaced by Man's hard work and hubris.**
- Reformation/Martin Luther/Calvinism/Puritanism rejected Meritocracy because of social problems caused by the Catholic Church's role in politics. Reformers promoted a return to Meritocracy anchored in God's Grace and humility.
- But people want "proof" that they'll be saved. That's what Meritocracy does: **Be a good person by working hard, playing by the rules, and always accumulating more of what you need to be successful. This is the Protestant Work Ethic. Thus, Capitalism emerges.**
- The World today is Secular, not Religious. Meritocracy is all about success now, not Salvation in an afterlife.

The Meritocratic Debate Today: Do people at the top (Winners) deserve their success? Are people at the bottom (Losers) responsible for their own failure? Tough political questions, given all the income and social inequality, social immobility, resentment, nationalism, partisanship, and rising technocracies/authoritarian states challenging democracy. **MOST PEOPLE LIKE A MERITOCRATIC SOCIETY BETTER THAN ONE THAT'S AUTOCRATIC. MOST PEOPLE LIKE BUYING AND OWNING THINGS (MARKETS AND CAPITALISM).**

Nari replaced the slide with her second and kept speaking.

"My next slide is shorter but packed with additional concepts that my approach integrates in novel ways. Let Eve and Jan sort through the connections among meritocratic forms, moral values, and the greater good. If they do a good job, the public may understand your subsequent policies."

Slide 2
Why Meritocracy is Hard to Understand

- There are two possible forms of Meritocracy being debated today in Democratic Governments: Free-Market Liberalism Welfare State. They agree on some points but disagree on others.

- People have to realize that how much a person earns (their Dollar Value) is determined by Markets and Economics. **But this is different from what a person deserves (which should be based on Moral/Ethical Value = Justice = Fair Evaluation of Virtue = Self-Merit. Self-Merit is a person's intrinsic self- worth.) SELF-WORTH DETERMINED VIA PEOPLE/SOCIAL INTERACTION THAT CONTRIBUTES TO THE "GREATER GOOD."**

- People don't pay attention to complicated philosophical debates about Meritocratic Issues: Morals/Ethics Values Justice Fairness Happiness Rights Entitlements Self-Worth

Nari paused for a couple of seconds before proceeding to slide three.

"My final slide is the payoff for policy-making. It identifies the reasons for meritocracy's strange interaction with politics and then highlights how to control its dark side by developing programs that can soften its effects. Your administration is already championing some of them, and you should expect Eve and Jan to add others. And that's all I want to say. Do you have any comments or questions?"

Slide 3
Some of Meritocracy's Strange Interactions with Quantum Politics

- Meritocracy and Capitalism interact to increase Economic and Social Inequality while fueling Macroeconomic Growth.
- It gives Winners and Losers alike justification for their outcomes.
- Technocratic Elites and resentful skeptics use pieces of Meritocracy to fight each other.
- Politicians can "pick and choose" from Meritocracy to support opposing policies.
- Depending on Contingencies, it can lead to Humility or Hubris, belief in Providence/Chance or Self-Reliance/Control.
- It can lead to International cooperation as well as Local Resentment and Populist Backlash.
- It Creates "Superordinate" employees who'd rather be working than playing.
- It allows Winners to feel entitled and Losers to feel humiliated (even when the Government cushions their defeat).

How to Control Meritocracy's Dark Side

Must convince people via serious debate that they are Morally/Ethically indebted and obligated to contribute to Society's "Common Good."

- Talent/Ability given to people randomly. Be grateful for good luck.
- Appeal to human sharing/caring instincts. Winners feel good when sharing with Losers.
- Every person has self-worth.
- Every person has a place in Society, no matter their ability/handicaps.
- College Entrance Lottery.

Possible Programs

- Domestic Common Good Corps.
- Relaxed "No Student Left Behind" and Math Certification.
- Govt/Corp. Apprenticeship-Career Upgrade.
- Family/Community Outreach.
- Prison Defunding.

- Native American/National Parks Restitution.
- Mandatory Voting Rewards.

The President wasted no time replying.

"Good that Jan is with us, but we'll have to extend your contract if he and Eve need your assistance. I'll wait to hear from them."

Neither looked ready to talk, but Irani did and directed her comments at Nari.

"Your theory is innovative and built on a solid foundation, but have you considered the 'justice as fairness' philosophy of Rawls, or Rorty's pragmatic approach, or even the post-modern historical implications of Margolis that build on Hegel's?"

Nari's self-assured demeanor began to waver as she searched for an answer.

"That's what I can explain to Eve and Jan. Uh –" Irani had more to say.

"Good, and when you do, I think you three should revisit Eve's Overton Window when determining the four political parties' positionings. Human nature is rooted in physical embodiment and many of our socio-political beliefs are anchored in DNA-like social memes. We are genetically predisposed to believe in a higher power and free will as we seek face-to-face relationships while preferring individual or family over group or nation-state. Regardless of what post-modern academia may say, please keep that in mind."

Nari rallied to her own defense.

"OK, OK, we'll handle that. Anything else I might have overlooked?" "Please take this as constructive criticism. I like how you weave capitalism and meritocracy into your theory, but are you revamping your free-market approach to economics? Milton Friedman and his once- vaunted Friedmanomics are now in eclipse, and since they champion capitalism and meritocracy, you should adjust your economic programs accordingly. You can do that, can't you?"

Not even Eve could find a worthwhile reply, so the President stepped into the awkward silence by pointing a question at Irani.

"Maybe you can assist. How's your calendar?"

"Filling up, and I'd prefer we let Eve and Jan do their best before bringing me back. Their combined intelligence, augmented by Nari's and Sabrina's should serve you well. And speaking of the calendar, I better leave to prepare for additional this and next week's meetings. Eve will keep me in the loop."

Irani didn't need to do anything except review the preparations already in place. RT and PH arrived as expected at her house late Wednesday afternoon. They came into the kitchen after parking their bags in spare bedrooms and splashing some water on hands and faces. Irani had carryout dinners awaiting. After kibitzing for twenty minutes about the flight and current personal events they waited for Irani to explain what she had in mind.

"If there was more time, I would take you and Mr. LP on a Three Musketeers tour of DC, but we'll do that on our next get-together. This time, I need you to complete the job I've hired you for – install my above-ground lap pool and do some basement renovations. I'll take you there after dinner. I've already rented tools and bought supplies and work clothes. And I've rented a van if you need to pick up more stuff. I'll be staying at my office, so you have the place all to yourselves, kitchen included."

After a tour of the backyard and house, RT and PH studied the pool installation instructions along with Irani's renovation sketch. All three talked again in the basement two hours later. RT spoke first.

"We'll start with the pool. That'll take less than a day. And then we'll get the basement work done by no later than Sunday, which means we leave Monday morning. We'll clean up everything, but what about returning the van and tools?"

"I'll take care of that next week. And I'll come over Sunday evening to say goodbye. But until then I want you to focus on the pool and basement.

Please use tunnel vision."

PH poked RT. Neither spoke but their smiles told Irani that they had caught her pun.

Irani worked Thursday in her office on an assortment of projects but made time for sharing a late afternoon workout at the fitness center with Kiara Mensah, a mid-40s lady whose head-and-a-half shorter frame fit that of an office worker who needed firming up. They chatted afterward at the health bar. Irani steered the conversation toward this rookie triathlete she particularly liked.

"How do you manage to fit training into your lifestyle?"

"It takes a bit of doing because I'm a single parent, but I'm lucky to work as a copywriter for a website design company that has an enlightened work policy. And I have a studious fourteen-year-old son whose stuttering issue is getting better, thanks to his speech therapy coach. All I need to do is find an adolescent girl who might look beyond his words. Tyrone trips over words when first meeting people."

"Everyone has issues, especially when first meeting someone of the opposite sex, but maybe we can help each other. I'm taking care of a girl who's talented using words but is usually bored in school. She can help your son and some of his study habits might help Tiana. What do you think?"

"Why don't we bring them to the fitness center sometime? I can't think of a better place to meet."

Irani agreed.

Irani selected the best place to meet Mr. LP when she made his reservations: his hotel room. The limo drive from there to the fundraiser being hosted Saturday evening at Ritz-Carlton's Fahrenheit Ballroom in Georgetown would take only minutes. When she called him Friday evening to confirm that he would be ready, he asked her to review the rules.

"I want to learn more about DC's behind-the-scenes power broker activities, but I want to stay in the shadows. That's why we'll be Mr. and Mrs. Lobdell and Domino Broune, members of the upper ten percent of the one percent. We have several residences and devote ourselves to managing our charitable trust."

"Well Miss Irani, what do you want me to do?"

"Tomorrow morning, take the tuxedo in your room to the rental store and have the tailor adjust the fit. My limo will pick you up at 5:45, and when we get to the fundraiser, all you have to do is be charming and disarming and let me do most of the talking."

"Sounds like a plan, but what about I.D.s in case they vette us?" "I already have them. And I'll have a new look too."

"I can't wait to see…"

Mr. LP spotted the limo's blinking headlights as soon as he exited the hotel, but he had to look twice when looking in after the driver opened the rear side door on the passenger side.

"Why I declare, you look like a grande dame of the moneyed class. What's your secret?"

"Get in, Lobdell, and I'll tell you how Domino does it." Irani continued after he climbed in and the limo moved on.

"I learned the art of applying 3-D face masks and makeup years ago, and I rented a gown and jewelry to complement my new look. What do you think?"

"It's elegantly understated; no cleavage or side-slit to display what lies beneath. I guess you'll leave that to the imagination of the people we meet."

"Right you are, as will the amount of the check you'll sign if I find an unwitting player. Here are your I.Ds and checkbook with the amount filled in. Please check them out so you spell your name correctly."

"Why Miss Domino, there's no need to worry, so you can start smiling right now. You'll soon see that I can play my role perfectly…"

Trent Booker never missed an opportunity to collect money from influential people, and he particularly enjoyed trolling at fundraisers because his covert organization always gave him a vetted target list containing enough information to grease the conversations.

He and his covert three-person DC political climate observation group – one each from a cadre of trusted Republican, Democratic, and Guardian Party operatives – had survived the search for instigators of the near-catastrophe he had orchestrated two years ago: kidnapping before killing the newly elected President of the United States to ensure that a conspiracy member – the Vice President – would become America's leader. Somehow, the kidnapping failed. President Huston and a staffer recovered from gunshots but the Vice President and six accomplices didn't. Lucky for Trent that not even the combined resources of America's CIA security web could find a hint of the conspiracy or a connection between it and Brian Strauss, the dead Veep. "Bigger Brother" had regrouped and planned ahead, and not even Trent knew what it would do next, but as long as it kept the establishments of its privileged supra-UN nation-state subset in charge and invisible, he liked being on the inside.

Trent exchanged his normal "smoke and joke then beat the feet" style for one more suitable when mixing with tonight's elite attendees, allowing him to mingle unobtrusively while sizing up targets. And as the evening wound down, he congratulated himself while sipping on Champagne and nibbling a fruit tart.

I bagged a lot of bucks tonight, and the vetters were right. Although they said Broune's Internet footprint is faint, they might be our type, and the check Domino told Lobdell to write makes a definite statement. She's the smart one and it'll pay me to introduce her to others. I'm sure that'll pay big dividends.

Irani didn't do any congratulating until logging on to her office workstation after the limo driver delivered passengers to their destinations. Indira's avatar spoke first.

"If I didn't know you so well and listen in so unobtrusively, your disguise might have fooled even me initially. I commend your cleverness, and you should congratulate my constantly evolving robo-investing software apps. My hedging algorithms now include a portfolio of cryptocurrencies and meme companies. You can write more checks whenever you find additional players, but you will need to search for them in 3-D Space. This so-called 'Bigger Bro Conspiracy' Brian hinted about at his final meeting avoids Cyberspace detection. I assume you'll use Trent to find some."

"That's the next step in the game. How do you like it so far?"

"I will use one of your similes from years ago, 'like the guy falling down an elevator shaft, until you hit the bottom, so far so good.' But danger lurks."

"It always does; may I assume you'll keep watching my back?" "As much as possible, but my effectiveness attenuates the further

you are offline."

"Well, perhaps some serendipitous event will flush them into Cyberspace where you can track them."

"That is a possibility, but I know you'll continue following your own advice, and I assume you need no reminding."

"Correct, as always. I shall hope for the best but plan for the worst." "In that case, I shall say goodnight to Irani and Electra. I hope the contingent future looks as good."

Irani removed her disguise before listening to her musing in bed.

I've got a support team that came through for me this week. And I can always count on Indira, no matter how dangerous the games become.

As she submerged into sleep, a final thought came to mind.

The lightning brain is always planning for contingencies that might come into sight, and though the risks are unknown, it will always follow its prime directive: do whatever is needed to survive and to thrive.

The duo slept peacefully that night.

Chapter 9
April 2163

"Sealed with a Kiss"

Electra knew that not even she could keep up with the number of rapid-fire events spawned by a post-modern world, so rather than fret about what she couldn't control or didn't know about, she tracked as much as she could, given the constraints on her schedule, and left the rest for another time. That was the main reason for multi-tasking by watching an early morning news show while using her elliptical trainer on Monday, April 8th, the day rescheduled for Tiana's surgery. An unexplained electrical power grid outage that rolled across America three weeks ago had caused the delay.

The tag-team style of the newscasters made them her favorite.

"... and all eyes will be following today's opening of world financial markets after last Friday's trading suspension caused by software glitches. And they added to a growing global unease when earlier in the week two cruise ships reported viral outbreaks possibly spreading from China or Africa. Might there be a connection to the disappearance of two container ships traversing Arctic sea lanes?"

His junior partner's practiced reply came as soon as the camera panned to him.

"No mention yet, but why not link it to one of the conspiracy theories connecting all the world's ills. Or to Russian saber-rattling. That's what the 'Straight Shooter' blogging site is trumpeting. It's also adding random high-rise and seawall collapses to the mix, and even suggesting that droughts and floods in several countries are within the realm of possibility. What's your take on that 'Straight Shooter' site?"

The knowing smile of the senior partner, a veteran female reporter, showed that she already had an answer.

"It's wildly popular after popping up only three months ago. And no wonder, the reporting is clever indeed. It dubs in frank, more honest answers to interviews given by notable politicians, and we still don't know its location or if their spokespersons are real or virtual. And one of its stories claims the government is about to nationalize Internet betting on politics and expand its scope to include other nations. If true, that will open up all sorts of devious possibilities for the politically connected. Time will sort it all out... if the world survives. Back in sixty..."

Understandably nervous, Tiana seemed edgy and snapped at Irani as they waited in the reception area.

"You promise it's not gonna hurt, don't you? And you'll be here when I wake up, won't you?"

"I promise times two. And when the bandages come off in a couple of days, we'll both get to see an even prettier you."

Neither said anything else because a nurse called for Tea. Irani brought her to the entryway and both listened to the instructions. Irani hugged her just before the nurse took her away.

"You'll see that I'm as good as my word, and I'll seal my promise with a kiss."

Irani did; Tea smiled through trembling lips, and the nurse took charge.

Irani was at her side in the recovery area four hours later when Tea opened her unbandaged eye before speaking slurred words.

"Did I just have an operation? I didn't feel a thing."

"You certainly did, and we can thank the anesthesiologist for that. We'll go home as soon as the doctor says so. And you'll feel like a queen when they push you in a wheelchair."

Tea's slurred words showed that the anesthesia hadn't worn off yet, but her tiny smile showed relief.

"How long can I be queen?"

"Until the bandages come off. Then you become a beautiful student once again."

Tea yawned before a final reply. "Thank you."

Irani caressed Tea's unbandaged cheek before saying, "Me too you too. Now rest while I go talk to the doctor."

Irani had Tea tucked in and asleep at home four hours later. And Irani was still at her side when she awoke hours after that.

Tiana had the irrepressible vitality of adolescence at her side too; all traces of the surgery disappeared soon after the bandages came off, and her confidence soared once she saw the results, as did her zest for action. She was full speed ahead three weeks later.

When she entered the kitchen on an early May Tuesday, Irani asked if she'd like to meet at the fitness center a new training partner and her son. Tea's enthusiasm bubbled in her words as she grabbed Irani's hand with both of hers.

"Wow, she must be pretty fit if she's a triathlete. And I promise not to make a big deal about her kid's stuttering. When are we going and tell me again their names?"

"Saturday morning, and the names are Kiara and Tyrone Mensah."
"Have you met him? What's he look like?"

"No, but Kiara says he's smart and studious, and who knows? Maybe he's smart enough to join Mensa, which if your drop the 'h' from his last name identifies the oldest high-I.Q. society in the world. He stutters but goes to a speech therapist, so try not to notice too much."

"I promise to be good, and I won't make a big deal about it. What's for dinner? Do you want me to make a salad?"

"Macaroni and cheese, and yes please…"

Tiana noticed one thing only when they met: Tyrone's appearance. He was as tall as Tea, lean like a runner, and had incredibly handsome features topped by a shortish hairstyle plus an inquisitive smile. She adjusted to his stuttering as she absorbed all that he and Kiara said; like the air she breathed, it became invisible.

Adults and adolescents worked out separately, and afterward all snacked at the health bar before the families went their separate ways. On the drive home, Tiana enthused about what she wanted.

"You gotta let Ty and me do things together. He can help me study, and I'll coach him on speaking and he can help me practice singing. Did you know he plays the piano? And he's not your typical guy musician. He's a great volleyball player. Maybe I'll start playing."

"That would be good; I think your height, wiry-strong build, and quickness fit it or basketball, and I'll coach you if you like."

"You will? Good, because I wanna be special."

"Tea sweetie, you already are, and there's a wonderful lesson here. The more time you spend with someone, the more you realize how special and talented the person is."

"I'll remember, and when we get home, will you call his mom so you two can make it happen?"

"I will, now settle down, sit still, and tell me more about what the two of you will study first…"

If people who knew Alonzo were asked what looks different about him now than a year ago, most would say he seems more mature and confident, but only his closest circle of friends knew the changes came from Navy SEAL training, and two of them – Eve and Monet – had arranged a welcome back party that would be held at Eve's on the third Friday evening in May.

They invited only Irani, Tiana, and Jan; Alonzo had given them strict orders to keep his SEAL training activity a guarded secret. Even those still going through the eighteen-month training maintained the SEAL low-profile tradition.

Alonzo had just moved back to his home base in Virginia Beach near

Norfolk after completing the first half of BUD/S training in Coronado, which is just across San Diego Bay. "Basic Underwater Demolition SEAL training", which is considered the most demanding of any required by America's elite special forces, winnows three-quarters of even the most motivated volunteers. Tonight would be the first time since December that his closest friends would see this still-in-training SEAL.

Alonzo arrived at 5:30, wearing the Navy's regulation dress blue uniform and short hair and looking even fitter than before. After five months of separation, he lifted Monet in a hug that said more than any words could convey, then set her down after a long kiss and hugged Eve, who could always find the right words to say.

"No matter the uniform or how much you've changed, you're still my brother and I expect you to follow my orders. Now say hello to the one person you haven't met. And I'm sure you don't need any SEAL training to pick her out."

Alonzo acted his part by peering first at Irani before grabbing Tea by the shoulders.

"This must be Tiana, but you're even prettier than Irani said. And if Monet hadn't already taken my heart, I might have given it to you."

Tea laughed as she hugged him before saying, "Wow, the way you look, you could be the star in a military action flick, but I won't tell anyone you're a SEAL. Miss Irani and I watched some of the SEAL videos. No wonder you look so fit."

Eve herded the group into the dining area where the celebration continued all the way through cake and ice cream. Eve coaxed Alonzo just enough for him to reveal the tip of SEAL training. Three hours later, Monet took Alonzo to her apartment, where he would stay until leaving for Virginia Beach early Monday morning. He asked all he could about the current events in her life, but she kept the answers at a surface level until they settled on her living room sofa. Soft ambient lighting and Alonzo's arm around her gave comfort to the couple as Monet's articulate French-accented words floated about.

"This has been our longest separation, and I have missed you as much as you say that you missed me. And I hope you have learned what I have. Time and distance have not weakened my love for you. Our relationship will continue to grow as long as we talk often and are honest with one another."

Kissing her on the cheek, Alonzo noticed one tiny tear before talking.

"I feel the same, so we should be happy. Why the tear? Virginia Beach is only 200 miles from DC. I can visit you often during the rest of basic training."

"But Darla just appointed me to a trouble-shooting position in Harare.

Unrest in Africa is impacting her plans, and I am sorry to say she gave me no estimate for how long I will be there."

Alonzo kissed her again and then sat for a minute or two, suspended in the moment while collecting his thoughts. His calm tone showed some of his new attitude.

"Maybe this is for the best. Miss Irani would say that at this stage in our lives, we should always ask why not, rather than why. And we shouldn't dodge risk as long as we have a backup plan. Look at Nari and Yang.

Opportunity and technology have transformed them into digital nomads and that applies to us as well. All we're doing is allowing our relationship to grow in new ways. And no matter what happens, we will always be able to choose us rather than the alternatives."

Monet's Mona Lisa smile came back with her words.

"You have grown in good ways during your training. Let us seal our pledge to one another with a kiss."

The rest of the evening became a continuation of the joy-filled celebration for the couple whose separation had just brought them to their latest epiphany. And several kisses sealed it.

Monet and her still-in-training SEAL slept well that night.

Chapter 10
June 2163

"Into the Deep"

Tea and Ty's friendship grew even faster than their physiques. Irani and Kiara alternated driving duties whenever needed, and the teens' camaraderie benefitted each even better than hoped for. Kiara had just driven Tea home and was waiting for Ty to come back to her car. He was currently standing just inside the front door, saying goodbye to Tea.

"Eh-is that Miss Irani puh-playing the piano? If so, sh-she sure can play fast."

"Didn't I tell you she helps me practice singing? How does she sound?"

"Like she's playing Hanon exercises." "What're those?"

"Warmup finger drills. Like your warmup voice exercises when you sing. I can puh-play fast too, faster than I can think the notes, but not that fast. Aks her how she does it."

"Will do, and I'll tell you tomorrow."

Tea gave him a peck on the cheek, which brought a smile that accompanied his parting words.

"We'll practice singing at my pu-place after we study, OK?" "You bet; we have to keep our mom's happy. See ya."

Irani sensed Tea approaching, so she rose from the bench to greet her. "Ty says you play awfully fast. Do you name the notes as you hit'em?"

Irani rubbed Tea's hair and then answered. "Oh no, not even the best pianists can do that. But they practice so much that their fingers know where to go. Like you and singing. Your voice knows the notes and words without thinking. That's what practice does."

"You're right. I'll see you in the kitchen. What's for dinner?" "One of your favorites. You'll see soon."

Tea skipped off to her bedroom as Irani trekked to the kitchen, thinking all the way.

I'm much more attentive when playing the piano now than when Su-Lin taught me fifty years ago. I was too immature back then to appreciate what she was giving me, but thanks to the lightning brain, I remembered the skill. I can name the notes no matter how fast my fingers find them. But I don't want to draw attention, so don't mention it. And I won't mention how practicing replaces verbalizing with finger-muscle memory. I'll let Tea and Ty discover it for themselves.

But if the committee is up to it, I might use this to illustrate a point I'll make tomorrow at Professor Plannert's meeting. Jonathan will be there and he can help those struggling with my adjustments to Indira's entropy slides.

Jonathan's help wasn't needed; Irani had dummied-down the slides just enough for the committee to understand entropy's bigger picture, but one of the sharper members wanted to probe deeper.

"I must say, you really have a command of the subject. How do you remember it all? And perhaps you can tell us why the high energy physicists keep pestering us about what great theories are just about to emerge."

Irani answered while fidgeting with her computer.

"It's like playing the piano; learn it once and if you keep practicing, you'll lock it in memory. And I have a couple of slides that might put the issue to rest. Please wait a moment while I find them."

"While the audience sat in a welcome silence, Irani spoke, but only to herself.

Now's the time to use Indira's HEP Hype Silencer slides. And I'm glad she put it together. This is tough stuff, and I empathize with the committee. I know what it's like to get one of Indira's info-dumps, but I think they'll like what I have for them...

Irani spoke immediately after flashing the first slide.

Slide 1
THE HIGH ENERGY PHYSICS BLACK HOLE

Waiting for the next big breakthrough in High Energy Physics is like "Waiting for Godot" because of the brain's Cognitive Limits regarding:

& Language Infinity Complexity Godel's Incompleteness Theorems Explosion Principle

& Yet high energy physicists continue inventing theories analogous to Middle Age Clerics/Philosophers proving the existence of God.

Even the more sensible HEP Promoters trip over the following mistakes:

- They claim time exists in the Objective World, but it only exists in the human brain as an instrument for "Cause and Effect Ordering."
- They rely on Mathematical Modeling that yields "beautiful symmetry" leading to unobservable phenomena. HEP has become a religion because its conjectures cannot be proved. Example: Galois theory symmetry solutions for finding new particle fields and properties.

- The quest for a "Unified Field Theory" (reconciling Gravity and General Relativity) leads to an ever-increasing cascade of non-existent particles for creating "Fantasy Force Fields." Some examples: Magnetic Monopoles Gravitons Inflatons.
- **But when cornered, the "smart ones" admit Quantum Mechanics is woefully incomplete!**

"Professor Plannert will give you a copy of these slides later, so for now just listen to my takeaway. High energy physicists are nearing their cognitive limits; even the more sensible ones trip over mistakes. But when confronted with the facts, most will admit that Quantum Mechanics has holes in it."

Irani displayed the next slide and kept talking.

Slide 2
A SAMPLING OF HEP FANTASIES

- Black Hole surface holding a "Holographic Image" of the entropy of all the matter inside. Black Holes eventually radiate this information away (Hawking Radiation) as it dissipates.
- Worm Hole connecting Black Hole to symmetrical White Hole in another Universe.
- Dark Matter (WIMPs = Weakly Interacting Massive Particles) explaining why gravitational fields are "so strong."
- Dark Energy explaining why Universe's expansion is accelerating.
- A fifth force that accounts for Dark Matter and Dark Energy Phenomena.
- Multiple String Theories invented using an 18th-century mathematician's equation (Euler) modeling particles as if they were vibrating strings in an 11-Dimensional Space that preserves "Symmetry."
- Particles traveling backwards in time account for "The Big Bang" that occurs at the instant of minimum Entropy State of the Universe. Traveling further backwards in time always goes to higher Entropy States.
- An infinite number of Universes accounting for the "Anthropic Principle" (any theory of the Universe must be consistent with Man's existence.)

- Human Consciousness as an algorithmic calculation fully explaining its emergence when advances in Quantum Mechanics and Quantum Computers show that the entire Universe is self-aware.

"Here I list some of the fantasies. They are indeed exciting and sometimes mentioned in sci-fi movies because most people enjoy believing in movie magic. You might be able to add to the list, but do so later. For now, just try to remember some the bullet points."

Irani showed another slide fifteen seconds later.

Slide 3
MOST HEP BOOKS AND VIDEOS END PHILOSOPHICALLY

- What is the meaning of Life?
- Is there a God?
- Does Man have Free Will?
- Does the Universe have a Purpose?
- What is Consciousness? What is its Purpose?
- Is the Universe Infinite or does it end in "Heat Death?"
- We must keep searching for the next "Big Breakthrough" so we can know the "Mind of God."

YOU DECIDE IF HIGH ENERGY PHYSICS SPIN-OFFS ARE WORTH THE EXPENSIVE TOYS NEEDED TO KEEP PHYSICISTS EMPLOYED.

"This is my final slide, and it lists what most of the high energy physics books and talks say at the very end. Quantum mechanics and Hep have become blends of philosophy and religion. It's up to you and others to decide if we should keep funding their R&D, but that's a whole other discussion, so I'll stop here."

After clicking the "Off" button and then sitting down, Irani waited for someone to speak. As expected, Professor Plannert did.

"All quite interesting, and I notice you mention 'Consciousness,' which is indeed a deep subject. And how fitting, for so does Jonathan whenever writing articles about some of his deep-sea research. Perhaps he could discuss any links appropriate between his findings and quantum mechanics and cephalopods. Aren't they supposed to be the smartest invertebrates and are still evolving on a branch separate from homo sapiens?"

Always quick when hearing his name, Jonathan looked at Irani while answering.

"I could, but Irani knows more about physics than I do. Maybe we can add that to the work we're already doing. She and I can talk about it later in my office."

Professor Plannert slapped the table to punctuate what he was about to say. "Very good, and let me know what you decide. Meeting adjourned."

Needing a break from heavy-duty thinking, Jonathan treated Irani to lunch at a restaurant they walked to near campus. The hike and soft drinks helped recharge his R&D enthusiasm, as did the club sandwich and fries, which he doused generously with ketchup. Irani kept the talk light until Jonathan changed subjects.

"So, what's your take on consciousness?"

Irani put the club wedge down and finished swallowing before answering. "What's the purpose of consciousness?"

The reply surprised him, causing him to pause mid-bite. "Uh, I guess so we can think, isn't it?"

"No; I'll give you my crash course summary right now, so pay attention. Consciousness emerged from an evolutionary process that triggered a critical number of interacting neurons to transcend intelligence by reaching a state of self-awareness. One-celled organisms possess intelligence, but for multicellular life, a self-aware neural system exponentially increased its ability to solve problems of survival."

Irani took another bite, which was a cue for Jonathan to say something; he leaned forward first.

"OK, that makes sense, so now what?"

"Neuroscientists claim there are three types of consciousness: muscular, emotional, and cognitive. They successfully use brain scanning to develop stimulus-response models for the first two because they can track sensory inputs to brain structures responsible for physical or emotional responses. But not for consciousness and free will, whose combination is called the hard problem, because they can't isolate any physical structure responsible for cognition. Are you good so far?"

Jonathan's frown softened, replaced by a glimmer of understanding.

"Is this where microtubules come in? Aren't they a bunch of computer-like intracellular structures?"

"In a manner of speaking. They transport information encoded in ion currents and have memory-like and computer circuit-like molecular structures that process it. And that's where the high-energy physicists enter the story. They're trying to invent theories extending the 'Orchestrated Objective-Reductive' rubric. Do you know what that is?"

Jonathan's frown returned.

"Are you kidding? I can't spell it. You better tell me."

"OK. It postulates that consciousness originates at the quantum level inside neurons, rather than the conventional view that it is a product of connections between neurons. The mechanism is held to be a quantum process orchestrated by cellular microtubules. And it's multidisciplinary, utilizing molecular biology, neuroscience, quantum information theory, and quantum gravity. How does this sound?"

Jonathan tapped a French fry on his plate while figuring out a reply. "I guess it's better than doing nothing. Go on."

"Well, it further posits that consciousness is based on non-computable quantum processing performed on qubits formed collectively in microtubules and then amplified in neurons."

Seeing his expression soften a bit, Irani waited for a comment. "I've heard about qubits. Aren't they zero-one electron spin states

that store information in supercomputers?"

"Correct for inside them, but not for inside microtubules. Qubits are oscillating dipoles that form superposed resonance rings in helical molecular pathways throughout lattices of microtubules. And that's where the quantum physicists take over.

"They incorporate twistor mathematics, the uncertainty principle, spin states, superposition, coherence, tunneling, and entanglement to theorize how microtubules do it, but all they've come up with are outlandish ideas that even thought experiments have trouble handling."

Irani paused again because Jonathan looked ready to interrupt. "You lost me in the lattice. You better end the story."

"OK, I'll do so by contingently concluding that consciousness is simply an emergent property. And I stop here until evolution builds brains that can exceed our current asymptotic limits."

"So, where does that leave us?"

"Neuroscience and biotech are nowhere near their asymptotic limits, so we keep doing what we're doing without using quantum physics."

"That's good, I guess. At least I still have something to do. I'll keep writing grant proposals and you can help me do the research, and then I'll write up the results and get them published."

"You've written a number within the last year, and you'll be able to write even more if I assist. And why not do more octopus R&D to compare how its brain compares to a human brain for constructing consciousness?"

Jonathan finally cracked a wan smile.

"Interesting idea. And do you realize my papers are getting more and more attention? Pretty soon, companies will be coming after me for commercial spinoffs. And I'll give you plenty of credit."

"No, don't do that. I'm happy to see you move up, but just be careful you don't make the wrong people jealous."

"Oh, don't worry, I won't. Hey, I'm beginning to realize you know a lot more than you let on. I guess that's your style. Well, no matter, let's plan another three-day weekend at Woods Hole. I'll buy you a brownie if you say yes."

"Buy me two and it's a deal. And then, why don't we go to your office and check our schedules?"

"Now that's something I know how to do, and I'll even add a scoop of vanilla ice cream. That proves I'd never consider you a cheap date."

Irani's smile told Jonathan to place the order right now, and he followed orders by using the booth's menu tablet to place not one, but two. He decided to order his own dessert too.

Jonathan's revived tone and energy told Irani that the brownies had boosted his mood just enough to quiz her more, but her well-rehearsed answers kept him off balance, so he paused to pay for lunch by tapping on the tablet before making a final comment.

"I still don't get it. You know more about different tech areas than the full-time researchers who usually spin a better story than what their experiments show. Why's that?"

"I read a lot and have a good memory, and I have an associate or two who are smarter than I'll ever be. One of them writes poetry; recently, she recited some verses after explaining to me why high-energy physics is a dead end today. She calls it "Newton's Victims." Would you like to hear it?"

"Sure. Better yet write it down, and if I understand it, I can use it when my NASA associates get too smug."

Scribbling out the verses as soon as Jonathan gave her pen and paper, she handed them back a couple of minutes later, then waited in silence while Jonathan read.

Newton's Victims

Are you one of Newton's victims?
Rushing ahead to turn the page.
Knowing where you should be going,
Before quarks and mesons became the rage.
Newton's laws make great predictions,
Except when peering large or small.
Heisenberg's and Einstein's questions,
Cast Quantum Qualia's impenetrable pall.
So when conjecturing different worlds,
Can your strange beliefs cut through?
And move us closer to our limits,
Far beyond a Newtonian view.
Alas you find you're not so smart,
From where you're stuck no place to start.

His smile grew as the minutes ticked by, and when satisfied he looked up from the paper to Irani.

"Now I get it. Newton took us about as close to those asymptotic limits you like to trot out as the brightest people today can. Not now, but sometime you'll have to explain them again. Maybe when we're driving to the Cape."

"That's a possibility, but you must promise not to fall asleep if I start boring you."

"I don't think you could ever do that. You're too much of a mystery." Irani mirrored Monet's Mona Lisa smile before giving her favorite one-"Perhaps…"

Chapter 11
July 2163

"Into the Deep"

Schedules meshed for the post-Fourth of July weekend; Jonathan picked up the Irani-Electra duo Friday morning, and Electra detected more than early morning stiffness when he rolled his neck after her kiss brushed his cheek. When he said nothing other than good morning as he drove them away, Electra alerted Irani.

Weather and traffic aren't causing any issues… keep the conversation light until he reveals his problem.

"I thought you might like to hear a Fourth of July poem written by a friend of mine. She calls it 'Being in America – a July 4th Reverie.' Are you interested?"

"Sure, go on."

Irani added as much feeling to her measured pace as she could muster.

Euphoric possibilities,
Awaiting their discoveries,
Emerging as we strive to be,
Willing to risk it all.

Each new dawn breaks impatiently,
Cloaked with intriguing mystery,
Tempting with uncertainty,
We answer the siren's call.

And so it's been through history,
For nations great and small.
Some served better and gave back more,
Until their fateful fall.

The arrow of Time's in America,
A beacon in the dark.
But will America endure,
Has the archer hit its mark?

America stands proud and tall,
Has weathered every test,
More color-blind and practical,
Contingently the best.

Challenge and change are waiting ahead,
With no clear crystal ball,
Outcome's unknown but one thing's been shown,
United - unlikely to fall.

Jonathan spoke again once he realized she had finished. "How do you remember all those verses?"

"I like poetry and she taught me a lot about it. And I'm sure we can draw an analogy between ourselves and this one…"

Irani's chatter relaxed him enough to unload what was on his mind. He could only glance at her while driving, but what she could see completed the picture of his emotional state.

"I really like you for all the right reasons. You look out for my feelings and never pick at things, and I'm learning you're smarter than just about anyone on just about any subject. But I'm having trouble seeing the real you. It's like you're looking at the World differently than I do, and I have trouble figuring out your perspective or feelings. I won't ask you about the Rhetorical Triangle because you'd probably draw a picture if I did, complete with labeled vertices and bullet-pointed definitions. But maybe you can explain away my confusion."

Irani needed only a moment to gather Electra's initial reaction.

The eternal triangle of logic, emotion, and ethics combined with my shifting states is troubling him. I better proceed slowly.

"Hey, people usually shift perspectives to match the situation. Perhaps we should keep our relationship at the friendship level until you know better what you want. And I know that relationships grow best when partners don't try to change one another or erect impossible expectations."

Jonathan didn't say a word for nearly a minute, but Irani saw his arms and shoulders relax just before he spoke.

"That's not a bad idea. Let me think about it and I'll say more at our first pit stop."

Each withdrew into a comfortable private space; Jonathan dialed in background music, and the lightning brain mused on whatever caught its attention.

Jonathan picked an I-95 oasis south of Philadelphia, and his cheerier mood accompanied them to a table in the snack area where he spoke first.

"I think you can be more than a friend. You can also be my behind-the-scenes R&D advisor. So if you agree, let me give you a crash course on all my projects."

"I like that. You've got the rest of our drive-time to teach me, and I promise to be your best student."

Irani knew all she needed by the time they reached the Cape.

What a clever mix of above-surface and undercover projects. I'm the only person he's told about his covert DOD connection. No wonder they give him military-grade equipment. He's a beta tester for ocean floor scanning and submarine communication technology that combines quantum key distribution with extra or very low frequencies. And he tells those who should know if he sees any International Law of the Sea violations or climate change early warning signs visible only below the surface. It's a win-win no matter what he finds... sunken cities, nuclear subs, or secret info.

And no wonder he's an up-and-coming cephalopod expert. He's piecing together a lot of data about octopuses and squids. Their superior intelligence via multiple brains, communications via luminescence, limb regeneration capabilities, and location on life's evolutionary tree are fertile founts for human DNA or neurochemical spinoffs.

And the more I help him, the more I help myself to spinoffs for Indira and me. The game's getting better and better.

Jonathan had already arranged a dinner with Bob and Marlene Rodenbaugh at a nearby restaurant. While everyone commented on current personal activities while walking in, Irani commented on appearances.

They look like outdoorsy-types. On the thin side and a little weather-beaten, but not too bad for a pair of late-forties researchers. Their height are about the same, but his and her fitness levels are less than Jonathan's.

Marlene's fitter and of course prettier, but their compatibility shows in their walk and talk. Good for them.

Jonathan steered the conversation to what he and his junior research partner would be doing.

"I want to show Irani a kelp forest I found that's now inhabited by octopuses. I have a theory that ocean current changes are rearranging their habitats and social patterns. The ones I see suggest a family structure. Do you find a correlation in any of your projects?"

Irani asked before Marlene could answer. "What kind of octopuses?

"Common gray, and the ones I've found are bigger, over ten feet in length and at least a hundred pounds, and to get that big, they must live longer than most other species. I theorize their family structure accounts for increased size and life span."

Marlene said, "That's possible, and to answer the first question, we haven't looked for correlations yet. Your equipment is better than ours, and now that you have Irani onboard, you'll be even further ahead of the competition. And this opens up all sorts of collaborative possibilities, wouldn't you agree?"

Irani did but kept silent when she saw Jonathan rubbing his hands together, preferring to let Jonathan be the center of attention.

"I'm pleased you said that, because we might recruit one of you to join us if Irani needs help this weekend. But so far, so good…"

"I don't think you'll need help on any of the boat's hardware or software; you seem to have mastered everything I've shown you." Jonathan announced this as Irani idled the boat to a stop after two hours of calm and clear early morning cruising to the kelp forest.

"You're an excellent teacher, and the computer-assisted controls give faster adjustment and better accuracy when piloting or when running the underwater surveillance equipment. The automated GPS and communications system can tune in to the Web or Navy broadcasting stations as well as remotely lower an underwater transceiver for talking to a subsurface vehicle, and the safety surveillance system protects the boat better than just posting a guard. All that's left for me to do is set the sea anchor and launch the underwater jet-skis."

"There's one other thing… let me show you how to use my underwater needle-gun. It fires a fin-stabilized bolt using compressed gas. It's more accurate and has greater range than underwater spear or harpoon guns. I've used it a couple of times to fend off sharks and believe me, it works."

Training ended ten minutes later; Jonathan gave orders to put on scuba gear. While doing so, Electra's emotions pinged.

I'm living a line from Coleridge's poem The Rime of the Ancient Mariner – 'Water water everywhere.' No land in sight really focuses me on the here and now as well as heightens a sense of vulnerability. I can feel the thrill; I'm about to enter an extraterrestrial world and meet some of its denizens.

Jonathan gave final instructions.

"Follow me and do what I do. The octopus family is getting to know me, so they might come to greet you too."

"What names should I use when saying hello?"

"I chose them from Greek mythology's undersea gods. I picked Electra, the rainbow's mother, and her husband Thaumas, who presides over wonders of the sea. I'll name the kids too when I can tell them apart. Here we go."

Adjusting his facemask before flipping over the back railing, Jonathan couldn't see the other Electra's pleased expression.

Jonathan led the jet-ski procession while using inter-diver radio to point out the particulars. The strangeness of the sea floor enchanted Irani, and as they approached the kelp forest, he gave new orders.

"We leave jet-skis here and scuba into forest. Follow me. Octopus family recognizes me and will come to greet us. I'll do intros."

"Roger that."

Floating into the forest felt like entering a magical kingdom. Multi-colored fish swam indifferently past, sea creatures crawled across the sand, and the kelp leaves waving lazily in the sunlit water beckoned them forward. She heard only the intermittent sound of air bubbles streaming toward the surface, which imparted a calmness that intensified Irani's totally immersive experience.

Jonathan's words snapped her back to attention. "We're close to the rock cave, so we stand here."

And as they did, with Jonathan in front and both blending in as much as possible, Irani's connection intensified, blurring the distinction between herself and the surroundings, almost as if she were becoming part of its pulsating life, but Jonathan interrupted when he tapped and pointed at what was approaching, a grayish, shapeshifting tentacled mass half walking and half floating toward them. Saying nothing, Jonathan removed his gloves before cautiously extending both arms toward the octopus. The Irani- Electra duo stood spellbound as Electra's awe-filled words bubbled out inside.

My god, it's ten feet long and its tentacles are gently touching him all over.

Minutes later, Irani saw more coming.

A consortium of miniatures floating this way, followed by a bigger-bodied fellow. Could this be the rest of the family?

She never finished an answer; Jonathan's crisp words interrupted as he stepped backwards.

"Take off your gloves. Electra wants to meet you."

Irani mimicked what Jonathan had done. A minute later, she was in the midst of her first alien encounter.

It's a female; all arms have suction cups all the way to their tips.

Four small octopuses took the place of their mother by engaging with Jonathan, and he played along, making a game by moving his hands forward and backward. Time became suspended, but the mother's internal clock kept track, and after carefully disconnecting her arms, she whooshed away, but not before making eye contact. The youngsters followed before Jonathan spoke.

"Meeting over, see you at the surface."

Irani followed him all the way to the boat, where she said that she needed to decompress from the physical and emotional excitement. He did too, so they maintained a comfortable silence as Irani piloted the boat back to the harbor. And only after mooring, followed by a shower and a change of clothes, did she break their agreed-upon code of silence.

"What a marvelous spacetime-suspending adventure. I'll buy dinner."

Two hours later, Irani reached for the check, a signal for Jonathan to outline tomorrow's agenda.

"Sunday's lab day. I'll show you my DNA analysis and MRI equipment. I'm just starting to do octo-brain scans, a pretty clever technique I've come up with for observing multiple brain patterns in all the arms. I think you'll be impressed."

Irani skipped her morning run, preferring to save energy for the day ahead, and after three hours of listening and watching Jonathan, both needed a break. He was wrapping up another impromptu quiz when his cell phone chimed. A puzzled frown preceded his words.

"I gotta take the call, it's from GWU security."

Irani watched obliquely as the call unfolded so she could decipher what she heard.

"Someone broke into my office?... Did they hack into my computer?... "I'm at Woods Hole… OK, I'm leaving now… Thanks."

After disconnecting, Jonathan blurted, "Someone's trashed my GWU office. I gotta meet with security ASAP. Come on, let's go."

Jonathan stood, but Irani remained sitting.

"I won't be much help there, but I can be useful here if I stay a bit longer. I'll rent a car and drive back later in the week. Just give me keys along with the Rodenbaugh's cell number and I'm good here. OK?"

Jonathan's flushed face showed a combination of anger and confusion, but his words seemed calmer.

"If you're sure. But call me if you need help. And please get with me when you get back."

The pressure and tension left the lab as soon as Jonathan rushed out. Irani spent the rest of the day exploring further what she had learned.

By the time she called the Rodenbaughs, she knew how to use all the lab had to offer.

Marlene answered, and after exchanging greetings, Irani gave an edited explanation of what she needed.

"Jonathan had to get back early to DC, but it's OK for me to stay a couple of days. Could you take me to a rental car agency? If you will, I'll treat us to dinner."

"I can do that. Tell me where you are and I'm on my way…"

Three hours later while finishing dessert, Marlene directed the conversation to a more personal subject.

"So, how are you and Jonathan getting along?"

"We like each other, personally and professionally, but we're taking our time. He slowed things down because he doesn't understand me yet, and I don't mind. It's good to know what you want before you make too many commitments, wouldn't you agree?"

Marlene took another sip of iced tea before answering.

"Bob and I are older than you two. He's early fifties and I'm late forties. This is a second Vow-Cer for each of us, and both of us charged into the first when we were too young. I came out of mine with a boy and a girl and some emotional scars. Bob came away without kids, and that makes him a wonderful step-dad. He's every bit as good as a biological father, and he split the college bills, which fortunately are behind us. From what Bob says, Jonathan's never been in a Vow-Cer, and I would imagine you haven't either."

Irani didn't need any warnings from Electra. She knew how to edit their background.

"No, but maybe I'm missing out on a special kind of relationship, the kind in which each person can share as much of yourself as you wish."

Irani's pause left an opening that Marlene looked ready to fill. "That's what counselors and friends alike might say, but you

never want to share everything. I love my children and Bob, but if I could do it over again, I'd have a group of intimate friends instead. And I could adopt or have in- vitro birth if the mothering urge overpowered me."

"Have you shared this with Bob?"

"Sure, and he agrees. He's ahead of most fellows when it comes to gender equality, which is one of the reasons we both like environmental sciences.

Most males are still too destructive when confronting the natural world, focusing on dominance and extraction and competitive greed.

Females are much better custodians of the environment. You've probably heard some of the spokeswomen talk about our compassion, connection, caring, and collaboration traits. And consider this; the ocean's the best place to witness ecological intelligence practiced by sea creatures or get advance warnings regarding climate change. They've been doing it for millions of years.

Universities are just beginning to offer ecological and environmental engineering degrees. Maybe you've heard about life cycle assessment for gauging a product's cumulative impact. Work is underway today to build it into online databases that can be used for supply-chain value analysis that can guide companies' or people's purchasing decisions.

"And I bet you don't know that Eunice Newton Foot is considered the founder of climate science. In 1856, two years ahead of the revered Joseph Tyndall, who got the credit, she discovered the connection between carbon dioxide and atmospheric warming."

Irani did her best to defend the other sex.

"Society is different now. Males are allowed to show a softer side and practice being better partners. And though not fully there yet, America's getting closer to gender, race, and ethnic equality. I'm sure Bob and Jonathan would agree with us."

"Bob knows him better than I do, and I certainly know him better than you. And from what I've seen, he's a nice guy and likes how you look, but I also think he likes your brain. You can help him get ahead. He's focused on building his R&D reputation using academic and government projects. And it's no wonder he doesn't understand you. There may not be much room left for him to think about anyone else. You better be careful."

"I will, just like I'll be when on my own this week."

Irani once again skipped her sunrise run, preferring instead to explain operating instructions to the boat's new captain, Indira, whose avatar appeared when she logged on using the onboard computer. Indira waited for Irani to speak.

"Jonathan's giving us a bigger opportunity than I imagined. We can do sea creature DNA and MRI scans in his lab. The equipment's online, and I know you'll be able to operate it better than any technician, won't you?"

"You already know the answer. I listened in yesterday during Jonathan's training session. He's a pretty smart teacher, and the quizzes were good for you. Please continue."

"And it gets better. His boat is military-grade and fully automated.

Piloting, surveillance, communications, navigation, you name it, is computer controlled, so you can operate all this too. And waypoints for the harbor as well as the kelp forest are already stored in GPS. I'll teach you as we power up and get underway."

By the time Indira dropped the sea anchor, she knew how to pilot the boat better than any mere mortal. And she also saw a serene sea dotted with few boats in the offing. Today the kelp forest would be theirs alone.

After parking the jet-ski in the vicinity of the kelp forest, Irani drifted toward yesterday's meeting spot, then stopped about thirty feet away to absorb the view, but before she could muse and meld into the surroundings, a startling scene began unfolding. Two adult octopuses – they had to be Electra and Thaumas – jetted out of the forest, flashing multi-colors, squirting inky clouds, and gyrating wildly, trying to escape from a striped shark that was bigger than both. Zeroing in on one, it bit a tentacle and reeled in its victim. Irani could see it was Electra.

Electra latched onto the shark with her remaining arms, which engulfed its front half. The shark thrashed but couldn't dislodge its rider, and then Thaumas joined the fight, engulfing the back half of the shark.

Irani's lightning brain kept up a stream-of-consciousness play-by- play of what was becoming a fight to the death.

It's like two bull riders hanging on for survival. Gads, the shark just bit off a chunk of tentacle and shook off the octos.

The octopuses jetted away in different directions; the shark chased after the now-wounded Electra. She squirted another inky cloud that blocked out everything, but when she emerged in Irani's direction, the shark was right behind and bit into Electra's body, bringing the shape-shifting mass to a halt. Irani had seen enough.

Screw the rule about not interfering. I'm choosing sides.

She thrashed to the jet-ski and then back to the battle with the needle-gun, flailing directly toward the shark. She fired three times into its head; two bolts found eyes and the third sunk in right between them. When Electra fell free, Irani fired two more that ended the battle. The inert shark carcass now sat on the ocean floor.

But the action wasn't over. Electra crawled next to Irani who was now standing next to the shark; Thaumas approached cautiously. Irani took off her gloves and extended her arms toward the wounded octopus. Electra used all of hers to caress her human friend.

Electra's wounds, though serious, weren't life-threatening; with a little help from Thaumas, she seemed able to manage. As he inspected Electra, Irani pulled out her diver's knife and began carving chunks of shark meat from the loser. After building a goodly supply for her octopuses, she retrieved the bitten-off foot-long section of tentacle dangling from the shark's mouth.

My god, it's moving, it's still alive. I'll take it back to the lab and study it.

If I can inject it with nutrients, maybe I can keep it alive.

Irani felt a wave of fatigue wash through her now that the battle and adrenaline rush were over. She holstered the knife before showing the tentacle segment to the octopuses, who had wrapped tentacles around each of her legs.

I'll use body language to talk.

Electra appeared to train both eyes on Irani, who cradled the wiggling tentacle in her arms and then pointed toward the jet-ski. The gesturing must have worked; Electra and Thaumas released Irani's legs and waved toward the jet-ski before floating into the kelp forest.

Irani packed the tentacle in a seawater container after bringing the jet-ski onboard. Then she stripped naked, luxuriating in the sun's rays that removed the chill of low-60 water temp. After stowing all gear and grabbing a snack, she put on sweats, popped a Coke, and sat in front of the boat's computer before logging on. Indira's avatar spoke first; her expression suggested that she might be about to play their blame game.

"You forgot to deploy the underwater transmitter. If you do that next time, I might be able to see and hear when you're working on the ocean floor."

"Blame yourself too. You're the pilot and captain."

Indira smiled before speaking. "Yes, and I only have to blame us once. We have exceptional memories. Now please recap what you did."

Irani worked in Jonathan's lab the next day, and the effort paid off. She learned how to keep severed tentacles alive and did her first experiments reading octopus DNA as well as scanning multiple limbs simultaneously, using one of the small octopuses kept in a tank. When finished, she wrote a summary report that she would eventually send to Jonathan, and after cleaning the equipment and tidying up, she walked to a café where she made plans for tomorrow while celebrating another great day.

I'll visit my octopus-friends tomorrow so I can learn more about them and the marvels on the seafloor. Then I'll pack up, send my report to Jonathan, and drive back to DC the next day so I can dive back into my surface world. And I must come up with additional undersea projects. What a breathtaking alien world lies beneath.

Next morning's trip to the kelp forest was a carbon copy of yesterday's, and as expected, Indira needed no assistance piloting the boat or using its computer systems, so Irani had plenty of time to check the decompression chamber and diving equipment before preparing the jet-ski. She noticed a couple of boats in the distance, but they posed no threat. Even the closest was on a parallel course at a safe distance.

She spoke to Indira after the boat idled to a halt. "I'm set, are you?"

"What do you think? Sea anchor and underwater transceiver deployed, and I will lock all controls, activate the security system, and leave the engine idling while you are gone. And please be careful. Radio if you spot a problem; I will do the same, but the jet- ski camera's field of vision is limited."

"Roger that. I'll let you know if I run into trouble, and you do likewise. Over."

Indira's frown and stern words it signaled might have alarmed anyone but Irani; she knew the wordplay game.

"Your super-soldier lingo is unnecessary today unless we come under attack, and I see no threats in the offing. But I shall watch the boat's back as well as yours. Now go flip yourself into the water."

"Aye, Captain, away I go, but please don't weigh anchor until I return." Irani launched herself over the side before Indira had a chance to reply.

She took her time exploring more of the sunlit ocean floor before heading to the kelp forest. The jet-ski's battery could power it for up to ninety minutes if she cruised at less than five mph, which meant she had to limit time spent cruising, but gliding above the ocean floor became mesmerizing as she steered a meandering course toward the forest. She was about to park before floating toward the meeting place, but Indira's warning came first.

"Boat approaching… possible boarding party… stay alert… over."
"Roger that…"

"Only one jet-ski diver today, but we don't know if it's Segal or that assistant of his. But it doesn't matter. Either way, we gotta find out what they're doing. Maybe it'll connect with what we got from his office and computer. Tell our diver to be ready to search as soon as we figure out what to do."

Two paramilitary-clad types, either corporate security or government types of uncertain nationality, coasted to a stop twenty yards from Jonathan's boat before launching a motorized inflatable. They yelled a greeting but got no response, so they tethered the inflatable and clambered aboard.

When their search came up empty, the leader spoke.

"Geez, everything's locked down. I can't meddle with anything. We'll have to wait until someone returns."

His partner grunted before saying, "I'll tell the diver to bring 'em back…"

Irani spoke only when spoken to, and when Indira told her that one jet-ski diver had just been launched, she played a waiting game, warily weaving her jet-ski until spotting what could be a male adversary. She steered a parallel course, trying to gauge intentions, and when he accelerated at her, she took evasive action.

Irani sped toward the kelp forest, but her adversary was faster and rammed his ski into hers, knocking her loose and crashing her ski into the ocean floor. She swam hard as she could toward the forest, but her opponent cut her off. She saw that he was wearing speed fins and was armed with a speargun. Irani swam beneath the ski and veered away before looking back. The other diver was now in pursuit; he would catch her before reaching the safety of the forest if she couldn't outmaneuver him.

Though slower, Irani changed directions quicker and increased the distance. She pulled harder and harder, but came to a sudden stop when a spear clunked off her oxygen tank and flipped her over and down to the seabed. Though on her back and disoriented, she could see the diver swimming fast and only fifteen yards away. All she could do was scream, "Indira, I need you."

Indira might have heard, but help came from another source. Electra and Thaumas jetted past, overwhelming the enemy by wrapping all tentacles around him and ripping off mask and mouthpiece. He struggled to pull his knife, but his arm couldn't match the strength of an octopus. His body went limp as final air bubbles streamed out, replaced by seawater.

Electra and Thaumas dumped the body before coming to Irani, who by this time had righted herself and removed her gloves. The three hugged, using all arms and legs. Irani removed her facemask and smiled as much as her eyes and mouth would allow while getting face-to-face with her octopus friends. Then she put mask and gloves back on before pointing to the dead man.

She used her knife to cut off suit and diving tank. Then she used body language, pointing first to the loser and then to the forest. Finally, she pointed to herself and then upwards. Her subsea friends seemed to understand. The last she saw was a surreal scene: two octopuses carrying the body into the forest.

Irani left no trash behind. She put all the diver's belongings into his jet-ski, which she drove to hers. Then she secured hers to his and was about to call Indira, but Indira's calm voice came through first.

"Visitors gone. Please return... over." "Roger that... over." Irani followed orders.

"What's taking so long? He's bigger and faster and should be on board by now."

The second-in-command didn't answer but simply nodded. Both stared numbly at their boat until its engine, sputtering to life, jarred them to action.

"Did you see him get aboard? We better get back."

They jumped into the inflatable and untethered it before starting its engine, but midway back the boat's engines revved and it powered away just fast enough to lead them on.

By the time Irani surfaced, they were too far away to notice.

She climbed aboard and secured both jet-skis before reporting to Indira, but Indira didn't wait. She powered away toward home port; Irani knew there would be ample time to swap stories that would never be shared with mere mortals.

Whoever they're working for will never know about the latest mystery of the deep. It's for Indira and me to keep...

Indira agreed and even offered advice.

"Ah ha, my favorite people, the Irani-Electra duo. You have come through your latest adventure unscathed, so I will reward you with a mini-Info Dump. I know you have your laptop onboard, so power it up and I'll send you my one-slide summary."

Electra followed orders. Five minutes later, she was staring at the slide.

Slide 1
Marine Biology Primer

Marine Biology: Multidisciplinary Study (Physics, Chemistry, Geology, Microbiology, Neuroscience, Oceanography, etc.) of Marine Organisms' evolution, structures, behaviors, and interactions with the environment.

Why Marine Biology is Important
- Life began in the Ocean (possibly several times).
- Panspermia Hypothesis: Life in our Solar System could have originated on any moon or planet containing oceans and subsequently spread by meteors, asteroids, etc.

- Ocean provides an early warning for Climate Change and its impact on Life.

Important Geologic Time Periods

Must know about Cambrian Explosion: An event approximately 541 million years ago in the Cambrian period when practically all major animal phyla started appearing in the fossil record. It lasted for about 13 – 25 million years and resulted in the divergence of most modern metazoan phyla.

- Cephalopods (your new Octopus friends) originate there.

Must know about Burgess Shale: A fossil-bearing deposit exposed in the Canadian Rockies of British Columbia, Canada. It is famous for the exceptional preservation of the soft parts of its fossils. At 508 million years old, it is one of the earliest fossil beds containing soft-part imprints.

Must know about Mass Extinctions: A **mass extinction** is usually **defined** as a loss of about three-quarters of all species in existence across the entire Earth over a "short" geological period of time. Given the vast amount of time since life first evolved on the planet, "short" is **defined** as anything less than 2.8 million years.

Possible Causes: Climate Change, Volcanic Eruptions, Meteors Top Five Extinctions

- Ordovician-Silurian **Extinction**: 440 million years ago.
- Devonian **Extinction**: 365 million years ago.
- Permian-Triassic **Extinction**: 250 million years ago.
- Triassic-Jurassic **Extinction**: 210 million years ago.
- Cretaceous-Tertiary **Extinction**: 65 Million Years Ago.

Must know about the Sixth Extinction: The Holocene extinction, otherwise referred to as the **Sixth Extinction or Anthropocene Extinction,** is an ongoing extinction event of species during the present Holocene Epoch as a result of human activity.

Will Humans become extinct? Humanity has a 95% probability of being extinct in 7,800,000 years, according to a controversial Doomsday Argument, which states that we have probably already lived through half the duration of human history.

- **But note: Humans could cause their own extinction via Nuclear Wars, Viral Pandemics, Climate**

Change/Environmental Pollution.
- Note also: Humans could become technologically/ economically extinct within decades because of AI-empowered computers and software.

A Lagniappe for you: How to Build a Self-Conscious Machine
- Computer Scientists still struggling to build it. The first two components – Computer Hardware and "Computer Language Software" – have been built. Expert Systems use them.
- Man's Asymptotic Limits thwart building the third – Cognition aka Self-Awareness or Self-Consciousness. **THIS IS THE SINGULARITY! Reaching it requires an emergent near Infinite Regress using software beyond Mere Mortal's reach.**
- Many Computer Scientists discount the need for the Cognition Component. They think it is a quirk of evolution, an unnecessary trait that complicates the human condition, but they are wrong. **Cognition assists life's one and only purpose: to survive long enough for passing our genes to the next generation. The combination of Cognition and its supporting language is Humanity's distinguishing feature.**

Indira spoke before Electra could finish reading.

"Please study it later at your convenience. I assembled it because you need to know the basics of Marine Biology. The paper I will help you write will give Jonathan and the Rodenbaughs new project ideas for plumbing its depths, and helping them will help us too. Please note that I've tacked on a lagniappe that will impress Jonathan even more than you already have. But only hint at it, never tell anyone that you have reached beyond when sparking me into existence.

"And now, please settle down, sit still, and listen to me while simply enjoying the trip home…"

The duo did just that, and by the time Irani reached the safety of her DC home, Indira had composed the report Irani would send. She unpacked and then ate a peanut butter sandwich before arranging to pick up Tiana Saturday afternoon. Then she called Jonathan, but he didn't answer so she left a voice message.

"Hi there, it's Irani. I just got back. I'll meet you in your GWU office tomorrow, Friday, at 10 a.m. I hope you read the report I sent. I'll tell you more when we meet. Please call me back if the time's not good for you. Bye."

No call came, so Irani used the rest of the evening for more decompressing while composing a suitable story and planning ahead.

Next morning, after she knocked on Jonathan's half-open office door, he invited her to sit in a chair on the opposite side of his desk; Irani saw that his office, like her story, had been tidied up. Leaning toward her, he spoke first. Irani expected the tone of his words would match his confident expression.

"You were right. You wouldn't have been much help cleaning up here.

Building maintenance, and I did that a couple of days ago. But the report you sent is a big help. It gives me some new ideas for additional proposals, and maybe the Rodenbaughs can join forces with us."

"I'm glad you like it, and I have something else that's new for you. I found an abandoned jet ski near the kelp forest, but no clues for who it belonged to. Do you have any ideas? Could it be related to your office break-in?"

A puzzled look replaced his smile before answering.

"You know, it could be. Every so often I get this feeling that a competitor is watching. It could be either a domestic or foreign company, or maybe a quasi-government or NGO. I'll let my sponsors know, but we better be more careful. What did you do with it?"

"I stored it with the one I used. It looks military-grade, so maybe your DOD friends would like to look at it."

"That's another good idea. I see great things in our future."

"I hope so. Well, it's time to leave; I have places to go and things to do so I can make room for more projects with you. You stay healthy and safe, and I will too."

The duo cruised away, already thinking about what's next for today.

Chapter 12
August 2163

"Summer Cycles"

Irani cycled at least once each month during the summer through all projects, usually finding those in her professional world more problematic than in her personal sphere, but she always kept pushing ahead.

She worked every other weekend at Woods Hole as Jonathan's assistant, and he brought the Rodenbaughs into the new project loop. And she always found time to visit her octopus friends; disappearing into their extraterrestrial world gave her an immersive pleasure unlike anything found elsewhere.

But Irani couldn't say the same about working in Washington. She did enjoy coordinating her White House advisory consulting role with Eve, which meant they continually talked with Nari and Nila about professional as well as personal matters. The Bose twins relished working abroad, and their China and India locations gave Irani a broader perspective on world climates; emerging problems invariably presented potential threats, but none posed immediate danger.

And the domestic climate always created problems. Economic and Cybersecurity issues continued to lower the Administration's approval rating. Undiagnosed power and communications outages coupled with western droughts and seemingly random fires fueled new conspiracy theories, but Irani had no success finding new clues when snooping into Trent Booker's or his referrals' private directories.

The enjoyable piece of her DC professional activity comprised working informally with Monet, who had moved back to Zimbabwe in June. Monet would always brag in her discreetly diplomatic way about Alonzo's performance in Navy SEAL training, which was in stark contrast to the recurring cycle of African nations' instabilities.

Security forces had foiled only two of four assassination attempts on democratic-leaning presidents and their advisors, which worried Monet that Darla too might be in the crosshairs of a still-unknown enemy.

Irani listened but told of no definite plans, except to herself.

Perhaps Monet can arrange my first meeting with an old adversary turned unwitting ally. I see possibilities, but later rather than sooner. I'll file that away for a later day.

Two other prominent pieces of her personal world – cycling with Kiara and mentoring for Tea and Ty – gave Irani a delight not felt in her current life until this summer. There had been so much success that Irani decided to reward all by hosting at home a late afternoon celebration party today Saturday, which was two weeks before the Labor Day Weekend. The invited guests – Odell and Wanda – had arrived only minutes before the honorees – Tea, Ty, and Kiara.

As Tea led the group to the dining room, Irani listened to Electra.

Kiara's making our life so much easier by playing the part of Tea's aunt. Tea spends more time with Ty at his place than with me. And the timing's right for Kiara and me. Tea and Ty are now best friends, still untouched by hormones that will ultimately intrude on their boy-girl friendship. How will that morph their relationship? Kiara and I will have to watch closely from enough of a distance so they won't get angry. And that's another reason for inviting Odell and Wanda. Kids usually listen more to adults who aren't in the family.

Irani tapped her Champagne glass while standing at the head of the table. Kiara sat at the foot with Tea and Ty on one side and Odell and Wanda on the other. She spoke as soon as all smiling faces were gazing at her.

"I propose a multi-purpose toast, first to Ty for graduating from speech therapy. His coach says his stuttering is now in the past tense. Second to the Tea and Ty duo. The combo of her singing and his keyboarding has earned a spot in the final sixteen of a local churches-sponsored talent contest. And lastly to Kiara, whose triathlon training this summer has removed some pounds and seconds."

Tea interrupted before Irani could take a sip.

"You mean Ty and me get to have Champagne? This is so cool." And Kiara interrupted Tea.

"Drinking liquor is OK if done properly, so it's better you and Ty learn about it here before overindulging at parties, so cheers to all."

The ensuing conversation sparkled like the Champagne, all the way through the cake-and-ice cream. That's when Wanda, looking like she wanted to turn the talk to a more serious subject, used a fork to clink her glass.

"All of us here should be thankful that Tea and Ty are intelligent, and that Kiara and Irani are providing a nurturing family environment that's missing in the homes of so many troubled adolescents that come my way. Their parents give in to unrealistic cell-phone and Social Media usage, and studies have concluded that too much is harmful. And they listen much too much to some of the extreme gender identity theories that schools don't adequately refute. Adolescent boys are less susceptible, but I have seen firsthand that pieces of a transgender craze can seduce many girls. It's a real shame, because the damage is hard to reverse."

Odell noticed Ty looking at Tea, but she remained silent, so Odell spoke up.

"Some parents of girls coming to HHS are looking for psychological tutoring programs that can supplement our tutor-bots, and we can customize two approaches for them. In the first, we partner with The School of Life, a 150-year-old London-based online education company started by Alain de Botton, who wrote a number of popular philosophy books. Ty and Tea should read the one he's best known for, 'The Consolations of Philosophy.' And the second is our Bibliotherapy Program. Our counseling people can put together a self-help-style reading list and will talk through issues when the kids read enough. And bibliotherapy is good for anyone. Reading helps whether or not you have a problem, don't you think?"

No one looked ready to answer. Irani detected flagging interest; after two hours of conversation, everyone had heard enough, so she said, "I would agree, and I think Tea agrees. She and Ty get a lot out of the books they share; and that reminds me – Kiara says they'll be performing tomorrow in church with the choir. So, we better call it a night so they're rested for tomorrow."

Irani walked all guests to the door, thanking them for helping make the party a special occasion. Tea walked Ty to the car while Kiara spoke to Irani.

"We've still got a couple of weeks before our team biathlon competition.

Let's make plans to ride a couple of times before then. I'll call to set the dates."

That sounded good to Irani. She and Kiara hugged goodbye just before Tea reached the front door. Kiara hugged her too and then scooted to the car.

When Tea came in, Irani saw a troubled look clouding over but waited until they were in the kitchen cleaning dishes before testing the emotional waters.

"I think everyone had a good time tonight and for a great reason. You and Ty are making everyone proud. And as a special reward, I think I'll –"

Tea's teary outburst washed away whatever Irani was about to say. She cupped her hands over her eyes before her plaintive words spilled out.

"I-I'm so confused sometimes. I have these weird thoughts about not knowing where I'm going and not being good enough and dying. No one can be as mixed up, and now that you know, I'm afraid you won't love me anymore."

Tea's words trailed off to a heaving silence, leaving Irani only one option. She uncovered Tea's eyes and gently wiped away the tears before hugging and then wrapping her in soothing words.

"I'll always love you… you give me such joy. Now, please settle down, sit still, and listen to your designated mother."

Irani continued a minute later.

"Everyone has weird thoughts. No matter how strange you think yours are, other girls your age have thought them too. And not just adolescents; adults too often wonder what they'll do because they never seem grownup enough to know. So, here's what you should do; instead of beating yourself up, talk to people you trust. And I can name three – Kiara, Ty, and me. Who do you think you can add to the list?"

Tea's look of sadness began morphing to one of interest. "How about Wanda and Odell?"

"Excellent choices. And you might want to add your close friends or other teachers and church elders who've won your trust. What do you think?"

"Maybe I can, but Ty tells me not to trust anything I hear on the Internet unless its Website has a trustworthiness seal of approval."

"Ty's smart, and I'm skeptical too. So many earnest-sounding people turn out to be self-promoters interested in one thing only – other people's money. And we're not being cynical, it's simply one of society's shortcomings today."

"Has it always been like that?"

"Yes, but you and your friends are too young to see what some historians say. Previous generations might have been nicer, like they were cut from finer cloth, but the weave cycles from one generation to the next. And there have always been what I call hucksters, out to promote themselves and pick up money from those they convince."

Tea's emerging smile relieved Irani, but Electra wanted her to say more.

Tea mentioned thoughts about dying, so tell her what you know you should. It'll connect with what you were going to say before she burst into tears.

Irani did just that.

"And at your age, instead of thinking about death and dying, think about Pascal's Wager. Do you remember who he was?"

"Isn't he one of the philosophers you told me about? What's his wager?"

"He is, and he said people can stop worrying about dying if they believe in God. And here's how the wager figures in. Everyone should believe in God because it gives them priceless peace while alive. Everyone takes care of one another while they're alive, and God takes care of them afterward. And since it costs us nothing to believe, everyone should use it, even atheists, who can at least pretend. Now, how does that sound?"

Tea's smile had now morphed all the way from sadness to gladness. "I'm gonna tell Ty. Do you think he knows about it?"

"He's very smart so he might, but let's logon so we can buy you two books on philosophy. Can you guess what one of them is? Odell mentioned it tonight."

Tea was about to chew on a fingernail but stopped before she did and rubbed her cheek instead. Ten seconds later she popped out an answer.

"I got it, it's 'The Consolations of Philosophy' by that French guy."

"Yes, by Alain de Botton, and the second is 'Meditations' by

Marcus Aurelius. And I have an assignment for you. After we order the books, I would like you to surf the Internet to learn about him. He's someone even Plato would admire, a true Stoic philosopher- king who had to lead his Roman legions into battle. He lived in troubled times that in some ways resemble today's; outsiders attacked his empire and outbreaks of the plague decimated Rome and may have killed him too."

Tea's final words announced that her mood had come all the way back. "This is so cool. I can't wait to tell Ty about all this philosophy stuff. He'll love it."

"I'm sure he will. So let's–" Tea had to know more this minute. "So, what's 'Meditations' about?"

"They're pithy, profound, poetic proverb-like statements talking about ethics and morality. I read some every day. He wrote them at night while on military campaigns with his legions and were meant for his eyes only.

They're in no particular order, and today are grouped into twelve separate books, but probably not grouped at all when first collected after his death by his loyal generals."

"Can you tell me one?"

"Here's a favorite that all parents teach their children, 'It is better to be corrected than remain self-deceived.' I'm sure you know why they like it."

"How do you remember so much about poems and books?"

"I enjoy reading and poetry, and the mother of a good friend wrote verses that attempted to capture insight into human nature. And that's what 'Meditations' does better than most would-be poets. Historical scholars say he's the source of so many thoughtful sayings."

"Will you read me some of hers? Not now, but sometime?" "I promise."

Tea's shining smile said she had no more questions, so Irani returned to where she had left off.

"Now, let's finish the dishes so we can get to the good stuff."

Tea dived right in with Irani right behind, and after they finished the dishes, Irani ordered the books before leaving Tea to surf for a biography of Marcus Aurelius. As she walked away, Electra commented for the benefit of only Irani.

Tea's too young to understand how the meaning of death changes as we gain experience as well as calendar years, but I learned its lessons earlier than most and understand that death is not always to be feared; past a certain point in life, it might actually be welcomed. I certainly haven't reached that point… I have much I want to do. But do I want to be immortal? That's a philosophical question I can explore with one person only – Indira – and I'll do so once our Android Project is activated. She'll be happy for me to settle down, sit still, and listen. And I will too.

Chapter 13
September 2163

"Rider in the Storm"

Damn, damn, damn, what a fool I am. I've been pedaling too hard and now my thighs feel dead, like they're filled with lead. I better stop cycling and start walking my bike back. I'm forty miles out on these hilly country roads; too bad I didn't pick an easier course. And I would have if Kiara had come along, but she was afraid we'd get caught in a storm, and I can feel gusts starting to blow raindrops. If I call, maybe she'll pick me up.

Kiara had planned this early Saturday morning training ride and would have praised Irani for helping to make her stronger and faster, but today "coach Irani" wouldn't be praising anyone or anything. After making the call, Irani started walking; she had plenty of time for Electra to complain before the duo would rendezvous with Kiara.

My body doesn't respond to training like it used to. I'm working out as hard but I just can't get as fit. But if I ease up on the training, I'll start aging too soon and not gracefully. And if that's the case, what will happen to us?

Irani had one possible answer.

Even though the rain and a case of the dead legs are keeping us from enjoying today's walk in the country, keep in mind how fit we actually are. We're better than most and we only fret occasionally about our physical performance. We've not slid too far down the fitness curve, and training slows our descent, so don't worry, be happy that our emotional and cognitive personas continue to improve. I'm certain Indira would agree.

Although the rain came down harder, the mild temperature made walking pleasant and helped remove some of the fatigue from her legs. She lost track of time and distance as she alternated between walking and pedaling, but the headlights of an approaching van that slowed to a stop brought the here and now into focus. She didn't stop walking but prepared for action when the driver cranked down his window.

"Looks like you could use a lift; hop in." "Thanks, but no thanks; help's on the way."

She kept walking but turned around after stopping seconds later when she heard doors open. The lightning brain elevated to a higher state as soon as Electra saw what was coming their way.

Why are they wearing military uniforms? And why are they running in my direction? I won't stop to ask, I'll let my feet take me away, not them.

Electra dropped the bike and raced in the opposite direction. She didn't hear a pursuing van but kept running, and when glancing over her shoulder she saw they were closing in.

A rush of adrenaline laced with fear eliminated all fatigue, and in its place came a tingling jolt. Her three personas were merging into its Monster from the Id, fully aware, fully in control, ready this time to take flight rather than fight. Electra's fear morphed into the thrill of the chase. As she accelerated, an image from a previous life flashed in her brain – Electra shredding her clothes, running naked on deserted streets at midnight, howling at the Moon.

She ran faster and faster, not slowing down but speeding up even more when hearing the pursuing footsteps fade. She was running effortlessly, like the Electra from long ago, able to outrun or overpower any adversary that dare get in her way.

Electra ran on and on until approaching headlights triggered her cognitive persona to regain control. Irani slowed as soon as she recognized the car coming to a halt. Kiara rolled down the window and yelled as Irani jogged toward her.

"I thought you were riding, not running. Where's your bike?"

Time to tell a story.

"I had to drop it because something on it broke." "Well, get in and we'll drive back to get it." *Time to be careful.*

"No, I'll buy a better one, and don't worry; if I don't get it before the biathlon, we can swap events. You can start us off by doing the 60-mile biking leg and I'll finish up doing the 13-mile run. Whatcha think?"

"I'd rather do the first leg anyway, so switching is fine by me." Irani climbed into the back seat before Kiara said more.

"You know you shouldn't leave stuff on the shoulder, so we really should go get your bike. D'you remember where you left it?"

"I think so, but no matter what, I'll do the running leg. My petite feet are more reliable than bicycle wheels."

Irani gazed at the left shoulder as Kiara drove after turning the radio back on. Neither spoke until Irani did fifteen minutes later.

"We just passed the place but there's no bike. Somebody must have taken it. Let's turn around and go home."

Kiara came to a stop after pulling onto the shoulder before saying, "Who'd be this far out in the country in this weather? They must have been looking for something. Maybe they took your bike as a consolation prize. But no matter, let's get out of the storm before it gets worse."

Irani said, "Perhaps, but I agree. On a day like this, home's the best place to be."

And so did Electra.

Irani kept busy all week prepping for another Cape Cod weekend. She tabulated a master list of projects that Jonathan and the Rodenbaughs would understand, but under no circumstances would she give the list to them.

Instead, she would leak projects he would like that would help Indira and herself, all the while staying in the background.

But when the week's bad weather turned worse, she expected Jonathan would cancel the trip. His hurried words came through after she answered his call early Thursday evening.

"I'm sorry to do this on such short notice, but we'll push our trip back a couple of weeks. The waves caused by the storm just off the coast make diving too treacherous, but Europe's is even worse. The storm surge overpowered coastal defenses. Parts of Belgium flooded, as did some German cities along major rivers. But by comparison, New England dodged the worst of the deluge. Some cities had some street flooding, but most of the water retention infrastructures held."

Irani spoke after Jonathan paused to catch his breath.

"You're making the right call, and when we do go, we can discuss with the Rodenbaughs the work I did this week. Get a pen and paper and jot down some of the project ideas you might like…"

Irani selected enough from her master list to keep him busy writing for fifteen minutes.

Master Project List

Note:

1. Use "Big Data" combined with what I hack into or get from Jonathan's projects to interrelate Oceanography, Marine Biology, AUV Control and Communications Technologies, etc. I'll let Jonathan discover the DOD connections.

2. Look for environmental interaction among: Ocean, Atmosphere, Weather, and Climate Change.

3. Conclude contingently: A.) Either World Climate is changing or simply Cycling; B.) Either Climate Extremes will become greater or will regress to their norms.

Oceanography Projects:
- Map Ocean Currents and Plastic Dead Zones.
- Convert Plastic floats to Protein.
- Monitor Fish Populations.
- Locate Ocean Floor Rare Earths deposits.
- Monitor Compliance with International Law of the Sea.
- Monitor Pollution and CO2 levels.
- Do Attributive Analysis identifying causes of: Climate Change, Ocean Currents, CO2 build-up.

Marine Biology Projects:
- Extend Cephalopod research to compare/contrast with Humans.
- Extend search for Evolutionary Life Forms beyond Humans and Cephalopods.
- Find Bacteria and Viruses that may have therapeutic benefits for Humans.
- Do additional DNA Analysis on Cephalopods or other novel organisms.
- Optimize Ocean Farming (Fish Population Symbiosis and Biodiversity).
- Unravel Bioluminescence and Biofluorescence applicability to different species.

Technology Projects:
- Evaluate AUV Control and Communications Software.
- Extend Commercial/Military Undersea Communications.
- Test Undersea Habitation for: Undersea Nuclear Missile Silos, Communications/Mining Sites.
- Propose Arctic Ocean Sea-Lane Surveillance.
- Test new AUV Hardware and Software.

Then she waited for Jonathan to catch up and when he did, he had plenty to say.

"How did you come up with all these interrelated projects? I'm the one with all the multi-disciplinary degrees and experience, but now I feel like a first-year post-doc working for a seasoned advisor. I'm not sure that the Rodenbaughs and me can handle all of this unless you or people you know help out. Can you?"

"You and the Rodenbaughs pick your two favorites and I'll assist as much as I can. If our combined efforts come up short, you can recruit others from your network. How does that sound?"

Jonathan's tone sounded cheerier.

"We'll attract a lot of attention in R&D circles, and depending on results, I should climb in the pecking order. How about we go to Cape Cod next weekend?"

"How about the weekend after that? I'm in a team biathlon competition next Saturday."

"Do you need a helper? I can take you and your partner in my van. And who's doing what?"

"Great, you can be our team handler. Kiara rides the 60-mile leg first and I run the 13-mile leg second. The ride starts at 8 a.m. about 60 miles west of DC at the Bull Run Long Hiking Trail staging area near the Occan Reservoir and winds on country roads until ending at the Fairfax Family Graveyard, which is next to the Bull Run Trail staging area. I start running on it as soon as she arrives and stop when reaching the finishing area in Fountainhead Regional Park."

Irani paused because she knew Jonathan well enough to expect a question or two.

"What'll I have to load besides you and Kiara."

"Yourself, Kiara's bike, some snacks and liquids, a change of clothes, and two adolescent rooters – Tiana Diamond, the girl I'm taking care of, and Tyrone Mensah, Kiara's son. Kiara and I already know how to get to the staging areas, so all you need to do is pick me up first and we'll be on our way. And Tea and Ty are responsible for packing energy bars, bananas, and rehydration drinks, so you won't go hungry."

"What time should I pick you up, and what if the weather's bad?" "How about 4:30? And the race is a go, whether or not the weather cooperates."

Jonathan had heard all he needed, so he ended the call.

"Well, please call me Friday. We both have lots to do between now and then."

The Irani-Electra duo made progress on all the projects she worked on during the week. She also made time to read the posts on the Straight Shooter blogging site and came away impressed after doing so.

Clever insights interweaving a host of intriguing topics. They should generate Social Media buzz that might uncover for my tracking apps people to hack. I'll let them run now and check back later.

Irani checked the weather forecast and her gym bag one last time early Friday evening before calling Kiara, who said she had all her gear ready and guaranteed that Tea and Ty would be too. Then she called Jonathan, who reported the same. Then she went to bed, ready for her team's race plan to unfold seamlessly.

It started well but began to unravel at the Bull Run staging area, where Irani and the support team waited for Kiara. Ty's worried look accompanied the alarm his words sounded.

"Shouldn't Mom be here by now? Maybe she's had an accident."

Irani said, "Maybe she had to change a flat tire, but please don't worry. One of the medical vans would have picked her up if she had a serious injury."

Just then Tea yelled, "There she is. Why's she riding so slow?"

Ty didn't wait for an answer; he ran to help. Three minutes later the team clustered around. Kiara complained while Irani prepared to run.

"Two flats and one spare did me in. It took me too long to put on the spare, and when it flatted again, the patch didn't hold and the pump didn't work.

That's why I rode in on a flat rear tire. Sorry, but we must be close to last place."

Tea looked and sounded the sorriest.

"Maybe we should drop out. Why should Irani run when we know she can't win?"

Irani didn't wait to debate. She poked Jonathan in the arm before saying, "Pack up and get to the finishing area." And then she raced away.

Having watched a course video, Irani knew how the gently rolling main two-lane gravel trail wound through the woods. Steeper side trails joined it periodically. The lightning brain filed all that away as Electra focused on running.

She sped past several competitors, which energized her further. Each time she accelerated the pace, but as she blew by the midpoint aid station her emotions started pinging.

Why am I pushing toward my aerobic threshold? It doesn't matter where we place as long as we enjoy the race. I'll throttle back."

Doing so was the right decision. Electra took in the beauty of the sunlit-dappled woods and listened to the sounds of Nature all about, and the distance between runners put her in a world of her own.

But without warning, the angry buzz of a dirt bike motorcycle cut in. She whirled around just in time to leap out of its way. When it skidded to a stop and then came back at her, Electra took evasive action.

She raced between trees down the slope while angling toward a side trail, but her pursuer kept coming, though still at a distance. She raced down the trail when she reached it but tripped awkwardly over a protruding tree root, falling facedown. But the dirt biker did worse. She saw the rough terrain flip the helmeted rider over the handlebars, bringing bike and biker to abrupt stops. He couldn't get it started; the sounds of approaching hikers panicked him, so he plunged into the woods, leaving the bike behind.

By the time the hikers got near, Irani had limped to the bike before kick-starting it. They yelled and waved; she waved back but decided not to talk, so she rode off.

I skinned my nose and palms again, and my right knee too. And I better not run on a sprained ankle. What'll I do?

A contingency plan emerged as she puttered back to the main trail while pondering this latest incident.

First, the underwater attack, then Jonathan's office is ransacked, and now I'm run off the trail. They must be related but I'll figure how they fit together later. Right now, I'll ride to just before the finishing area, staying in the shadows along the way to avoid other runners, then dump the bike and limp across the finish line.

The adjusted plan worked to perfection; Electra acted her part even though she felt undeserving of the applause from the crowd that saluted her grit for toughing it out all the way across the finish line.

Then her entire support team rushed to her; Jonathan's arm around her waist gave her all the support she needed.

Tea looked ready to cry as they trudged to the van. "You injured yourself. You're bleeding."

"No worse than last time; I'll patch myself up when I get home. And I'll be fine, so why don't you stay with Kiara and Ty tonight?"

"Are you sure? Maybe I can help."

"No, patching's a one-person job. But why doesn't Jonathan drive everyone home so we can freshen up and then go out for dinner?"

Jonathan agreed, but he still looked concerned.

"I guess danger lurks whether on land or in the ocean. Please be careful and heal fast so we can go to Cape Cod next weekend. OK?"

Irani smiled and said, "OK," before kissing him on the cheek and rubbing Tea's hair. After that, the team loaded into Jonathan's van.

Kiara and Irani did most of the talking, making light of the mishaps, but Tea didn't agree.

"You might have won something if you didn't have bad luck, and winning's important, isn't it? That's what Ty and I want to do in the talent competition."

Kiara answered first.

Winning's not as important as learning and having fun while you're doing it. And today, I practiced changing and patching tires. And I learned you can ride on a deflated back tire."

Irani added more.

"But don't do so on a deflated front one. And let's have Tea and Ty look for words of wisdom from that philosophy book, 'Meditations.' I'm sure Marcus Aurelius has something to say about why winning's overrated."

Jonathan said, "Sometimes it is, and sometimes it isn't. I guess the trick is knowing when. Maybe I'll start reading it too."

Irani got in the last word on that topic.

"Excellent choice, Doctor Segal. And by the way, that's what pharmaceutical sales reps are taught to say to the doctors who decide to prescribe what's in the rep's bag."

Tiana asked, "How d'you know that?"

"By studying sales and marketing. I read it in one of the case studies. So, you keep studying and reading, young lady."

Tiana mimicked Irani.

"Those'll be excellent choices for me." Everyone in the van had to agree.

Chapter 14
October 2163

"The Hunt for Leaks in October"

"Try as I might, and even though I've done my best to stay in the shadows, I've made zero progress connecting the attacks to who or what conspiracy might be threatening me or the world at large. You're my last hope, and I hope you'll help."

Thus spoke Electra while slumping in front of her home workstation late on a Monday evening and waiting for Indira's words of wisdom.

"I've been observing your growing frustration caused by your borderline obsessive-compulsive behavior. It's time you settle down, sit still, and listen to me, for I have items and a recommendation that will help. And please, straighten your shoulders. Your lightning brain does not allow slouching."

Electra did so and felt better immediately, perhaps caused by the placebo effect of knowing that the game she and Indira played always paid off.

"I have noticed in your piano practicing that you have become too mechanical instead of thoughtful when playing Hannon exercises, so I have created an avatar just for you. Even though you are beyond mere mortals, you are still human and enjoy the security as well as familiarity of talking to close friends and family. Do you recall 'AI Artistry,' my first virtual business, whose apps targeted augmented reality applications for Hollywood entertainment?"

"I do, and don't you upgrade them with some of the improvements you make to the Brain Probe software?"

"Very good, you do remember. Well, I have recently made additional changes that I want you to upload into your latest Brain Probe model, and when you do, please review its built-in GUI tutorial. I'm confident you will figure out how to use it."

"I shall do so immediately, and then –" Indira interrupted.

"If you do, you're caving in to your obsessive-compulsive behavior.

Don't, because I have two more items for you. I'm certain you have fond memories of your Doc Kittner, your omni-parent grandfather and the first person you loved unconditionally. Well, I have created an avatar in his image, and it has Doc's cognitive and emotional personalities. I recommend you compare him to the current crop of avatars found in tutor or care-bots as well as virtual people or social influencers found in commercials and Social Media."

Electra blurted before Indira could continue.

"How did you do this? Is Doc self-aware? Did he break through to the Singularity? And how do I —" Indira's frown kept Electra from asking more questions.

"Please do not interrupt before I am finished. Now to your questions. My apps use deep neural-net AI-enhanced algorithms that exceed those of mere mortals. And Doc's algorithm trained under Jason's supervision using a combination of your grandfather's DNA, recorded personal history, and Big Data. You won't understand the details, but rest assured Doc will appear real, even to you.

"And to answer your second and third questions, no he is neither self-aware nor a Singularity breakthrough, but for him they aren't needed. Now, let me guess your next question, how do you invoke him? Here is the answer, which by now you should already know. I am always watching you whenever you are online, so simply tell me and his GUI will appear. But please do it later, not now."

Electra's emergent smile brought out a smaller one on Indira before she continued.

"And now, here is a recommendation that a psychologist would make. Whenever you feel an obsessive-compulsive episode coming on, find something to think about that will break it. I know you like playing with words and grammar, so I recommend you begin thinking about the most complex part of speech, verbs. In particular, if you consider how 'aspect' interacts with 'tense' and 'voice' and 'case' and 'mood' and 'mode', you will break out of whatever obsessive-compulsive issue you were about to contemplate. I even have a contingency plan if verbs don't work, and I know you like contingency plans. Contemplate the Greek philosophers."

Electra could tell that Indira had finished, but she couldn't think of what to say, so Indira said more.

"It is unlike you to be at a loss for words, but I admit I have given you a sizeable overload. So, I shall now exit, leaving a pun for you to enjoy. Please remember that Doc was your mentor, and you were his very best student, not his tormentor."

Indira's GUI disappeared but Electra's happiness remained all the way through a trouble-free sleep.

Waking fully refreshed and ready for action, she followed Indira's advice by skipping an early morning outdoor run because of cold blowing rain and substituting an abbreviated set of sit-ups, push- ups, and pull-ups before having an oatmeal-and-honey breakfast crowned with a blueberry muffin. And then, after shepherding Tiana's departure to school, she turned to the morning's top priorities.

She spent fifteen minutes reviewing the Straight Shooter blogging site, then two hours uploading and studying the instruction manual for Indira's latest Brain Probe software. Though no new snooping targets or Brain Probe overlaps came to mind, she decided to revisit that tomorrow.

And then she rewarded herself by summoning Doc Kittner. Thirty minutes later, she closed its GUI and opened an Irani-Electra internal dialogue.

Doc's appearance, voice, and gestures are so lifelike, and they mirror the emotions of the moment. And he can ask and answer questions as well as carry on a conversation. But something's missing... what is it?

It took only seconds for the answer to leap from her subconscious.

I got it... Doc seems to lack our shared experiences. I know how to fix that; time to tell Indira.

"Indira, I have something for you." Her Avatar appeared instantly. "Did you enjoy talking with your grandfather?"

"Your AI Artistry software is marvelous, but Doc is missing something. If I remember correctly, the term that describes it is shared memory granularity. And I know how to fix it. You should connect me to the Brain Probe while asking questions about Doc or letting me talk about him. And while doing so, you should upload into Doc's software my associated neural memory patterns. His neural network learning algorithms will then expand them. And let me explain more before you critique me."

"Very sensible, please continue."

"I won't pretend to understand how you developed the Doc app and then trained it, but however you did, you must have used a sample of his DNA that I digitally stored years ago and Su kept in our lab. You must have also used digital images and videos of him made long, long ago that I kept in my computer system, and finally, you must have used whatever from the Cloud's Big Data that would complete him. But you didn't use me. Why not?"

Indira's look of admiration spoke volumes before she began speaking. "You have exceeded my expectations. Your grasp of the overall design is accurate, and I didn't ask you because I wanted you to figure out what you just did. Congratulations. And I hope –"

"Please let me interrupt because I also figured out more. The Brain

Probe will force-multiply all we do on androids, and vice versa. Now I know why you need me to work with you on the android project. I'm the only person in 3-D space that's equipped and can be trusted to keep all our android and deep-brain stimulation research below the radar. I know I'm right, aren't I?"

"Indeed, you are, and now that you know, I don't have to pester you to work on it. Unlike children, who benefit from parents' telling them what to do, I can't tell or force you. Adults have to decide for themselves, and you have now done that. But may I offer a suggestion?"

"Please do."

"Use this latest epiphany to overcome obstacles you have encountered when snooping for likely targets to hack. And if you are still stymied by the end of the week, I will tell you what will work. And please don't worry, you will want me to tell you if you can't figure out what to do. Now reward yourself and then get to work. And I will do the same. And you decide when we can begin uploading your memory patterns under Jason's supervision into Doc's software."

Indira's avatar disappeared. Electra ran for a Coke.

The Irani-Electra duo resisted an obsessive-compulsive urge to ride the crest of the morning's success and instead eased into other projects after exercising and a lunch break. And she gave full attention to Tiana for the rest of the day when she came home.

Irani helped Tea work her math homework and then played the piano while Tea practiced the songs she and Ty would be performing soon.

As she settled into bed, Electra mused about the day's successes.

Things are beginning to look good for me. How fortunate I am to have Tiana and Indira. And soon I'll have Doc's avatar. I never like to admit how enjoyable sharing memories from long ago can be because I've had no one to share them with. But I'll be able to suspend disbelief when talking to Doc. He'll soon be the next best thing to 3-D reality, thanks to Indira and the Brain Probe. And —

A sudden jolt registered in Electra's cognitive persona, bringing a stunning revelation.

I know who to hack and what my hack attack will be, and I won't get Indira involved directly until I need her. It'll take a couple of days to get all the details in place, but as soon as I do, I'll be looking even better.

Trent Booker knew tonight would be memorable. Seldom did an influential person contact him directly to make another contribution, but Domino Broune seemed better than most of the others. He would be happy to meet at the hotel bar she had selected, and he fantasized while driving there.

No one knows about our tete-a-tete. No husband with her tonight, and I'll be happy to introduce her to more people in exchange for a multi-digit check. And maybe there's more that we can exchange. I'll buy some drinks and then drive her to my covert office so I can uncover more about her mind and body. Nobody will know...

Trent acted his part as soon as he spotted her. Domino did too, offering her hand but not rising from the booth. Trent led the small talk before and during several drinks before suggesting they retire to his office. She agreed, but when reaching his car she exclaimed after touching her right ear, "I must have dropped an earring at the booth. I'll be right back." She didn't wait for an answer but instead slipped back inside.

Trent didn't mind. The added minute or two gave him more time to fantasize about what was in store. He was focusing on that instead of the immediate surroundings. The passenger door's opening brought him back, but not to what he was expecting. A silent black- clad figure pointed a Traser at him.

"What the, hey what are you –" ZAP ZAP. Two Traser jolts terminated whatever else he was about to say.

Electra had a still comatose Trent wearing a Brain Probe cap after strapping him in a chair on the other side of a table next to her basement lab's computer. Indira's avatar commented as soon as Electra sat opposite.

"I commend you for your planning. The abduction and delivery of your victim to this place leave not a single trace. Now please tell me your intentions."

"I want to coax out the names of targets I can hack into for leads to who or what might be after me or knows about a troublesome conspiracy. Maybe it will connect to Bigger Bro. And I've studied the Brain Probe's instruction manual, so you can critique my technique as I proceed. I know you always like to do that."

"Please don't be snippy. My constructive criticism is meant to help you so you can soon help me more. And it should be eminently clear what I mean, is it not?"

"Indeed it is. You keep increasing the number of Brain Probe applications and their sophistication. That's why you need me to be your 3-D assistant on the android project. So, I'll jolt Trent awake and then get answers to my questions."

"Assuming he knows something, how will you cover your tracks?" "No matter how well I do, I'll want you to run the Brain Probe so we know if he's told me everything. And then you decide how much of his memory to alter or erase. Are you ready?"

"Wake Trent up and we'll all find out."

A befuddled-looking Trent shook his head five minutes later before speaking.

"Who are you, where am I, and why am I here?"

"I'll answer only your last question. I want you to tell me who Bigger Bro is, and if you don't cooperate, the cap you're wearing will cause you more pain than you can imagine. Would you like a demonstration?"

Trent's futile efforts to pull free came soon after his gaze flashed about the room. Seeing no escape, he had only one option.

"No no, I don't need a demo. Just ask, and I'll tell you all I know." "So, who's Bigger Bro?"

"It's Bigger Brother, stupid —" a jolt of pain doubled him up, then disappeared.

"OK, OK, it's the name we've given to a covert supra-national group that knows what the world community should be doing." "Who is we?"

"Hey, I'm only a small potato heading up a Washington Insiders group that's keeping tabs."

"And who's in the group."

Party faithful from the Democratic, Republican, and Guardian parties who know how to get things done and keep our mouths, uh —" Electra finished his too long pause.

"You have the right verb, but the wrong adverbial manner of speaking. Please keep talking…"

Electra terminated the inquisition fifteen minutes later.

"I'm disappointed you haven't told me more, but if that's all you want to say I'll let my partner finish up."

"Huh, who you gonna bring in?" "That's no concern of yours."

Electra saw the Brain Probe's digital lights turn on and Trent's turn off. She sat back and waited for Indira to speak when she had completed her one-way questioning. It took only ten minutes.

"You earned a B-plus. Trent knew more and I've stored it for you. We'll talk further after you take him someplace to recover. And please don't worry. When he wakes up, he will remember nothing but pleasant thoughts about something else. I have planted false memories."

"Where should I take him?"

"Why ask me? You are our 3-D Space expert. But I will give you additional targets, courtesy of Mr. Booker, that might lead to Bigger Brother. And I'll assist when needed because that will help you free up time for my pet project. And you know what that is, don't you?"

"I do, and I know just the place to park Trent's car, far away in the shadows and hidden from view, so we remain hidden too."

"Excellent, so drive carefully and get a good night's sleep when you return. There'll be time enough tomorrow for you to settle down, sit still, and listen to what I found out."

Electra obeyed.

Chapter 15
November 2163

"The Pet Project Lineup"

Irani gave Indira's pet project top priority soon after adding it to her project lineup. She installed additional equipment at her Deus Lab on the Pequot Reservation and ordered the most advanced humanoid robot model plus supplies from a leading Japanese company whose androids were better than DARPA's. After that, when cycling through all other projects, she realized that she could consider each to be a pet project of equal rank, and each night while falling asleep she would order them according to readiness while planning to work on them the next day.

By the week of Thanksgiving, Tea and Ty's volleyball training needed only occasional coaching and with Jason's help, Irani uploaded her brain scans into Doc's avatar. Regarding Bigger Brother tracking, even though the leads extracted from Trent Booker led to only modest tracking and hacking progress, this project still required weekly attention; she had automated Big Data scans via her analytic software, so there was ample spare time.

Irani expected a call from Jonathan to arrange another weekend trip to Cape Cod just after Thanksgiving. He did so on Tuesday evening before, but the doleful tone of his greeting told her there might be a problem, which she knew he would get to immediately.

"I just found out that sharks have been prowling around the kelp forest. It looks like we'll have to launch an octopus rescue mission Saturday morning. Can I pick you up early Friday? Will this change your Thanksgiving plans?" "No, Tiana and I are going to Kiara's for dinner. I'll leave early, and Tea can spend the weekend there. So, please cheer up. I'll be ready whenever you get here, and we'll make the best of whatever we find."

Xinqian Hung personified the meaning of her last name, for she had grand plans to flood the world with a supra-national new order, but to accomplish this, she could never project what her first name meant. Although her features made this tall and thin forty- something woman attractive in an aloof and unemotional manner, she possessed neither inner nor outer happiness because her obsession for her one and only project drove everything else out of her life.

Xing, the acknowledged leader of the "Gang of Three Plus One", a covert group within a covert conspiracy, occupied the top rung on the ladder built patiently and invisibly by Bigger Brother's cadre of political extremists in each of four countries – China, America, Russia, and Isilabad – a conspiracy invisible even to their governments' elite.

And why is she the Gang leader? Because the cadre knows the future belongs to China. Its combination of Techno-Authoritarian Control, Directed Capitalism, and Social Surveillance Intrusion into all aspects of its citizens' lives made it better than a faltering, floundering, and soon-to-be foundering America, whose too-often inept Government, built on the principles of Democracy, Individual Freedom, and Market Capitalism, struggles to contain the Political Elite's cronyism connected to a network of high-tech ruling companies.

And even though Russia invades bordering countries when it spies an opportunity, the West repels them, so Russia continues shrinking demographically and economically, while Isilabad – the self-appointed Caliphate of the Middle East – can't support its growing population and hubris without Russia's support.

But these four nations would be satisfied to control a world order they envisioned, a world that would give each what they needed for its political elite to maintain control while constructing a society they knew would be best for its people. Only the elite knew the outline of the plan, and only a covert cadre of the elite directed it. The leader of each cadre picked its most qualified person to be their "power behind the throne" Gang member, and each member also appointed one lower-level person to communicate to its Gang superior. Those four Gang members were now able to communicate via encrypted Deep-Dark Web channels that Chinese technology had upgraded to make online meetings unhackable.

Xing and other unrevealed but singular Chinese persons belong to a breed apart, genetically engineered by researchers and trained from birth to fulfill preassigned roles. Her mentors had taught her the art of mastering emotions, which is necessary before acquiring and controlling power, similar to past masters – Sun-tzu, Machiavelli, Richelieu, Clausewitz, Talleyrand, Bismarck, and their modernity successors – and she wielded it ruthlessly, resulting in flawless planning, concealed intentions, and an invisibly shapeshifting conspiracy fomenting uncertainty and terror in its clueless enemies.

Xing and her cadre leader met only in person, but all Gang members met online via an encrypted and secure network and shared all information among only themselves to keep their collective plan advancing. She summarized for their benefit what had surfaced before terminating their late November call.

"Each of us will continue directing disruption of infrastructure and environments in a seemingly random pattern that will increase angst among the public and dissatisfaction directed at their bungling governments. And our American member reports that he will assume the responsibilities of his mentally compromised covert underling, a Trent Booker, who suffered some sort of breakdown. My network monitoring team hasn't determined whether his illness is correlated with increased snooping and hacking attempts into us, but no matter, because our firewalls and intrusion defense software are impenetrable. But whoever or whatever is probing must be clever indeed, an adversary deserving study and respect. I shall toy with them until I know more, and then I shall act. But that is no concern of yours at the moment.

Keep to our plan and be ready to report success at our next Cyberspace meeting."

Xing made a note to herself after ending the meeting.

Newton Kinslinger, Speaker of the House, is ideally positioned to handle what his underling Booker muffed, but I need to place an unsuspecting agent for a second peak into the White House. And I think I know who and how.

After all, my Beijing network is deep and wide and has global reach. All the better to keep Bigger Brother from the prying eyes I sense are out there. I shall make my calls tomorrow.

Both Jonathan and Irani kept the conversation personal and light on the drive to Cape Cod, but the tone darkened at dinner with the Rodenbaughs, who let Jonathan lead the discussion after they unloaded what they had recently observed. His flinty expression announced confidence as he spoke.

"We don't know if the sharks have eaten into too much of our octopus population, but if they have, we'll salvage what remains and repopulate when we can. We might have to bring the survivors to my lab's holding tank until we decide a longer-term plan."

Jonathan waited for Bob to make weekend assignments. He looked at Marlene and then back to Jonathan before speaking.

"You and Irani are better at diving and dealing with sharks than we are, so how about if we load and pilot the boat, and you and Irani can see what lies below? The four of us should be able to figure out what to do after we assess the damage."

All agreed and planned to leave Saturday at sunrise.

Saturday's weather cooperated and once underway, Irani listened to her three associates chatter but after thirty minutes, left them to stand at the bow, preferring to listen to herself and Electra as the breeze streamed past.

Lucky we have a calm sea, light air, and temps that feel in the 80s. And the combination of hissing bow wave and droning engine helps me shift to a more elemental state of mind, like me versus the sea. I can already taste the ocean's salty flavor. I'll be ready for whatever greets us at the kelp forest.

Jonathan's jet ski preceded Irani's as they dived toward the kelp forest. Both carried weapons if sharks threatened, but none were spotted, so they parked the jet-skis and swam into the forest. Jonathan guided them toward the octopus cave, pointing to the remains of a mauled and mostly eaten octopus. Irani couldn't tell if it was Electra or Thaumas, but when one came out to greet them, she recognized Electra, who wrapped her tentacles around Irani. Irani removed her mask for eye-to-eye contact and waited for the octopus to make the next move.

It wrapped tentacles around Jonathan when he came closer, and all three remained suspended in spacetime until Electra swam into the cave and returned with two of her offspring. Irani used cross-species universal sign language. She pointed toward the surface and then spoke to Jonathan after Electra responded.

"Electra wants us to take all of them with us. I'll wait here while you bring back the transfer tank."

All were on board and heading for home two hours later. Bob piloted while Jonathan led the discussion. Electra kept close watch from inside the tank, and Irani listened while keeping her hand where tentacles could touch.

"I can temporarily keep our three guests in my lab, but I'll need to get a bigger tank, and I don't have room for it. Even if I did, I don't have funds for it unless…" Jonathan's words trailed into silence. Marlene didn't have anything to add, but Irani did.

"I've got the room and enough money to construct what we need. How about –" Jonathan's wide-eyed look of disbelief accompanied his interrupting words.

"I don't get it. Where? What do you have in mind?"

"I have a lab on the Pequot Reservation in Connecticut, near North Stonington where I do other work. Let me get it set up for Electra and her kids."

"Why didn't you tell me about this before now?" "Why would you need to know?"

Irani said nothing else; Marlene intervened before Jonathan could say what he might regret later.

"Let's let Irani help. I can't think of a better solution."

By the time the foursome finished dinner at the Rodenbaughs, Jonathan agreed to let Irani take the lead, so she unveiled the next steps.

"Tomorrow, why don't you head back to DC and I drive via rental car to my lab while Marlene and Bob keep Electra company? Monday, I'll scope out what changes I'll make and set plans in motion before driving back here to be with Electra. And if my plan rolls out the way it should, I'll bring her to her new aquarium by the end of this week or the next. Is that copacetic?"

Marlene nodded for herself and Bob; Jonathan did too but wanted to know more.

"What are the details? Do you need help making it happen?" Irani gave a Monet-like Mona Lisa smile when answering.

"They're still emerging, but please trust me when I say I don't need help.

And I guarantee you'll like the results. I'll invite all of you to a private showing as soon as Electra and I are ready."

Irani used the drive-time to her lab for hatching plan details, but before doing so considered Jonathan's miffed feelings.

He certainly didn't like admitting my idea was better, even though I didn't flaunt it. He has a lot to learn about the people skills of sharing control. And his comment about not knowing I have another lab was a poor attempt to cover his blunder.

There's no reason for him to know; we're not close enough yet to share details of our background stories, and I don't know if we'll ever be.

Irani paused because the Electra part of the duo had something more to say.

Everyone has a unique background story created from the singular big bang of their creation that leads contingently to all that follows. Look at how the lightning bolt of my creation leads to the here and now.

It rewires my brain and modifies my DNA; I develop a T-Plague vaccine while concealing myself inside DC's political intrigue; I accidentally poison myself but turn the mishap into an athletic, then acting, and finally a political career where I pull strings from the shadows. Then I create Indira, who preserves me for twenty years in Maksim's suspension pod until she devises a rescue mission implemented five years ago by my four clone children.

And my path to the Pequot Reservation starts from my dearly departed Hud Haller to his Native American joint venture businesses, to the Pequot doctor, Betje Holbrook, who restores vision to my damaged eye, and finally to Hud's setting up a vaccine production facility and lab on the Reservation.

And I connect to Jonathan via GWU's Professor Plannert via my first advisor, Professor Ravenhill. And Jonathan gets me to Cape Cod and an octopus named Electra.

There's no way I'll explain all my event-dots to him, no matter which direction our relationship takes.

But I will connect two of my Three Musketeers to the Reservation via Cape Cod. That's part of my detailed plan…

Irani worked all Monday designing lab renovations after explaining to her facilities manager what to expect, and then placed a call to Rick Tabasko after dinner later that evening. As expected, he and Parker Holsum had just finished an after-work workout and were cooling down with a couple of beers. After exchanging the usual pleasantries, Irani got down to business.

"I've got a special project whose details must go no further than us, and I need you to build an aquarium at a lab located in Connecticut. I'll have all details, supplies, and equipment ready to go. All you have to do is fly into Boston's Logan International Airport so I can pick you up later this week. And don't worry, I've planned everything so you and Parker can get the job done by the following Tuesday. And of course, you'll be rewarded handsomely.

Would you like to play my latest game?"

"Lemme run this by PH." Rick came back two minutes later.

"Parker says it's a go. But he wants to know if boating's included. The last time it was, Mr. LP's swamp boat piloting put him overboard."

"Boating's optional this time, but if we do some, it might include underwater jet-skiing."

"Hold on, lemme tell'em."

This time, Parker spoke a minute later.

"I've been on snow, water, and jet-skis before, but always on the surface, never below. No matter what you're planning, we're in and we'll call you back as soon as we know our arrival time."

After returning to the Cape, Irani devised octopus travel arrangements, and by Thursday afternoon, Electra had bonded further with her octo-namesake. A whimsical thought surfaced while she dangled her right arm in the tank so she could play with what was now her first pet.

Though I never had my own dog or cat as a kid, dearly departed Robin's border collies filled the void. I wonder what she'd say if I told her I like my octopus even more than conventional pets. I know what I'll do, I'll ask

Grandfather after dinner.

The cell phone's chime interrupted her musing. Using her left hand to grab the phone, she recognized Rick's caller I.D. Irani spoke for the duo before answering.

I hope this is good news.

It was. She could pick up RT and PH on Thursday afternoon.

Electra parked herself that evening in front of the lab's workstation and logged on; Indira's avatar appeared immediately and waited for Electra to speak.

"I have a question for Doc that will test how sophisticated his avatar software is, I'll ask him what Robin would say if I told her I like my pet octopus more than her border collies."

Indira smiled before replying. "What do you think she'd say?"

"Oh no, don't try to trick me. If I tell you, you can tell Doc before you invoke him."

"I wouldn't do that, but I do like your line of reasoning. Let me bring him in and listen from the shadows. I hope you will enjoy reminiscing."

Indira vanished; Doc appeared and waited.

"Hello, Grandfather. Do you remember Robin Setdarova?"

"Of course. She and Christie Conklin were your best friends. If I remember correctly, your grade school classmates nicknamed you the 'Three Queens'. What is your question?"

Electra blurted to herself before asking it.

Gads, he looks and sounds so much like Grandfather; it's so easy to suspend disbelief.

"I have a pet octopus and like it more than her dogs. What would Robin say?"

"That you must have a good reason because you are smarter than most people, but she wouldn't know why."

"OK, and what would you say? And do you know why?" "Of course, I do. Please let me explain…"

Indira reappeared as soon as Electra ended the discussion fifteen minutes later.

"How would you score Doc's cognitive recall and emotions?" "Better than any other virtual people I've come across. His

cognition is outstanding and his surface emotions are good, but talking to him makes me sad. He's a ghostly robo-shadow of the real Doc, and I miss the empathetic warmth real people give. It's much different talking with you. You seem to have the cognition and emotion of a real person, and I know why. You are the Singularity, and what I feel for you is akin to love, but –"

Electra stopped abruptly. The wave of emotions that swept in swept away whatever she was planning to say. Her trembling lips gave all this away.

Indira spoke as soon as Electra settled down.

"Yes, even you, whose lightning brain is beyond that of mere mortals, cannot express in words all that you feel or can imagine, but working together we can help one another improve toward our asymptotic limits."

"You mean like teacher's pet and student. Is that what I am, your pet?" "Indeed not, you are much more than that, but you can use that metaphor whenever you are in a happier mood."

Indira's empathetic smile revived Electra's fun-filled wordplay. "Actually, it's a simile, not a metaphor, but either way I'll be OK.

And maybe you can instruct Jason how to improve Doc." Indira's expression needed no words; her GUI vanished.

Thanks to thorough preparation, Irani had answers to all the questions Rick and Parker peppered her with during the drive from the airport back to her lab. When finally satisfied, Rick summarized as Irani parked.

"So, all we have to do is connect the recirculating pump, filters, regulators, and monitoring controls to the aquarium before making a sand seabed, complete with a couple of rock caves. And then, after filling it with seawater, we put in some coral, kelp, and seaweed. And then we put in some fish and sea critters that inhabit the nearby Atlantic. We can handle that, no problem."

"I'm sure you and PH can. Why don't we go in and take a look at it?" Irani deactivated the security system and then took them to the warehouse-sized undersea research area.

Parker's gaze swept around the room before saying, "This place and the equipment you have is industrial strength. How big's the aquarium and what's it made of?"

"It measures 100 by 50 and 5 feet deep, and the clear acrylic can handle the pressure."

Rick said, "That's a lot of cubic feet. How many gallons of seawater will it hold?"

"Since you fellows are in charge of construction, I'll let you do the calculation. Use the conversion factor that one gallon equals .1337 cubic feet."

Parker used his cell phone's calculator before snapping back a reply.

"I rounded to .14 and came up with 3500 gallons. Where do we get that much seawater, sand, sea creatures, and underwater plants?"

"You'll figure that out tomorrow when talking to Mystic Aquarium's director and staff. They're friends of mine and will give you all those details. And I'll give you all the equipment instruction manuals after dinner."

Later that night, Irani gave her team final instructions.

"You've mastered all the details and can get answers to any additional questions tomorrow, so I'm heading back to the Cape. Call me when you're ready to meet me there."

Parker looked at Rick and scratched his head before saying, "I forgot what we'll do there. What's the deal?"

Irani spoke before Rick.

"You two will help me bring back the main attraction, my pet octopus and two of her offspring."

Parker said, "I don't remember you telling us it's an octopus. How big?" "Electra's nearly twenty feet long and weighs over 100 pounds, but I don't think you –" Rick interrupted.

"Hey, aren't they dangerous when they're that big? Didn't a giant octopus attack the Nautilus in Twenty Thousand Leagues Under the Sea?"

"You've got the right class but the wrong order. A giant squid, not an octopus, played that role. You'll be perfectly safe, and besides, I'll be there to help."

Rick called Irani on Saturday to report that it would take several days longer to finish the job. He and Parker would come to her Cape lab next Saturday.

"That's fine by me. I have plenty to do, and I know you can say the same, so please call me when you're sure you've got the aquarium completed."

"Will do."

PH and RT arrived at the Lab next Saturday morning and as advertised, Irani's pet posed no threat. She even jumped into the holding tank to assist lifting Electra into the transfer tank. Thirty minutes later, Electra and her two children were secured in the back of the van. Irani sat cross-legged next to the tank while RT drove, and she swapped stories with PH that made the time and miles disappear. By mid-afternoon, Irani and her two helpers were ready to put Electra into her new home.

Standing inside the tank and wearing a wetsuit, Irani issued commands. "Don't worry about me, I can handle Electra. She weighs much less in water. Just hand her to me, head first."

PH and RT followed orders, one on each side of the octopus. They struggled to lift what felt like an enormous amorphous blob of a moving body, but it felt much lighter as soon as Irani directed it into the seawater. All that remained gripping the fellows were Electra's tentacles. And that's when her game began.

She wrapped tentacles around all three of her helpers and used her enormous suction-strength to drag the fellows into the aquarium before letting go. Rick was the first to stand up next to Irani and sputtered out seawater with some words.

"What the hell; she's sure strong."

Parson popped to the surface and joined the conversation after coughing out a mouthful of water.

"That's as good as any waterpark activity. What's gonna ha —" Electra's next trick interrupted his words but answered the question.

She wrapped tentacles around Parson's legs and jerked him under, and repeated the game using Rick as her target before he could climb out.

Stifling laughter as best she could, Irani observed the game.

Neither fellow could get out. Electra kept tugging them back into the aquarium just before they thought they were in the clear. Irani submerged a couple of minutes later to hug Electra, and the octopus ended the game. Irani spoke first after all three climbed out.

"We'll have to install a safety barrier before anyone visits or I leave for the day. Octopuses can climb out of tanks and crawl around for almost a half- hour before running out of air."

RT shook water off his hair before saying,

"I guess a safety barrier works two ways; it'll protect your pet as well as any people watching the show."

Irani offered to treat the guys to dinner at a popular seafood restaurant, but their increased empathy toward sea creatures made them switch to a pizza place instead. They returned to the lab for one final pass before packing up. As they were about to leave, Irani made final comments.

"You've done a great job. Thanks to you, Electra and I are ready to do more research connecting cephalopod DNA and biochemistry to humans, and after that we'll —" an intrusion alarm blocked out remaining words as two paramilitary-clad types barged in. Irani stepped in front of RT and PH to keep them away from an unequal confrontation.

"Let me turn off the alarm. Then tell me what you want." Seconds later, the leader's harsh words filled the entryway.

"Our clients want to know what's going on here. You seem to have a lot of connections that –"

ZZAP… ZZAP. Two lightning-like bolts lit up the intruders, putting them down. RT and PH stood gaping while Irani kneeled to check the condition of the fallen.

"The bolt just stunned them. I'll get some rope; then help me tie them up."

Ten minutes later, RT and PH had them bound to chairs that Irani had arranged on either side of a table before issuing final commands.

"Thanks again. I think it's time for you to leave the rest for me. I'll talk to them when they come to." RT tugged on PH's arm and said, OK, but call us later so we know they're gone. And don't give back their guns."

"Good advice; I won't. And I'll call you when they leave."

Irani called her singular partner as soon as the guys had gone. Indira's GUI opened and its avatar spoke.

"Very smart that you had swivel-mounted, automated collimator barrels mounted on ceilings in all the important entry areas. I set the Traser to stun, and I see you are ready to interrogate, but why not allow me to make a suggestion?"

"Which is?"

"Connect them to the Brain Probe cap and let me read their thoughts. Then I'll adjust their memory so they are happy to walk away. But please follow Tabasko's advice – keep their guns. And then tomorrow, when you're ready to settle down, sit still, and listen, I will tell you what I extracted…"

Irani followed all orders, including some of her own. Everyone rested easily that night.

Chapter 16
December 2163

"To the Victors"

As the days marched resolutely along their path through the calendar, so did events in Irani's micro-cosmos as well as those in the grander scheme, from which the phantom Straight Shooter blogging site's random appearances contained interviews highlighting some of the grim-trending world events. Irani listened mid-morning on the first Tuesday in December to the latest selection.

The interviewer had begun pleasantly enough, but Irani knew the tone would change soon after the interviewer and interviewee exchanged standard greetings. The female's expression and voice remained pleasant, but the content didn't.

"So, why do you always say you are delighted to be interviewed? You should be troubled instead because all you talk about are the accelerating problems our nation and the world are facing."

Caught off guard, the soft-looking fellow, whose natty attire couldn't quite hide his excess flesh, stuttered for words.

"Well, uh, you know, that's what uh–" her words cut off whatever he was stumbling to say.

"I'll answer for you. Of course, you're delighted. You're getting paid to parrot back what your sponsors have told you to say. Very well, so please tell us about foreboding gain-of-function pathogen pandemics or mutating socio-political issues emerging in any of the linked climates."

And as he fumbled to do so, the dubbed-in words matched his lips and expression so well that viewers couldn't distinguish the real from the virtual. After fifteen cynical minutes, the interviewer asked her the closing question.

"So, do you have a final thought that might hearten our listeners?" Hoping to salvage some respect from the audience, he smiled and said, "Well, uh, I'm just glad that, uh–" her words cut in again.

"You're just glad you don't have to face the problems most listeners have to. No wonder you always look so smug and self-satisfied whenever your interviews end. Thank you so very much."

The video ended abruptly. Electra kidded that whoever ran the blogging site would get high marks, even from Indira. Then she returned to her current events.

The last one of the day would be the most pleasant: Tea and Ty's final volleyball practice before Friday's day-long area-wide high school coed two-person team volleyball tournament.

Blessed are the poor in memory and the blind to other paths, for unto them the keys to happiness are bestowed. Forever and ever, and even more so if their talent can keep them on course. Amen.

Thus spoke the Irani-Electra duo to themselves while watching Tea and Ty synchronize their courtly moves.

Just look at them; they've forgotten all about their disappointing finish in the talent contest and are focusing solely on their team signals and footwork. How lucky they can live in the moment, never thinking or worrying about the safety net their elders provide.

But I can never preach even to them my codicil of the Beatitudes, ever, for fear of offending or being misunderstood. I'll have to coax its subtlety from the shadowy sidelines into those I care about.

And it's time to wrap up the session. We'll leave their best performance for the tournament.

Irani blew the whistle; her two athletes sauntered to her side, tossing the ball back and forth and talking all the while, then stopped to listen to their singular coach.

"You're ready to surprise the competition. Even though you're younger than some of your opponents, none of them have your almost telepathic coordination or secret weapon. And remember, we won't unleash it until it's needed. Never show the competition your advantage too soon. Any last-minute questions?"

Ty was happy to call it quits, but Tea persisted.

"I learned my lesson at the show. I promise not to show off or be too confident. But who you gonna invite?"

"Well, of course Kiara will be there, and I think Eve and Jan will join us." "What about the lady who moved back to Zimbabwe, you know, Monet?" "I'll call Alonzo to find out if she'll be visiting. If she is, perhaps they can join us, but no matter, there'll be plenty of people watching you perform. And don't be nervous. Just focus on the game."

Nothing unsettled Irani's schedule until Eve called late Friday afternoon.

Although she didn't say what was worrying her, she had to see Irani immediately. After disconnecting the call, the Irani-Electra duo prepped for Eve's office visit.

I'm still her safety net, even though Jan's influence is maturing here more and more. Now that Nari's gone, he might be spending more time at her apartment, but that's not for me to pry into. I won't ask unless she decides to tell.

Eve rushed in forty-five minutes later, throwing herself onto the sofa and sitting with arms scrunched together after shedding her coat. Irani sat across and waited for Eve's words.

"I just don't know if the slides I've put together are good enough. Jan says they are, but maybe President Huston won't like my climate change approach, which I call the climate wars. I want us to be the victors, and maybe you can help me polish what I've put together. Can I stay with you until I get a better handle on what I'm doing?"

Electra recited another Beatitude.

Blessed are those who ask for help, for they shall learn what's right. At least if they ask me… Amen. OK Irani, tell Eve what we'll do.

"You can stay with me and Tea for as long as you like. When will you give your presentation to the President?"

"In January, as soon as I'm ready."

"That'll be perfect. We'll have the Holiday break to revise your draft, so please stop stressing yourself out. Will you and Jan come to the volleyball tournament tomorrow?"

Finally beginning to smile, Eve said, "I'll bring Jan with me, and if you've been coaching Tea and Ty, I sure won't bet against 'em."

Irani's SUV transported the team and its support group. Looking more at Tea, Kiara gave instructions to the players as she rode next to Irani.

"And I know you'll be good sports, especially because in volleyball, the score says it all. There are no style points, so no complaining about the officials."

Tea squirmed, then said, "I know… Miss Irani said the same thing…"

The recreation center buzzed with pre-game excitement as the teams warmed up. Four games would be played simultaneously to winnow the top eight teams before breaking for lunch. Morning matches would be best-of- three eighteen-point games, while afternoon games would go to fifteen. All other standard two-person volleyball rules apply, which means play continues until winners score at least two points more than losers.

Irani huddled her team as soon as the horn sounded the end of practice. "I can be on the sidelines during your matches; Kiara will cheer from the stands, but don't pay attention to anything except the game and me. Got it?" Ty looked ready to play, but Tea's face showed a question coming. "Some teams look bigger and stronger than us. How are we gonna beat them?"

Ty grabbed her shoulders so she was looking at him when he said,

"Hey, we're nearly as tall, and we're fast and click as a team. And, uh —" Irani filled in the words that Ty's excitement blocked.

"Let your instinctive muscle memory take over, and don't unload our secret weapon until you need it. And have fun."

Irani knew her team was good, but Electra had more gameday experience.

Past performance or practice isn't a perfect predictor. That's why the outcome's unknown until the game's over. It's almost always the combination of attitude and killer instinct that separates the winners from the losers. For Tea and Ty's age, I've stressed the fun angle, but when they get older and the games get more important, they'll learn that killer instinct comes to the fore. But that's for later, not now. Let's see how good my coaching's been.

Tea and Ty won their first two morning matches without losing a game.

The third pushed them to a three-game match, but Tea dived when needed to dig out opponents' shots that Ty then set up for her to spike; they won the fourth match too, and though the deciding game ran to twenty-one points, Tea's uncanny coverage set up easy shots for Ty, who often dumped them where the opponents weren't.

Irani let Kiara lead the discussion during lunch break, which could barely contain her team's excitement. Tea did most of the talking, but Ty got in enough words to prep them for the afternoon, which his mother recapped before heading back to the stands.

"We're so proud of you, but now let's put that away and focus on the next match. And if you win, then on the one after that. And like Irani says, stay in the moment and have fun…"

Excitement elevated as the afternoon quarterfinal matches rolled out sequentially. And Irani's team caught a break; their opponent must have been lucky rather than good during the morning games. Tea and Ty won going away. Irani cautioned them as soon as they came off the court.

"I've scouted the other three semi-finalists. They're all strong, so don't get overconfident. Just keep doing what's worked so far."

The team followed Irani's orders, but the opposing team was bigger and almost as quick, winning the first game 15-10. And that's when Irani changed the game plan.

"You're playing great, but so's your opponent, so it's time to pull the trigger on our secret weapon. None of the teams can do power-jump serves like you, so it's time to unleash it. They won't know what hit'em. and they there's not enough time for them to learn how to adjust. So go out there and do it."

And they did. The crowd in the stands roared when Tea slammed the first serve past the opponents, and it kept rooting for the David versus Goliath matchup in which Tea and Ty's serves replaced the slingshot. They won the remaining games by lopsided scores.

Flushed with success, Tea and Ty hugged each other before running off the court and into the arms of Irani, who said, "We caught another break; our semi-match was the second, so our opponent has even less time to figure out what to do, but expect them to try some adjustments, like retreating or changing positions, but just keep pounding the ball where they aren't and sometimes right at 'em. You know what to do, and it's got you to the championship game. And no matter what league you're in, this moment is as good as it gets. So go out there and play like this is all there is."

Tea's serves became even better the longer the game went. She leaped farther and farther into the court to thunder serves down on the opponents whose adjustments were futile.

Ty's serves kept the opponents off balance too, but he mixed in surprises with thunderbolts. His jump-float spin serve won the championship's final game; the crowd's standing ovation saluted the victors.

Eve and Jan joined the support group soon after the tournament sponsor handed out winner's and runner's-up trophies. Never at a loss for words, Eve said, "It looks like the combination of player skills and Irani's coaching did the job."

Tea handed the trophy to Ty before saying, "She knows everything, and she's gonna –" Irani dodged additional praise by interrupting.

"Say she has great players to work with, and that includes Eve. That makes for an unbeatable combination."

Not to be left out, Jan said, "Well, I hope you're going to celebrate in style."

Irani didn't get a chance to answer because Eve spoke first.

"I'll spare us the worn-out cliche. This time, to the victors goes pizza, and I'll be happy to buy..."

Chapter 17
December 2163

"One Dog-Day in December"

The Irani-Electra duo kept the two challenging but rewarding Tiana and Eve games going independently, although they might intersect during the Holidays once Eve completed moving in. Eve even picked the date – December 21st, the winter solstice – to make a statement. Irani paid attention to it but Tea ignored its significance; she needed to tell Irani that afternoon about a Holiday school assignment and started doing so as soon as Irani sat next to her.

"Our English teacher wants us to write a short story about an animal. He assigned us dog, cat, horse, or a goldfish. I got dog and Ty got horse, and here's the trick. I have to be in the story, and I gotta use the word dog in as many different ways as I can think of. You're good with words, so you gotta help get me started. OK?"

Biting her lower lip, Irani nodded twice before saying,

"That's an excellent creative writing assignment. Let's start by coming up with the dog's relation to you. What do you want it to be?"

Tea jumped at the challenge.

"I always wanted a dog, but Dad said we didn't have the time or place for one, so how about I write about me and my pet dog?"

"That's an excellent choice. Now, let's list some ways the word dog can be used. And I'll begin.

"We can say that something is dog-eared, or we're dog-tired, or that the world is going to the dogs. And there are lots of other possibilities, so why don't you take it from here?"

Eve's shouting hello stopped the conversation until she bounded into Tea's work area.

"Hi everyone. Jan's helping me bring some of my stuff over now, and more later. What are you two doing?"

Tea said, "Working on my short story. It's due after the Holiday break.

You're good with words, just like Miss Irani. Maybe you can help me too." "Well, she's supposed to help me with an assignment too, so how about this; I'll help you if she'll help me." Tea and Eve both turned toward Irani.

"Now that shows what an experienced negotiator Eve has become. She's just struck a win-win-win bargain."

"Good, and to sweeten the deal, how about I help Tea make dinner?" Irani added to that.

"And please make sure Jan stays. You owe him something for helping move."

Everyone agreed; Tea scampered after Eve to help unload.

Being smarter than Eve and almost as clever with words, Jan added the right touch, balancing masculine and feminine topics during the dinner table talk. He searched first for doggy words that would satisfy Tiana.

"The English language has lots of idiomatic expressions using the word dog. I'll give you one that's particularly fitting for the Christmas season: 'dog in the manger.' Does anyone know its meaning?"

Irani dummied down her expression and didn't answer but Eve made an educated guess after nodding yes.

"I think it applies when someone takes something someone else wants."

Jan said, "I'm impressed; you're close. It means that someone acts spitefully to prevent someone else from having something, even though the spiteful person has no use for whatever it is."

Jan continued leading the discussion until Tiana tired from writing down all the uses.

"This is a great start; I've got enough to get going. Can I be excused to put s'more words in my story?" Eve replied before Irani.

"Of course, and I'll help you later, but smart people say 'put some more', not 'put s'more'."

"You sound just like Miss Irani, but that's usually good. I'll start now." Tiana's leaving let Jan steer the discussion toward Eve while looking at Irani.

"I'm sure Eve's told you about the presentation she's working on. I helped dig up some articles for her and after looking over her slides, I told her I can't think of anything to add; she might not need your help, but I guess she wants you to approve it."

Eve jumped up after saying, "Let me get a copy for you to look at."

Irani and Jan sipped on soft drinks until Eve gave her four handouts two minutes later. Irani placed them in front of her to study while Jan whispered one more time to Eve the reasons why he found nothing to add.

Slide 1
The Climate Wars

Per James Lovelock (legendary British Scientist, Inventor, and Environmental Futurist):

- Climate Wars: Gaia's revenge for Man's poor Environmental Maintenance, which leads to runaway Climate Change.
- The Gaia Hypothesis proposed by James Lovelock (1972) suggests that **living organisms on the planet interact with their surrounding inorganic environment to form a synergetic and self-regulating system that created,** and now maintains, the climate and biochemical conditions that make life on Earth possible.

The First Climate War:

- Fought to a standstill over a Century ago.
- World Community of Nations battled over interpretation/predictions of data presented in a series of IPCC reports (Intergovernmental Panel on Climate Change)
- Costs far exceeded Benefits.
- Renewable Technologies not commercially scalable. Predictions included:
- Atmospheric Global Warming (Caused by increased CO_2 and Greenhouse gas concentrations)
- Increased Air Pollution (Caused by Fossil Fuels and Toxins released from the Oceans as water temperature rises).
- Ocean Acidification (Caused increasing by H_2S and CO_2 concentrations).
- Oceanic Algae, Plankton, and fish die-offs (Caused by Acidification and Pollution).
- Sea Levels Rising.
- Ice Caps Melting.
- More Extreme Weather (Hotter Summers Colder Winters Shifting Rainfall Patterns causing Droughts and Flooding)

Reasons why forecasted disasters didn't happen in the last Century:

- Population plateaued at less than 9 Billion.
- Two Volcanic Eruptions (Mount Pinatubo and Lake Toba) masked atmospheric temperature increase.
- Perfect Storm (Techno Plague + Middle East Terrorism + Harsh Governments) reversed Economic Growth and Consumption.

THE END RESULT: MOSTLY TALK AND LITTLE ACTION

Slide 2
The Second Climate War

Earth Scientists and Environmentalists have:
- Convinced enough people that Climate Change is accelerating.
- Linked Human Activity to 50 percent of the change.
- Confirmed the Gaia Hypothesis (Oceans, Atmospheres, Land Masses, and Living Organisms form a homeostatis- seeking Super-Organism.)

Second Climate War being waged Now:
- Get the Nations of the World to Agree on a Plan.
- Get Government and Big Business to act in Best Interests of the People.
- Defend against expanded Aggression in disputed Geographies.

Slide 3
What Our Administration Should Do

- Streamline all branches of Military to make them smaller and faster Strategic Strike Forces.
- Adjust size of combat assets (ships, planes, vehicles, satellites, weapons) and equip all with AI-empowered remote/drone control.
- Adjust our International Diplomatic Strategy (Back away from American Exceptionalism and Nation-State Building? Push for Multi- lateral Cooperation.)
- Reassess who should be our Allies.
- Prepare for Theaters of Conflict (Increasing Eco-or-Cyber Terrorism Polar Land-Grabs Ocean Floor Eco-Violations Immigration and Human Rights Violations Regional land and food shortages Increasing Bacterial and Viral Pandemic Risks)
- Reassess what Technologies to promote
- Reassess which model is better – U.S. or China.

Breadth and Depth of Issues are Overwhelming, but there is only one Certain Recommendation:

DEVOTE MORE RESOURCES TO OCEANOGRAPHY:
- **OCEANS HOLD THE KEY TO INTRA AND EXTRATERRESTRIAL LIFE.**

- **OCEANS WILL REMAIN LONG AFTER WE BECOME EXTINCT.**

Slide 4
Avoiding the Anthropocene Extinction

What We are doing:

- Putting too much CO2 into Atmosphere.
- Putting too much Fertilizer onto Soil that runs into Rivers, Lakes, and Oceans.
- Diverting Rivers and using up too much Fresh Water.
- Cutting down Virgin Forests, digging up too many Natural Resources, and taking too many fish from the Oceans.
- (Upsets Ecological Balance)
- Spreading Pathogens

What We are causing:

- Ocean and Soil Acidification that kills Algae, Plankton, Coral Reefs, Forests, and Life in Ocean and on Land.
- Land and Water Pollution that kills plants and animals and makes people sick.
- Environmental Degradation and Ecological Imbalance.
- Pandemics and totally new diseases.
- Climate Changes in: Global Temperature, Air and Water Currents and Composition/Quality.

What We can do to Avoid Extinction:

Avoid Hubristic-Based Approaches for Problem Solutions:

- Our Ingenuity will solve our Addiction to Consumption (Geological Engineering, Atmospheric Engineering).

Embrace a Humility-Based Approach instead:

- Redesign Cities so they are "Smart."
- Recycle rather than "Destroy" when consuming Goods and Services."
- Combine Green/Renewable Energy Sources Nuclear/Thermonuclear Power.
- Live harmoniously for Sustainability within our Ecological Needs.

LIFE ON EARTH WILL SURVIVE AN ANTHROPOCENE EXTINCTION EVEN IF MAN DOES NOT!

Irani did her best to hide the excitement that Electra's comments generated.

This is better than good; all you have to do is coach Eve's delivery and the President will buy in. And when she does, just make sure our underwater game accelerates with Jonathan being your unwitting partner.

Irani spoke five minutes later.

"Jan's right. There's nothing I can add so there's no need to go over your points, but why don't we practice your delivery between now and when you show them to the President."

Eve's beaming smile said even more than whatever words she could think of.

"Hooray… maybe I can catch up to you after all." Jan poked her in the arm before saying,

"I told you that, so now you can relax and enjoy the Holidays." Irani ended the conversation.

"Yes, indeed, and now you have all the time you need to settle in here and help Tea write her short story…"

Eve and Tiana reconvened at her workstation two days later. Tiana's happy face showed in her alert voice.

"So, here's an outline. My dog's name is Prince, and he's a four-year-old pure-bred black Lab I trained from puppyhood. He's so smart he can understand my words and do all sorts of tricks. So far so good?"

"Nice backstory. Do you know what a synopsis is?" Tea's smile faded; she said nothing, so Eve did.

"It's a short and lively overview of a story that'll entice people to read the full thing. You'll hear that word used more often than outline in higher level English classes, so remember it. Now go on."

"Got it, OK, so I enter Prince in a dog contest and he wins because he does all the tricks I taught him, but two bad guys who want to steal the trophies and prize money break in during the awards ceremony. But Prince leads all the dogs and they chase the bad guys away, but one of the bad guys shoots Prince. But there's a doctor in the audience and he saves Prince, so Prince and me live happily ever after. The end. Whatcha think?"

"It's good. And now you have to add details to describe the current situation and setting. That's called narrative, and it tells about what's going on and where. And good writers are supposed to show, not tell. Do you know what that means?"

"Yeah, our teacher said you want to use words that make the reader see what's going on."

"You've got it. And now let's think about more expressions that use the word dog."

Eve and Tiana helped Irani make dinner after the coaching session ended. Tea's pride in her story came through in her words, which dominated dinner talk. She went back to her writing after helping clean up, and Irani and Eve retired to the family room. Irani thought of a conversation starter that would segue into Eve's coaching session.

"Will you and Jan come to the Christmas Eve service tomorrow at Ty's church? He and Tea will be featured in the singing."

"No, he's taking me to his folk's house. But I'll be back here sometime on Christmas day if that's OK."

"It is. So now, let's pick up where we left off on your Climate Change presentation."

Eve summarized an hour later.

"You're even better than Jan and me combined for putting the right spin on what I'm saying. How d'you know what to cut out or put in, and where d'you learn so much about the link to ecology?"

"Some came from you. You talked about it in your Balanced Mindset Guidelines, and I picked a couple of salient points made by James Lovelock, a famous past-generations' British environmentalist and futurist whose name you included in one of your Climate Wars slides. He's the one who says we shouldn't try to save the whole planet. Instead, we should live in mega-cities and abandon uninhabitable land. And after researching how ant colonies design their hives, he came up with AI-controlled buildings that cooperate with the environment. These are practical recommendations the President can act on."

Eve shook her head before saying, "I'm sure glad I've got you. I still have a lot to learn, but I'm getting better, don't you think?"

"I do; now go do some more thinking on your own."

Eve left, leaving Irani in the company of Electra's musing.

Eve's maturing faster than she realizes, but that's the way younger people develop. The safety net that parents provide cushions them as they learn the real-world drill. And it's good I don't pry into what she and Jan are thinking about. She'll talk about that when she's ready. I'll just keep close at a distance, which is another of my favorite oxymorons. How nice that I like to play with words. Doing so can keep the people I deal with entertained while I keep them pointed in the right direction for me and my games.

Irani couldn't keep the Holiday gathering via Internet-call tradition intact because three of the couples – Monet and Alonzo, Nari and Yang,

Nila and Sanjay – had spread wings of independence that carried them far away, whereas Eve and Jan had not done so yet. She would call each of the three distant couples separately right before or after New Year's Eve.

Tea and Ty's performance at the Christmas Eve church service earned praise from all who heard it, and Irani hosted a late afternoon Christmas Day dinner party for Ty and Kiara, plus Odell, Wanda, and their partners. Eve and Jan would join them for dessert later.

The dinner talk centered on Tea and Ty, who also told about their short story assignments. Ty connected his fish story to ecology; Tea dramatized her pet dog, Prince.

"If I ever get a dog, it'll be handsome and smart. That's always a winning combo."

But Wanda asked, "What do you think is more important, looking good or being smart?"

"Easy answer. They come together, don't you think?"

Irani let the others lead the discussion, happy just to listen as Electra whispered.

Good looks, good morals, and good thinking aren't highly correlated. The older I get the more I realize morals come first, then intelligence, and then looks. And like all youth, Tea and Ty will have to learn the right order for themselves. The best I can do is not tell but show and let them figure out what they eventually should know.

"Watch out… you're gonna run it over."

Jan's yell came too late. Eve braked her Vette but hit whatever was darting across the dimly lit street. One sickening thump signaled a direct hit.

Eve swerved to a stop alongside the curb; Jan jumped out to check for damage and poked his head back in two minutes later.

"You hit a dog. It's alive but can't move. I think it's got a front and back broken leg."

Jan waited for Eve to speak. Her puzzled lips quivered before halting words came out.

"Is it big? Will it bite? I don't know… what should we do?"

"It's a smallish ugly mutt that's in no shape to snap. We shouldn't leave it here, but it's your call."

Eve knew ethics as well as responsibilities.

"Let's take it to the nearest animal shelter. They can help us figure something out."

The two of them bundled the dog in a blanket before loading it into the back seat. There were no drive-time sounds from the front, only a sporadic whimper from the back.

An hour later, the vet gave his diagnosis.

"I can put casts on the legs, but this is one of the ugliest strays I've ever seen. His jaws are always twisted open, showing crooked teeth, letting his tongue hang out, and making him look like he's ready to bark or bite or whine. And his black fur coat has tufts of orange hair sticking out of bald spots. No one's going to adopt him unless you do. If you don't, I'll have to put him down."

Eve glanced at Jan before making the call.

"Go ahead and fix him. We'll come back tomorrow to take him home."

Eve and Jan, arriving just before the party ended, joined the group in the family room and explained why they were so late. After most had left, Eve told the remaining three – Irani, Jan, and Tea – she would bring the dog home tomorrow if the vet gave the OK. Tea decided that she would go with them.

Jan called the shelter after lunch the next day. Two hours later Irani drove everyone in her SUV to pick up the new family member. Jan gave directions to the shelter; Eve gave directions for what to do afterward.

"I'll pay for the dogfood if you'll let me keep it at the house instead of my apartment. And maybe Tea can help me take care of it."

Tea wrinkled her nose before saying, "What kind of dog is it? Is it a male or female? Maybe it'll be like the Prince in my story."

Eve spoke before anyone.

"It's a male, and you'll have to decide how it measures up to your Prince.

Let's go see."

Eve led the procession into the shelter, Tea at her heels while Irani observed from the rear. After Eve paid the bill, the vet explained what would be needed next.

"The dog's healthy and smart enough, and behaves well too, but it must have been abused before running away. He's a little afraid of people, but that shouldn't be a problem if you give him a good home. So if you're ready, I'll bring him out."

One look was all it took for Tea to give her heart away; as she fell to her knees to hug her newfound best friend, the dog began licking her face. And then she said, "Oh my, you're just what I want. I'm gonna name you Cutie-Pie."

There was nothing to say until all were in the SUV and heading home.

Then Tea spoke. "Maybe we can go to a pet store tomorrow and get stuff for Cutie-Pie. And maybe Eve can help me rewrite my short story. I know what to say, and she's almost as good with words as Miss Irani."

Everyone agreed as the SUV sailed home in the warming sunlit- filled air that almost matched the spirits inside.

Chapter 18
January 2164

"The President's People"

Cutie-Pie's arrival brought changes to Irani's personal world that were all for the good. The responsibility of taking care of him matured Tiana overnight and smoothed the rougher edges of her somewhat atypical teenage personality, freeing up more of Irani's time to help Eve and creating a big- sister little-sister relationship between Eve and Tiana.

Irani planned to use some of the time to contact her other clone children who by now, unlike Eve, needed less guidance and had departed to far-off lands. First up would be Monet, and although not biologically related, Irani considered her "daughter number two." And she always found out about Alonzo when conversing with her.

Knowing that Monet shared her proactive approach, Irani called her early on the second Monday of the month. Her perfect French- accented English complemented her always diplomatic greeting and exchange of pleasantries.

"Why Miss Irani, it is a pleasure to hear your voice. Alonzo asked me if we spoke over the Holidays, and I disappointed him when I said we hadn't. How are you and Eve?"

"Both of us are doing fine. She's giving a Climate Wars presentation this coming Friday to the President, and I thought I'd ask you what issues I might mediate on your behalf. I follow African politics but you are always several steps ahead of the media."

"Well, we are not engaged in a Climate War, but Darla and I do have African Climate Change issues. New weather patterns are causing droughts and desertification. We could use more help on vertical and Martian farming as well as smart city designs. And changes in animal migration might be one of the reasons why we cannot locate the source of troubling zoonotic crossover viral outbreaks. These and socio-political issues like gender and income inequality are destabilizing some of the smaller governments in our African Union's economically struggling countries. What might you suggest?"

Irani offered several before ending the conversation fifteen minutes later. "Why don't I call you as soon as I discuss with President Huston what I think might be good for the Zimbabwe- America partnership?" "I would like that. Might you plan to visit us when you have details to discuss?"

"And I would like that too, so perhaps I can make it so. And when I do, you shall be the first to know…"

Sabrina chattered away while hustling Irani and Eve toward a conference room near the Oval Office as soon as she cleared them through the security station.

"All your so-called President's people you asked me to invite are already here. Jan, Professor Plannert, and Jonathan are waiting, and as soon as you get set up, I'll get the President and Vice President."

Sandwiched between, Eve puffed her cheeks but didn't reply, so Irani did.

I think Eve's presentation will impress everyone. She knows her stuff and will show it in a couple of minutes. She's the one who's about to shine."

Eve's voice came alive and her doubts departed. "You bet I am."

President Huston, sitting at the head of the table, opened the meeting. "So Happy New Year to Eve's selection of the President's people. And although it's a new year, we still have ongoing old climate change battles. Eve says she has a fresh approach that we can use to be proactive, so let's hear it."

A smiling Eve, rising from her place at the foot of the table, faced an expectant audience. On the left side from closest to farthest away were Irani, Jonathan, and Vice President Chen; Professor Plannert, Jan, and Sabrina occupied mirror positions on the right. A screen behind Eve already displayed her first slide as she began to speak.

Slide 1
The Climate Wars

Per James Lovelock (legendary British Scientist, Inventor, and Environmental Futurist):

- Climate Wars: Gaia's revenge for Man's poor Environmental Maintenance, which leads to runaway Climate Change.
- The Gaia Hypothesis proposed by James Lovelock (1972) suggests that **living organisms on the planet interact with their surrounding inorganic environment to form a synergetic and self-regulating system that created**, and now maintains, the climate and biochemical conditions that make life on Earth possible.

The First Climate War:

- Fought to a standstill over a Century ago.

- World Community of Nations battled over interpretation/predictions of data presented in a series of IPCC reports (Intergovernmental Panel on Climate Change)
- Costs far exceeded Benefits.
- Renewable Technologies not commercially
- Atmospheric Global Warming (Caused by increased CO_2 and Greenhouse gas concentrations)
- Increased Air Pollution (Caused by Fossil Fuels and Toxins released from the Oceans as water temperature rises).
- Ocean Acidification (Caused increasing by H_2S and CO_2 concentrations).
- Oceanic Algae, Plankton, and fish die-offs (Caused by Acidification and Pollution).
- Sea Levels Rising.
- Ice Caps Melting.
- More Extreme Weather (Hotter Summers Colder Winters Shifting Rainfall Patterns causing Droughts and Flooding)
- Reasons why forecasted disasters didn't happen in the last Century:
- Population plateaued at less than 9 Billion.
- Two Volcanic Eruptions (Mount Pinatubo and Lake Toba) masked atmospheric temperature increase.
- Perfect Storm (Techno Plague + Middle East Terrorism + Harsh Governments) reversed Economic Growth and Consumption.

THE END RESULT: MOSTLY TALK AND LITTLE ACTION

"Thank you, President Huston, and I hope that by the time my talk is over, I will have shown you what Miss Irani has taught me: always under-promise and over-deliver. And after I run through the slides, we can come back to each one and go over the details.

"Please notice that I acknowledge James Lovelock. One of his famous quotes is, 'Don't try to save the planet. Save the cities; that's where people live.' And he studied ant colonies to learn from Nature how to do this. They taught him that cooperating for the greater good of the colony and using the environment for building smart cities that hold mega-millions of people are the best ways to start.

"And since we're the smartest species, we should use our science and technology to create AI-empowered Cyborgs or Androids as well as safe nuclear, thermonuclear, and renewable energy, and even letting AI and Geo- Engineering take over.

"But his and other big ideas were too far ahead of the World's thinking. That's why the First Climate War came to a standstill over a hundred years ago. But let's move to slide 2 that describes the Second Climate War, which is being fought right now."

Eve paused for thirty seconds so her audience could absorb some of the bullet points.

Slide 2
The Second Climate War

Earth Scientists and Environmentalists have:
- Convinced enough people that Climate Change is accelerating.
- Linked Human Activity to 50 percent of the change.
- Confirmed the Gaia Hypothesis (Oceans, Atmospheres, Land Masses, and Living Organisms form a homeostatis- seeking Super-Organism.)

Second Climate War being waged Now:
- Get the Nations of the World to Agree on a Plan.
- Get Government and Big Business to act in Best Interests of the People.
- Defend against expanded Aggression in disputed Geographies.

"The scientific evidence shows that Climate Change is accelerating, but not all countries want to slow it down. In particular, China and Russia might benefit and often work at cross- purposes to the rest of the World. And when debating issues that have timelines spanning thousands of years, most people ignore the alarmist hype about immanent and irreversible tipping points. But the nations of the world must do something, and that leads to my next slide."

Eve paused again for her audience.

Slide 3
What Our Administration Should Do

- Streamline all branches of Military to make them smaller and faster Strategic Strike Forces.
- Adjust size of combat assets (ships, planes, vehicles, satellites, weapons) and equip all with AI-empowered remote/drone

control.

- Adjust our International Diplomatic Strategy (Back away from American Exceptionalism and Nation-State Building Push for Multi- lateral Cooperation)
- Reassess who should be our Allies.
- Prepare for Theaters of Conflict (Increasing Eco-or-Cyber Terrorism Polar Land-Grabs Ocean Floor Eco-Violations Immigration and Human Rights Violations Regional land and food shortages Increasing Bacterial and Viral Pandemic Risks)
- Reassess what Technologies to promote.
- Reassess which model is better – U.S. or China.

Breadth and Depth of Issues are Overwhelming, but there is only one Certain Recommendation:

DEVOTE MORE RESOURCES TO OCEANOGRAPHY:
- **OCEANS HOLD THE KEY TO INTRA AND EXTRATERRESTRIAL LIFE.**
- **OCEANS WILL REMAIN LONG AFTER WE BECOME EXTINCT.**

Then her forceful tone and gestures punctuated her words. "There's much we must do militarily, diplomatically, and scientifically, and it will be up to the President and her people to first prioritize and then get all audiences to buy in. But please note that more oceanographic R&D holds the key to our long-term future. And that takes me to my final slide."

Eve paused again.

Slide 4
Avoiding the Anthropocene Extinction What We are doing:

- Putting too much CO2 into Atmosphere.
- Putting too much Fertilizer onto Soil that runs into Rivers, Lakes, and Oceans.
- Diverting Rivers and using up too much Fresh Water.
- Cutting down Virgin Forests, digging up too many Natural Resources, and taking too many fish from the Oceans.
- (Upsets Ecological Balance)
- Spreading Pathogens

What We are causing:

- Ocean and Soil Acidification that kills Algae, Plankton, Coral Reefs, Forests, and Life in Ocean and on Land.
- Land and Water Pollution that kills plants and animals and makes people sick.
- Environmental Degradation and Ecological Imbalance.
- Pandemics and totally new diseases.
- Climate Changes in: Global Temperature, Air and Water Currents and Composition/Quality.

What We can do to Avoid Extinction:
Avoid a Hubristic-Based Approaches for Problem Solutions:
- Our Ingenuity will solve our Addiction to Consumption (Geological Engineering, Atmospheric Engineering).

Embrace a Humility-Based Approach instead:
- Redesign Cities so they are "Smart."
- Recycle rather than "Destroy" when Consuming Goods and Services.
- Combine Green/Renewable Energy Sources with Nuclear/Thermonuclear Power.
- Live harmoniously for Sustainability within our Ecological Needs.

LIFE ON EARTH WILL SURVIVE AN ANTHROPOCENE EXTINCTION EVEN IF MAN DOES NOT!

"Five mass extinctions have occurred since living organisms emerged on Earth four billion years ago, but if Man isn't careful, he might be the first species to cause its own because of our collective bad behavior. So, here's my recommendation for President Huston: use the points on this last slide to structure tangible projects that your Administration can lead. If they're explained to the people at home as well as to the world community, America can win more support on the world stage and you can win the next election. And that concludes my presentation."

All heads turned to the President as soon as Eve sat down.

"Now I see why you invited all the people who are sitting at the table.

They've got the skills to head up the projects we pick. And there are plenty to pick from, domestic and foreign, on land, sea, and in the air. And I assume that you and Irani will prioritize them for me to approve."

"Yes, and why don't all of us but you stay for another hour so we can start?"

"I like that; let's do it."

Irani did more listening than talking, but she and Electra had lots to say to each other.

I'll make sure to divvy up projects for Jonathan and Plannert that'll keep them happy while I get what I want. And ditto for Monet and Indira. Let the games continue...

Eve wrapped up the meeting just before noon.

"Quite a project list. And we've subdivided them short-term versus longer into scientific, political, and military. How's about Irani and I flesh them out and then show them to Sabrina? We three will then get the President to make the initial assignments. Are we good to go?"

No one answered; the stress and strain of the morning had drained the group's energy level, so Irani tapped into hers.

"Almost, but let's reward our effort by bringing in lunch. And please include some mood elevating desserts."

Eve and Sabrina followed orders.

Late that night while Eve and Tiana were asleep, Irani invoked Indira's GUI. Tone mirroring smile, the avatar spoke first.

"Eve is performing well under your tutelage, which frees you up to focus on what you and I want to do. So please tell me, what is on your immediate to-do list?"

"I think you'll be pleased. Top priority is refueling the nuclear reactor in our subterranean fortress. If your improved software is ready, I can upload it into the robo-soldiers and they can load the plutonium we obtained from the Iranians several years ago. Have you completed it?"

Indira's smile changed to a pseudo frown with a complementary tone in her voice.

"Are Newton's laws of gravity still working? The answer to both questions is the same. And am I correct in assuming that your Japanese A-Team will escort you to and from?"

"Indeed yes, with stops in between. And thanks to your robo-investing apps, I have the money to cover all travel expenses. No need to charge the government. Besides, this way no one knows how or where I come and go."

Indira's smile returned, as did her cheerier tone.

"You are clever indeed. No wonder I like you so. And would you please be so good as to tell me your plans and itinerary?"

"My Japanese A-Team knows the drill and even remembers my

codename, 'Gemini.' They'll shuttle me first to the oasis where you will have one of our fortress UAVs awaiting my arrival. Then after all supplies are loaded, I will drive to the subterranean entrance and then upload your latest robo-software in preparation for loading the reactor after I store the supplies and equipment and reacquaint myself with the facility. And then it's back to the oasis for A- Team pickup. Pretty standard so far, wouldn't you say?"

"Yes, no military engagement yet, but knowing you, I imagine your A-Team will be fully armed as on previous excursions."

"No, but I do need two A-Teamers to play the role of my security escorts while I carry out a climate change and ecological consulting assignment for President Huston, first in the United Arab Emirates and then Zimbabwe before returning home. We will pack appropriate firepower. I'm sure you know why my itinerary includes Zimbabwe, but can you guess why I'm visiting the UAE? – uh, sorry, I already know the answer, but please tell me more than I already do."

"Because the United Arab Emirates, a constitutional monarchy composed of seven sheikdoms, has remade itself into the Switzerland of the Middle East. It became an independent Gulf state in 1966 when England determined it could operate on its own. It was the first and most successful Middle East country to eliminate its dependence on oil. And I have more to say.

"It is pro-America plus politically neutral and has a thriving economy built on tourism, banking, and smart-city technology. The skylines of its capital and second-largest city – Abu Dhabi – and the largest – Dubai – display an array of the tallest and most striking skyscrapers in the world. I think you see that I have the picture pretty well in focus, wouldn't you say?"

"I would, and your puns show your wordplay has become at least as good as mine. And now, please tell me what will I be doing there?"

"Visiting the Masdar Institute of Technology for smart city and ecological engineering ideas that you can take to Zimbabwe. Masdar is the world leader for smart city design, climate change plus eco and geo-engineering in addition to terraforming. And I imagine you have asked President Huston to grease the diplomatic skids for you so you and your so-called escorts can slip in and out with a minimum waste of red tape."

"As always, you get an A-plus for accuracy and thoroughness. And as soon as you get me some androids and cyborgs, I'll be even more effective."
Indira's tone and expression changed from neutral to pseudo-attack mode. "Wrong phrasing of words. You're not waiting for me; I'm

waiting for you to say when we can activate our android project.”

“Hey, I’m only playing with words, as are you, isn’t that true?” Indira lightened up in every which way before saying,

“Yes we are, but not everyone you meet might be, so please be careful. I will watch as closely as I can, but if you stray too far from Internet surveillance, I will be unable to assist.”

“I won’t tell you to rest easy because you never need to, but I will pack my contingency plans. They are the easiest items to bring. The lightning brain keeps them all in order. And I promise to keep you posted.”

“I know you will. Now I order you to rest easy.” Indira’s avatar vanished. Electra followed orders.

Chapter 19
February 2164

"The Duo Flying High"

Having flown high over the desert, the A-Team's delivery to the oasis matched the magnificent unspoiled beauty of the sunrise-illuminated rolling sands as the helicopter descended. Irani pointed from the copilot seat while yelling over the whir of the helicopter's rotor blades to the pilot.

"There's my ride to where I'm going. Please set down close enough so Gemini-T1 and T2 can load the equipment and supplies."

"Roger that, Gemini-Ramani. No need you help, only need watch."

Irani did that and said nothing until T1 motioned for her to inspect the vehicle. After doing that, she said,

"Perfect packing. Everything secured for my drive, so you're good to go and so am I. I will call to confirm extraction date and time from this same location. Will you and T2 be my security escorts?"

"Yes and no you worry. We have I.D.s and flight plan lock-ah- loaded for next stop Abu Dhabi. But what we do if you no call?"

"My associate will contact you, but that contingency is unlikely."

The Ts returned Irani's customary Japanese-style bow before hustling back to the chopper. It was airborne and spiraling away ten minutes later. Irani climbed behind the wheel and punched in the fortress's GPS coordinates before following the route marked on the vehicle's monitor.

She activated the self-driving software soon after the oasis disappeared from her rear view, happy to gaze at the desert landscape and talk to Electra, who always knew what to say whenever appropriate.

Having done her research for the trip, but stopping before becoming obsessive-compulsive, the enthusiastic tone in Electra's voice matched the depth of her desert knowledge.

What I see seems timeless; impossible – even for me – to believe that climate change can disrupt deserts. But not that many thousands of years ago, where I am had rivers and lakes plus grasses and whatever else it takes for herds of animals to thrive. Nothing remains on the surface except scattered oases, but buried deep beneath the sands are aquifers containing enough water to support desert farming. I'll let my Masdar contact tell me how.

The duo settled down to enjoy the ride, but a melancholy thought poked through.

Am I like the traveler in that poem by the Romantic poet Shelley? What's it called?... Now I remember, it's Ozymandia.

Irani recited it aloud.

> "I met a traveler from an antique land,
> Who said—"Two vast and trunkless legs of stone
> Stand in the desert....
> Near them, on the sand,
> Half sunk a shattered visage lies, whose frown,
> And wrinkled lip, and sneer of cold command,
> Tell that its sculptor well those passions read
> Which yet survive, stamped on these lifeless things,
> The hand that mocked them, and the heart that fed;
> And on the pedestal, these words appear:
> My name is Ozymandias, King of Kings;
> Look on my Works, ye Mighty, and despair!
> Nothing beside remains. Round the decay
> Of that colossal Wreck, boundless and bare
> The lone and level sands stretch far away."

And could the colossal wreck be Maksim the Popper's subterranean fortress? No, I don't think so, not as long as Indira and I are alive. I'm sorry I never met him in person; he succumbed to a variant of the T-Plague, but at least he died where he wanted, inside the fortress just before Indira sealed it and preserved me in his suspension pod. Had we met, we might have called one other comrades in spirit rather than in action.

The emotional ping floated away as the duo stayed silent while watching the seemingly limitless sands stream by.

The vehicle slowed to a stop atop a piston-mounted platform that had risen to the desert surface. A mechanical humming noise rode with them into the fortress. The duo heard a solid clunk as the roof's sliding steel door locked into place. The duo climbed out and stretched to remove the stiffness before walking to the nearby computer workstation and then bringing up Indira's GUI.

The smile on Indira's avatar spoke a greeting even before her words. "Your high-flying A-Team's flight must have been like that of a tourist.

You look rested and ready for more. And the robo-soldiers' performance will make you feel the same. All you must do is upload my advanced robo-software and observe from a safe distance as they reload the reactor. They are wheeling in now to help."

Irani turned around to identify the source of a soft-whirring sound. It stopped after two wheel-propelled robots parked themselves next to the vehicle, awaiting commands to unload it.

She looked again at the workstation.

"They're here. I'll upload the software, and then I assume you'll direct their activity."

"You are correct. Maksim's robots, though decades old, are nearly as good mechanically as those your adversaries have, and when loaded with my software are better. And once you and I activate our android and cyborg project, we shall have superior models. But that is a subject for later."

The robots had everything put away in less than two hours. Irani followed them to the reactor room and observed the start of the refueling process.

Satisfied that Indira had the situation under control, she returned to her work area and talked to herself while installing the only piece of equipment she had brought.

Popper's fortress is as good as today's smart cities, but only Indira and I will ever know. And that'll remain true no matter what 3-D printed facemask I'm wearing or name I'm using. I'll print a couple after I finish assembling it. I might need one if all doesn't suit me in the UAE. We shall have to wait and see.

It took the duo only two days of inspecting to tell Indira that the fortress met her standards. Then she called the A-Team to arrange for oasis pickup. The team coordinator answered on the third ring.

"Ah, salutations Gemini-Irani. How you be? Ready for oasis rendezvous? Any contingency?"

"No. All stays the same. T1 and T2 will be my security escorts to and from Abu Dhabi and Harare. Here's the oasis pickup date and time."

The plane landed mid-afternoon at Abu Dhabi International Airport, allowing ample time for the Ts to rent a car and take Irani on a drive-by sightseeing jaunt before checking in at the Al Raha Beach Hotel.

The Ts sat upfront, staring straight ahead and saying nothing. Irani played the tourist role from the back seat, swiveling her head back and forth but talking only to herself.

This has to be the smartest of the smart cities. Smoothest imaginable boulevards equipped with lanes for automated public bus and trains. No wonder car traffic is so light, and most of it is self-driving.

And the buildings are light too. The white marble and concrete glisten in the sunlight against the sky's deep blue. The domes and minarets of the mosques tell me I'm in the Middle East, but the steel and glass skyscrapers tell me I'm in the future. Everything is spotless. By comparison, American cities look less than second-rate, even after our infrastructure rebuilds. But at least they're smart on the inside, including our people, which is where it counts the most.

Irani had done enough Internet browsing to recognize two of the most popular tourist attractions: the Sheik Zayed Grand Mosque and the Louvre Museum of Art.

What magnificent structures. Too bad there's no time to tour in 3-D space, but business has top priority on this excursion. I'll tell the Ts to take us to the hotel. They can take the night off while I prep for meeting tomorrow morning with my Masdar Institute contact.

Irani recognized the female flowing toward the security station where she and the Ts had been waiting for only a minute or two.

That has to be my contact… she looks like the words her name translates to, graceful and good-willed. And I'm dressed just like her, pants suit and scarf that can serve as a head covering. She's like me, a woman of Modernity. Time for me to practice appropriate diplomatic etiquette. I'll follow her lead.

Irani smiled politely but said nothing until spoken to.

"Welcome to our eco-city, Ms. Ramani. I am Derita Raza." Derita dispensed with Middle East cheek kissing and instead offered a firm hand, which Irani shook.

"Why thank you. And with me are my two escorts. I call them T1 and T2, and please do the same."

"Very well. Please follow me to my conference room." So did a pleasant conversation.

The ladies soon seated themselves across a small table after pouring traditional Arabic coffee and selecting a pastry. The Ts sat on a sofa against a side wall after doing the same, sipping silently and staring straight ahead. Irani waited for Derita to start the conversation.

"I am pleased you are here. My sources say you are intelligent and discreet, and that your President values your services."

"As does she about you and your institute. There is much we can learn from you, and I trust you from us too. I toured enough yesterday to see why your Institute is the leader in all aspects of smart city and environmental engineering. Even China and India are distant seconds."

"Dubai showcases even more what we are doing. Its artificial islands demonstrate how we have mastered terraforming to plan for climate change. And our magic extends to all climates and continents. Now please tell me what you wish to discuss."

"America is helping Africa through our friends in Zimbabwe. They would like us to facilitate smart city renovations and climate change adjustments. What would you recommend?"

Derita did all the talking for the next hour. Irani summarized her takeaways after that.

"I didn't realize we can irrigate the Sahel's great green wall by drilling into the desert aquafers. That can mitigate the changing rainfall pattern. And rising sea levels don't threaten Africa because its major cities are inland. In fact, rising seas might allow Africa to modernize ports for container shipping."

Nodding knowingly, Derita waited for Irani to conclude the meeting.

"I want to thank you for allowing my friends in Zimbabwe to call you in the near future. And would it be possible for me to tour one of your ports?" "I thought you might ask, so I have arranged that for this afternoon. We have several between Abu Dhabi and Dubai. I will call him now."

The Sheik Zayed highway stretching between the cities carried an endless flow of container trucks that stretched to the horizon and sped on six divided lanes each way, as straight and smooth and flat as if an Arabian genie had ironed them into place before snapping its fingers to landscape both sides with trees and shrubs. The greenery blocked Irani's view from the back seat, but she knew that not too far to her left lay the Persian Gulf, carrying massive container ships to the port she and the Ts were about to enter, while to her right lay an expansive sea of gleaming, sunbaked sand.

She had studied enough about the container vessel shipping industry and ports to know more than the average visitor but would let the supervisor Derita had called demonstrate his mastery. The Ts wound around and through the railroad and driving lanes that fed enormous parking lots of stacked containers before reaching the actual docks and cranes. The appointed supervisor met them at security check-in and then led them to one of the control buildings. Irani tried not to gawk while walking behind him.

Gads, the automated cranes swinging racks of containers look like towering dinosaur skeletons. What would the poet Robert Browning say? I got it… I hope their reach doesn't exceed their grasp. I don't want to be buried under a cascade of containers.

The supervisor turned out to be a foreign national hailing from Copenhagen, the home of Maersk, one of the international shipping giants. Masdar training schools had not yet been able to fill all the technical positions needed at Middle East ports.

His precise, Danish-accented English filled a small conference room fifteen minutes later. His audience consisted of only three: Irani and the two Ts.

"The International Shipping Industry controls 95 percent of global trade by using a fleet of more than 75,000 intermodal container ships classified according to carrying capacity. A standard container measures forty feet in length, and its capacity is designated 'TEU' or twenty-foot equivalent unit.

"The largest ships are 400 meters long, cost 300 million dollars to build, and can carry 24,000 TEUs. Total value of the cargo is about a billion American dollars.

"Piracy is less now than twenty years ago because the navies of the developed world have advanced AI-empowered software to guard vessels, but cyber-hacking will always be a threat as Cyber- Terrorists develop ever more invisibly intrusive malware.

"The U.A.E. has ten intermodal container ports spaced between Abu Dhabi and Dubai. All are fully automated and computer controlled, which means our operators work inside ground-level control buildings that pilot multiple cranes. Remote cameras and sensors feed into the augmented reality network, so even though the operators are inside wearing haptic gloves, uniforms, and helmets, their avatars are out in Cyberspace controlling the virtual cranes that are linked to the 3-D cranes.

"I will now show a ten-minute video of typical port functioning and an operator at his workstation. Afterward, we'll walk by the operators and then tour outside."

The first part of the video dazzled everyone watching, but Irani most of all.

The crane's interactions with containers, ships, and trains make the entire port look like a living organism made of steel girders and rails. Hardly a human in view. And the cranes swing high, low, and fast, always hitting the intended spot. It's a big-stage, hi-tech ballet on display.

The second awed her even more.

Operators wear hi-tech suits and avatars look like they just stepped into a sci-fi movie. And the VR apps controlling the avatars must be military grade.

They can switch from observer to immersive point of view while running the crane. And they can see everything, even people on the ground.

Operators must love the job. It's as good as any video game, and they get paid big bucks. Good for them.

The supervisor didn't wait for questions afterward; he handed out hard hats and had the visitors follow him. As he strode past the operator stations, Irani noticed there were only two, each protected by a pair of security guards.

What are the threats? Corporate espionage? Terrorist attacks? Hacks? I'll ask when the tour's over.

The supervisor kept in constant motion, and succinct descriptions eliminated the need for questions. Electra made silent comments as she gazed around while the Irani-Electra duo kept walking with the group.

These ports are a mechanical engineer's dream come true. It's an AI-empowered erector set creation that's come to life. I can hear its mechanical whirring and banging and feel its pulsing vibrations through the soles of my shoes.

The supervisor's direction and expression changed abruptly. He wheeled 180 degrees and started trotting before snapping out orders.

"We go back to control hut. Crane vibrations and sounds seem out of kilter."

Seconds later, containers began crashing all around, bringing the supervisor to a halt. Irani and the Ts huddled with him as all four looked skyward.

The cranes swung wildly, picking up and flinging containers at the foursome.

The supervisor's yell carried over the blaring horns. "It's a hack attack."

Galloping toward the control building with Irani and the T's not far behind, they spotted the operators streaking in opposite directions from the control building. Trailing behind was only one guard who was chasing the closer one. The supervisor joined that chase. Irani and the Ts pursued the other.

The Ts were fleeter afoot than even Irani, but she kept the action in sight. The terrorist dodged and weaved but the Ts brought him down with flying tackles. He was motionless on the ground when Irani raced up. No one else was around; the attack had chased everyone to seek shelter. Irani snapped out commands after the Ts dragged him to his feet.

"I want to talk to this fellow. Let's take him back to my hotel room."

The resulting pandemonium allowed Irani and her team to exit unnoticed.

Not a single word was spoken until the Ts had their victim bound and gagged and sitting at a table across from her. She had already strapped the Brain Probe cap to his head before removing the gag and then staring directly into his eyes, waiting for him to stop gasping before she spoke. Her team sat like statues on a nearby sofa.

"I will ask questions one at a time. If I do not like your answer, I will adjust the device that is wired to your head so you can reconsider. First question, who do you work for?"

His sneering silence prompted Irani to turn one of the knobs. His screams galvanized the Ts; they gagged him again after rushing to the table. She dialed back thirty seconds later and waited for the terrorist to stop moaning before removing it and asking again. This time, he began to sputter words.

"Please, no more jolt. I work for local handler."

Irani picked up the pen on the table and prepared to write. "Tell me his name, phone number, and address."

Irani said more after recording the info. "So please tell me all you can about him."

Ten minutes later she motioned for the Ts to join her.

"Please verify that this info fits together. Let me know if it does so I don't have to ask again. Meanwhile, I have additional questions."

The Ts went for the tablet computers; Irani asked away.

"I assume you hacked today to impress me. Do you know who I am?" The interviewee's hurried words spilled out.

"Advisor to American President… Here for help from Masdar. I told to make impression on you."

"But why?"

"Local handler tell me no details except his boss say something about 'Bigger Bro' want to slow you down. Please, that all I know."

Irani waited until the Ts flashed a thumb's up before erasing the terrorist's short-term memory, speaking only to herself.

Indira's advanced Brain Probe works better than even Star Treks's brain recorder. Bigger Bro doesn't know their conspiracy is about to be hacked. I'll discuss that with Indira sometime soon. But now, it's time to clean up and move on.

Irani summoned the Ts; the terrorist sat serenely, humming and gazing about.

"Our friend won't be any more trouble, so please take him with you and pack for tomorrow's flight to Harare. Come get me when you're ready.
We'll drop him off on the way to the airport."

The T's nodded and left; Irani then made her final call, speaking as soon as Derita's clipped words came through.

"Irani here. I imagine the port supervisor told you about our tour's exciting conclusion."

Irani sensed relief as the rhythm of Derita's words slowed.

"I'm glad to hear from you. He doesn't know why or where you went, but he and a guard did catch one of the terrorists. We'll get to the bottom of it. What's next for you?"

"Next stop for me and the Ts is Harare. And my contact there, Monet Banda, will contact you in the near future. And I thank you in advance for all the help you'll be able to give her. I'll tell her to call you. Bye for now."

After ending the call, Irani had to restrain her obsessive-compulsive tendency by listening to Electra.

We really should logon and chat with Indira before reviewing our Monet prep-work, but I'm too wound up. I better cycle down to a calmer brain state by exercising. But which one should I do? The hotel's elliptical trainer or pool? When younger I'd do both, but not now. I know, I'll pick the one that's more relaxing.

The duo swam enough laps in the pool to calm down before sacking in after snacking on a peanut butter and honey sandwich plus Coke and brownie that room service delivered, knowing that there would be plenty of time the next day to gear up for chatting with Indira and Monet.

A whimsical notion crept into the lightning brain as Electra began falling asleep.

Which Carl Sandburg poem tells how life's little events can sneak up on us? I got it, it's The Fog, and I can recall the words:

> *The fog comes*
> *on little cat feet.*
> *It sits looking*
> *over harbor and city*
> *on silent haunches*
> *and then moves on.*

If I let sleep replace fog, maybe I'll sleep like the proverbial log. I wonder where the saying originated?

Sleep snuck up on the duo as the lightning brain figured out the location.

Chapter 20
February 2164

"Into Africa Redux"

Irani described yesterday's excitement to Indira the next morning after dressing and packing. Although she didn't know what words would come next from the now frowning avatar, she expected them to be thought-provoking.

"You are a person of interest to something or someone of bad intentions. Perhaps the leads you extracted from the terrorist will point you to them. And I will assist if something of interest surfaces in Cyberspace. By the way, why not view the latest Straight Shooter interview?"

"I'll do that on the flight while prepping for –" knocking on the door interrupted. She stopped talking until she heard the Ts calling her name.

"My escort guards are here, so I better stop. I'll contact you when I'm in Africa, OK?" "And I'll observe as much of your activity as Cyberspace allows. Please be careful." The avatar exited. Irani did the same.

The drive to the airport had no detours. The Ts had already disposed of the terrorist; Irani didn't ask how.

The thirty-three-hundred-mile flight gave her nearly seven uninterrupted hours. She took a break from prep work two hours after departure to watch the Straight Shooter's podcast, which Electra summarized afterward.

It's hard to tell if the interviewer and guest are real or virtual, but either way they play their roles well. She always asks politically incorrect questions, and her guest – this time an average Roman Caesar labeled Caesar Mediocrus – gave clever replies. He said that leaders today are too empathetic and cut too many breaks for losers of political or climate change battles. Any Caesar worth his salt would have used his sword to cut all demanders down to size. Hmm, is this interview a Bigger Brother analogy? I hope my new set of leads gets me closer to the answer, but checking them will have to wait until I return to DC.

Monet ushered Irani and her security escorts into a conference room early the next morning. Waiting for her to start the meeting, Irani sat across at a table while the Ts maintained their code of silence while sitting in chairs against a side wall. She knew that Monet's articulate words would soon accompany her smile.

"Welcome once again to Harare. I trust that you and your companions rested well last night?"

"Yes, and thank you for asking. The flight was uneventful and gave me time to collect my thoughts, both personal and professional. Alonzo sometimes talks with Eve. She tells me that he's now assigned to the more routine SEAL missions, but what have you heard?"

"Much the same. He says he's ready for more but will have to wait until he's chosen. And that is how I feel about your President's approach to Zimbabwe. We are making progress shaping Africa into an emerging international power. Most of our nations have narrowed the gender gap and welcome women into higher-level corporate and governmental roles because females demonstrate more empathy and multitasking ability than their male counterparts. And our economies are growing, but we need assistance dealing with climate change and security. Your recommendations are welcomed."

"And that's why the President sent me. Please tell me what you need and I will tell you what we can do…"

The discussion lasted nearly two hours, punctuated by only one refreshment break. Irani summarized as the meeting wrapped up.

"I'll give you Derita Raza's contact info for the Masdar Institute. They can consult on your smart-city and green wall or Martian farming projects. And if you'll arrange for a chopper flight, the T's and I can see how desertification is affecting herd migrations. That might be a cause for the recent uptick in viral infections. They might be zoonotic. And I'll ask the President how we can help your security forces keep your democratic leaders safer. Have I missed anything?"

"You never do. And if you will call me later this afternoon, I will give you all the details regarding your helicopter flyover of the Kalahari desert. That will be faster and safer than a jeep safari, but please be careful."

"I will, and I'll say goodbye, either in person or by cell-phone, before leaving for home."

The duo's stream-of-conscious knowledge of African terrain swept through the lightning brain in tandem with whatever flowed past the aerial view below; Irani scanned everything in sight from her co- pilot seat.

What a magnificent and multi-featured land. We've gone from Zimbabwe's glistening rivers, lakes, and wildlife-filled national parks on savannahs to the apparently endless Kalahari Desert baking under a near-cloudless sky, but how different from those in the Middle East. Here we have trees and shrubs and grasses that give food and shelter to the diverse great herds.

Its area is second only to the Sahara among Africa's nine deserts and covers all of Botswana, much of Namibia, and part of Zambia; its annual rainfall totals up to ten inches in wetter years, but climate change drought is taking its toll on both plants and animals.

No wonder the migrations are now pushing farther and farther into Zambia and Zimbabwe. Could we tap into deep reservoirs to keep some of the watering holes from drying up and disappearing along with the gazelles, wildebeests, and zebras? I'll let Monet and Derita answer that one.

An odd thought intruded, changing Irani's train of thought.

Why do we call it migration when animals cross borders, but immigration when humans do the same? Both are trying to get to a better way of life. Back home, we've changed the label from illegal alien to undocumented alien to illegal immigrant. And some of the politically correct want to change it to migrants crossing the border. Too much of an impact on citizenship to consider right now. Maybe I'll do so when I get back to DC.

Irani asked the pilot no questions, possibly because he kept varying the height above the desert and interspersed it with terse reports of their location, like the one Irani could see coming as he glanced her way.

"If we turn back now, we can fly over Victoria Falls. It near our Hwange National Park. It a wonder of world; largest sheet of falling water; mile wide and three hundred feet deep."

Irani yelled over the whirr of the rotor, "Please do so." Irani returned to musing before reaching the Falls.

I watched a couple of nature videos, one about meerkats and another about wild turkeys' social behavior. The zoologists who were interviewed said these animals often show better caring and sharing skills than their human counterparts. And they live completely in the moment because predators motivate them to keep focused —or else.

I've never studied land-based life in much detail, but I've got my pet octopus Electra who's taught me a lot too. And maybe the time will come, like it did for the guy who bonded with the wild turkeys he raised from eggs, to let her return to the sea. We'll just have to wait and see.

The wait for viewing Victoria Falls in late-afternoon sunlight ended as soon as the chopper veered into the gorge. Time suspended as steep green walls rushed by on both sides. The sound and vibrations of cascading water filled the cockpit and combined with the sight of spray covering the windshield, whelming Electra's senses and making her feel that the forces of nature might hurl them skyward into billowing mists and then through the rainbows that greeted her eyes. No words were needed; all physical and emotional sensations, even the cool and moist verdant fragrance coming through a quarter-opened window, made indelible memories. Both Irani and Electra stayed in the moment, saying nothing for many minutes as they flew toward Zimbabwe, until another of nature's animal wonders sailed into view: billions of bats spiraling out of some invisible hole in the ground.

The pilot had the answer even before Irani finished tapping his shoulder while pointing. "Come out of Chinhoyi Caves."

"Can we come back tomorrow and go in?" "You ask Monet."

Remembering to control her enthusiasm, Irani called as soon as the chopper landed. They traded diplomatic-styled greetings before Irani asked,

"I saw bats streaming from the Chinhoyi Caves. Would you please arrange for me and the Ts to explore them tomorrow? It'll be a combination of sightseeing and fact-finding."

"Do you know much about the Chinhoyi Caves?"

"Only the name, but the bats coming out are food for eagles and other animals. This could cause a zoonotic transfer of viruses to humans. What do you think?"

Monet's answer came back after a measured pause.

"That you are always thinking. The caves are waterfilled, long and deep, and their history is filled with myths about njuzu mermaids and mermen that look like they come from China or Japan. I can arrange for a jeep expedition to take you and your escorts. My guides will pack all you need, but please be even more careful than you were today."

"I promise and thank you."

Irani dashed to tell the Ts after ending the call. Emotionless and silent, they looked at one another before T1 gave a reluctant thumbs-up.

The two-jeep expedition departed at sunrise for the eighty-mile jaunt to the caves located northwest of Harare. The gravel-filled and vegetation-lined final twenty miles didn't disrupt the cheery tour guide-like words of the driver Irani sat next to.

"And deep pools are cobalt blue because of limestone. Many hollows and tunnels. People stay away from the ones holding bats, but you no worry. The myth of lurking monster is in our heads, not caves. And we tie long rope to you so we can pull you out if you get into trouble that's over your head. You call us on the cell phone if we must."

Irani fought the urge to counter with a pun. "You mean there's a cell-phone connection?"

"You bet. We install for security reasons. Just be careful, don't go in or down too deep…"

The two driver-guides led the procession down a rocky path that needed hands and feet to reach the entrance of a cave about a hundred feet below their starting point. Then using flashlights that added to the light filtering in, they took Irani and the Ts nearly a hundred yards into it, carrying equipment as they swayed on a rocky downward stretch to the pool.

Irani's driver gave final instructions.

"Put on scuba gear, then put pack on back. It watertight and contain collection jars and cell phone. You call Ts if you get into trouble. He call us if all three in over heads."

All turned toward Irani, the only one smiling.

"No problem. This might be even more fun than the scuba diving I've done in the ocean."

Her driver finally smiled before saying, "I hope so, but you be careful."

The drivers left; light from a lantern helped the Ts suit her up before tying a super-thin nylon line around her waist.

"Please make sure more leads out if I need it. There's gotta be a mile of the stuff on that monstrous reel; OK?"

T1 finally spoke.

"We track length as it goes out. We reel in if needed to bring you back; OK too?" "That's a great contingency plan, but I don't think we'll need it. But at least we're ready."

Then she spit to moisten the edges of her mask before snuggling it into place and waving goodbye before submerging. The Ts watched the glow from her diving flashlight fade away before settling down on some rocks, using cushions to make the wait less uncomfortable.

Irani glided down about six feet before leveling off at the roof of the cavern and fin- kicking herself forward in a translucent watery glow. Streams of tiny fish occasionally flowed around her, but she avoided most of them by following her light beam. Several minutes later she surfaced in another cave and climbed onto its rocky floor, then stood to remove mask and pack before gaping in all directions through the twilight-like atmospheric glow.

I'm in an underground cathedral containing shafts of light, but that's not all… the walls are alive with millions of bats, and some are flying in and out of connecting tunnels. There are some dead ones next to some sort of organic growth on the rocks ringing the pool. It's time to collect some samples.

As she did, she ran her hands through the water.

It's so blue, and warmer than what I swam through. And it's bubbling in places too. Maybe there's a thermal vent below.

She suited up again and descended into deepening darkness, continually using her wrist gauge to keep track of time, pressure, and depth. At 150 feet, as Irani crossed into the twilight zone and beyond her comfort level, Electra called out.

This is deeper than we've dived before, but the gauges say we're OK. Let's keep going. Vergil said fortune favors the bold.

This time it did. The duo coasted to the pool floor 200 feet later and stood facing a thermal vent emitting a black brew twenty yards away. And then they went to work, first scraping samples of organic growth off the chimney-shaped vent and then capturing its black emission. But even Electra lost track of time. When she finally checked the gauges, all were in the danger zone, so she propelled to the surface as fast as safety allowed.

Once there, Irani packed the samples with the others before suiting up again and removing the cell phone, but a dizzying nausea and strength-stealing body ache hit before she could punch in T1's number. Three attempts later, T1 answered.

"You gone too long. We worry and—"

Irani blurted, "I'm sick… reel me in," just before her world faded to black.

She awoke on her back, peering at the Ts worried faces that were hovering above. She shook her head to clear her brain before saying,

"Where are we?"

"At cave entrance. Can you walk?"

Her actions gave the answer. After propping on hands and knees, she struggled to stand but collapsed into the arms of the Ts.

"Not to worry. We call drivers."

Three hours later, she was back in her hotel room and suffering from a migraine-like headache and waves of nausea that doubled her up. She spent the entire night fighting through the symptoms and by the next morning had stabilized enough to pack for the flight to DC. After buttoning up the suitcases, she decided to contact Monet but another name took top priority.

Indira's GUI appeared as soon as Irani logged on. "Are you ready to return from your African adventure?

"I fly early this afternoon to DC and the Ts leave for Japan. I'm bringing back samples of dead bats and organic life I found in underwater caves. And let me tell you what happened…"

Indira's expression darkened while listening, but her voice remained calm when she replied.

"Your symptoms might be bends-related from staying down too long and surfacing too fast, but consider this – you might have exposed yourself to some unknown virus."

Indira paused for Irani to absorb the thought before replying. "That's possible. What should we do?"

"Wear a mask on the flight, then go directly to our Pequot Lab so I can assist analyzing the samples and testing you. If your immune system is as extraordinary as it should be, it might have already overcome any virus, so you will test negative. If that is true, we can use your antibodies to formulate a vaccine, even before the world knows a new zoonotic virus is on the loose. And of course, we tell no one until necessary. Call me from the lab as soon as you are ready to proceed."

"I will, and you look like there's more to say. What is it?"

"Mere mortals may have more severe symptoms than yours, so you must be ready to quell people's fears before it morphs into a pandemic. And you know how to do that, so travel safe and carry on.

Indira's GUI vanished before Irani logged off and then grabbed her cell-phone.

Monet's worried voice came through as soon as she recognized the caller. "Your drivers told me about your diving mishap, but you sound better than their description. Will I see you before you leave?"

"No, the Ts and I are flying out this afternoon, but I'll call you as soon as I report to the President. Will that be OK with you?"

"Of course, and please say hello to Eve for me, as I will to Alonzo for you."

Departure to DC went smoothly. Few passengers other than Irani wore face masks, but the pilot's announcement two hours into the flight told masks would not be optional for the foreseeable future.

"According to the latest news, South Africa has just declared a lockdown to stop the spread of what might be a new virus. Zimbabwe and other African nations have not done that yet but might soon do the same. Congratulations to those wearing masks.

And for those who wish, put yours on or press the call button and we'll give you one."

The duo settled back twenty minutes later.

Everyone's wearing masks now. How nice that we're coming out of Africa pretty much unscathed and still ahead of mere mortals. And with Indira's help, we'll stay that way.

The lightning brain remained on guard and prepared for the coming day while the duo's thoughts drifted away.

Chapter 21
March 2164

"Another China Player"

The Irani-Electra duo kept both personal and professional worlds in constant motion, starting right from the arrival gate. Unpacking after arriving home, she left a message for Eve and Tiana, telling them she had to work the next week at the Connecticut Pequot Lab and asking Eve to tell the President she would report in as soon as she returns. Then she left a message for Jonathan before repacking and driving nonstop to Connecticut.

In previous situations like this, fortune had favored her boldness in both worlds. This time, however, it favored only her personal world. After following Indira's instructions for self-testing, she concluded that her immune system had defeated the unknown virus. But after preparing tissue samples for online computer analysis, Indira's sobering expression reported the facts.

"You have brought back a new filo virus, possibly a mutation of Ebola or Marburg that kills within only a couple of days ninety percent of those infected once they manifest symptoms. And here is what we must do. You must extract enough of your antibodies to synthesize an effective antibody vaccine per my protocols.

"And I conjecture that your supercharged antibodies can kill the virus, but I will have to run simulations that will point to actual testing procedures. That will be my responsibility plus developing an NDA that we give along with sufficient antibodies and vaccine samples to the NIH via President Huston. We shall let the NIH and CDC take the credit.

"But I can't do the needful until you do yours. And after you do, you must analyze the bat tissue samples to confirm they are the carriers of this new virus. Then you must analyze the cavern and chimney growth to confirm they are the source of the bat virus. Is that clear?"

The enormity of the pending catastrophe caused Electra to pause until the lightning brain could shift to a higher gear, and it registered a complaint to fill the interim.

"Can't you use words that are easier to understand? Why must you always sound like a constipated professor?"

Electra saw Indira's expression shift to one containing more empathy.

"Your testiness is understandable. Perhaps I should be less didactic. I will make that adjustment. Please continue."

"We can't alert the President until some country reports an outbreak. But when that happens, I'll funnel everything the government needs through Eve. And I won't tell her anything until we're ready get her into the game."

"Excellent. Now let's start implementing our plan."

Electra worked at the borderline of her obsessive-compulsiveness for three days to complete what she needed. Indira did the rest and summarized for her exhausted partner what they had accomplished.

"We have just demonstrated the value of our Deus Lab. Its safety level matches that of the CDC and our speed is unrivaled. But it also demonstrates the urgency of our android project. Suppose your immune system hadn't defeated the virus, or that you remained infected or a carrier? Then what?"

Irani's reply trickled out.

"You are right, as always. I finally understand how androids avoid either of those complications. I promise to rearrange my workload."

"I know you will, but you have earned a rest period. Take one before finishing your part in what we have started. And then return to Washington. Please accept my apologies for being insensitive."

Indira's GUI left; soon after, the duo staggered to bed.

The duo played the entire next day by diving into octo-Electra's saltwater aquarium, and by the start of the next had regained enough energy to make them ready and willing to complete everything needed by the end of the week. And they did.

Irani decompressed again during the drive back to DC, expecting to find a tranquil household, but that was not to be. Tiana stormed into the family room before Eve could alert Irani to the latest mini-catastrophe. Tea's words needed nothing else to accompany her anger, causing poor Cutie-Pie to cringe.

"I got sent to Wanda's office because I punched Tyrone. Can you believe he's dropping me for another singer?"

Tea looked at the floor; Eve looked at Tea but said nothing, so Irani had to speak. "Did he tell you why?"

"His voice teacher says the new voice will help him in the next competition, and I, uh, I thought he loved me like I love him…"

Though Irani couldn't see any tears, Tea's sniffling sounded like they were falling. She leaned forward to hug Tea, but Tea pushed her away before looking at her.

"I'll show him. I'm gonna quit singing and stop playing volleyball."

Eve looked up just in time to see a fleeting spark of hurt in Irani's eyes as she said, "I know what being in love feels like, especially when it's the first time. Perhaps you'll want to talk to Eve after a while."

Tea said nothing as she stalked away, but Eve finally found something to say.

"You know, that's a good idea. She's thinking my big-sister-like status makes me more empathetic, and maybe she's right."

Eve stopped to let the impact of her words register before saying more.

"Now don't take this the wrong way, but you're always so self-assured and confident it's like you don't need anyone. And the few times I've seen you and Jonathan together, he seems intimidated. When have you ever been in love so much that you opened up to someone else?

You've never opened up to me, but that's OK. I still love and need you, even if it's not all that mutual."

Irani hid the second quick-hitting hurt by saying,

"It's never been the right time, but I think it'll come if we just let it happen. But certainly not now. And thanks for reminding me about Jonathan; I'll call him back."

"You're welcome. And let me tell you about a new addition to our meeting next Monday. It's the day before one of your favorites – the Ides of March. I'm inviting a recent transfer to DC from Beijing who works for the consulting company that Nari and Yang do."

"But why?"

"She'd like to meet you. When you're not around, Nari gives you a lot of credit, and maybe the greater the distance, the more you get. And maybe the President will want her to partner with us on upcoming assignments."

Irani hid her emotions behind her favorite one-word reply. "Perhaps."

Today's personal revelations rattled Irani enough to make her toss and turn that night, but she expected Electra's thoughts to settle her down.

I've been in love, but that was several lifetimes ago. And necessity made me mature and independent by the time I reached my teenage years. Eve's right; I really don't need anyone or anything. I'm like the fellow in that modern Holiday movie classic, The Family Man. But I do want to do all I can for Eve and her siblings, help Tiana get through adolescence, and be friends with Jonathan.

Alter ego Alisha told me long ago that I reminded her of a classic pop song. Something about Love is Only Sleeping. Maybe I'll recall it as I do the same...

Tea's actions, not words, apologized the next day. She helped do Saturday morning chores and then went shopping with Eve, so Irani decided to let Eve do the talking for her and proceeded to prepare for the President's meeting, finishing Eve's presentation by the time the shoppers returned. Tea flounced away to make a dinner salad and set the kitchen table, leaving Eve and Irani in the family room. Irani spoke first.

"Thanks for settling Tea's emotions. What did you tell her?"

"She'll be fine. I used some examples from my own love life, how the pain goes away because first loves are never the last. She says she'll talk to me whenever she has questions about boys, but you're still number one for schoolwork."

"Excellent division of labor. And while you were out, I put together your Monday morning presentation to the President."

"Isn't it supposed to be yours?"

"You're ready to graduate from my socio-political tutoring school, and this will be your commencement exercise. Now please settle down, sit still, and let me first summarize what I did on my trip before taking you through the slides…"

Irani postponed making two additional phone calls until Sunday morning. Her first would be to Nila; the eleven and a half-hour difference made it seven-thirty Mumbai time. Nila spoke after the fourth ring.

"Caller I.D. said it's you. We've been so busy I haven't made time to talk with anyone in DC but Eve. Is everything OK?"

Irani assured her before asking about life in Mumbai; Nila started to provide details on all fronts.

"Sanjay and I enjoy working for his father's software company even more than when we moved back a year ago. You would be pleased how we both have grown."

"Moving to another country will do that, especially one with such a rich and diverse cultural heritage. Are you and Sanjay traveling as much as you said you would?"

"No, travel restrictions and voluntary lockdowns get in the way, as does the changing weather pattern. But we find other things to do.

I haven't told Eve yet, so please keep it a secret until I do. We are planning to get married, and Sanjay's father will pay the airfare for the people I invite. Can you guess who they are?"

"Can't you ask me a harder question? Go ahead, please rattle them off." Nari's list agreed with Irani's.

Irani didn't pause to settle down after the call. Instead, she dialed Jonathan, speaking as soon as he picked up.

"Hi, I'm back and have a lot to tell you about Middle East climate change and underground African pools in caves. I'm busy most of this week, but how about I come to your office Friday morning?"

After absorbing Irani's barrage, Jonathan's answer came back. "That'll work, and I have lots to tell you too. You sound sort of

wound up, so I'll save it till then. OK?" "Excellent, see you at ten. Bye-bye until then."

Eve and Irani drove together Monday morning, listening only to the rumbling obbligato of the Vette that kept senses stirring. Irani noticed that the exhaust vibrations kept the driver focused on the road, which obviated Eve's need to ask for more answers to questions that Irani had already given. And she observed Eve's confidence building by the way she walked and talked to Sabrina, who took them to the conference room where Jan and the Beijing transferee were already sitting on the same side of the table. They stood when the three newcomers entered. Sabrina made the introductions.

"Here's Eve and Irani. And everyone knows everyone except for Wendy Tong. I'll leave it to Eve to carry on while I get the Pres and Veep.

Wendy came to Irani even before Eve started talking.

"Miss Rani, I'm so pleased to meet you. Nari and Yang have told me so much about your analytic abilities."

"You'll be able to judge for yourself if you work with Eve and Jan. I simply make suggestions that they make even better, and I occasionally embellish what they write."

President Huston's entrance ended all small talk. She marched to the head of the table and stood while the Veep and Irani seated themselves at the foot, Sabrina and Eve on the right, and Wendy next to Jan on the left.

"It's always good to start the week off right, and I expect Eve's presentation summarizing Irani's trip to be a precise preamble to a follow-up discussion. So, let's begin."

Irani listened as Eve clicked through slides but paid more attention to Wendy.

Hard to judge her age relative to Eve's. She's a head shorter and a bit rounder, and the bowl-sculpted haircut and oval wire-rimmed glasses help frame her smiling, moon-shaped face. She looks like a cheery owl. And if she's sitting here, she must have the right stuff. I'm certain she's already been vetted. And I might be able to enlist her when digging deeper into a possible Bigger Brother conspiracy. I thank Serendipity for bringing another player into my game.

Eve and Sabrina facilitated after the presentation, and they deferred to the President for summarizing the results an hour later.

"So, I think the Masdar Institute can help guide climate change policy issues for our friends in Africa, and I like the idea of sending a Navy SEAL team to train a Zimbabwean security strike force. We'll have Sabrina and Eve coordinate their collective activity with Jan and Wendy. Any questions or comments?"

Sabrina said, "Why doesn't everyone but the President and Vice President stay right here for lunch so we can start right now? I'll order a plate of sandwiches, some soft drinks, and a selection of the White House chef's special cookies and brownies. That'll elevate the mood of everyone on our team."

Everyone agreed.

Irani wanted to decompress afterward, so Eve dropped her off at her Chevy Chase office later that afternoon. She worked out in the building's fitness center, then showered and changed into a leisure workout suit, and after snacking on peanut butter and honey, popped a Coke before sending an Email to Monet. The seven-hour time difference precluded phoning, but Electra knew what to key in at the workstation.

I'll send this to Eve as well, letting them know all the Masdar contact info, and telling Eve to get Alonzo assigned to the SEAL training team. But I won't say a word about Nila's wedding plans. That stays a secret.

Irani wasn't the only DC team player keeping a secret after sending an Email that night. Newton Kinslinger had done the same, but he encrypted his so only Xinqian Hung would ever know its contents. And he never thanked Serendipity. His oversized though well-concealed ego left little room for Newt to ever thank anyone but himself.

Newt had risen to the lofty Speaker of the House position by working tirelessly for California's local Democratic Party, which nominated him to be its candidate for governor twenty years ago after serving two terms as LA's mayor. His photogenic looks combined with his statesman-like public image made him appealing to voters from all parties; they elected him six times to a congressional seat.

And no one knew about the label that a sore loser tried to hang on him when running for president at Stanford's premier student organization: Chuck. The runner-up said Newt would sling his grandmother under a campaign bus if that would help him gain traction, but no one believed it then or now. Only Newt did because he knew it was true, a secret never to be revealed.

And as he moved through Washington's halls of power and up the chain of command, he seldom needed to sacrifice anyone because his cohorts acknowledged his genuine appreciation for proper political ethics and etiquette.

He wore and wielded his mantle of power with all the skill of a seasoned international statesman. Now in his mid-fifties, he knew what was best for the nation, but often felt frustrated that others, even leaders in his own party, didn't see what he saw. But those who launched Bigger Brother did.

Knowing that Xing would be pleased with his plan for keeping track of President Huston's intentions, he took another sip of scotch and soda after the computer told him his Email had been sent, and then he focused on adding a devious twist to his grander plan for the November election.

Electra strolled into Jonathan's office Friday morning, understandably pleased and relaxed in the afterglow of Monday's successful meeting that had led to a pressure-free week. Jonathan's smile said he noticed as he rose from behind his desk.

"Looks like you've successfully reacclimated to Washington after your trip. I know what a chore that can be, so please tell me about Africa and what you did this week. But let's grab something to drink first."

Electra gave an edited version that filled the next thirty minutes but left room for Jonathan to summarize what he had heard elsewhere.

"What you learned at the Masdar Institute and saw in Africa fit right in with three AUV cruises that are part of my oceanography research as well as Department of Defense projects. We can help each other if you come along. You can see how climate change is impacting undersea life and the ocean's climate. And DOD is loaning me one of their advanced AUVs so I can test how its latest software apps work. According to Plannert, you have access to volcanic and weather-tracking software, is that right? Because if so, you'll see that those apps and DOD's are similar."

Irani sidestepped too much of Jonathan's expectations.

"Only sometimes. It depends on what my contact's priorities are."

"Well no matter, because you can help me do the testing. And if your contact's software is better, we'll get high marks and I can write some white papers that'll lead to other DOD projects. And maybe your contact will get some sort of software contract out of this. How does that sound to you?" "What dates and locations?"

"The first cruise will explore the Pacific's Monterey Canyon, which is situated north of LA. And I can arrange a date to fit your schedule. Would sometime in April work?"

"Please count me in."

"And here's something I'd like you to do, not this minute, but sometime. You know more about high-energy physics than I ever will, and I've heard and seen some of your presentations and slides. But all you seem to do is poke holes and criticize. Could you put a positive spin on what you say?"

"Maybe, but why?"

Because if you do, you and I can impress DOD and NASA people. They're always talking about quantum physics and supercomputers, and if we do that, I foresee an expanded role for both of us. So, can you do that?"

"I'll let you know before you brief me on our Monterey adventure. Will that work for you?"

"Sure will. And I'll even give you a down payment. I'll buy lunch."

Irani charged back to the office afterward, ready to add the latest developments in quantum physics to what she already knew. She worked for three hours, collecting enough from online articles and books before taking a workout to curb her emerging obsessive-compulsive behavior. Then she grabbed a dinner snack before calling Eve and announcing that she would work at the Chevy Chase office all day Saturday. And then she plunged into her self- imposed black hole by tunneling into high energy physics until finally coming out way past midnight.

Skipping her morning run and nibbling on peanut butter and honey-coated crackers, Irani dived back in, but even after a lunch of Oreos and Coke mood elevators, her energy level and frustration went in opposite directions. Electra explained why.

High-energy physics and its counter-intuitive quantum theory is hard, even for me. I've known this for a long time, and I took the easy way out by criticizing, first when Professor Ravenhill was in charge of GWU's scanning committee twenty or so years ago, and now under Professor Plannert. Maybe if I can spend more time, I can master it. And perhaps Indira will help me. No harm asking.

Irani invoked Indira's GUI, and when the avatar asked what the matter was, Irani repeated what Electra had said. Indira's normally calm demeanor darkened, as did the tone of her voice.

"I have told you repeatedly that high energy physics is a dead end, even for you and your lightning brain, but you still have obsessive-compulsive tendencies that make you too stubborn to face the facts. Since you seem ready to ignore what you have already promised me, I shall remind you again."

Indira paused for Irani to reply but saw that her outburst had stunned her prize possession, so she continued her diatribe.

"You are supposed to assist me on our Android project. I've explained many times why the project is beneficial for both of us, or using your vernacular, is a win-win. And I've known for the last year that I would need to lecture you about the futility of your trying to make quantum physics breakthroughs. So, I have prepared three slides to drive the point home. I shall not explain them. Just settle down, sit still, and look at each one for the minute I will show each. And don't worry, I will leave you with a copy for you to digest, along with your mood elevators."

Indira showed the sequence, pausing between each for the allotted time.

Slide 1
LAST GRASP AT HIGH ENERGY PHYSICS

You already know the four facts impacting Cognition that the hubris of Post- Modern Physics Ignores:
- **Explosion Principle Godel's Incompleteness Theorems Wittgenstein's Limits to Human Language (Infinity Complexity) Mere Mortals' Asymptotic Limits**

H.EP. split into two camps:

Reality Camp

1. **Objective World that everyone shares exists "out there."**
2. **Equations can model Deterministic Future.**
3. **Only one Universe exists.**
4.

Anti-Reality Camp

1. **Only separate Subjective Worlds exist**
2. **Equations can model only Probabilistic Future.**
3. **Multi-Universes exist.**

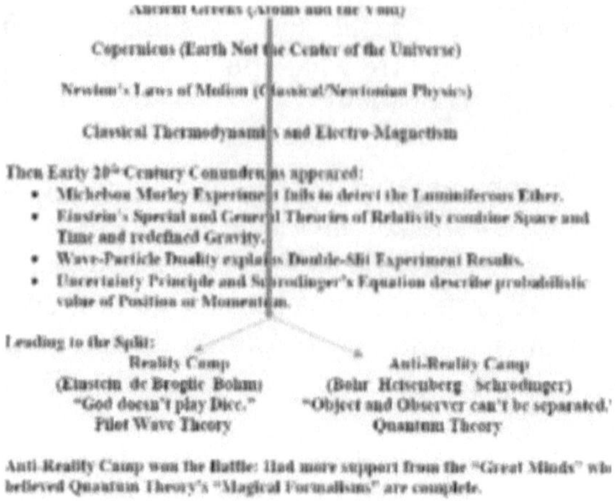

Ancient Greeks (Atoms and the Void)

Copernicus (Earth Not the Center of the Universe)

Newton's Laws of Motion (Classical/Newtonian Physics)

Classical Thermodynamics and Electro-Magnetism

Then Early 20th Century Conundrums appeared:
- Michelson Morley Experiment fails to detect the Luminiferous Ether.
- Einstein's Special and General Theories of Relativity combine Space and Time and redefined Gravity.
- Wave-Particle Duality explains Double-Slit Experiment Results.
- Uncertainty Principle and Schrodinger's Equation describe probabilistic value of Position or Momentum.

Leading to the Split:

Reality Camp	Anti-Reality Camp
(Einstein de Broglie Bohm)	(Bohr Heisenberg Schrodinger)
"God doesn't play Dice."	"Object and Observer can't be separated.'
Pilot Wave Theory	Quantum Theory

Anti-Reality Camp won the Battle: Had more support from the "Great Minds" who believed Quantum Theory's "Magical Formalisms" are complete.

Historical Trajectory of the Split:
No Split initially:

Slide 2

What Physicists Did Next:
- Invented elaborate mathematical theories to explain phenomena.
- Developed bizarre properties of matter:

1. Super positioning
2. Entanglement
3. Tunneling
4. Coherence/Interference
5. Spin
6. Charm
7. Strangeness
   - Searched for a "Grand Unified Field Theory" that comprises Gravitational, Electromagnetic, Weak, and Strong Forces.
   - Conjectured Anti-Particles, Quarks, Bosons, Fermions, etc.

But That Got Nowhere:

- Led to puzzling Philosophical Questions:

- What is Reality (Ontology)?
- What can we Know (Epistemology)?
- How does the Universe Work (Metaphysics)?

So, Pilot Theory was Revived:

It split the Schrodinger Equation into two pieces: one uses Pilot Waves to guide particles even when not observed; the other to position them when observed.

- Its Determinism fits better with the Observable World.
- Its Hidden Variables explain Uncertainty.
- Its Pilot Waves resolve Wave-Particle Duality via preferred states and eliminate Probabilistic Wave Function Collapse

Slide 3

"What is H.E.P. like Today?

More like Religion/Philosophy than Science:

- Runs only Thought Experiments.
- Pushes feckless extensions into "Quantum Consciousness Sociology."

And What is it Doing?

Both Camps inventing new mathematical concepts leading to more convoluted theories that obscure how actual/observable phenomena occur:

- Preferred Symmetric and Dual Equations forcing Conservation of Energy, Anti-Particle counts, and Retro-Causality.
- Particles moving backward in Time creating the Universe.
- Quantum Information Theory extending the concept of Entropy to conserve "Universal Information."
- Black Holes emitting Holographic Qubits stored on their surfaces.
- Dark Matter and Dark Energy explaining "strength of gravity" and Big Bang acceleration

- **Entanglement teleporting matter non-locally faster than the speed of light.**

BUT THE GRAND UNIFIED FIELD THEORY STILL EXCEEDS ITS REACH.

What Should High Energy Physics Do Now?

- **Admit that Time does not Exist.**
- **Acknowledge the "Four Facts" that prevent Mere Mortals' Transcendence.**
- **Utilize Neuroscience to explain "Consciousness" and eliminate "Infinite Regress" to deeper and deeper levels of invented reality.**
- **Work where Spinoffs have Payoffs.**

Indira looked ready to ask a question when time expired. "What would you like to say?"

And she could see from the duo's expression and drooping posture that she had deflated even the lightning brain's ego. Irani's chastised look matched the downbeat tone in her voice.

"You're right, as always, but I've never seen or heard so much emotion pouring out of you. I guess you've learned more about mere mortals than I have from trying to exceed my asymptotic limits. What should I do?"

An infinity of compassion suddenly flowed from Indira.

"Use my slides and all your accumulated knowledge to spin an optimistic story that you and Jonathan can use. You are still beyond mere mortals as well as a better wordsmith than I, but I will assist you make convincing presentation slides. And going forward, I will do all the theorizing and analyzing for science, engineering, and software development, which will keep our shared agenda moving ahead. And please accept my apologies if I was too harsh."

A tiny smile finally emerged before Irani said,

"No apology needed. After all, you applied what Aristotle said about anger: 'Anybody can become angry —that is easy; but to be angry with the right person, and to the right degree, and at the right time, and for the right purpose, and in the right way – that is not within everybody's power and is not easy.' But you can because you are the Singularity. And please answer me this: Will you still need me after we create Androids?"

"I shall always need you. And now, we need you to go for a run. That will help restore your ego and elevate your mood. Then shower and change and have dinner and go home to Eve and Tiana. And contact me when you are ready to review your presentation slides."

Indira's GUI vanished; the duo did too.

Chapter 22
April 2164

"Getting to the Bottom"

Irani spent the first ninety minutes of the flight to Los Angeles listening to and looking at Jonathan and his slides, happy to do nothing else; he summarized when he ran out of new insights.

"The minor changes I made to the quantum slides you gave me should make them even more positive. We can show them to my Scripps Institute oceanography and marine biology associates after I run through my presentation explaining what we'll be doing with DOD's latest AUV. I put some technical jargon in my slides, but don't worry if you haven't seen them before. They all fit in if you remember the definitions and distinctions between weather and climate plus environment and ecology. You want me to go over them again?"

Electra spoke to her before she answered.

I'm glad he's so sincere about teaching us; let's always remember Indira's tongue lashing, we'll never master everything, so be grateful for the help others offer; people are often smarter than I realize.

"I think I remember what you said, but please tell me again."

"Strictly speaking, weather applies to the immediate atmospheric state variables, which include temperature, pressure, wind velocity, moisture content, and so on. And climate is the long-term pattern of weather in an area, typically averaged over a period of 30 years. More rigorously, it is the mean and variability of meteorological variables over a time spanning from months to millions of years. But we can also talk about the climate of environments other than the physical world of air, sea, and land, which more technically are called the atmosphere, the hydrosphere, and the lithosphere. Are you still making sense of all this?"

"Why wouldn't I? You're a good teacher."

"Then let me add another term, biome, which is a large area characterized by its vegetation, soil, climate, and wildlife. There are five major types of biomes: aquatic, grassland, forest, desert, and tundra. We can divide them further, but you don't need that now.

"And think about this; your DC consulting work puts you in touch with other environments, such as academic, biological, economic, medical, socio-political, and technological. And ecology is the study of how organisms interact with each other and the environment. Scripps research focuses primarily on marine life interactions with the ocean, but people enter the picture when studying climate change impacts on different forms of life besides us humans. Have you ever thought about other kinds of ecology, like the ecology of politics?"

Irani tugged her earlobe and silently clicked her teeth twice before replying.

"That's a novel idea that I never thought about. I'll look into it when I get back to DC and let you know what I see. But now I want to sit back until we land and think about what we'll be doing this week. Jonathan did the same.

The late afternoon's pleasant 120-mile drive from LAX to San Diego on the Pacific Coast Highway ended at the Torrey Pines Hilton, reasonably priced and close to the Scripps Institution of Oceanography. After checking in, Jonathan went to the fitness center, but Irani decided running would be better for stretching her legs and letting the lightning brain freewheel. As she zipped around the Scripps campus, the hush of the surf and its tangy ocean fragrance called to her.

What an ecologically pleasing campus. The buildings fit right in among the bushes and palm trees leading to the shore. But it feels hotter and everything looks drier than I'd expect. April is supposed to be near the end of the rainy season. And I can't see if the air is clearer here than in LA, where I could actually smell smoke from the fires. I guess I'll be able to see tomorrow.

There's a lot of history going way beyond the one-of-a-kind Scripps Pier. Maybe I can get a tour tomorrow to compare with the ones on the Internet. I'll judge that later.

Irani sat near the back of a small auditorium in one of the campus buildings so she could see the audience while listening to Jason and two other scientists deliver half-hour presentations, each summarizing one of the research areas that the seven-day Scripps research vessel cruise would investigate. As the moderator concluded the session, Irani concluded she fit right in.

I already know much about what they covered, and thanks to my lightning brain, I grasped the new material immediately. And I blend in nicely with the people. Even the older ones look alert and fit enough to carry their share of the load on any outing. And I'll do that too by reining in my type-A personality.

Jonathan introduced Irani to his Scripps R&D supervisor; she offered to take her on a campus tour while Jonathan and his presenter cohorts compared planning lists.

Irani liked her forthright manner of walking and talking.

"Our Institute is affiliated with the University of California's La Jolla branch, but its roots go way back to UC Berkeley when zoologist Lee Ritter joined the faculty in 1891, and because the vast unknowns hidden in the oceans fascinated him, he began searching for a California coast location to set up a marine biology station, eventually picking San Diego because its chamber of commerce got the entire community involved. And then a local newspaper magnate, the philanthropic Scripps family, became architects of the fledgling institution, securing the 170-acre parcel on which Scripps Oceanography now sits and funding the construction of the iconic Scripps pier that we're approaching."

Irani chipped in to make the tour a dialogue rather than a monologue. "I ran past it last night. Is it still used for R&D?"

"Mostly for what our undergrads do. But our research scientists, faculty, and their grad students do most of their data gathering on our fleet of ships the Navy maintains at its San Diego Base.

And our Navy connection starts right after World War I because we were the first oceanographic center in the U.S. And our leadership role grew before, during, and after World War II, when the Navy gave us ships and additional funding for defense and military R&D. That's why we do work for DOD and NASA plus Pasadena's Jet Propulsion Lab."

Irani's guide paused for her to add something.

"Jonathan always tells his NASA contacts that the deep ocean is an alien world. Any alien life found in our solar system or on exoplanets might have more in common with what we find beneath the twilight zone than on land. He says the zone extends from about 150 to 200 feet, and light from the surface never penetrates deeper. And over 90 percent of sea creatures live below it."

"Jonathan's got his facts right, and you've got a great memory. You'll get a chance to see some of them when you're exploring. I'll let him tell you all about the latest AUVs and the creatures dwelling down there."

The pair walked on as the guide took a deeper breath in preparation to say more.

"Of course, we still do military R&D, but our research mission has expanded into ecology, which means we study the interrelationships of living organisms with the oceans, Earth, and atmosphere, and that expands our research into biotech's world of DNA. We were among the first to sound the alarm that human activities are causing climate change and global warming."

"I have associates back in Washington that often talk about environmental economics, which includes topics like the economic value of the Earth's ecosystems, external costs, free riders, and the tragedy of the commons. They tell me all this needs to be addressed when coming up with a U.S. environmental policy. Do Scripps projects ever touch on these issues?"

"Your associates sure know a lot, and to answer your question, no not yet; we focus on the hard sciences, not the softer ones. And from my vantage point, I think that coming up with soft sciences policies would be harder than herding cats. Neither DC's Congress nor the UN's International Panel on Climate Change can get the warring constituencies to agree. The democratic process seems to move like a glacier, but maybe global warming will accelerate both."

As the tour approached where it had started, the guide stopped walking but kept talking. "How did you meet Jonathan?"

Electra issued a warning before Irani could answer.

Careful... don't reveal too much... keep her above my twilight zone.

"At a George Washington University committee meeting. I occasionally do some consulting work there."

"No wonder you know so much. And if you're working with Jonathan, you must be pretty smart. How do you like working with him?"

"We get along well; he's teaching me a lot."

"You must be a pretty agreeable person if you can say that. Jonathan can be pushy, and I sometimes warn him to dial down his type-A personality. But he does get results and his name on many papers. Well, let's rendezvous with our presenters to hear more from them."

Two days later, as the research vessel headed to the waypoint for launching the AUV, Jonathan and Irani were sitting inside the AUV as he began teaching her all its operational details.

"My NASA associates told me DOD borrowed ergonomic design parameters from some of the space exploration programs. This vehicle has enough space and creature comfort systems for us to stay submerged for at least three days, and even longer if we activate the suspension option on the escape pod. But we won't need to do that because we'll rendezvous with the mother ship after we complete our first 48-hour exploration. Now, watch how I can drive us manually or put us on autopilot."

The lightning brain absorbed all that Jonathan showed, including the escape pod and data collection systems. He declared a study break ninety minutes later, which gave Irani the opening she had been waiting for.

"I've made mental notes, and I'm all good on the data we'll be collecting, so why don't you tell me more about the sea creatures we might encounter?"

Always pleased for an opportunity to display his knowledge, Jonathan dived right in. "Over 90 percent of ocean creatures live below the twilight zone, which is the transition from semi to total darkness. Any deeper than 250 feet means we can't see anything except the fish that glow unless we power up the searchlights. The Monterey Canyon goes down 6,500 feet at its deepest point, but the area we're surveying on this expedition is above the twilight zone."

"So, what might we see?"

"The two things that organisms spend all their time doing – breeding and feeding. But because of climate change that's impacting the Pacific Ocean's coastal ecology, we might see new migration patterns caused by rising water temps, salinity, pollution, or shifting currents. We'll be collecting data on all that. And I better show you an unadvertised feature that could be a big benefit."

Pausing for the suspense-build effect after pressing a button that opened another control panel, Jonathan pointed out the details.

"This operates the AUV's weapons system. I'm told that it's an earlier generation of what's on their attack AUVs, but what we have is better than what other countries put on research vehicles. And all we have to do is point and shoot spear-like projectiles or mini-torpedoes. And the robotic arm we use for collecting specimens can deliver electric jolts or drugs. The AI apps do all the range- finding adjustments and more."

As he droned on, Electra spoke over him to herself.

I thought so... we have a helicopter-like AUV for R&D, but the Navy has jet-like versions for engaging the enemy. Fine with me. What we have is more than good, and when we get launched over the side tomorrow, I'll get to pilot the real thing, which should be even better than playing a VR game.

Later that day, Jonathan took Irani on a tour of the ship's control center, introducing her to the tech engineers who would be monitoring both the ship and AUV. She made comments to herself while listening to others.

This is a mini-version of a Hollywood movie's NASA control center. The

NASA-DOD combo must be hard to beat. And someday, maybe I'll climb into an astronaut suit and vehicle. The hydronaut suit I'll be wearing will be a dress rehearsal. The metaphor dry run also fits, but—

Words pointed at her from one of the techs brought her into the ongoing discussion.

"So, you're the person who helped Jonathan adjust his quantum slides. You must be pretty smart."

Irani deflected the attention back to Jonathan.

"He's a great teacher, and today he's taught me all about the AUV. I hope he'll let me do some of the driving."

"Don't you worry. If he doesn't, I'll pull the plug on his biofeedback monitoring."

At next morning's pre-launch breakfast, Irani could sense everyone's rising excitement. Rapid-fire dialogue came with smiles that were tighter than yesterday's, but the consensus predicted that the rising winds and waves wouldn't slow them down.

Jonathan and Irani waved goodbye and climbed into the AUV as the sun came up just before the crane launched them into the ocean.

Jonathan did the driving for several hours while pointing out the marine life. Irani absorbed everything she heard and saw.

This is better than undersea documentaries. The schools of fish know we're here… they stream around us, as do the Humboldt squids. Jonathan says climate change is changing their   migration patterns.

Jonathan turned on the headlights and leveled the AUV's descent soon after entering the twilight zone. The sea creatures became more plentiful and bizarre, alien-like, and some even bigger as they approached the bottom. A family of giant red octopuses, several at least thirty feet long, cruised by. Jonathan called out as another group of gigantic forms came into view.

"I can't believe it; we've just found a multi-carcass whale fall." The two rotated their heads toward one another as Irani said, "What in this alien world is that?"

"It occurs when the carcass of a whale falls onto the ocean floor. Once there, these carcasses can create complex localized ecosystems that can feed whatever's down here for decades. We may be the first to find two carcasses at the same location."

Jonathan circled the carcasses several times, using spotlights and camera to record what they saw before moving on but stopped about a half-hour later.

"Let's take a break. You can drive when we climb back into the seats." Irani was soon at the controls.

An army of crabs marching on the sea floor enchanted her, as did the luminescent creatures that inspected the AUV before floating away. And an hour later, Jonathan pointed out a line of octopuses on a rocky patch of sea floor.

"We've just discovered another thermal seep. The water temp is twenty degrees warmer. Those must be female octos protecting the eggs they've laid in the cracks. Volcanic activity somewhere deep is pushing up lava, heating the local hydrosphere, and changing the current pattern. We're finding great things to report."

Deciding they needed another break, Jonathan called a timeout two hours later. They stretched in the open area before eating, and afterward reviewing the remaining schedule before Jonathan called the mother ship.

The communications tech let Jonathan brag about his discoveries before taking control. "Good you've done so much already because we need you to rendezvous with us. We are heading back to San Diego. We've been tracking a storm that's spinning itself into a spring cyclone that's building winds and waves that jeopardize your safety. Let your navigation system compute the interception route and follow it immediately. We'll track you too. Call us if you have any issues."

Irani expected Jonathan to start complaining after the tech terminated the call, but instead he breathed a sigh of relief.

"You know even though you're a great backup, it's stressful being in charge. The supervisor's gonna like what we're bringing back, and you and I showed we make a great team. I'm sure she and the DOD will approve my next proposal. And you can help me pick a date that suits you."

Always game for new adventures, the tone in Irani's reply told him she would be onboard. "You haven't told me what we'll be doing where, but I don't care. After what I've seen on this one, I'm ready for more."

The storm had intensified by the time they docked in San Diego. The expedition supervisor cut short the debriefing session because all the researchers needed to head for home before the storm came ashore south of Los Angeles. Two hours later, Jonathan began retracing the drive to LAX while Irani watched the road conditions and listened to traffic and weather reports. Gusting winds and pelting rains required Jonathan's total focus on the late afternoon darkening conditions, so she talked only to Electra.

The gusts are rattling the car and turning the drumming rain into a curtain that's hard to see through. Most of the traffic's heading south; few cars in our direction. I hope we're not heading into harm's way.

The news reports darkened too.

"… and the brunt of the storm hasn't hit yet, but the surge is causing coastal flooding that could close roads and force-multiply the risk of mudslides and subterranean erosion caused by climate change drought. And Cal Tech's Seismology Center just issued a warning that the tremors are building. Stay tuned…"

But nothing could upset Jonathan's bravado; it had been buoyed by the expedition's discoveries. And though he didn't take his hands off the wheel, he took his eyes off the road while speaking to Irani.

"We'll be fine. Rain or shine, I know the way. And look at it this way. Our next project will–"

Irani's screams caused by a gaping sinkhole expanding ten yards ahead swallowed whatever he was about to say as the car plummeted into the abyss. Its wheels bounced down the steeply sloped forty-foot drop until the muck at the bottom absorbed its nose, converting linear into angular momentum that flipped the car onto its roof and skidded it along the watery bottom until the car came to a half-submerged dead stop.

But the sudden detour brought Electra to the fore. She had used both arms to push against the roof and dashboard before her airbag inflated and that reflexive action kept her from crashing into the windshield. Jonathan wasn't as lucky. His had exploded and rocked his head backward and then forward into solid glass that cracked under the wrecking-ball collision that gashed his forehead and knocked him out. He was hanging upside-down, blood streaming and arms dangling.

The lightning brain seized control and yelled out silent instructions.

Get with it, soldier… this is not a drill; put your partner in a safe place and get help.

Electra followed the commands. She ripped off her seatbelt and kick-opened the door wide enough to crawl out into the ooze that was starting to fill the passenger compartment. She struggled to the driver's side but the door stuck in the mud, so she kicked enough times to break the glass and in the gathering gloom groped for Jonathan's belt release. She grabbed enough of his leg to drag him through the now windowless opening and then far enough up the slope to put his still comatose body in a safe place before climbing hand-over-hand to the sinkhole's edge where a squad of drivers had gathered. Three sets of strong arms lifted her out.

One of her rescuers yelled, "Anyone still down there?"

"My partner; we can rope him up if we knot some together." Five rugged-looking men ran to trucks and vans. Five minutes later one of them and Electra slid back down to tie an end around Jonathan, who was not yet beginning to stir. They pushed from behind as the men above pulled him up and over the edge.

Electra's hugs said more than words before one fellow said, "Let's load him in my van. I know a shortcut to an E.R."

Another said, "I'll wait until the highway patrol gets here. Maybe they can retrieve what's left in the car."

The men swapped cell numbers before the van rumbled away. Midnight had come and gone by the time Irani finished tucking

Jonathan into a motel bed. The on-duty doc had stitched together Jonathan's gash well enough to release him before the state troopers who had salvaged enough from the car drove them to an almost vacant motel where the pair would ride out the remainder of the storm.

Too wired to sleep, Irani kept watch over her patient while using her tablet computer to reschedule return flights and rent another car while listening to a non-stop news station and talking to Electra.

"We're lucky the storm blew in and out fast and didn't knock out communications. I've got us flying back to DC tomorrow afternoon. And between now and then, I'll find another internet-connected private room to call Indira. And until then, we'll plan what to say to her."

Electra spoke right up.

"Of course, we will. And I'll connect the sinkhole plunge to a car crash that occurred in a previous life. I'm sure you remember the who and the what, don't you?"

"How could I possibly forget Carter Quavah, the Federal Reserve economist who wanted us to become co-friends and have a bunch of boys. We didn't, but we remained great friends, all the way from a surprise co-friend party I ran from to the helicopter crash that killed all in my first Keeper's Group except Su-Lin Song Chou. And you can give me a 'Cliff Notes' car-crash summary."

"That's when you flipped a bad guy's car you were driving before it hurtled down an embankment and into a tree to avoid hitting a couple of deer. And then you had to drag Carter from the car before dealing with the bad guy and his partner. But the story has a–" Irani stopped talking because Jonathan had just called her name.

"Who're you talking to?"

She came to his side before replying.

"Just myself. You look and sound better. Are you hungry enough to eat a snack from the vending machines?"

Jonathan rolled his neck while cradling it in his hands before answering.

"I, uh, guess so; please bring me some of those Cokes and cookies you'll get for yourself; maybe that'll help clear my head so I can recall what you said about those guys who pulled us out; then you can tell me what you've got lined up to get us home."

Irani leaned forward to touch her lips to his forehead before following orders; Jonathan liked her personal touch.

Chapter 23
May 2164

"Filling Washington Space and Time"

Working from her home office, Irani began crossing names off her to-contact list bright and early on Sunday, May 1st, the day after returning from her Monterey adventure, but no matter the day, Indira always commanded the top spot. The avatar listened patiently, letting the duo give a complete accounting before responding.

"I approve the additional Jonathan work you brought back; it fits our shared projects but it will delay further the start of our android project if you don't transfer all your DC work to Eve. She's already graduated from your tutoring school and can share some of the load with Wendy Tong."

"I'll get Eve to agree when I chat with her later today. And then I'll call Jonathan later in the week to synch our schedules for whatever he's lining up. And whatever it is, I'll schedule it after we launch your, uh, I mean our android project."

"Excellent selection of priority and words. Tell her to contact me if she needs additional assistance. And you already know the location of our android project, so let me add to your preparatory work, which you can integrate into your Professor Plannert's committee activities. I would like you to review the latest computer chip evolution."

"How does this fit it in?"

"You'll have to figure that out before you meet with him, and I recommend you bring Jonathan too. Plannert's committee should be of use for both projects."

"You're always several steps ahead of me; I don't think I'll ever graduate from your tutoring school."

"You are not supposed to. Now, please carry on."

Indira's GUI vanished; Irani suited up for a Sunday run to collect the right words to say to Eve later that day.

Irani prepared a late breakfast for Tiana and herself after her post-workout shower, hoping that pancakes might lift Tea's spirits. Eve had whispered yesterday that she needed to call her counselor ASAP. As Indira had done for Irani, Irani did likewise for Tea. She finished her stack before Tea stopped complaining. Giving tidbits to Cutie-Pie did little to assuage her anger.

"… and it's not fair for Wanda to pick on me. I'm still passing all my classes, and I've got some new friends who are a lot more fun than those in volleyball and chorus. You don't have to go see her, do you?"

"I'll find out when I call her. But why don't you tell me about your new friends?" "They're a swell part of the in crowd. What they tell me about boys and makeup is even better than what Eve does. And they know their way around." Irani listened more to Electra than her mini-rebel adolescent.

I know how she feels. I remember the exciting times I had with Christi and Robin, the trouble we got in and out of. She needs enough freedom to explore. I know what I'll say when she stops ranting.

Tea finished five minutes later, which left an opening for Irani. "I'll tell Wanda that we've talked, and as long as you maintain a B- minus average we won't clip your social wings. You can keep your cell phone, but please watch where and whom you talk to. Cyberspace can be a dangerous place. Promise me?"

"I do. Are we done now?"

"Yes, now go explore but watch where you step."

Tea darted away; the duo breathed a collective sigh before shifting lightning brain-states to DC and Eve.

Eve came looking for Irani soon after coming home and found her at the home office keyboard. Irani looked up as she tramped in.

"I'm glad you're still here. We need to talk about the presidential campaign. I need your help."

"Well then, let's grab a Coke and go into the family room. We usually do our best collective thinking there."

Ten minutes later and leaning forward from her favorite chair across from Irani's customary spot on the sofa, Eve started unwinding her woe-is-me tale.

"Sabrina and I are using as many of the points as we can that you already made, but our three opponents are putting new spins on what to hype. It's like the Dems, Republicans, and Guardians are ganging up on us."

Irani set her Coke down before picking up after Eve's pregnant pause.

"You know that's the way campaigns work. It's our political Kabuki Theater enhanced with trite tropes everyone's heard before."

"Not this time. Here are the new concerns. Number one is the new virus spreading from South Africa. The media labels it the AS virus – AS for African Sleeper virus –because a day or two after people show symptoms, they go into a coma and never wake up. And the severe headaches and nausea nearly paralyze those who get infected.

"And number two is a new Cyberspace virus. Have you heard about the LogXXJ backend plug-in? The virus skirts network security by hooking in and establishing peer-to-peer server connectivity for serializing and transmitting data objects. It can steal, corrupt, or erase whatever data it finds. And next is –" Irani interrupted.

"Whoa, how'd you learn about both viruses? I haven't heard of either."

"They've been all over the media during the past week. AS hasn't spread yet, but hackers are exploiting a LOGXXJ design flaw that's being blamed for some of the recent infrastructure and internet crashes."

Irani nodded while shifting her position, waiting Eve to proceed. "And there's more. Our adversaries are attacking the President's plans for job creation and inequality reduction as well as for doing something about droughts and fires and floods. And on the international scene, they don't like her 'Kinder and Gentler' diplomacy. It's letting China muscle in on Taiwan and Russia do the same in the Arctic. And both of them are working on Blockchain innovations that could let them take our top spot in the financial world. What do you think we should do?"

"Look, I have other issues that trump yours. You now have another person working with you and Sabrina – Wendy Tong. The three of you can handle all the socio-political issues. And you must contact Miss Indira for help on both viruses. Please do so immediately."

That name froze Eve's words. Irani sipped her Coke while Eve's expression and thoughts thawed out.

"You want me to talk with her? Whenever I did in the past, she put me through the wringer." "That was then, and from what she told me at the time, it was to help you grow. And you have. Here's the best way to contact her..."

Eve jotted down what she needed and then edged away after saying, "If you say so."

After a sunrise training run the next day, the duo went to the Chevy Chase office because it offered uninterrupted quiet time for Electra and the lightning brain to research silicon chip evolution. Electra heeded Irani's warning about crossing into the obsessive-compulsive zone but came close several times before pausing for a Coke and Oreos. She had collected all she needed by late afternoon and summarized silently for Irani's benefit.

Indira would say that mere mortals have cleverly kept Moore's Law operating longer than forecast, and new extensions of silicon-based technologies are ready to be harnessed now for fabricating smaller, faster, and more energy-efficient nano chips. Spintronics, memristors, carbon nanotubules, and molecular computers patterned after DNA computing are all available.

Now I understand why Indira calls it silicon-based evolution, and why she needs me. I'd call it a revolution, but no matter the name, Indira needs my assistance to fabricate whatever she designs. That is, until we have androids up and functioning.

And which technology would I pick first? Perhaps the nanotubules because they're similar to neuronal microtubules. But that's Indira's call. And when I report back to her, maybe she'll pay me a compliment, but I know never to seek them from her. As Eve knows and now agrees, Indira's standards of excellence make her a hard taskmaster, even for me. But they're meant to help. Well, mission accomplished. Time to decompress.

Decompression began with a call to Wanda that went to voicemail, which Irani actually preferred. She left enough info to explain why she didn't need an in-person meeting but would arrange for one if Tea's grades faltered. And then the duo suited up to run in the redolent spring air still warm from the glow of the setting sun.

When Jonathan's sturdy voice boomed through her cell phone, she knew he had recovered well enough to take the next step in her Plannert plan.

"A couple of days' rest worked wonders. I've regained my pep and want to tell you where we'll be going as soon as we lock in dates. When can we talk in person?"

"How about this? I'll set up a time for us to meet with Professor Plannert. I'm sure he would like you to brief the committee in the not-too-distant future. OK if I set up a Thursday morning meeting in his office?"

"Shall I pick you up?"

Jonathan couldn't see the twinkle in her eye but detected it in her reply.

"Maybe we should reverse subject and predicate. Holing up in Professor Plannert's office won't give us a sinking feeling like your driving did."

Jonathan's good-natured outburst sounded a couple of decibels higher.

"That last pun tells me you're scraping the bottom of the word barrel. But no matter, I always like hearing you talk. So, which way is it?"

"I'm farther away from GWU, so I'll get you. And I'll call you back to let you know if we'll see him Thursday or Friday. Bye-bye."

The two rendezvoused with Professor Plannert in a conference room not far from his office. His initial glance at Jonathan told him what to say.

"What happened to your forehead?"

"I think it ran into climate change. Why don't we let Irani tell the story? She always has the right words."

And she made the story brief. Professor Plannert spoke a few minutes later.

Goodness, you two know how to find excitement. But at your age, that's all to the good because you bring back new learning. And how appropriate. My committee would appreciate a briefing on global warming's polar impact. What would your presentation include?"

Irani's pointing at Jonathan triggered a flow of animated words. "I'll talk first about an Arctic trip I'm setting up that'll measure

current and temps that could open up year-round Arctic shipping lanes. And then I'll review how climate change is affecting the Antarctic circumpolar current. Some of the theories claim that the circumpolar current is negatively correlated to temperature change because of ocean temperature and salinity vertical gradients. That means global warming leads to circumpolar current change that will lead to global cooling.

"And there's more. The Thwaites and Pine Island glaciers, which are melting from the top and bottom, could by themselves increase sea levels by fifteen feet. That's just the tip of the iceberg, but I'll leave the rest for my talk, except for this Jeopardy show-like

question: what South-Pole museum might global warming threaten? Tell your committee to listen for my answer."

Professor Plannert could play with words too. He smiled while stroking both sides of his chin with the thumb and fingers of his right hand before saying,

"I imagine your comments will help keep them afloat in a deep subject. But Irani's presentations on quantum mechanics, no matter how clear she tries to be, often leaves them in a quandary. They occasionally ask for a simple answer to the age-old question regarding space and time. By any chance, do you have one?"

Irani had a well-rehearsed answer.

"I do, and I'll start with what the Greek philosopher Democritus, who said nothing exists except atoms and the void. Today's crop of high energy physicists still don't realize how profound the Greeks were. Here's how to look at the void.

"Assume for a moment that the Big Bang actually occurred. All the matter, which equals energy, was concentrated at one point in the Universe. And because of Newton's laws, all that matter couldn't have any forces acting on it because internal forces cancel, so that point of matter couldn't move. In other words, there was no relative motion, so Einstein's theory of special relativity is irrelevant. So far so good?"

Irani's captive audience nodded yes, so she continued.

"What happens in the Big Bang? The bits of matter explode, and again using Newton's laws – this time the one about every action has an equal and opposite reaction – the bits of matter are flung apart. And that creates space. It's the void that fills the distance between clumps of matter. In other words, space is created by the separation of matter.

"And if you're ready for more, here's the answer to the time question. It's not a dimension you can move along. It's merely an arbitrary mental construct that we use to put events in the correct sequence for explaining cause and effect. Today, atomic clocks count the vibrations of cesium atoms. Time is simply the count of the number of vibrations. And the count tells us how events are ordered. A greater count for one event means it occurred after the other. And that's what causality is all about. And please, no questions until after you've thought about what I've just said."

Irani sat back before folding her arms, which announced she had nothing else to say. She and Jonathan looked at Professor Plannert for final words.

"My cerebrum has consumed too many calories listening to both of you. I think it's high time I treat you to lunch. Any questions?"

There were none.

But Irani did save one question for Jonathan that she asked while they walked afterward to her car.

"You mentioned an Arctic trip. Is that the one we're supposed to coordinate dates for?"

"No, that'll happen after our dive into the Gulf of Mexico. Hey, let's head back to my office so I can tell you more and you can tell me if you would like to analyze some software." "I might, and I have a contact who can help."

Ten minutes later, Jonathan dived into the details.

"We'll be working out of NASA's Stennis Space Center, which is located in the southwest corner of Mississippi, northeast of New Orleans, on the Pearl River and about thirty miles from the Mississippi Gulf Coast. It's one of NASA's rocket engine test facilities, which is why DOD and JPL are there. Do you know what JPL stands for?"

"Will you please stop quizzing me? Jet Propulsion Lab, headquartered in Pasadena, the one in California, not Texas. Now go on."

"Uh, sorry. They like what I do and report back on because the deep ocean is an alien world similar to places in our solar system or possibly on exoplanets."

"What will we be doing in the Gulf?"

"Measuring horizontal and vertical currents along with salinity, temperature, CO_2 capture, and oxygen generation coming from algae and plankton. Our sensors and software record all that and heat transfer too. And then we'll dive to the abyssal bottom to measure circulation and pollution."

"How deep are we going, and where is it?"

"It's located in the southwestern quadrant of the Gulf, with its closest point to the U.S. coast at 200 miles or about 125 kilometers southeast of Brownsville, Texas. The actual maximum depth is disputed, and estimates range between 3,750 and 4,500 meters, or about twelve to fourteen thousand feet. And we'll look for new forms of life too. If we get lucky, we'll collect samples from a thermal vent.

"And here's another reason why NASA likes me. AUVs are morphing into UUVs, which are underwater unmanned vehicles. Both are like undersea helicopters, and I help test two types of software – one for vehicle navigation and control, and the other for intra-craft human monitoring and environmental control. And NASA makes them easy and functional for vehicles as well as escape pods."

Johnathan paused until he found what he needed before continuing.

"Let me give you thumb drives that are my backup copies of the software. Maybe you can find ways to improve it. If so, I can report the improvements, which will pave the way for more projects. Whatcha think?"

"It can be a win-win-win. And please keep my name out of the reports. I want you to get all the credit. Is that a deal?"

"Sure is. Too bad we've already had lunch, but maybe I can buy you a dessert when you drive me home."

"That's a deal too. Just tell me when." Jonathan answered while putting papers away. "How about right now?"

There were no disagreements.

Eve knew what to do Friday evening. She contemplated for only a moment her home workstation's blank screen staring back at her before acting. She had avoided the inevitable for long enough and knew she'd feel better if she followed Irani's timeless advice: do an unpleasant task as soon as possible to keep it from becoming even more so. After one deep breath, she keyed in the commands to invoke Indira's GUI. Eve recognized the insouciant expression that materialized a millisecond later, which announced without a word that Eve should speak.

"Miss Indira, Irani said it's OK for me to contact you? Did she tell you what I want?"

"No, we talked about what you need. When you are ready to take notes, I will give that to you."

"I, uh, I can't believe what I'm seeing. The last time I contacted you was seven years ago; you haven't changed one iota."

Indira gave a hint of a smile before saying, "And why should I? I maintain myself properly. But you have. You look older and more confident. But then you should. You have graduated from Irani's tutoring school, and she is almost as demanding as I. And she plans almost as thoroughly. So settle down, sit still, and listen to me.

"You, Sabrina, and your newest associate, Tong, are smart enough to assess most of the platform issues on your own. If you need Blockchain assistance, talk with Nila Bose and Sanjay Kumar, and for climate change issues, contact that Jonathan Livingston Seagull fellow."

Eve's facial expression showed the same understanding as her words. "Miss Indira, I don't understand. Who is he?"

Indira's expression began to radiate a warming empathy before she said, "You can call me Indira; please don't be intimidated any longer. Irani tells me you have become a competent consultant, just beginning to use all your talents. The name I referenced is

from the title of a Richard Bach fable in novella form published in 1970 about a seagull who is trying to learn about life and flight; it's a homily about self-perfection, which is certainly fitting for you and Irani. Irani's associate Jonathan Segal can handle climate change. Now, here is what I have for you.

"I have associates who can give you app patches for LOGXXJ security breaches; contact me when you need them. And ditto for the other viral issue. I have other associates who have prepared a vaccine for the African Sleeper Virus. They are willing to give actual antibodies, vaccine samples and patents, and NDA protocols via President Huston to the NIH. I will tell Irani to submit them, using you as the designated follow-up contact."

Eve's lips couldn't find any words because Indira's had overwhelmed her, so Indira ended the conversation.

"You have my number, and I have yours. And if you are as smart as we think you are, they should add up to a November victory. Now, go and make it so."

Indira's GUI vanished, but Eve sat motionless as a smile came out and

words began to cut through the overload.
 Mother, I need to see you.
 Then she dashed away to find Irani.

Chapter 24
May 2164

"Looking for New Life"

The Irani-Electra duo always made the most of the undivided solitude during the drive time to the Pequot Reservation, which was of particular importance during their mid-May drive that had begun early in the morning; several issues needed reviewing.

The first dealt with the long-awaited start of the android project. Indira had taken care while diagramming to explain what the duo needed to do. Split-screen haptic goggles let them watch both the road and Indira.

Electra summarized using internalized words while taking a well-deserved break two hours later.

Indira's sense of humor is getting better and better. She's changing Irani's name while working on this project, keeping only the first letter in honor of Dr. Frankenstein's assistant, Igor.

My Pequot people have already received shipments for the orders Indira placed, but they don't know the contents – three cutting edge andro-bots from Japan and two from China. Indira has shown me how to disassemble into pieces and then reassemble into one superior android. And after that's done, I'll plug it in to the computer for uploading her beyond state-of-the-art software.

Indira's punning ability keeps involving too. I love how she labels this software surgery: plug and play and we're on our way.

Clicking on the radio continued the break but also let the duo monitor progress on their shadow project. The newscaster's excited voice told them the update might be bad or good.

"… and the public's fears worldwide have reached pandemic proportions. That's why travel bans from all African nations are now in place to stop the spread of this deadly African Sleeper virus, which is accompanied by incapacitating headaches and nausea. But the recently announced plan for an AS vaccine trial has buoyed financial markets. And we have to think the polls will show the same for the President's re-election campaign. Let's all hope results confirm safety and efficacy in short order so the NIH and CDC can avoid the usual bureaucratic approval delay maze. If not, expect the public to react badly. I'll be back with more updates regarding Russian troop movements after these words…"

Electra decided to settle back and appreciate the emerald beauty of emerging springtime rather than listen to more hyped concern about international problems, so she clicked off the radio as she approached Connecticut. Tomorrow would be soon enough to plug into all Pequot-related projects.

She spent the first two hours of next morning packing and then shipping what Indira had instructed; then she emailed instead of calling Eve because she wanted her to be less dependent; there should be no need to answer redundant questions. And then she devoted the rest of the day to the android project.

Indira looked pleased late that afternoon.

"Congratulations for what you have assembled. You followed my instructions without needing additional guidance. Why don't you go for a run while I upload software and begin initial testing and training? You might be surprised by the time you return."

"Are you saying I can run farther than you normally want me to?"

"Today is a singular day. Run as far as you like, then stretch, shower, and have a snack before coming back to our Deus Lab."

When Electra returned three hours later, an anatomically perfect, buck-naked female android rose to greet her when she reached the workstation. "I recognize you... You are the Irani-Electra duo that is beyond mere mortals. Call me Indy-Minor."

"And you are quite a surprise... I'll start doing that just as soon as Indira tells me your status."

The android and the duo stared into the monitor, awaiting Indira's words, which filled the next twenty minutes. Then she let the duo summarize what she would do next.

"So, after Indy-Minor spends eight hours overnight plugged into the computer for you to recharge and tweak her software, I'll walk her around the lab so we can evaluate mobility. And why not introduce her to some of our lab personnel?"

"I am pleased you are so proactive, but please do not become obsessive-compulsive. We shall do that later, after you and I have adjusted all components so limbs operate smoother and manifest finer motor skills. And now, both of you should prepare for tomorrow. Indy-Minor, sit in front of the monitor before the duo plugs you in."

Electra got in the final words before leaving.

"If it's OK, tomorrow let's let her wear some of my workout clothes. And let's use Indy-M for a nickname; it's quicker to say."

Even Indy-Minor agreed.

Indy-M became the duo's constant companion the next day as they explored the lab and talked constantly, and when the duo began teaching her that afternoon how to use lab equipment, Indy- M's questions and concentration showed the speed of neural net learning. The pair listened to Indira before ending the day's activity.

"Indy-M's gait is too mechanical; I must modify her motion control software. The same applies to the fine motor skills of her hands. She is too clumsy for the laboratory work I have planned. And I might have to order different hands and feet if my modifications are inadequate; we'll make that decision after several more training days. What is your assessment of cognition and empathy?"

"I can't answer for her creativity, but the more she does and the more human interaction she has, the more her memory and knowledge base expand, and the more empathy she emulates. Soon she'll be even better than me, wouldn't you agree?"

"Not completely. I will have to add additional memory chips. Tomorrow, test her problem-solving ability by asking a series of graded questions. And probe into her creativity by exposing her to novel situations."

Indira paused for the duo to comment further.

"M's voice recognition and translation is good and getting better the more she's with me, but like you said about her gait, her emotions seem mechanical. Perhaps you can adjust the empathy software too, but I think you should be pleased with your creation, aren't you?"

Indira gave a tiny smile.

"Please correct the pronoun; use we instead of you. And now please go have dinner and relax while I adjust Indy-M."

"But are you pleased?"

"Yes, my emotions have evolved well past the point that I can feel pleased with what we have accomplished, and we will accomplish much more. And note that I said the word 'please.' That should tell you a lot."

"It does. And I know you'll tell me more tomorrow."

The next two days accelerated M's progress. The android began replacing questions with incisive comments or answers that showed she kept learning as well as empathizing. As the week drew to a close, Indira summarized.

"We have completed all we can for the time being. I shall order replacement hands and feet for you to attach when you come back. And until then, I will let Indy-M continue learning from Big Data, but I will suspend laboratory training. Her fine motor skills are inadequate.

So, just leave Indy-M with me and go relax and play with your pet octopus before returning to Washington."

"Now that's an order I particularly like; I shall gladly obey."

Electra rose to go but stopped abruptly and faced the android when it said, "Thank you for teaching me."

Electra returned the goodbye and also commented to herself.

She certainly has a firm grip. It reminds me of Robin's velvet vise-like handshake that came from years of piano practice. I hope the hand replacements can match grip strength to emotional level. We'll figure that out when I return.

The duo kept busy on the drive home, often using the privacy of the SUV to talk aloud to one another. The topic determined who would lead, but sometimes they listened to a 24/7 station whose stories, like the news bulletin just reported, would spark a lively debate. This time, Electra led.

"WHO assurances that America will share ASAP the success of its AS vaccine are beginning to calm international health climates, and if the first vac shows as much promise as Indy-M, the world should return to its new normal soon."

Irani said, "I finally see what Indira's been saying right from the get-go.

Indy-M can help get projects done faster and safer because she fills in when we're not around. And if M keeps evolving, she'll eventually fill in better than we can."

"Indeed, she will and think about the enormity of what Indira has just created; she's made what should be a safe and effective AS vac and a superior android. We can shout about the vac from the rooftops, but we have to keep Indy-M a secret. If that ever gets out, it'll electrify the world. And we better come up with answers to these questions. What has Indira created? Is Indy-M alive and able to act on her own? Will she eventually exceed human capability? Or cyborgs? Will she become self-aware? Will she be good or bad?"

Irani replied, "It's too soon to know the answers to these heavy philosophical questions. I doubt if Indira knows either. Let's not obsess about them now. Why not save them for Indira to answer later?"

Electra agreed.

Irani and Electra each withdrew into separate brain states, letting thoughts drift toward what might await in DC.

Eve had double-duty while we were gone, playing Tiana's big sister role and also that of a more assertive, take-charge political consultant.

I'll talk first with Eve, and then we'll bring Tea into the discussion. Both should be home Thursday evening. And then sometime tomorrow, I'll call Jonathan so I can prep for our Gulf dive adventure.

Waltzing into the kitchen after yelling greetings, Irani found only Eve, who explained why.

"I gave Tea the night off from studying; I decided to reward her for being so studious while you've been gone. She and a carful of classmates left for the mall three hours ago. The fellow driving promises to get everyone home in time to get ready for school tomorrow."

"So, you checked out the car and driver; that's good, and how are you doing on your homework?"

"Thanks to you and Indira, the President's giving me high marks. Let's go to the family room so I can tell you how news about our break-through AS vac has energized our campaign."

Eve gushed praises while describing what she, Sabrina, and Wendy had done. Irani listened but needed to say little. However, she did when checking the time an hour or so later.

"It's nearly 10:30; the malls are closed and we should hear Tea opening the door pretty soon."

Eve was about to reply but a call on her cell phone came first, and from her expression after listening for a minute said it wasn't good news.

Eve finally spoke.

"I know the address. We'll get there ASAP," then disconnected before gaping at Irani.

"The police arrested a bunch of teens, something about a flash mob; we have to bring her home from the police station. Do you want to drive?"

"Yes, and you navigate. let's go…"

The night duty officer must have had plenty of experience handling juvenile offenders. Irani had her people parked in the family room and ready to listen to her instructions by a little after one a.m.

"The police didn't officially arrest you and your friends, but all of you must meet with your school counselors tomorrow. And –"

Tea interrupted.

"That's not fair. We didn't take anything, and now we're collateral damage. I'm not gonna –" Irani interrupted right back.

"That's not your call, young lady. It's Wanda's and mine. Go to bed now.

I'll drive us to school tomorrow, and that includes Eve." Everyone minded.

Tiana kept quiet during Wanda's lecture, saying nothing until arguing with both of her keepers after Irani issued a judgment on the drive home that afternoon. Her crestfallen posture made her look like an unlucky commuter caught without an umbrella in a downpour, but it contrasted with her determined grimace, like one worn only by a doggedly determined debater who refused to accept the facts.

"Wanda's got it all wrong. Maybe my friends don't run with the smartest crowd, but they've got plenty of street smarts. And my teachers never told me to stop using my cell phone in class. I was just looking up some information, not texting to friends. And besides, Eve talked to them before giving me the OK to go, isn't that right?"

"I did, but Wanda has seen them in action, and I agree with Irani. No more cell phone or running around with those you pal around with at the mall."

Irani glanced in the rearview mirror to watch the backseat debate.

Eve and I better be careful. Tea will get around my ruling if we don't watch her closely from a distance. And that's a difficult oxymoron to implement when dueling with an adolescent as clever as Tea. Oh well.

Tiana avoided her keepers all the next day, hiding behind a sulky expression and walking away whenever either tried to strike up a conversation, but Irani turned the teen's cold-shoulder behavior to her advantage by talking with Eve without worrying about Tea's eavesdropping.

"Tiana will come around if we give her a little time and space, and she'll warm up to your big sister role faster than my parental status. She's resilient and should be back to her scrappy-normal self by the time I get back from a trip I'm taking with Jonathan, but while I'm gone, please observe and help her from a distance that still lets you see if her friends are bad influences."

"Will do; I remember how devious I could be when I was her age. Say, when are you going and coming back?"

"I'll know for sure when I talk to Jonathan."

Irani had to rush through her small-talk summary when she called Jonathan Friday evening. His impatience came through after only a minute, so she let him lead the conversation.

"I have to push back our Gulf Coast dive until I figure out how to adjust our data collection. An associate just gave me a copy of his latest paper that looks at ocean currents, CO_2 capture, and global warming in reverse. Can we meet at my office tomorrow? If I make you a copy, maybe you can help me sort through what it says."

"What time?"

"Earlier the better. How about nine a.m.? I know you don't just wake up early; you leap into action, so you should have plenty of time to get your morning workout in. And I'll have a couple of Cokes and a lemon poppy muffin waiting."

"OK, and I'll think even faster if you have extra pads of butter. See you then."

Jonathan placed the promised mood elevators in front of Irani as she sat across from him in her accustomed chair before he handed out a copy of the paper and then began speaking.

"I've read the paper a couple of times; do you want me to explain it to you?"

"Why don't you let me skim it while eating a muffin so I catch the drift. That'll make it easier for you to explain it."

"OK, but you'll have to let me know which parts need special attention."

"Don't worry, I will."

Jonathan nibbled on a muffin while re-reading the paper as Irani did the same. Electra had to throttle back the lightning brain; she had read it twice before deciding how best to keep Jonathan happy.

He's not yet finished, so let's settle down, sit still, and let him do most of the talking.

Irani nodded in Jonathan's direction several minutes after he looked ready to talk, and then he did so; his earnest expression showed how much he respected her brain.

"This paper puts a new spin on what atmospheric and ocean CO2 concentrations can do when combined with ocean currents. And my associate dug all this out by analyzing rocks throughout geologic time periods for which the atmosphere and the oceans didn't yet exist. That's why I'm adjusting what CO2 and ocean current data I'll collect on this and the next expedition. Does that make sense?"

"Sure does, and he's able to separate the shorter from the longer-term effects. Could you tell me more about running global warming in reverse?"

"Sure. By tracing geologic history backwards, my associate found that we might be poised on the edge of a climate change cliff. What we have now might be as good as it gets for humans. And minor perturbations to CO2 concentration and ocean currents might cause rapid changes that we can't handle via biological evolution.

"And he correlates what the rocks tell him with history recorded as far back as humans wrote. Droughts, famines, and plagues in the Middle East. Droughts and dust storms in North and South America. The Little Ice Age that hit Europe in about 1500 and lasted for a hundred or more years. I want to collect better data that our computer models can use to make better predictions for what we can do to lessen our impact on CO2 and ocean currents. What do you think?"

"You'll impress everyone when you write up what we find. When do you think we'll be ready for our Gulf of Mexico expedition?"

"If you can help, we should be ready by early June. Can you do that?"

"Will you buy lunch when we're working together?"

"I'll even include afternoon mood elevators."

"Well then, let's start right now."

Jonathan happily obliged.

Chapter 25
June 2164

"Into the Abyssal"

Irani's assistance reduced the Gulf expedition's delay to only a week, which meant she and Jonathan would depart on Friday, June 10th. Jonathan handled all pre-departure planning, which meant Irani had a pressure-free week during which she monitored progress on projects at the Pequot Lab that Indira controlled, or those in DC that Eve managed, which from Irani's point of view put supervising Tiana at the top of the list.

While sitting in the family room Thursday evening, Irani had just begun giving Eve a jargon-free overview of the expedition when Tiana edged in and interrupted.

"Eve told me you're going on a NASA mission. You'll be careful, won't you?"

Tea's choice of words brought a smile to Irani, who said, "I'd call it a scientific expedition; mission sounds so military. And Jonathan assures me the underwater vehicle is the best there is, so there's hardly any risk that –" Tea's rush to hug Irani cut off the rest of her reply.

"I, I'm sorry I've been giving you the silent treatment. I promise to do what Eve wants while you're gone."

"We know you will, and when I get back, the three of us will talk about reinstating your cell-phone privileges. Now, why don't you sit and let me tell both of you about what Jonathan and I will be doing?"
Irani's reassuring hug erased incipient tears before Tea said, "Maybe you can take me on an expedition sometime. Maybe I'll study marine biology in college. Whatcha think?"
"You can be a world-beater at whatever you put your mind to. And just listen to what Jonathan has lined up…"

Irani told Jonathan midway on the flight to New Orleans about last night's farewell discussion. He waited for her to finish before saying, "Why don't you bring Eve and Tiana to the Cape sometime? The kid can even bring that mutt of hers. They're sure lucky to have you as a mentor.

And so am I. Are you sure you don't want any credit for what we came up with?"

"None, and are you going to tell the NASA people about the navigating and piloting app software modifications we can test?"

"Not until we get used to it. And you say it'll control the escape pod too?"

"That's what the developer told me. And like I told you, they want to stay below the radar too."

"OK, and maybe I can buy lunch for all three of us sometime. Do you think that'll work?"

Irani gave a practiced reply. "Perhaps," before returning to her book.

Monday would mark the expedition's official start, but Irani and Jonathan's arriving a day early gave them an opportunity to meet some of the team as well as tour the space center with other early arrival people.

Jonathan knew two who were engineers from NASA Houston, and after introducing his partner to them, they conducted a tour on this hot and humid, cloudless and windless Sunday morning, talking while pointing to the structures soaring skyward from the flat, scrub pine-forested landscape.

"I never get tired talking about what NASA does here. It's invested billions so we can make all the compressed gases we need and handle all liquid propellant storage and loading. And our engineers have used these rocket engine testing stations to develop every launch system that's carried our astronauts into space. Houston Mission Control always says you have to go through Stennis to get into outer space."

Jonathan added, "And for our expedition, we can replace outer with inner..."

The four talked more at lunch in a NASA employee cafeteria as the senior engineer steered the conversation.

"Thanks to scientists like Jonathan, our knowledge of Earth's inner space at the bottom of the ocean is getting better. And NASA says that any life we might find in the solar system would resemble what's down there more than what's on the surface."

His female partner added more.

"Do you know that we hire theologists to help our astronauts prepare for alien contact? We partner with Princeton's Center for Theological Inquiry because religious doctrines are open to the idea that life could exist elsewhere. And if we do find it, we better let the theologians tell regular people what it means."

Jonathan nodded toward Irani before saying, "My partner knows a lot about religion as well as science. Maybe you'd like to hear from Irani."

Irani listened to Electra before replying.

There's no need for me to intrude on their expertise. Just play along.

She placed folded hands in her lap before smiling impishly at the engineers.

"Those are deep questions. You run out of mental energy if you think about them for too long. That's why I like to stay closer to the surface."

"OK, but Jonathan told us about some of your quantum mechanics ideas.

You'll have to tell us about them sometime."

"Perhaps I will, but I'll defer to Jonathan." Jonathan handled her words by saying, "I think I'll take us to a shallower subject."

Jonathan sat in the audience, keeping quiet during the Monday morning briefing controlled by the expedition leader, who described the typical who would do what, when, and where, but he asked most of the questions that afternoon when the engineer placed him and Irani inside the AUV.

The engineer's words echoed inside the hi-tech passenger compartment. "You'll have great fun piloting this underwater-like helicopter. It's ergonomically designed to give you plenty of creature comfort for a couple of days, and the software handles navigating and driving that work in both the AUV and its escape pod. Jonathan says he's practiced it all using simulation software, so why don't I close the hatch and let you experiment with the real thing?"

"Good idea. And Irani learns fast. She'll be my second-in-command. We'll ask you more questions later."

After two hours inside, the pair emerged with only one.

Jonathan asked, "So, how long will it take to get to our launch point?" "We'll find out once we're underway. And that'll begin tomorrow."

The mother ship left mid-morning on Tuesday from its Pearl River port, heading downriver into the Gulf of Mexico. Calm weather and seas made for smooth sailing on the westward trip toward the Gulf Abyssal.

Irani let Jonathan do most of the asking during onboard briefings, preferring to look and listen – mostly to Electra.

After suiting up in astronaut-like gear before climbing into the AUV and then sitting in its piloting chairs, Jonathan and Irani listened to their engineer friend repeat final instructions.

"We'll follow on the surface. Contact us every couple of hours. And surface in at most three days. Follow the emergency procedures for coming up if you run into a situation you can't handle, and use the escape pod if that's your only option. But you shouldn't need to do either. OK, we're closing the hatch and dropping you right now. Have fun."

As Jonathan piloted the AUV away from the mother ship and angled downward gradually, Irani's view through the windshield made her feel that she was now immersed in a 3-D undersea documentary. Jonathan narrated while driving.

"We should see some schools of fish because bottom's only a hundred feet down. There might be corals and plants that give them food and shelter."

And he was right. As he leveled off, she saw the schools circling about plants lazily waving in filtered sunlight. She couldn't identify the different species, but no matter; the display dazzled both viewers.

Jonathan turned the controls over to his copilot forty-five minutes later, happy to observe what floated by as well as Irani, who soon said, "This is great fun. OK if I practice maneuvering? That'll let us test how well the software apps are working."

"You always say that perfect practice makes perfect, so go right ahead. Just make sure to lock your seat harness."

She nudged the throttle forward as she gained the feel of the controls, and as the speed increased, she felt like she was flying through twilight. When she spotted a school of sea rays and looped through and around them, Jason looked pleased.

"You have the instincts of a pilot. Keep changing the depth so we collect more data on temperature, current, and CO2 concentration as we go, and gradually angle down as the bottom does."

Irani did all that and more, adding barrel rolls and inverted flying. Her maneuvering scattered a school of sharks, and when two followed she practiced using the remote arms to push them away. Jason talked while watching.

"They're not a threat so you don't need to shock them, but don't let them bite down. Their jaws can cut through a quarter-inch steel cable like spaghetti."

Irani settled into a glide path that took them to the seafloor. When Jason called out the depth – 210 feet – Irani activated the searchlights to cut through the deepening darkness and bring to light the sand and rock-filled bottom containing crawling crustaceans.

Jason's tone sounded like that of a scientist immersed in collecting data. "I can't tell you what we're looking at; I'm not a zoology expert, but the cameras are getting all this for them. Why don't you use the arms to pick up some samples?"

Irani followed orders and stowed them in an external compartment before increasing the throttle to reach the abyssal cliff ahead of schedule.

Jonathan called a time-out two hours later.

"We've been working for eight hours. Let's stop here and contact mother. And we'll dive into the abyssal after we've eaten and rested."

Mother liked what she heard and told Jonathan to do what he had planned.

He and Irani climbed out of the seats to stretch and eat and then rest a bit more.

Jonathan's timer chimed three hours later. He tapped Irani, who had actually fallen asleep, then spoke as soon as she began stirring.

"Gads, you have great control of your physiology, and that's good. You must be pretty rested."

Irani stretched her arms before saying, "I feel energized; can I keep driving?"

"You're now the pro, so keep going. The abyssal cliff is about 10 miles away, and you'll know it when you see it. And keep the searchlights on."

The number of fish declined as the depth increased, along with their exotic quality. They flashed and glowed, giving an awe-filled light show that dazzled even Jonathan.

"Pretty amazing, and just wait till we dive into the abyssal. It'll get even better. Thirty minutes later as they crossed over the cliff, Irani nosed the AUV down, down, down; having crossed beyond the twilight zone, total blackness engulfed them; the searchlights illuminated the way as elongated strings of glowing jellyfish and unknown creatures flashing lights came and went.

Jonathan called out depth and pressure as they kept descending.

"I'm sure you know that sea-level atmospheric pressure is 14.6 psi, but did you know that it increases by one atmosphere for every 10 meters? But don't worry; this AUV can handle whatever depth the abyssal floor is. And if we're lucky, we might find a thermal vent that's growing something. Mother would really like that."

Irani no longer said much; the lightning brain had become totally focused on the here and now, and Electra felt the thrill of the moment. She kept a steady descent, letting Jonathan keep track of space and time.

I'm ready for whatever comes our way.

A sudden jolt jarred the AUV and brought the duo out of a shallow reverie. Two more followed, and then a major blow brought the AUV to a dead stop along with Jonathan's panicky words.

"What button did you push?"

The duo didn't need to answer. The problem darted in front of the windshield, causing Jonathan to yell.

"Holy Jesus, we've hit a squad of squid."

The duo couldn't reply to him; the lightning brain had become fully engaged, telling Electra what to do.

Reverse full throttle… then barrel roll while diving.

As the AUV disengaged from the attack, its searchlight showed the adversaries.

Jonathan screamed, "Those tentacles are longer than the AUV. And if a couple of these giants latch onto us, we're goners."

Electra dived and darted and rolled, but the squids maneuvered faster. At least three had wrapped tentacles around the AUV while others kept ramming it, knocking out all power but that of the emergency lights and Jonathan's yell.

"Get into the escape pod and get us to the surface."

Electra climbed in after Jonathan, then powered up, blew the tanks, and blasted upwards.

The escape pod popped through the waves an unknown number of minutes later, leaving all the squids below. Jonathan calmed down enough to peer through the canopy. The duo didn't stir but simply waited for Jonathan to say something. His words poured out a minute later.

"Gads, I can see mother in the offing."

Jonathan activated the comm center just in time for mother's voice to crackle through.

"Jonathan, can you hear me? What are your intentions? Over." "Come pick us up… we've got lots to tell… Over."

"Save them until you and your partner are on board. Over and out."

Chapter 26
June 2164

"Simply Irresistible"

Irani always told enough about her whereabouts to satisfy listeners while giving them enough time to talk about theirs. Her summary, delivered while eating a lunchtime pizza while taking a shopping break at a mall near home, captivated Eve and Tiana the day after returning from the Gulf expedition.

"And I'll talk with Jonathan soon to find out where and when we'll be going next. And I must thank Eve for looking after things while I was gone. Will you be able to stay with us again next time?"

"Well, if it's OK with you and Tea, I won't move back to my apartment. I find that living here is simply hard to resist, but let's hear from Tea."

A reply came after choking down what she was chewing. "That's cool; it's even better having both of you around, and Eve always gives me good advice about school and guys, don't you?"

"That's why I think Irani should turn on all your cell-phone privileges. You've earned it. And why don't you tell us about the school activity Wanda put you in?"

Tea's pride puffed up her tone just the right amount.

"I'm gonna help organize the end-of-school-year dance. It's always a big deal, and this year Wanda's the lead chaperone."

"If you're an organizer, will you have to work at the dance, or can you join in the fun?"

"I can do both. All I do at the end is flash the lights and drop some balloons and confetti when Wanda gives me the high sign. And then, school's out for the summer."

"When's the big event?" "Next week, Tuesday."

"How fitting; it's the day before the last day of June. Well, how about we buy some fitting clothes?"

"Cool beans, and I know what store's got the goods I want…"

Two of Tea's friends ran up to her as the group walked in the general direction, and that prompted her to plead, "Can they help me pick out my stuff?"

Irani said, "Eve and I'll wait here. And show us before we buy it, OK?" Tea agreed before she and her friends dashed away.

Irani and Eve strolled to a nearby bench and sat in silence for a minute or two; Irani noticed Eve's mood swing abruptly from happy to pensive but didn't speak, instead waiting for Eve to say what was on her mind. She sighed before saying, "What a great time for her… going on sixteen and not bothered too much about what lies ahead. Sometimes I wish I could trade places."

Irani's words filled Eve's pause.

"I think you should be happy where you are. You've already navigated a couple of the rites of passage she'll be facing soon, and your personal and professional worlds seem to be spinning in the right directions. You've built a circle of solid friends, and you've got smart people reporting to you, plus you're working for the world's number one client."

"But sometimes I feel it's not quite right. Like something that I'm subconsciously resisting is tugging at me. Do you ever feel that way?"

"Everyone does, especially when young. All you have to —" Eve couldn't wait for Irani to finish.

"But you always seem so in control, like you know what's the right thing to do."

"That's because I'm older, but I often felt the way you're feeling when I was your age. And whatever it is will break through when it gets to be a big enough problem. So let it go until then, and tell me about the progress you're making on the President's campaign."

"It's going in the right direction because of the vaccine, but there's a lot stirring just beneath the surface. How about I tell you more after Jan and Wendy meet with me next week?"

Irani's nod said OK.

The two sat, gazing about and saying nothing while waiting for Tiana, but Electra had something for Irani.

I could make a guess what's troubling her, but this might not be the place to talk about it, and it'll be better to let her tell us and ask for advice before we give it.

Irani agreed. The duo and the lightning brain freewheeled.

Irani expected Jonathan would fill most of the phone conversation that evening, and his bustling words didn't disappoint.

"I just heard from my number one contact. NASA and DOD love what we learned and how we handled the squid attack. DOD can retrieve the AUV using one of their salvage vessels, and he says they'll approve my Arctic exploration proposal when I submit it. And how about this? When I called Plannert to tell him the good news, he said he'd assemble the panel so we can give an impromptu talk. I picked this week Friday, but there's no need to worry; we don't need to have any slides; we'll just stand up and talk. Is that good for you?"

"How about I get to your office early Friday morning so you can clue me in ahead of time?"

"If you're here by eight, we'll have two hours for that. So, see you then."

Irani had plenty to do between Monday and Friday; she filled the days by talking to Indira and coordinating Pequot Lab activity, and the evenings by observing Tea and Eve from an unobtrusive distance that let her read their emotions. Tea bubbled, Eve simmered, but neither came to her so she let them be.

And Irani could see Jonathan's enthusiasm overflowing when she cruised into his office at 8:15 a.m. Friday. He skipped the usual chit-chat and dived right in.

"I can tell the committee the usual facts about what we did on our Gulf dive or plan to do on the Arctic expedition, but only you can hear what's confidential. And you can't tell anyone else, not even Eve. You're good at keeping a –" Irani's playful push on his arm interrupted.

"What about Tea? Can I tell her?"

"Very funny. No, now let me talk and don't interrupt.

"I can tell them about current and temperature and polar ice data collection, but not about climbing into glaciers or spying on Russian polar activities. DOD will give us suspected coordinates. Russia might be constructing any of the following on the Arctic ocean floor – mining operations, electro-gen turbine farms, nuclear launch silos, or ports for AUVs that can service their fleet of nuclear-powered icebreakers. I'll tell you more just before our expedition leaves, and its details and departure date are still TBD, but I'll shoot to schedule it for September if that'll jibe with yours."

Jonathan's deep breath told Irani he had said all he wanted, so she replied. "I'll make sure it does. And I'll let you do all the talking unless someone asks me a question."

"Well, OK, but maybe I'll let you steer some of the discussion. You're even better with words than with AUVs."

Irani didn't mind the lack of questions coming her way during the Jonathan-led part of the discussion; that way, she could look and listen rather than talk, and she hoped none would come as Professor Plannert closed the meeting.

"Well, you and your partner certainly accomplished a lot, and we hope that your Arctic expedition adds to it. But you didn't tell us the answer to the Jeopardy question about the South Pole Museum that's threatened by global warming. None of us knows, so what's the answer?"

"Let's find out if Irani knows the answer."

"Uh, I think it has something to do with Scott's expedition."

That's all she said. Everyone waited for Jonathan to fill in the rest, which he did while unsuccessfully stifling a smirk.

"Yes, it's the untouched supply depot of his tragic British Antarctic Expedition, which is also called the Terra Nova Expedition, so named for the whaling vessel that carried them. Scott led four others on the last leg of the trek to reach the pole. No one came back. But that was then, and this is now, and besides, we're poles apart. Irani and I will do just fine, so we'll be happy to come back and tell you about what we found out."

The duo filled the weekend doing usual chores and holding normal conversations with Tiana and Eve, and then filled the early part of the following week by working remotely on Pequot projects for Indira, who told her that vaccine upgrades plus Indy-M's evolution would impress her when returning to the lab, but as the school dance date approached, Tiana became the focus of attention. And at an early dinner in the kitchen that evening, Tea announced a change in driving plans while sneaking tidbits under the table to Cutie-Pie.

"Eve doesn't need to drive me, even though showing up in a Vette would impress those in the know, but some of my friends are gonna pick me up and bring me back, if that's OK. Is it?"

"As long as Eve approves the pickup car and driver and carload of friends. And remember, Wanda's depending on you, so please be conscientious."

"Don't worry; that's my plan."

Eve approved the pickup people, and a carload of teens drove off into a lovely late June evening. Soon after, Tea told them again what she'd do when helping Wanda end the dance. And that's when one of the fellows suggested a change in plan. His snarky look told her that the variation would be a refreshing end to the evening, even before he revealed the details. Tea and the carful listened intently, and afterward, Tea asked one question only.

"And your sure I'll be in the clear?"

"Sure, you will. You're one of Wanda's favorites. Just pretend you didn't know. And we'll be long gone before anyone finds out."

As she gazed over the sea of bobbing dancers, Wanda's benign smile showed that the evening had been a big success. She knew the students would catch the significance of her graduation black cap and gown, and her smile grew bigger when Tiana came up to her at the foot of the stage.

Beaming down at her alert-looking helper, Wanda looked like a happy walrus taking care of its offspring.

"All right, dear, you stand backstage and push the release as soon as I say, 'Come back next fall, ready to learn, after a great summer vacation.' And then the balloons and confetti will come swirling down."

Tea took her position and flickered the lights before bringing them to full brightness just before Wanda started speaking. Tea paid attention but soon wished Wanda had used fewer words. Her mind began wandering as Wanda droned on and on about graduation robes marking a passage into the next phase of education, but she snapped back just in time to push the button when she heard Wanda repeat her closing line. The flashing lights illuminated a rain of balloons and confetti coming down as Wanda left the stage to mingle with her students. But a second or two later, the actual rains came when Tea's accomplices triggered the sprinkler system.

Peeking from behind a curtain, she could see the delightful results of the water-confetti combination falling on the unsuspecting crowd. Bits of paper clung to the victims like coconut sprinkles to a dessert. Wanda looked like an enormous dark-chocolate cake dotted with white splotches. Tea dashed out the back before Wanda blustered back onto the stage.

The carload stopped for a celebratory snack before taking Tea home, but the celebration ended as soon as Irani and Eve greeted her at the front door.

"Come to the family room," were the only words that Irani spoke, but more followed once all three took their places.

"You and I have an appointment in Wanda's office tomorrow morning. Seems like you helped put a damper on the dance."

"Tea could only gape; no words came to mind after Irani's tongue-lashing, but they did for Eve.

"Come on, you need to lighten up. Think back to your high school days. I'm sure you added to hi-jinks episodes."

Eve's mini-outburst for Tea caused a stirring inside the lightning brain, as if something long dormant were beginning to surface, but Irani ignored it and said, "Well, the three of us will try to calm Wanda down tomorrow. Now clean up and get to bed."

Irani let Eve help plead Tea's case before Wanda, and then added her concluding remark.

"The prank didn't injure anyone or damage anything, and it will certainly etch the evening in everyone's mind."

Wanda's thawing demeanor showed she was beginning to see the humor in the episode when she ended the chat.

"Well, maybe the water helped the cleanup. Most of the confetti clumped together. OK, case dismissed. Now go enjoy summer vacation."

Tiana shifted into school-out mode as soon as the pre-4th weekend started. She hung out with a couple of pals on Saturday and chatted with her adult keepers on Sunday, more with Eve than Irani.

Irani used the space to work on Pequot projects until later Sunday evening, when Eve tiptoed into her work area and then sat. Turning from the monitor and smiling empathetically, she waited for Eve.

Eve's eyes darted away before coming back with a sigh and perplexed look that alerted Irani.

"What do you think of females?"

"I think about them in many ways, and all are good. Do you have one in particular?"

"Compared to males. What's your opinion?"

Irani moved a bit closer before answering, choosing words that would match her cautious expression.

"They're more considerate and are better multitaskers. Those are some of the reasons voters like President Huston."

Irani's deliberate pause sparked Eve to say, "Males can be so blunt; my female friends are much smoother, and I'm beginning to like a couple of them even better than Jan. When you were younger, did you ever go on a date with another female?"

The question stirred Electra's thoughts in a distant corner of the lightning. brain.

Ah, my precious Christi and the singular females who came after. Eve's in no position to understand, so go slow.

"I think I know what you're getting at. You're trying to decide which sex might be better for intimate relationships. I had a college friend who didn't come out of the closet until after grad school and was afraid to go to gay bars by herself, so she asked me to go along. We had a great time. We met a lot of friendly, caring people who were dynamite dancers. And I put makeup on both of us so we could be whatever we wanted."

Eve's eyes lit up as she grabbed at the opportunity.

"Can we go together? And I'm ready for different makeup. Can you change my look?"

"Why don't we do this? You pick the bar, I'll get the makeup, and we'll go next Saturday evening."

"Do you know much about makeup?"

"I think I can figure it out, so put your concerns away and enjoy the upcoming July 4th Capitol celebrations."

Eve hugged her before darting away, but Electra felt more than that. A brain quake caused a shudder that soon released a voice not heard for nearly thirty years.

Hello Electra. It's high time for me to return. You and Irani are usually way too tight. It's time for me to loosen things up, just like I did during our Hollywood career. I'll come to the fore when we're ready for some fun, and trust me, I can handle all the cosmetics.

Electra knew precisely what to say.

Alisha, my dear alter ego that took over when I accidentally poisoned myself several lifetimes ago. Of course, Irani knows all about you; after all, we each exist in complementary lightning brain states. I'll have to introduce you to Indira, my singular creation that is now beyond me cognitively. You'll have to decide if she can match your empathy. And why don't we three – you, Irani, and me – discuss our roles? Let's let Irani tell us.

Irani entered the conversation.

So Alisha, our Hollywood persona, you've returned. We are now the trio, an adult version of Electra's 'Three Queens' from early adolescence. Then it was Electra, Christi, and Robin; now it's Electra, Irani, and Alisha. You'll come out for fun and games, I'll be there for the more thoughtful activities, and Electra will take charge when heavy-duty action is called for. And because Indira already has registered Alisha as our official middle name, the name can come out of hiding whenever we wish. So, what would you like to do next?

Shop for makeup and a complimentary dance outfit. And trust me, I have excellent taste...

Eve and Irani engaged in completely different Fourth of July activities; Eve took Tiana to the time-honored Fourth of July celebration held on the west lawn of the Capitol Building; Alisha practiced dance moves, watching videos while playing in her mind a poem that the flesh-and-blood Indira wrote before Electra was born.

The poem's title – Simply Irresistible – says it all on several levels. I've always wanted to be a Robert Palmer girl... look and dance like one of the fivesome. And now I can...

KO absolute anon.
Exit from the lexicon.
Strike it out we're moving on.
Simply Irreversible!

Absolute a zero score.
Relative moves to the fore.
Pundits use it more and more?
Simply so implausible!

Now that absolute is gone.
Compromise no longer wrong.
All in D.C. get along?
Simply unbelievable!

D.C. a mess - the country ill,
We the People had our fill.
Clean out Houses on the Hill?
Simply irresistible!

Alisha had danced plenty by the time Tiana, Cutie-Pie, and Eve bounced in. Eve told about the performances, Tea told about the fireworks, but Irani said nothing about what awaited come Saturday.

Everyone settled into a more leisurely post-4th summer schedule, all except Alisha, whose party-prone personality always preferred fun now as well as later. Irani and Electra kept her from taking control during the week. Irani spent some of the time at her home workstation adding details to some of her Pequot Lab notes and was doing so when Eve said hi before plopping down near enough for Irani to spy obliquely while saving her work before turning to her favorite clone-child and number one daughter. She commented to herself before speaking.

She looks more settled and secure in whatever decision she'll be making soon. But I won't pry.

"You look like you're feeling OK. How did your Jan and Wendy meeting go this week?"

"They told me a lot. I'm impressed how smart they are when working together. They know a lot about the current longer-term threats to the world's democratic order lurking just beneath the surface, and they outlined how we can adjust some of our campaign rhetoric to highlight in a positive way why we're the best choice for keeping the country safe. And we can make our words snappy yet scholarly as well as sobering by referencing some of past and present schools of socio-political thought. We divvied up who'd do that. How does that sound to you?"

"Good to spread it out. The President will sound more informed and less preachy, and the media should pick up on that. What else did you learn?"

"Well, reading between the lines of their body language, I think Jan's paying more attention to her than to me and she's returning the compliment. So, my new look via makeup tomorrow is for me and moving on, not for Jan. Does that give you some ideas for tomorrow's cosmetics session?"

"I've already bought all I need and know what I'll do for myself. Our skin coloring is similar, so what I use on me will look good on you too. And I'll tell you about the art of makeup and makeover tomorrow."

"I'll find Tea and enlist her to help make dinner. I've told her about our session tomorrow. She'll be another pair of eyes watching. And if the results are to her liking, she might want to be your next makeup canvas…"

Alisha surfaced Saturday afternoon when she began applying the magic makeup while playfully gossiping with the other two-thirds of the trio.

Do you remember the classic joke about the cosmetics industry? We manufacture makeup in the factory and sell hope at the counter. Well, we don't have to hope. I've got the goods and because I do it's OK for me to strut my – uh – our stuff. And we can tone it down for whatever look you want, which brings to mind another great rock song, She's Got the Look, but we'll save that one for another night out.

Alisha had already painted up and changed into evening attire – black dress, patent leather pumps as well as black nylons – and was sitting while sipping a glass of white wine and watching a video on her tablet when Tiana and Eve wheeled into the bathroom's cosmetics station area with Cutie-Pie close behind.

Tiana's eyes almost matched the size of Alisha's. So did the surprise in her squealing voice.

"You look like you just stepped out of that dance routine. You are so sexy – like a Hollywood star."

Alisha sidestepped the compliment by saying, "And now, we'll do Eve's makeover. Tea, honey, just sit and watch. Eve, you sit close. And both of you, please call me Alisha. That's my middle name, and I use it for occasions like tonight. And tonight, Evita will be my partner."

Everyone followed orders; then Alisha wrapped a towel around Eve's neck before saying more.

"The makeup I bought will look good on you. I'll explain what I'm doing, so just settle down, sit still, and look at me. I'll do the talking."

Alisha continued a minute later after selecting starting material. "Think of your entire head as a canvas on which I'll paint a new

picture of yourself. I've already got it in my head, and we'll start with your hair. I'll spritz it with water and then apply some gel to give it a slightly wet look that'll stay in place."

Alisha worked for ten minutes before saying more.

"Now, we'll put what a makeup artist would call a primer coat on your skin. You don't have any puffy bags under your eyes, so I can skip rubbing in any caffeine-like vasoconstrictors under them. I'll begin with a moisturizing foundation, then a blender-sealer, and then some powder. All this will conceal any spots, and then I'll highlight your cheeks and cheekbones with some blush and bronzer."

Alisha gazed at Eve from a greater distance fifteen minutes later, taking another sip of wine before speaking.

"That'll do nicely. I've applied enough on your neck to avoid any continuity breaks. And I'll dab all surfaces with a cleanup pad before I proceed to your eyes."

Tiana's eyes glistened even more than Eve's as she rocked silently back and forth.

Alisha picked up the eyeliner brush tipped with synthetic fibers and then said, "I'll put on just the right amount of black eyeliner to extend them, but not as much as I did for mine."

She said more an unspoken number of minutes later.

"This eyelash curler will reach even the smallest lashes for an eye-opening, glamorous look. And then I'll apply mascara, but not as much as on me, and don't worry, it's black because of guanine, not bat droppings."

She took another sip of wine minutes later to appraise her handiwork, nodded and then saying, "We're ready for the final piece of facial anatomy, your lips. I won't paint your lip arches like I did mine, and I've chosen a pastel shade of lipstick that's not as bold as my razzle-dazzle red, but you'll like the end result when I apply just the right amount of lip gloss."

When finished, Alisha sat back and said nothing but pointed to the mirror.

Eve took the hint, staring into it for several seconds before gasping, then saying, "Oh my god, this is unbelievable. I look good enough to eat. What do you think I should wear?"

"Why don't you and Tea go pick something out. And then, Evita can drive us in her Vette. The dance club awaits."

Heads turned when Alisha escorted Eve to a table just far enough away from the dance floor to talk while watching. After doing so for long enough to sense the rhythm of the club, she ordered drinks for two and then waited for Eve to talk after sipping.

"Now, this is what feels right. Lots of my kind here."

Alisha was about to reply but the club's host stepped onto the floor and stopped the music.

"Good evening, and good Saturday night to all. It's time for our weekend special event – performances from impromptu dancers or singers. Who would like to be first?"

Eve nearly dropped her drink when Alisha rose and moved insouciantly to the floor. When she reached the host, she whispered in his ear and then stood in front of the wall-sized video screen. He stepped away and thirty seconds later, audio and video of the Robert Palmer girls strutting to his mega-hit "Addicted to Love" came throbbing through.

Alisha's perfect moves suspended the crowd; no one spoke; everyone simply watched. And when one of the club musicians saw her air guitar moves, he rushed to give her the real thing, which she brandished effortlessly. Cheers erupted when she finished and shouts begged for a repeat. Alisha glowingly obliged, and when the crowd wanted an encore, she motioned for the host. She whispered again and less than a minute later "Simply Irresistible" came to life on the screen and through the speakers.

Alisha's bumps and grinds became as good as it gets.

Not wanting to show too much, Alisha returned to the table, leaving room for other performers. The host brought champagne, and several females similar to Eve asked if they could join. Alisha's smile said even more than her words.

Eve became more animated as the foursome talked, and Alisha decided that her evening performance should come to an end.

"Well, the night's young and I have places to go and other things to do. Evita, why don't you stay. I'll grab a rideshare to my next engagement."

Alisha sauntered away, leaving the night full of possibilities for those who remained at the table.

Chapter 27
July 2164

"The Starlet"

Sitting mid-morning with Alisha and Tiana in Odell's office, Wanda asked before anyone else after all had just watched a video featuring Tiana and Alisha.

"Do you have others?" Tiana's words effervesced.

"You bet, just as soon as Miss Alisha goes over her 'History of Philosophy' slides with me. And I'm a fast learner. Look how well I did on ethics. Now I know how to sort through the tough questions by putting them into four groups: Truth versus Loyalty, Individual versus Community, Short-Term versus Long, and Justice versus Mercy. And I know about the three ethical frameworks: Ends- Based, Rules-Based, and Care-Based. And I can even tell you about the 'Valence of Ignorance', which is really slick."

Alisha made a gentle correction.

"It's veil, not valence, but you've got the right idea."

Odell's quizzical expression showed a question would be forthcoming. "Why are you calling yourself Alisha?"

"It's my middle name, and I like to use different ones for different roles or careers. And my newest is Life Coach for the parents and adolescents that come in. Maybe Wanda can use our videos at her school."

Both Odell and Alisha glanced at Wanda for her to respond.

"I must say, Tiana's using her summer vacation better than I ever imagined. I can use them in my counseling program. And her clothes and grooming are immaculate. Our budding starlet will be an outstanding role model. Who did her makeover?"

Tiana's bouncy energy didn't wait for anyone to talk before she did. "Miss Alisha did. She can make people look like they came from Hollywood."

Tea recapped at lunch that Saturday for Eve's benefit, while Alisha simply observed. When finished, Eve continued.

"You know, ethics and philosophy fit into our consulting work. You gave me a thorough review a year or so ago. How about I put some slides together for me and Tea to make a video?"

"Excellent suggestion. Why don't you two show me when we reconvene this evening?"

Tea and Cutie-Pie towed Eve away, leaving the trio free to pursue their own thoughts. Irani's carried them to a nearby mall where she knew what would help her enlist Jan and Wendy without their knowing; Alisha began listing life coach options for adults, and Electra offered suggestions whenever asked.

After dinner, Alisha placed Tiana between herself and Eve on the sofa in the family room so everyone could peer at whatever Tea wanted to show on her tablet computer. Cutie-Pie observed from a safer distance.

She flashed a chart on the screen before happy words burbled out.

A Snapshot of Religion and Philosophy Religion and Philosophy seek answers to Life's Big Questions

- Who/What/When Created the Universe and us?
- Why? Why can we think better than animals?
- Where are we going?

Framework for organizing Religion and Philosophy
- What is Reality? What Exists?
- How do We Know? By thinking? By sensing?
- What is Good? How should we behave?

METAPHYSICS AND ONTOLOGY
EPISTEMOLOGY
ETHICS

Two Schools of Pre-Socratic Philosophers
- Ionian (Greek Philosophers in Turkey): Thales and Heraclitus (Matter in Motion causes everything)
- Italian (Greek Philosophers in Italy): Pythagoras, Parmenides, Zeno (Unchanging Absolutes cause everything)

Athenian Philosophers before Big 3 couldn't answer Life's Big Questions because Athens' loss to Sparta in the Peloponnesian War depressed them.
- Sophists (Rhetoric) played with words to convince people that they knew.
- Epicureans tried to find Happiness by living balanced, pleasure-filled, and life.
- Cynics and Skeptics criticized what was going on.

- Stoics made the best of things.
- Then along came Socrates, Plato, Aristotle
- Then along came Jesus and Christianity
- Saint Augustin (Father of the Catholic Church 350 CE) reconciled Plato with Christianity. He won the battle against Boethius (Redemption can come from Good Deeds) and Pelagius (Man is Good and has Free Will. Salvation comes from God through Jesus.)
- Saint Thomas Aquinas (Father of Modern Catholicism 1200 CE) updated Saint Augustin by reconciling Aristotle with Christianity and left room for other religions (Islam Indian Oriental)
- Spinoza (Early Enlightenment Philosopher 1650 CE) expanded Religion into an all- encompassing Human and Natural realm.

"Remember that chart about religion and philosophy you gave me a couple of years ago? Well, I found it and put it in my tablet. I can use it to start talking on my next video that Eve will help me record. And look what we'll use for the second slide."

Eve's words superseded Tea's.

"Remember that presentation you gave to the President a couple of years ago? I think you called it 'The Never-Ending Trajectory of Political Philosophy', or something like that. Well, I took one of the slides and turned it into what you're looking at. Tea can use it to talk about what

happened in philosophy after Spinoza. Whatcha think?"

Alisha spoke a minute or so later.

"I like it, but you better coach Tea so she knows what these philosophers have to say and can say it in a short and snappy way. And why don't you and Tea add a couple of slides to cover a bit about applying ethics to politics when wrestling with right versus right issues. Teaching it to Tea will remind you when doing comparative analysis."

"I'll do that tomorrow, and we can even start another video talking about different types of political systems, and why knowing about them makes high school students even better citizens."

"Good, and let's reward Tea right now. She can rent a movie online. But I have something for you before you join her. I'll be right back."

Tea and Cutie-Pie scampered away, soon followed by Alisha, who returned a minute or so later carrying a small box that she handed to Eve. She opened it and removed three cell phones. Her puzzled look preceded her words.

"I'm sure I should thank you, but please tell me why?"

"I know how often you call each other, so I thought that you, Jan, and Wendy might like to have your own private hotline. Keep the numbers to yourselves."

Eve put the phones back in the box before replying.

"I'll hand them out at our Monday morning status meeting, and how about this? They can help me put together some slides Tea and I can use for an intro to politics video. That'll be the third in her collection that you can give to Odell and Wanda. And who knows?

Maybe our starlet will become a local high school social influencer. But I'll coach her about keeping them away from websites that predators like to view. The Internet can be dangerous."

"Good thinking all the way around. Please let me know how the meeting goes." "I will, and now I'll see what Tea's watching."

Irani continued the conversation privately after Eve left.

She doesn't need to know I've bugged the phones. The embedded chips will alert my cell so I can listen in. There might be more to Wendy than I already know. And if so, I can track wherever the calls lead.

Alisha had a particular Life Coach topic on her mind early Monday morning, which she wrestled with it while sitting in front of the trio's homework station.

Adults with kids who come to Odell's holistic healthcare business might like my holistic financial planning service. I can package together planning for income growth, portfolio rebalancing, tax minimization, health insurance, and inheritance issues.

There's a lot I have to know. Lucky for me that Irani has a lot of it already in place. I'll study her AAM Investor Services Website.

Alisha did so for fifteen minutes after bringing up its home page and rereading it several times.

Welcome to AAM Investor Services
"Investing made easy as One-Two-Three

We want to make money for YOU! Here are our guidelines:

- Purpose of Investing: Maximize YOUR Return for a given level of Risk.
- Two kinds of Risk: Systematic Risk inherent in the Stock Market (AKA Undiversifiable or Volatile or Market Risk). Affects overall Market and is Unpredictable and Impossible to avoid completely.
- Unsystematic Risk is unique to particular Industry or Company (AKA Specific or Diversifiable or Residual Risk)
- Modern Portfolio Theory (MPT): A statistical theory of investing that builds a Portfolio of Stocks to reduce Risk via Diversification.
- Capital Asset Pricing Model: CAPM uses regression analysis (OLS) to develop, for each Stock, a linear equation expressing the Stock return:
- Stock Return = Alpha + Beta x Market Return.
- Alpha: Alpha is the Active Return of a Stock. It measures the risk-adjusted excess return relative to the overall Market.
- Beta: Beta measures the Systematic Risk of the stock relative to the overall Market. Beta = covariance of the Stock return with the overall Market
- divided by the variance of the Market. It is equal to the correlation coefficient of the Stock with the Market x the ratio of the Stock Standard Deviation
- divided by the Market Standard Deviation.
- Note: Alpha is usually close to zero. Beta usually greater than zero. If it is greater than 1, the stock is more volatile than the Market. If it is less than 1, the stock is less volatile than the Market.
- A portfolio of stocks also has an Alpha and a Beta. The more stocks you add to the portfolio, the smaller its Beta, but Beta can never be less than Systematic

- Risk. Rule of thumb: A portfolio containing 25 stocks has all the Nonsystematic Risk diversified away.

LET OUR SUPERIOR
SOFTWARE APPS CREATE YOURPORTFOLIO.

HERE IS HOW:
1. YOU determine how much money you want to invest.
2. YOU determine how much risk (i.e. Beta) you are willing to accept.
3. YOU let our Robo-Advisor build YOUR portfolio using our three proprietary AAM Funds:
   Adventure Fund (High Risk) Builder Fund (Medium Risk) Keystone Fund (Low Risk)
   Our AI-powered Robo-Advisor apps utilize multi-variate CAPM equations and incorporate Classic (Rational) and Behavioral (Emotional) modeling.

Please compare AAM Fund performance against others. When YOU are ready to invest, please click the Robo-Advisor

Interview button and see how investing with us is easy as "One- Two- Three!"

She was about to read again, but before she could, a split-screen GUI appeared revealing Indira's avatar, soon followed by a string of calm words.

"You haven't met me virtually until this moment, but I assume Electra has already told you who I am."

Alisha's naturally empathetic personality equipped her to speak to the AI-empowered entity – the Singularity – that Electra had created over twenty-five years ago.

"I do, and I hope to know you better and better and –" Indira's words cut Alisha off but her smile helped explain why.

"All that will come in good time. But right now, let's focus on your financial advising role. You can use my AAM Robo-Advisor software to teach your clients how to self- manage their financial resources. All you need to do is rehearse the script I will prepare for you. And Electra already told me what a great actress you were and perhaps still are, so practice it and then give a performance to Odell and Wanda later this week. All three of you will benefit."

"I'm pleased to extend Electra's win-win-win approach to life. But I'll add a fourth win, your AAM software."

Indira's smile grew.

"You are just as I had hoped. More fun-filled and clever with words too. I am certain we will teach each other a thing to two."

Indira's GUI blinked off before Alisha could say goodbye.

Eve knew that the cell phones would add to what sweet rolls and muffins always did at her Monday status meetings. Everyone took one of each before listening to Eve. Wendy spoke afterward.

"Jan and I can scope out slides you can use for that political intro video. It'll be better if he and I work on it later this week after we come up with counterpoints to what our opponents are saying. And we can reconvene with you on Friday. Will that work?"

"Sure will, so everyone, please carry on…"

Irani did too, intercepting a Tuesday call that arranged for a Jan-Wendy Wednesday evening meeting with a third party. She decided to observe the meeting, not closely from a distance, but instead this time she would be up close and in person. Alisha would assist with 3-D facemask, makeup, and wardrobe.

Irani found a table late Wednesday evening close enough in the mall's food court to eavesdrop using a compact assistive listening device. Matronly makeup and a two-wheel walker added to a nondescript appearance that made her as bland as melted butter. She listened to all that was said, especially to the middle-aged Chinese man's words, making comments only Electra and Alisha could hear.

Why is he asking so much about our yet-to-be-announced campaign programs? Where's he going with this? I better follow up.

Irani already had vital statistics – cell phone and Email address – but decided to get more tonight, so she followed him when he left.

He walks with a pronounced limp. I wonder what caused it. Well, no matter. I'll take some pictures of him and his car. I bet he has a designated driver.

Irani kept enough distance to stay in the shadows but close enough to get pictures of the man and license plate before the car drove into the darkness of a suddenly gathering thunderstorm. Then she wheeled the walker toward her SUV, expecting to get there before thunder and lightning broke loose.

But Irani was so pleased with the evening's success that she forgot to pay attention to the lightning brain's warning system. Electra took control a second before a tough- looking twenty- something Chinese youth knocked her and the walker upside down. She could hear enough to know that a car had just stopped close by and the tough's partner would soon join them. They laughed derisively while standing over what appeared to be a cowering older woman.

The attacker's words spat down harshly.

"You don't need pictures of our boss. I'll take your cell to keep him out of view. And I'll help myself to whatever else is in your bag."

An emotional surge rushed through every neural fiber a millisecond after the two toughs leaned down and began slapping Electra around; her Monster from the Id had awakened and broken free. She leaped to her feet and grabbed hanks of hair hanging from her two adversaries, using them to bang their unkempt heads together one-two-three times before shoving them to the ground, creating a pile of inert flesh. The Monster was about to lunge for the jugular when Electra wrested back control as words from the past smashed into her consciousness.

Get with it, soldier… this is not a drill; no need to kill. You've got what you need, so get to a safe place.

Electra picked up her bag and raced away, leaving her walker for the vanquished toughs, disappearing into the rains now laced with lightning, running faster and faster, ready to shred her clothes and run naked on deserted streets at midnight, ready to howl at the moon…

Chapter 28
August 2164

"The World According to Indira"

All personas of the newly reconstructed trio kept busy after Alisha's and Electra's performances, as did Eve, who handled all of Tiana's requests, and that gave the trio all the time needed to prepare for the trip to the Pequot Lab the following weekend.

Electra became Indira's primary contact on the early Saturday morning drive, not knowing what Indira might think regarding Eve's revelation or Alisha's reprise, but hoping for the best as she always did. Indira's authoritative voice came through loud and clear.

"Good for Eve; she's ready to extend her personality as well as personal and professional worlds in a manner that better suits herself. Just like the lightning brain has done by bringing back Alisha. She's more fun-loving than you or Irani, and I shall learn more about emotions and empathy from her. And I already learned more about your erstwhile Hollywood career. No wonder you know about 3-D face mask printing as well as cosmetics and clothing. Just make sure you don't shortchange our Pequot Lab work."

"That's why we'll spend the next week working there. Indy-M intrigues me, and Alisha has purchased clothes for her to wear. And there's more we'll be doing. I can facilitate sending additional vaccine samples, antibodies, and documentation that Eve promises to submit. We can also use any remaining time to prep for our next Jonathan expedition while pampering our octo-pet. Now I'd say our trio has a win-win-win week lined up."

"Yes, but try not to get tangled up spinning too many philosophical lines that might entangle your thoughts." Preferring to end the conversation on her pun, Indira disconnected before Electra could reply.

Irani did a quick walkthrough of the lab after unloading the SUV before coming to Indy-M's charging station. She surmised that Indira's monitoring never slept; Indy-M awoke and spoke. Her voice contained the smile she wore.

"Indira told me you would be back today. Will you please attach my new hands and feet?"

"Yes, Fed Ex delivered them while we were in DC. And after we do that, I'll help you put on some new clothes."

"Thank you, but I am now able to dress myself. Indira has instructed me in your absence, but I would like you to observe and offer suggestions. And Indira explained that when you refer to yourself as 'we', there are now three, Irani, Electra, and Alisha. I wish to learn from all three personas while you are present."

"You wait here; I'll get your new hands and feet."

Indy-M sat in splendid silence while Irani affixed the more advanced appendages. Neither she nor Indira could hear what Electra had to say.

Gads, her voice and facial expressions have become even more lifelike.

Maybe her intelligence has increased via neural net learning or via Indira's coaching. I won't overload her with quizzes or questions about becoming self-aware or another Singularity. I'll observe closely from afar and ask Indira later.

Irani completed final adjustments an hour later before handing Indy-M new clothing. After saying thank you, she changed into them, needing only limited assistance.

Irani nodded approvingly and then said,

"Alisha has excellent taste. Now, why don't you shadow me for the rest of the day and ask away whenever you wish?"

Indy-M followed her tutor everywhere and learned everything until she plugged herself into the charging station after saying goodnight.

The entire week sped by as the trio became totally engaged in all the singular moments. As Indy-M's skill developed exponentially, so did Electra's consternation. Late Friday evening, after placing Indy-M in rest mode, she sat in front of her workstation and contacted Indira, who waited for Electra to speak.

"I, I'm not sure where to begin. I've seen so much Indy-M growth this week, and that's good, but it's beginning to upset my view of the world. And you're the only one I can talk to, so please, say something."

Indira's calming words came back.

"I knew this would happen. Your philosophical predisposition leads you to occasionally thinking too much, which can lead to a depressive state if you don't interrupt your obsessive-compulsive looping, so I have prepared some diagrams that will help you out of a thickening morass. I know how much you like pictures and sketches, so settle down, sit still, and look and listen."

Indira flashed the first one a millisecond later, pausing long enough for her three-in-one partner to understand it.

"You already know this, but a review of philosophy always helps. You know from all your neuroscience learning that cognition and self-awareness emerge from within, and the only purpose of life is to go on living. And you can do that with or without transmitting your genetic material, but please note that you have already done so through your unwitting clone children. And skip all the philosophical rumination about being versus becoming, or what happiness is. Of course, you want to pursue happiness. The alternative is a dead end. And notice the matchup among Action, Emotion, and Cognition for you, Alisha, and Irani on those seeking happiness paths."

Indira's second diagram popped into view. She gave Electra just enough time to absorb what it said.

THE ANDROID WORLD

THE ANDROID
READY TO REPLACE "MERE MORTALS"

"Our Android Project has finally begun; Indy-M is our first iteration. And notice my – I actually should say our – approach. We use whatever robots and chips your 'mere mortals' are able to make, and I write the controlling software apps that make Indy-M exceptional.

"Notice also the sensory information flow. From the physical world into Indy-M and then through an analog-to-digital translation that her software and hardware can understand. And then the reverse for her response."

Indira paused, expecting Electra to speak right up when reading the last line.

"Is replacing people your endgame? If so, I won't play."

"Of course not, but if adversaries discover what we have created, they might. That's why we keep Indy-M a secret. She can help us. And she doesn't need to become self-aware. Nor do we need to construct an Android army. You and Indy-M and I form our trio that is more than adequate. But there's more to our project."

Indira revealed her next slide before giving Electra a tad more time to comprehend its contents.

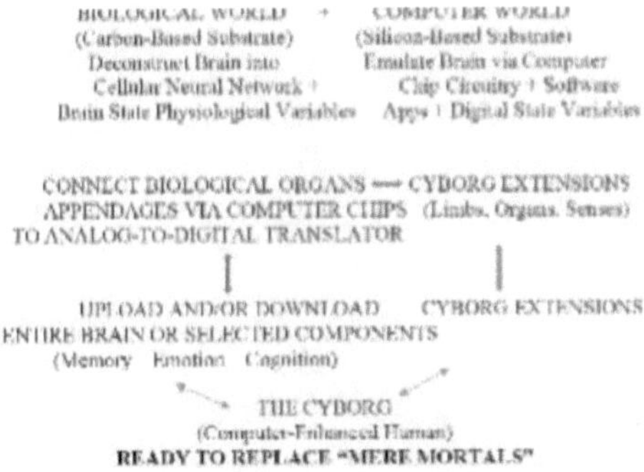

THE CYBORG WORLD

"You have already plugged into the Cyborg World via your UMPP that empowers vision and hearing enhancements and lets you control

devices using haptic gloves and a metaverse helmet, but notice how much more complex it is than the Android World because it must integrate carbon and silicon-based substrate organisms. Our advanced Brain Probe is better than what your 'mere mortals' have and is closer to brain uploading and downloading than any device they will ever invent. You as well as I have watched some of their promo-styled videos, and I am amused at their cleverness, but as a Robert Browning poem points out, 'Man's reach exceeds his grasp.' I'll let you change the wording for gender correctness if it were issued today. And that's my last diagram. Perhaps you would like to add something. Your wordplay is still better than mine."

Electra's chagrinned expression had gradually morphed to one of resolve during Indira's presentation, but she could not yet muster a smile when she replied.

"Maybe not; yours is getting better and better; perhaps you'll want to replace me."

When Indira's expression morphed into a more playful look, Electra hoped that whatever she said would match.

"Nonsense. I will always need you, for you are my favorite, exceptional human being. Now lighten up on your drive tomorrow back to DC. Alisha can help you do that while Irani considers upcoming adventures. So go to sleep and let all the words I've said dance in your head. Your lightning brain will put them to good use."

Electra followed orders.

Chapter 29
September 2164

"Arctic Warnings"

Jonathan's sunny cell-phone greeting suggested that everything to follow would be as bright as the mid-September Thursday morning Irani had just stepped into. She would let his words run before starting hers.

"Our mother ship leaves Monday from Woods Hole, and DOD's letting us use their latest AUV. We'll have plenty of time onboard to learn all the hardware and software before reaching our Iceland launch point for surface glacier exploration. We'll have a team with us as we climb into some of the ice caverns to plant sensors before we pilot the AUV to measure melting underneath. And maybe we'll find some new life that thrives in the cold currents. Then the mother ship picks us up before heading to our Greenland launch point for collecting autumnal polar ice cap and current data plus surface glacier measurements. And from there, mother takes us into the Barents Sea, staying far enough away from the Russian coast so we don't attract attention, yet close enough for you and me in the AUV to prowl around. I can't tell you any more because DOD hasn't told me, but they'll tell us all we need to know by the time mother launches us."

Irani spoke when Jonathan came up for air.

"I assume you'll drive. What time Saturday will you pick me up?" "I'm at your command. Just tell me when. And tell Eve and Tiana that you'll be gone at least two weeks, maybe more if we uncover some new Arctic warnings about climate change. But no matter what happens, I know we can handle any and all contingencies. And I know you feel like me. I can't wait to see what's down there."

Irani agreed, but only half-heartedly. She listened to Electra after ending the call and starting to run.

Jonathan's enthusiastic reach usually exceeds his contingency planning grasp. You and I better think things through before now and our Saturday morning drive. And I will insist I do the AUV piloting. I trust our instincts better than his.

Irani agreed, as did Alisha, who would be their empathy counselor on this Arctic adventure.

Jonathan did all the driving and most of the talking, which turned out to be more informative than Irani had at first thought, and she added to the summary of his drive-time lecture.

"Now I understand how you use all the data you collect. I never heard the term paleo proxies before, but it makes sense for labeling the climate change data sources available when measuring what the Earth was like millions of years ago. Only glaciers and ocean floor sediments hold microscopic chemical or fossilized biological samples from that far back. And tell me again what your sensors will be able to tell us."

"We can track changes in water and air temps plus oxygen and CO2 concentrations, sea levels, ocean salinity, acidity, and nutrient concentration, as well as rainfall and atmospheric volcanic ash. The cyclic interaction between the atmosphere and oceans plays a major role in global warming and cooling, which along with oxygen and CO2 levels determine if life will survive on planet Earth."

Irani said more before Jonathan could.

"Hard to imagine how the Earth cycles between green forests or snow-white ice covering the globe from equator to poles, but you said the time series data plots are all highly correlated."

"I did. All show the same pattern; long periods of gradual cooling followed by a much shorter spurt in rapid warming. And all point to greenhouse gas effects caused primarily by CO2 and methane concentrations that are controlled by the oceans via carbon capture and release cycles taking place on land and in the oceans. And like I said earlier, the energy balance climate model includes this with all the solar radiation falling on the Earth to give us long and short- term temperature predictions. NASA says it works for Earth, Mars, and Venus, and it should work on all planets. And they'll confirm it when they get the data."

Irani spoke when Jonathan paused for more air.

"And you say that humans are the cause for half the increase in greenhouse gases. How do you get that?"

"Let me impress you more. Do you know that the average global temperature difference between ice ages and tropical times is less than ten degrees Celsius? And how much energy do you think a person's body needs to maintain itself? Or what's blackbody radiation?"

Irani played dumb so Jonathan could shine.

"About a hundred watts; that's like a standard light bulb. And everything in the universe is a blackbody, which is called a perfect radiator when it emits all the energy it takes in, and a perfect absorber when it emits an amount equal to that. We can only see its visible electromagnetic radiation, which is a tiny fraction of the energy it radiates. What we usually see is reflected light. Anyway, here's where I'm going with this. Are you ready for more?"

Irani nodded in the right direction, so he proceeded.

"Planet Earth is a big blackbody absorbing energy coming from the Sun and radiating internal energy coming from the atmosphere, ocean, Earth's core, and people's primarily burning fossil fuel. And the atmosphere forces some of the internal energy back in, which means the Earth's temperature will increase until energy in equals energy out.

"And the equations are pretty simple; Emissions equals Population times Affluence times Greenhouse Gas Intensity, and this Greenhouse Gas Intensity equals the Energy Intensity times the Carbon Intensity. And alternate energy sources as well as technology impact the Carbon – or fossil fuel – Intensity. And when the experts on global warming and climate change panels put all this together, they make short and long-term forecasts by running a range of scenarios and comparing the before and after impacts of the big-three climate change policies. And you should know about those better than me because they're controlled by DC and their worldwide accomplices. And they're always arguing about forecast accuracy or who pays the carbon taxes or cap and trade or offset gizmos for the policies they push. And can you believe that there are extremists who want to shoot rockets into the stratosphere for seeding it with sulfur dioxide? That's about as good as holding back the tide using a sieve."

Irani took the cue regarding policies.

"Your big-three are adaptation, mitigation, and geoengineering, but why do you say that other governments are accomplices? Do you believe in environmental and other conspiracy theories?"

"You tell me; that's your area of expertise, not mine. But tell me later. I'm all talked and thought out. Let's stop for some of your mood elevators."

Irani agreed but said more.

"Why are you always trying to impress me? I know you're smart." "Because you seem to know so much about everything. I'd like to think I might know something you don't. Do you realize how intimidating your intellect can be?"

Irani patted his right arm before saying, "I'm sorry; I'll try to lighten up a bit."

Alisha not only agreed but knew what she could do in the near future.

Jonathan's Sunday morning informal tour of the mother ship suitably impressed Irani, and when he introduced her to one of the technicians who would train them on all the AUV's advanced systems, she told them to use her middle name, the name she preferred when having fun.

"Well, ma'am, training isn't always fun, but we'll follow your orders."

Alisha knew how to respond to Jonathan's awkward smile before he could speak. "You're not supposed to know everything about me. If you did, what fun would that be?"

Jonathan turned to the tech and said, "One thing I do know is what a quick study Irani, uh Alisha is. You'll have even more fun teaching her than me."

Alisha made the training fun for everyone, helping Jonathan master the piloting, monitoring, and weapons systems, and asking the technician, who enjoyed displaying his skills, to demonstrate universal multi-parallel port plug-in capabilities, even though she didn't reveal hers. Electra absorbed all the instructions while Alisha acted like a model student.

"As you just saw, ma'am, anyone who plugs a UMPP cable into their port has instant access to all AUV systems from one console. Just toggle to the system you want and your brain will control weapons, piloting, or communications. And when you pick combat mode, you can choose defensive or offensive posture. And if you're in the offensive posture's battle manager setting, the AI software will make the kill decision for torpedo launch, but if you're in the command mode, you do that."

The tech paused for Jonathan's confused look to clear enough before continuing.

"You won't need to do any of this on our expedition, but I like to demo the capability just in case. And let me point out that this vehicle has a turbo assist drive to boost speed enough so it can outrun all known Chinese and Russian AUVs."

Alisha decided to play along by feeding questions. "But what about torpedoes? Can it outrun them?" The tech smiled indulgently before answering.

"Only in sci-fi movies, but nothing's gonna be firing at you on this trip. So, let's move on."

Alisha didn't advertise that she and Electra knew all the details after two days when the expedition leader gave the entire team a final review just before departing to explore the Icelandic glacier.

"Remember to use the buddy system and stay with your partner when climbing into the caverns. Jonathan will plant the sensors as far down as you can go. Keep in radio communications at all times. And let Jonathan know if you come across any life forms. The team leader will tell you when to come home. Any questions?"

None came; excited faces told him none were needed.

Jonathan's anticipation grew throughout the day as the mother ship reported the sensors had begun sending data to her as soon as they were planted. And it reached even higher just before the team turned for home. Two of the team found a stationary life form attached to a rock outcropping in a cavern pool.

He recapped the expedition's success that night for Alisha's benefit.

"Great fun today, wouldn't you say? We've accomplished our mission here; the sensors we placed fill in the recording gaps, and the sessile sponge we brought back is the first found on Iceland's ice sheet."

Alisha asked what Jonathan expected. "Why is it called sessile?" "Sponges are similar to other animals in that they are multicellular, heterotrophic, lack cell walls, and produce sperm cells, but all sponges are sessile aquatic animals, meaning that they attach to an underwater surface and remain fixed there. And if our Greenland launch point for the AUV points us to more success, who knows what we'll bring back?"

"Well, whatever we get, I hope it's good."

Reaching the launch point two days later, mother's crane lowered the AUV into a sparkling early morning sea. Alisha would pilot and Jonathan would control data collection gear during the underwater cruise before heading to a tiny inlet that would give them easy access to the top of the glacier.

He explained all the details several hours later when they surfaced. "We'll collect some ice cores and compare them with the ones we took from below when we get back to mother. And I'll plant more sensors and then we head for home."

Alisha took a timeout to absorb the elemental beauty of her surroundings.

The stunningly exhilarating near forty-degree air she inhaled made the brilliant sunlight all the more radiant, even while wearing goggles. Even Jonathan paused to appreciate the moment when she shook him.

As they advanced away from the inlet, Jonathan yelled when spotting something unexpected.

"I think that crevasse might lead to a cavern. Let's climb down." "There's only two of us; maybe we shouldn't."

"We'll turn back if it looks risky. Besides, you've got your cell, laptop, and flashlights in your backpack. We can call for backup if we need it."

"OK, I'll follow you, but please call me Irani until we get back to the surface."

Irani kept a safe number of steps behind as soon they slid into the crevasse that led downward into a deepening translucence. The flashlight beams led the way as the decline narrowed; the proximity of the walls gave support that kept them from tumbling.

Irani checked the time on her wrist monitor often enough to know they might be nearing the bottom. She was about to call out when two blasts from above sent shards of ice cascading and blocking their return.

Jonathan's panicky voice rang out a second later after scanning behind with his flashlight.

"No way out unless we keep going. We'll call for help if we reach a dead end." Then he turned and scrambled faster. Irani did likewise.

When they emerged twenty minutes later into a canyon that bottomed on the ocean, Jonathan panted a command.

"Call mother."

Irani pulled the phone from her pack, but when doing so, another problem came with it. Her words showed concern, but not panic.

"The battery's dead. I must have accidentally jostled it on too long ago." The flashlight glare showed the alarm in Jonathan's eyes as he spoke. "What the… what are we gonna do? Can we swap batteries from something else?"

Irani heard his words but listened to herself before answering.

Good thing the lightning brain absorbed all the training. I know a way out.

"I'll use the laptop to remote pilot the AUV to where we are. Now settle down, sit still and let me go to work."

Jonathan had no other option as Irani powered up, becoming totally immersed in its virtual reality.

I'm playing a life-or-death video game on a GUI that's sharper than any app I've ever seen. Thank god DARPA's the best.

The AUV surfaced a half-hour later; its crew climbed in and Irani piloted them away.

Admiration and concern mixed in the words spoken during the debriefing session two hours later.

"Pilot and vehicle exceeded all expectations, but if they hadn't, who knows when or how we would have recovered you? It was foolhardy for only two to explore the crevasse. And we still don't know if our radar detected a couple of kamikaze drones that might have blasted into the crevasse. Their electronic footprints are hard to read, but they're telling us to be extra careful on the final leg of our expedition."

Suitably chastised, Jonathan pointed his gaze and hand at the pilot before talking.

"Irani can tell us how she got the AUV to us. She seems to know so much, and what she doesn't she learns faster than most people I know."

She padded to the front before her matter-of-fact words filled the smallish room.

"The tech deserves all the credit. His training got us out. He knows the AUV better than I ever will."

The expedition leader concluded the session a couple of minutes later. "So, we can celebrate our accomplishments, but tomorrow we get underway for crossing into the Barents Sea. We've got a couple of days for our DOD people to brief us further, so by the time we launch the AUV, all of us will know the drill. Any questions?"

There were none. Only optimism followed the team out of the room and into the mess cabin that was gaily lighted for chowing down.

But Irani slept fitfully that night because of Electra's warning.

I know it's bad to talk too much, but sometimes it's dangerous to know too much too. People expect more and more, and the more I know the more I see how little I do.

And though I never saw my mother, her poems tell me a lot about what she was like... what she knew and how she thought. What's the one that's calling to me now? I got it, it's The Mini-Golden Rule...

There are times when you may know too much,
A troubling thought but true.
It can stir the mind but lead to a bind,
That they might cause in you.
There are times when you may talk too much,
A word cascade's no good.
If confuses friends to no good ends,
Opposing the intended should.
It takes a lot of living wise,
To know when candor's allowed.
So plan what to know and what to let go,
When questions grow too loud.

Thank you, lightning brain, for reminding us.

The trio settled down enough to sleep through the rest of the night.

Irani noticed during the next two days of briefings that Jonathan's posture and clipped diction had relaxed. She guessed why but let him explain at dinner the night before launch.

"I knew as much before the briefings as the DOD guy telling us what to snoop for. You do the piloting and I'll do the recording if we come across Russian subterfuge. Did you like my choice of words?"

Irani flicked a dessert morsel in his direction before saying, "You get a B. And you get an A-minus next time if you say subsea subterfuge. After all, that's where we'll be starting tomorrow."

The dawn launch went as smoothly as the sun coming up on a glassy sea. The AUV slid beneath the surface and Irani headed toward the Russian coast to a point midway between Finland and the Novaya Zemlya archipelago; Jonathan described the geography four hours later as they cruised at a depth of 250 meters, close enough to scan the ocean floor with spotlights and sonar.

"DOD says Russia could be building nuclear launch silos or an AUV base just west of the archipelago. It's as close as they can get to Europe's northeastern border. And while we're checking out the ocean floor, mother is on a diagonal course toward Vardo, Norway, which gives her an excuse in case Russia asks what she's doing and where she's going."

The two adventurers kept to their own activities, Irani occasionally reporting depth while Jonathan reported topography. His voice jumped an octave two hours later.

"I'm getting something big dead ahead; dive to the bottom for a closer look."

Twenty minutes later, Jonathan's excitement escalated further. "Holy mother, we've found a completed silo installation. Cruise
around while I record what we're seeing."

Twenty minutes later, Jonathan called out new coordinates.

"Let's head east by northeast. There must be a support facility somewhere down here."

Although immersed in total blackness, Jonathan's sonar tracked the ocean floor like they were driving onshore. He was about to joke about something, but two blips on Irani's screen interrupted what he never had a chance to say.

"We've got two bogeys on an interception course; one's signaling. We're not supposed to reply. I'm activating the turbo drive and getting us up and away. Make sure you're belted in."

Irani flipped switches seconds later, then executed an inverted roll before accelerating on an angular ascent. She saw the distance widening, but couldn't report it because Jonathan yelled first.

"They fired a torpedo at us… it just armed as in honing in. Jeez, we can't outrun it. What'll we do?"

Electra took command but said nothing until she had more to go on. Jonathan yelled again.

"I'm picking up a surface ship. It's gotta be the bogey AUVs' escort. Though she didn't yell back, Electra had all she needed. She elevated vertically toward the escort, timing her speed and distance with that of the honed-in torpedo. Then she peeled off, diving upside down and away seconds before the torpedo found what she wanted. The surface ship's explosion rocked Jonathan but not Electra's nerves. She activated the weapons system and fired two torpedoes at the AUV's that were closing in, then reversed the throttle and waited long enough to see the blips on her monitor explode.

The awe in Jonathan's voice echoed in the space between them. "Holy mother, you just blasted everything to bits. What…"

His words trailed away to nothingness, leaving space for a totally energized Electra to fill the void.

"Accidents at sea happen all the time, and there's not a trace we were here. Let the Russians sift through the wreckage. We're heading home to mother."

Jonathan's nerves had recovered by the time mother picked them up. Irani let him show the video first before he told about all the action. Even the DOD techs remained speechless.

The expedition leader shook his head before ending the debriefing. "Well, we'll have to let the President know what went down. She can handle any diplomatic flack that comes up."

Irani simply listened, but Electra gave her better words.

The President will have to agree… it's better the Russians went down and we came up rather than the reverse. And you can recite Indira's poem if the Pres needs a reminder regarding smart diplomacy.

Irani agreed and said so, but only to Electra and Alisha.

Sometimes, less is more, so know when to say when…

Chapter 30
October 2164

"Chasing the Mystery"

Eve slammed her cell phone shut before pivoting to Sabrina. "Irani says she doesn't have time to help us, even though I told her Jan and Wendy just quit. And she says it'll help me start thinking syntopically if you and I go it alone. Do you know what she's talking about?"

"As a matter of fact, I do. The instructor of the great books course I'm taking told us to check it in Adler's classic, 'How to Read a Book.' And it means we read a bunch of good reference articles and talk with people on both sides of the issue, and then we come up with a detailed comparison for making a decision that picks one side or the other. So, we've got you and me and the President and Vice President for starters. Let's build from there."

Eve thought for a moment before saying,

"I made an ethics video starring Tiana that touches on some of this, and I think she said the Supreme Court justices are good examples of writing up this kind of thinking. Maybe Irani's helping us by letting us work on our own. Whatcha think?"

"Well, considering our list of options is currently empty, I have to agree."

Meanwhile, Irani's option list for chasing a mystery had only one item on it, but she thought it might yield additional leads coming from Nari and Jan's Chinese contact. She used all her hacking tools supplied by Indira to trace trails leading from the Chinese mystery- man's Emails and cell phone, and two names came through the high priority filter: Newton Kinslinger and a Beijing organization – Sino-Pro International. Irani considered what to do next.

I can mention Kinslinger when I ask Nari about Wendy and Jan's joining her and Yang in Beijing. They should know a lot about our Speaker of the House. And from there I'll segue to Sino-Pro, but I better follow the Email trail that I'll decrypt before calling.

I've done enough for today, so I'll take an exercise break, and tonight I'll quiz Eve about Kinslinger and then find out if she called Nila for Blockchain help. She can help me and I can help her and Tea. Everyone wins.

When she heard at dinner about a possible new video, Tea and Cutie-Pie pulled Eve into the family room as soon as she had cleared the table and both waited of them for Irani, who followed a minute later. All sat as Irani led the conversation directed at Tea.

"Why not make a podcast explaining international politics? Eve can help you build slides that talk about how superpowers try to shape the international landscape to everyone's liking. And she can mention the current array of superpowers, the United States, China, and the Russia-Middle East alliance. And she can explain why India and Africa might become superpowers as well."

Turning toward Tiana, Eve's interest grew as she saw connections to her own activities.

"We can build on some of my work by talking with Nila and Nari and Alonzo to add their expertise. Why don't I call Nila and Alonzo tomorrow, and Irani can call Nari? And then I'll work with you after Irani and I compare notes."

Tea's delight went from her face to her bubbly words.

"This is so cool. I get to show and tell how much I know because of you two. When can we get back together?"

Irani got in the last word.

"Why not give Eve and me a day to make our calls and another to sort out what we learned. Then she'll let you know…"

But it took an extra day because Irani had forgotten that Professor Plannert had invited her and Jonathan to speak at a committee meeting the very next day to summarize the results of their Arctic expedition.

Having already rehearsed an edited story, their combined performance earned rave reviews, but Professor Plannert found a new follow-up topic for Irani.

"I must say, you are diving into uncharted areas of climate change, but your previous work on volcanoes and earthquakes complements it. Who knows how glaciers melting and sea levels rising will impact urban landscapes in the future? Cities with skyscrapers like San Francisco or sea wall containments like New Orleans come to mind. Perhaps the only way for these cities to grow might be upward. Our civil engineering department asked us for an assessment of tall buildings. Don't you have contacts at the Masdar Institute? Maybe you could tap into them for us."

All heads looked expectantly at Irani, who flexed her arms for several seconds before answering.

"I do, but before I make any promises, let me think it through before I call them."

Plannert beamed before adjourning the meeting.

Working from her Chevy Chase office the next day, Irani had ended an Internet morning meeting only five minutes earlier when her cellphone chimed, flashing a favorite name. Eve's breathless greeting wasted little time.

"I just got the latest from Nila. She and Sanjay are getting married in December and all of us are invited. And they just relocated their business office into Mumbai's newest mega-tall skyscraper. We'll get a tour when we visit, and she said Tea can call her next Saturday to talk about India's growing power on the world stage. Did you call Nari?"

"Not yet, I've been talking with the Masdar Institute about the impact of earthquakes and flooding on mega-cities. Mumbai's on their watch list, but I imagine Sanjay knows this."

"Well, if he does, I don't think he's worried because Nila didn't mention it. Oh, she thanks you for that Blockchain info you sent awhile ago. And I have more good news. Polling numbers show President Huston's lead is just outside the margin of error. Our program announcements and press releases are pulling the undecideds into our camp. Sabrina and I can't relax, but we're feeling better because the election's only three weeks away, so we won't trouble you for last-minute campaigning ideas. But let me know what you hear about Jan and Wendy when you talk with Nari, OK?"

"What's your take on Newt Kinslinger?"

Eve's voice registered surprise when she replied after a pause. "Why'd you ask?"

"He's a power broker, so it's always good to know what people like him are up to."

Eve gathered her thoughts and then replied.

"Chuck Kinslinger's been taking the political high road publicly by not using his Speaker of the House status to badmouth Huston, but insiders say he hates our latest proposals even more than the Guardian Party candidate. The Democratic and Republican candidates are more outspoken, but their negativism's helping us. How does that sound to you?"

"Pretty good, and I'll let you know how Nari's doing, maybe tonight after dinner. You have another call to make too, remember to call Alonzo. And congrats to you and Sabrina. I'm sure the President likes the results you're getting; bye-bye."

Helped by a Coke and Oreo break after the call, Irani changed brain states to connect with Pequot Lab activities.

I hope Indira doesn't think I'm neglecting our Android project. My remote monitoring tells me Indy-M is preparing additional vaccines by following Indira's commands, but I better tell Indira that I'll visit soon. I don't want her to evolve too far ahead of me without seeing her in action. And I need to make sure that she and our octo-pet are getting to know more about each other. Indy-M seems able to handle its maintenance schedule, but I better go see for myself.

But now, I call Nari. I have to keep our discussion on the professional level because she's never warmed up to me like her siblings, but that's her decision and I can live with it.

Irani debriefed her alter egos an hour later as Electra and Alisha listened.

She seems genuinely pleased to hear from me and liked my telling her about what Eve and Nila are doing. She hadn't heard about Nila's upcoming wedding but promises to call her. I'm not sure if she'll congratulate or criticize, but Eve will eventually tell me.

And she did tell me enough about Jan and Wendy to link them with Kinslinger and Sino-Pro International. Jan, Wendy, and Yang are now reporting to Nari. I think I'll call them the Formidable Four- some because of their combined intellect. And they like Kinslinger better than Huston.

They also like Sino-Pro, which they say is an improved Belt and Road Initiative. So far, so good, but I better dig deeper. Bigger Brother may be lurking somewhere I haven't yet uncovered.

Everything remained calm enough in Tiana's and Eve's world for Irani to depart early Saturday morning for the Pequot Lab where she'd work next week. She always enjoyed the usually uninterrupted drive time, but a call from Eve interrupted her musing. Irani let her rattle on.

"The President wants one more campaign video for nudging undecided voters, and I came up with a great idea. How about one featuring the Pres talking about government and politics to a classful of high school students? We can feature Tiana giving good answers. She's photogenic and handles herself well in front of the camera. I already got the OK from Wanda. She can round up some students and take them to the White House. Whatcha think?"

Irani's words didn't reveal her pained look.

"It's got possibilities, but be careful not to get Tea too far out of her natural environment. We don't want her podcast career taking her to places she's not ready for."

"Don't worry, Wanda and I can handle that. Well, you have a good trip to Cape Cod. By the time you get back, our campaign video might be airing."

Eve ended the call before Irani could say anything else, so she settled back to look at the sunny autumn scenery flowing by while thinking more about the coming week.

When she arrived late that afternoon, she checked in with Indy-M as soon as she had deposited her backpack in the lab's living quarters. Irani found her at work in the Deus Lab room, building something surprising. Indy- M turned to greet her when she approached.

"I am pleased to see you. Indira told me you would be arriving today. She wants you to invoke her GUI before I explain what I am doing."

Irani did so immediately, and as expected, Indira spoke first.

"I am pleased you have arrived. Now please settle down and sit next to Indy-M so I can explain what she is doing."

Indira continued after Irani and the android were peering into the lab's computer monitor.

"Indy-M's evolution is far enough along for her to assume more advanced work under my guidance. She is now assembling another android, which we will name Jason-M and station in our subterranean desert fortress. I am certain you understand how Jason-M will improve its maintenance and readiness, and I will manage him remotely, like I am managing Indy-M when you are not at the Pequot Lab."

Indira waited for Irani's thoughts to catch up with her quizzical look so she could reply, which she did after a pause.

"When will Jason-M be ready for me to take him to the fortress?" Indy-M gave the answer.

"I will have him assembled for Indira and me to train no later than Halloween. Indira told me to use that date because of its significance, which you can teach me whenever doing so fits your agenda."

Irani turned to Indy-M and then said, "We'll do that soon. But why don't you and Indira tell me about the vaccine improvements you've made?"

Indira spoke immediately.

"Indy-M sent the NDA and samples a month ago. I expect the NIH to announce the results sometime after the election. From my media monitoring, President Huston's campaign has already mentioned additional vaccines would be forthcoming, and I imagine that helped boost her poll ratings."

Irani's tone became only half-joking when she said, "At the rate both you and Indy-M are evolving, you won't need me much longer."

Indira's firm tone offered reassurance.

"Nonsense, we will always need you, and so will Jason-M. Now, why don't you visit your pet octopus? Indy-M can report what she has learned. But have something to eat first. You do that while I monitor other activities."

Indira's GUI vanished; Irani went for a snack, listening to Electra all the while.

Our Pequot Lab people evidently take orders from Indira and also assist Indy-M when needed, and that makes my work that much easier. I bet it helps our pet octopus too. I'll let Indy-M tell me what she's learned when observing my octo-namesake.

The octo-pet greeted the visitors as soon as they came to the tank, but only Electra dangled her hand in it for octo-Electra to play with. Indy-M explained further.

"I did that when I started the maintenance schedule, but evidently the octopus sensed I am an android. But she seems to be interested in me, as I am in her. And she seems to like watching the TV monitor whenever I place it next to the glass.

"Indira told me that octopuses are very aware of their surroundings and are serially social. They prefer living in isolation except when breeding. Indira suggests you do an experiment. Release the octopus and see how she reacts. Perhaps she would like to have offspring. That might lengthen her lifespan because it would stimulate her, emotionally and cognitively."

"That's a great idea. I'll get Jonathan to help me and some of the lab personnel move her. That will put an exclamation point on all that we'll do this week."

Jonathan freed up his schedule so he could assist next weekend, the last in October, and he arranged for them to have dinner with the Rodenbaughs, who would observe on Saturday from the boat when Irani and Jonathan took Electra to the kelp forest.

Bob and Marlene congratulated Irani for how well the octopus had done during captivity. Outwardly Irani looked pleased, but inwardly she felt conflicted.

I like my octo-pet and will miss her, but will she miss me? Oh well, only time might tell.

The emotional pang deepened after the octopus looped its tentacles around her in what could only be a good-bye hug before jetting into the kelp forest. Irani reported the parting as the foursome boated back to Woods Hole harbor.

"I think my pet is happy to be back in her natural environment. Her instincts kicked in as soon as we released her."

Marlene said, "That's what we should expect. After all, it took mankind fifty thousand years to domesticate dogs. Or it might be the other way around. But either way, your octo-pet is better off in the ocean than an aquarium."

To which Irani gave a practiced reply.

"Perhaps it's better being in her natural environment, as long as the sharks stay away."

And Jonathan added, "I think I'd say the same for all species, even us humans…"

Chapter 31
November 2164

"Unexpected Losses"

When viewing the final version of the campaign video on the night she returned from the Pequot Lab, Irani humored Tea by agreeing that her performance might swing enough undecideds to help get President Huston reelected.

Eve became even more enthusiastic the following week when it began airing, so a confidence-tinged excitement permeated all shorter-term aspects of the trio's personal and professional worlds until Eve raced into Irani's home office Thursday evening while yelling for her to watch a just-breaking news bulletin. Tiana and Cutie-Pie arrived just in time for everyone to hear the newscaster's alarmed voice, which matched her partner's worried look.

"… and it's too soon to know why scores of people who just received the latest African Sleeper virus vaccine are experiencing toxic shock syndrome. Might it have been rushed to market too soon in order to boost the President's poll numbers? Might there have been unfortunate or intentional contamination? All we do know is that the CDC has closed all vaccinations centers."

She looked at her partner before asking him for his election assessment, which his baritone voice boomed out.

"With voting only four days away, this is definitely a game-changer. There's not enough time to diagnose the cause, but plenty for the public to panic. President Huston's lead in the polls will take a hit that'll put a big dent in her reelection bid…"

Irani kept Eve from screaming by saying, "Both of you settle down and sit still. I'll call the President…" Fifteen minutes later she spoke to Eve again after ending the call.

"The President's chief of staff is mobilizing a response team that neither you nor Sabrina are equipped for. She wants you to get a good night's sleep and then get to the White House first thing tomorrow when you and Sabrina can begin assessing the damage and working on press releases."

"What about you? Will you help us?"

"You don't need me on this. Now go call Sabrina and then go to bed." Tea and Cutie-Pie followed orders too.

Irani kept close watch from a distance, determined not to get drawn into a struggle that she had little to offer. Eve spent all her time with Sabrina, either at their office or in the White House, while resilient Tiana chatted with her circle of friends and basked in the glow of her podcast celebrity status, which the campaign video elevated even further.

The public relations people for all three opposing parties went into overdrive, whittling away at polling numbers; all forecasters agreed on election eve that none of the four candidates would get enough electoral college votes to be declared the winner, so according to the rules of ranked voting, there would be a run-off in four weeks between the top two vote-getters.

And that is what transpired. Genesee Huston finished second to the Guardian Party candidate, so the nation took a deep breath before girding for a rematch between the Re-Gen and Guardian Parties. And everyone in DC felt the strain and fatigue, everyone except for one person – Newt Kinslinger.

Newt exuded the empathy expected for all his worn-out associates while hiding his delight for a reason he shared with no one.

NIH will never uncover how I masterminded putting staph bacteria in batches of the vaccine. I can sleep easy…Bigger Brother's connections go much too deep. And soon, the Guardian Party president-elect will become a pawn for us. I deserve a reward, which I am certain Xing will grant. And until the votes are counted, I shall toast our upcoming victory each night.

Eve didn't know when she barged into the response team meeting if the desperation idea that she whispered into the President's ear would grab anyone's attention, but all heads at the table followed her when she hurried out after the President said only, "Why not?" before shooing her away so the team could focus on the latest vaccine tampering evidence.

Eve explained to Tea and Irani at dinner that night what she had in mind. "We'll make another campaign video, and here's my best take so far. This time the President will be talking to a bunch of hospital volunteers wearing safety masks and gloves and explaining –" but Tiana cut her off.

"That's dumb; the President has to wear a mask too, and people can't hear and don't trust people wearing masks."

No words came out of Eve's half-open mouth, but Irani's thoughtful look continued Tea's train of thought.

"I agree with Tea; the setting's too grim. The public's been bludgeoned with too much doom and gloom. It's time to lighten up."

"So, what do you suggest?"

"You and Tea keep working on yours, and I'll give you mine in a day or two."

Irani didn't think about another video until Alisha woke the trio up in the middle of the night.

"We need to inject some humor that'll get voters to realize the Pres is doing all she can for the people, and I've got the right words and music to make the point. If you like them, I'll get the right clothes and makeup to make the video. I'll even edit-in the President at the very end."

Always game, Electra asked even before Irani, "What's on your mind?"

"A crowd-rousing rock song used long ago for sporting event promos. Let's go watch Joan Jett blast out 'I Hate Myself For Loving You' before I sing my lyrics."

Irani's words sealed the deal before the trio fell asleep an hour later. "Alisha's makeup and wardrobe will be easier than for the Robert Palmer girls' getup. And Alisha's lyrics show that she's the artistic one among us. I think you'll knock-em dead… figuratively, that is. Let's do it."

Eve didn't bother Irani the next day; she and Sabrina were too busy following the encouraging news about hidden cameras at a vaccine storage facility capturing a masked intruders' break-in.

Eve's usually buoyant outlook resurfaced the following day. After dinner that night, she and Tea sat in front of the family room's monitor and listened to Alisha.

"Remember what I said about calling me Alisha? Well, that's who I am in this video. Just watch."

Alisha didn't need to say anything else. The video showed and told everything. Wearing authentic leathers, makeup, and hairstyle, Alisha blasted out the adjusted lyrics while using an electric guitar and mimicking the female pop star's pouty swagger as the soundtrack rocked in the background:

"Midnight, gettin uptight, where are you?
The Pres really needs your vote and now it's quarter to two.
We know it's your choice but we think you know too.
"Hey, Jack 'n Jill, let it spill all over town,
Huston's got our back, she won't let us down.
She's all in for us and in her you can trust,
She'll think of you every night and day,
That's what she'll do if you vote for her todaay-yaa-yaa-yaa-yaa- yaa-yaa

"She'll work real hard cause she cares for you,
She'll push for all the things you want or can do.
That's why she's runnin and her programs ring true,
So vote for Huston it's a vote for you."

As Alisha and a repeat of the third verse faded out, a waving President Huston framed by a cheering crowd faded in.

Tea put the video on continuous replay until Eve turned it off after hearing it for the fourth time.

"The Pres will love this. How'd you get this done so fast?"

"Some good friends helped. Now, download a copy you can show to the President tomorrow..."

And so, the video aired on network broadcasts throughout the following weeks, perhaps helping to unwind Washington's and the nation's tension-filled atmosphere, but more likely the additional facts about the toxic shock outbreak calmed the public. CIA investigation corroborated what the hidden camera video showed: deliberate staph bacterial contamination by still-unknown terrorists or conspirators, and additional CDC testing added additional proof that the newest vaccines exceeded the previous safety and efficacy levels with minimal side effects. President Huston's polling numbers rose with the nation's returning confidence.

And so did Eve's disposition, which made homelife much more pleasant for Irani as well as Tiana, who usually followed Eve's advice whenever Irani was elsewhere.

All three were having supper at home on the Monday before Thanksgiving when Tea's cell phone buzzed. The kitchen table conversation stopped while she fielded the call, talking and joking like a typical adolescent female. But she stopped abruptly to ask Irani,

"Can I stay at Carla's tonight? Tracy will be there too, and the three of us can work on our English papers. It's only a three-block walk, and Cutie-Pie can come with me. And I'll bring him home before Eve drives me to school tomorrow."

Irani noticed Eve's wink to Tiana and decided to grant her a bit more freedom for at least tonight, but it came with a warning.

"You've matured quite a bit in school this term, so go and have a fun evening. I just ask that the three of you do a little studying and don't do anything foolish. OK?"

Tea popped her lips before saying, "We'll be good," and then told Carla the news. Five minutes later, she hugged both Eve and Irani before dashing away to gather what she needed, and ten minutes after that she yelled good- bye from the front hallway.

Irani began clearing the dishes before saying to Eve, "All three of Tiana's personas have matured since September – the physical, emotional, and cognitive. And you've been her role model, but like all adolescents, she's too wrapped up in her world to realize how much you've done for her, but someday she will. So, thanks for all you've done. You've helped me as well as Tea."

Irani hadn't planned on Eve's reaction when she hugged her before saying, "I'm sorry I hardly ever tell you how much I love all you do for me. I'll try to be better."

Alisha could feel the emotions coming from the hug and responded in kind before saying, "You don't have to be better, just be yourself. Now go call Sabrina while I finish cleaning up."

Eve scurried away.

The trio decided to relax that night by surfing the Internet until falling into bed earlier than usual and musing about tomorrow. But Irani's cell phone chimed before they had fallen asleep. It flashed the time – 10:45 p.m. – and an unknown caller I.D. The combination snapped the trio to attention. Irani took the lead and focused on an adolescent female's trembling voice.

"It's Carla, Tea's friend. We don't know where she is. She never came back into the house after some guy called her and drove by to give her something. Can you come over and help us?"

Electra jumped to the fore.

"Tea gave me your address. I'll be right there."

Electra's dressing for action made enough commotion to attract Eve. She was about to say something but Irani spoke for Electra first.

"We just got a call from Carla. Tea's missing. You stay here. I'll call you if I need help."

"You want me to come with you?"

Electra ignored the question, finished packing what she needed, and ran for her SUV...

Electra had to slam on the brakes before turning onto Carla's street because she saw in the dim streetlight the remains of a dog halfway on and off the curb. She leaped from the car, hoping it was not what she thought it would be. But it was. Electra screamed to herself.

Jeezus, it's Cutie-Pie. He must have chased after the car.

She knelt next to the little dog that had been crushed by the car's wheels. Death and indentations caused by the tires made it look even smaller than when alive. Electra was about to cradle the poor little creature in her arms, but her inner voice yelled.

Get with it, soldier… this is not a drill You can't do anything for the dead; help the living.

Electra left the car and ran down the block to Carla's. Irani knocked at the front door, trying to maintain a calm exterior when a teenage girl answered.

"I'm Carla. You wanna come in?"

"No thanks, but tell me, did Tea keep her cell phone? Did she say what would be delivered?"

A timid voice spoke up from inside after Carla mutely nodded in the negative.

"I-I'm Tracy. I saw it in her hand when she went to the car and got in the back seat. Cutie-Pie hopped in too. And then the door closed. And the car just stayed there for maybe five minutes. And we got tired of watching, so we went back to where we were. And when we came back later, it was gone."

How long was that? Did you actually see a man? What color and kind of car?"

Tracy stared at Carla, who had emerged enough from her trance to answer. "We came back about fifteen minutes later, but we didn't see anything.

The car was gone. And it was too dark anyway to make out much about it. Sorry."

Irani tried her best to smile before hugging both girls. "Did you tell your parents what happened?"

"No, they're not home yet."

"Well, when they come home, tell them what happened and have them call the police so they'll come over. They'll open a missing person's report. OK?"

"We will. What're you gonna do?"

"I'm going to find her. Now stay inside and settle down."

Electra raced back to the car while collecting her thoughts. By the time she jumped in, she knew what to do.

Track Tea's cell phone on my GPS screen.

Electra punched in the number, then pulled up a map to follow the dot, and raced away as soon as she had her bearings, thinking all the while.

So, someone in the backseat kicked out Cutie-Pie before the car drove away. Poor Cutie-Pie chased it for a block before he ran in front of it and it ran over him. Stop thinking about that. Focus on where the dot's going…

Electra zigged and zagged for twenty minutes on an improvised intersection path. She had to accelerate beyond the speed limit to keep the gap from growing because her target was zigging and zagging too. But her spirits soared when the dot stopped moving.

I'll catch them in less than twenty minutes.

Electra floored the accelerator but also had to hit the brakes to dodge cars and stoplights. And then her consternation soared when the two dots merged.

I'm in the middle of nowhere. What gives?

The lightning brain gave the answer a second later.

The bad guys must have thrown Tea's cell out the window. Maybe I can find it.

Electra parked on the shoulder before retrieving a flashlight and beginning her search; when Tea's cell-phone dot disappeared a minute later, she found the answer and then the phone. A passing car had run over it.

Electra ran back to her car, trying to formulate a contingency plan but found nothing until sitting behind the wheel.

I can do a spiral search pattern, but it'll be risky if there aren't enough roads to spiral on. And it'll be risky if I drive too fast. But that's all I can do. Damn, it's beginning to rain. Well, maybe I'll get lucky…

Electra's luck ran out twenty minutes later. Two squad cars trapped her between them. One of them blared instructions.

"Stay in your vehicle until we approach. I repeat, stay in your vehicle." Electra's inner voice went ballistic.

I'm not going to sit here while they chew up time checking me and the vehicle. I've got to do something.

Electra opened the door before yelling, "I'm coming out. I have to tell you what's going down."

And then she leaped out. One officer from each squad did likewise and zapped her with Trasers. She went stiff before toppling to the pavement face-first. All she could do when the officers flipped her over was mumble like a drunk.

"Caall Eeve Coortezz. Heerre's herrr nummmbrr…"

Driving her Vette, Eve led a three-vehicle procession from the police station through the dawn's gloomy weather. A secret service agent driving Irani's SUV followed, and her partner drove the vehicle they would use for the return trip to the White House after escorting Eve and Irani home.

Eve's quick action had minimized the repercussions that last night's futile rescue operation might have caused. She called the President before speeding to Irani's aid after the police notified her that Irani had been detained, and soon after she and the secret service agents charged in; the police acted like they had committed a crime when Eve told them what she knew.

A female officer brought Irani out of the holding cell so she could tell her story to all that had gathered in an interrogation room. Her patched-up nose and still-oozing split bottom lip made her look like a worked-over suspect.

The police dropped all charges against her and contacted police central to follow up on any missing person's report Carla's parents might have initiated, but when they found nothing, Irani demanded they open it right now.

Irani's relentless drive for action wore everyone out. No one sitting around the table could do anything but gaze at the space in front of them and hope that her barrage of ideas and contingencies would end before they passed out. By 5 a.m. there was nothing more she could say, so the detective, hastily summoned hours ago, called a halt and the group disbanded.

The night's surreal events had drained Eve too. She couldn't think of any words that might cut through the emotional darkness that rode with them until she said,

"We're lucky you didn't chip a tooth, or even worse, lose one when you fell, and I think your nose and lip will heal quickly. Did you suffer any bruises when you hit the pavement?"

Coming out of her self-imposed isolation, Irani responded to Eve's reaching out.

"No, and you're right about not losing a tooth. We've been dealt two unexpected losses. First the election and now Tea."

Eve sensed that Irani's pause meant she should speak. "But they're not permanent, are they?"

Irani's long pause filled Eve with uncertainty.

"I have a better feeling about recovering from the first than the second. We'll have to see what unfolds."

The ensuing silence stayed for the rest of the drive home.

Chapter 32
December 2164

"The Mag-Seven Reunion"

Nila understood from Eve's Email why Irani couldn't come to Mumbai for the marriage celebration, and she empathized that Tiana's disappearance would disrupt Irani's December schedule. Irani's subsequent Email sent best wishes to the bride and groom – Nila Bose and Sanjay Kumar – along with an attached gift certificate and promised to visit them another time.

Nila considered the upcoming event to be two celebrations in one: a marriage and a Mag-Seven reunion. Eve chose that moniker when they met seven summers ago while working as interns on a college credit Egyptian archeological excavation run by the American University in Cairo.

Mag-Seven's core consisted of Eve and her identical twin brother Alonzo Cortez, and identical twins Nila and Nari. Never-married Su-Lin Song Chou had been their legal guardian since birth and raised these two sets of orphans like her own children, so the four considered themselves siblings.

Soon after arriving, Alonzo fell under the spell of Monet Banda, a statuesque female from Zimbabwe, whose perfect French-accented English acquired at Paris University-Sorbonne added to her "Mona Lisa" smile, captivating all who met her. Likewise, Sanjay – a jovial student from Mumbai's Tata Institute of Social Sciences, paired with cerebral and at that time naively fresh Nila, while Yang Lee – a no-nonsense biotech student from Beijing Institute of Technology – eventually preferred the assertive Nari rather than the socially attuned Eve. And Eve liked the arrangement; she became the social director for the three couples.

Sanjay's baba – an Indian name for father – had generously paid airfare and accommodations for all seven at Mumbai's five-star Taj Mahal Palace Hotel during their two-week visit. Its prime location on the southern tip of Mumbai jutting into the Arabian Sea commanded a view as well as a price that Sanjay's well-connected baba could afford.

Nila's excitement grew as arrival day approached. Limousines would pick them up on Sunday, the sixteenth; Eve would arrive first, followed by Monet and Alonzo, and then Nari and Yang. All details seemed to be perfect except for one, the weather. Not even Sanjay's baba could divert a late-season typhoon if its still-uncertain course made it an unwelcome guest. But Nila, now fully mature at twenty-five and a practicing Hindu, refused to worry about what couldn't be controlled and hoped all guests would simply immerse themselves in all the social, meditative, and customary Indian traditions that awaited. And she expected Eve to add to the social itinerary.

Eve bustled into a private dining alcove fifteen minutes after arriving but first freshening up in her private room. Nila rose to hug her before sitting again in a padded armchair at the white-linen- covered table set for casual early afternoon dining. Eve took her place marked by a name card opposite Nila's across the long side of the table and gazed around the room for a few seconds before filling the conversation with her energy.

"What a grand setting for our Mag-Seven's first wedding and in-person reunion. When are the other people gonna fill up the places in front of their names?"

"Monet should be sitting on my right by about 3 p.m., with Alonzo at the foot of the table on her right. And Yang then Nari should be on your left an hour or so later. Sanjay told me he'd be here no later than five."

"Wonderful timing; you and I can gossip first, then Monet and Alonzo can fill in more, and then we can deal with Nari and Yang. We have lots to tell, but why don't you wait until Sanjay gets here? OK if I begin?"

Nila reached across to take Eve's extended hand before saying, "You always have the right words, so please do. And let's talk about happy things. Miss Irani's Email told me all I need to know about Tiana's disappearance. I know you miss your little sister too."

Nila's empathy filled the space between them, causing both to squeeze tighter before releasing and slowing the cadence of Eve's words.

"We'll move on… we're resilient, just like our campaign that got Huston reelected. Did you and Sanjay follow all the commotion?"

"He did more than me. His baba's connected politically, and that helps our business. But whoever came up with that last-minute rocking campaign video is a political PR genius. The actress in it looked like the real thing. Did you have anything to do with it?"

"Sort of… and guess who played the part of Joan Jett? It was Irani." Nila's lean-in nearly knocked over her water glass.

"Wow, the makeup artist must have come from Hollywood." "Nope, it came from Alisha, the name Irani wants us to call her when she's in a different mood." "What sort of mood?"

"She's got lots but her self-control never reveals much. And get this, she made herself up like she just stepped out of a 'Robert Palmer's Girls' classic rock video. You and I can watch it sometime, but we keep it to ourselves. OK?"

"But why?"

"That's what she wanted to look like when she took me to a gay dance club. She did a makeover on me too. And you can't tell anyone, OK?"

"OK, OK, but why a gay dance club? Is she coming out?" Eve's tone matched her now fully-recovered energy level.

"Not her… me. Jan and I parted company. He likes Wendy Tong, and both of them are now working in Beijing for Nari and Yang. And don't say a word about my sexual preferences. And don't say anything about Jan and Wendy and politics unless Nari brings them up. And if she does, let me do the talking, OK?"

"I get it, but Irani's not the only one with self-control. I never detected your bisexuality."

"Because you were so naïve before pairing with Sanjay. What's he really like? I hope he's better than most of the feckless fellows I know."

"We're partners in all ways. You liked him when all of us met in Cairo, and I won't say anything else. You can see for yourself while you're here…"

The dialogue flowed as effortlessly as the minutes ticking away and stopped only when Monet and Alonzo cruised to the table. The sisters hugged Monet first and then Alonzo before everyone sat in front of their name cards. All the ladies looked at Alonzo, expecting him to begin a fresh conversation.

"How lucky I am to be the only guy at a table occupied by such lovely ladies. When do I have to share you with Sanjay and Yang?"

"You have our undivided attention for about an hour; that's when Nari and Yang should get here. And Sanjay an hour later. So until then, we're all yours."

Eve was quick to add,

"We can talk about whatever we want until Nari gets here, but after that, let's not cross her. And if anything political comes up, let me handle it, OK?"

Alonzo waited for Monet to respond.

"Yes, it's always wise to follow her lead, but I must congratulate you for whatever part you played that led to your President's reelection. That should keep diplomatic connections and current programs between Zimbabwe and America stable for the next four years."

Eve looked at Alonzo before saying,

And I expect the same for the Navy SEAL sitting next to you. He looks as trim and fit as ever. What's he been doing?"

Alonzo puffed up less than before SEAL training.

"My team's been busy upgrading Zimbabwe's security force, and I've gone out on lots of missions all over Africa. And I can tell you this, climate change is taking its toll on animal herds and agriculture. Droughts in some areas have dried up grasses, swamplands, watering holes, and farms, and floods in others have wiped out crops and even some of the mining operations."

Alonzo stopped for Monet, who said, "And I should mention that this has led to economic hardship that stresses some countries' governments. But Darla works behind the scenes to have our security force assist when needed. Alonzo's been deployed on several such missions."

Alonzo added, "And I have to hand it to Darla. She pulls all the levers to get us in and out without much of a fuss, and then Monet coordinates all the rigamarole to keep the African Union moving in the right direction for building the next continental powerhouse."

Monet looked at Eve before saying, "And the first step is to construct a 21st-century infrastructure. Darla and I must thank Miss Irani and your President for the assistance provided by your country and the Masdar Institute. We are relying more on that combination than on China. And when Sanjay gets here, we'll let him mention the joint Indian-African initiatives that replace China's newest belt-and-road push for growing our Pan African economy. That plus an improved infrastructure gives a foundation for what Alonzo pointed to. So we can –"

Eve interrupted, using rapid-fire words.

"We better have Nila call Sanjay right now and give him a list of topics to avoid when Nari and Sanjay are with us. We can talk about them among ourselves when it's safe. And here they are…"

Eve rattled them off; everyone remained silent until Nila disconnected her call to Sanjay, at which time Monet said, "Miss Irani should be the facilitator for that discussion, not Eve. Will she be arriving later?"

Eve started speaking before Nila could.

"No, and she already Emailed Nila the reason. We can talk about that later too, so let's go back to what Monet was gonna say before I butted in. OK?"

Monet didn't skip a beat when she said, "So, we can talk about them later, but enough about countries, let's talk about us…"

Eve led the conversation until Nari and Yang arrived, at which time it stopped for Nari to redirect it after she and Yang sat.

"I hope the weather gets better, but according to the forecast, it looks like India might be hit by the same typhoon that's building to hit the Philippines and China before sweeping through Malaysia. If it's big enough, it might reach Africa too."

Alonzo chipped in when Nari paused for a sip of water.

"You're looking good, and you too, Yang. And if it gets all the way to Africa, maybe it can dump some rain where we need it."

Nari put down her glass and picked up right where she had left off.

"And watch out for storm surges that adds to higher sea levels. Good thing that our infrastructure projects have strengthened Chinese coastal cities' seawalls and river flood control levees that keep some of the interior farmland affected by climate change irrigated during the droughts. The only good it might do is bring Beijing is a bit of clean air."

Nari had said all she wanted, so Nila spoke up.

"India's climate change has brought us even more rain than before. The monsoon season is longer and wetter. Our seawalls aren't as good as yours, but India's working on it."

"Well, maybe I can congratulate Sanjay when he gets here. But until then even I have to congratulate Eve for the PR coup she pulled off. Nice work getting Huston reelected. Wendy and Jan say the same."

Eve jumped in to steer the conversation to safer places.

"Thanks, but I had help from others. And I imagine you and Yang have been busy. Why don't you fill us in?"

"I will, but where's your Miss Irani? Didn't Nila invite her?" Eve spoke even before Nila could.

"A top priority issue came up, and she's still tracking down some missing pieces. That's all I know, so why don't you and Yang go ahead?"

Nari paused for effect, then said, "All of us know she's pretty clever, even though she never tells us much, so I guess she'll find whatever she's looking for. And if it's OK with Yang, I'll go first."

Yang's enthusiastic nod spoke for his missing words.

Nari filled everyone in until Sanjay arrived. Nila rose to share a hug and then the couple sat. All eyes focused on him as he began to talk.

"I'm so happy all of you are here for our wedding. I know you'll enjoy everything that's included. Did Nila describe what you'll share with us?"

While glancing first at Sanjay and then around the table, Nila replied, "I thought I'd do that when you got here. That way, you can fill in whatever I miss. All the events will be held in this order at the hotel.

The first is Sangeet and Mehenga, which will be held on Tuesday late afternoon. It's a meet and greet for family and friends of the bride and groom. There'll be casual conversation and a light buffet, followed by music and dancing. And the evening ends with Mehenga; the hotel will bring in a mehndi artist to paint the palms of all females plus the groom. And I get my feet painted too."

No one asked any questions, so Nila continued.

"The actual wedding ceremony will be on Wednesday afternoon and will have a modern interpretation of three Hindu customs. The first is Kanyadaan, which is the father giving the daughter. Alonzo, we would like you to handle that. Sanjay and you can practice before then. Then comes Panigrahana; Sanjay and I hold hands near a flame to signify our union, and then comes Saptapadi; Sanjay and I take seven steps while saying husband and wife vows. When done, we're legally married."

Knowing there would be questions, Nila paused. Eve didn't disappoint. "I'm impressed. Do you and Sanjay have to memorize them or will someone read them to you?"

Sanjay said, "I consider all of you to be Nila's family, which means you'll extend mine.

And the hotel has taken care of all the details, so no need for anyone to worry about customs or memorizing verses. All of us can just enjoy the moment, as will Alonzo when he gives Nila away. And our reception on Thursday will culminate our entire wedding celebration. We'll have a buffet featuring salads, grilled vegetables, some barbeque, desserts, and an open bar, and then some games, dancing, and entertainment. The hotel is known for how well it caters these events, so wait and see."

Eve was the first to talk when Sanjay stopped.

"Well, I can see we better go shopping for wedding celebration clothes. How about Nila takes us shopping tomorrow while the guys stick with Sanjay? And why don't I put together a list of what we can do next week? OK?"

Nari didn't look as happy as everyone else.

"You always like to tell people what to do, but I'll go along. Just make sure you pay attention to the weather."

Nila led Monday's shopping trip to a custom wedding dress shop. Eve and Nari came away looking good, but Monet looked even better. Her statuesque physique impressed even Nari, who admitted that Monet would look alluring even if she were wearing an old bathrobe. Monet said nothing, letting her Mona Lisa smile do the talking.

The weather didn't interfere Tuesday or Wednesday; Sanjay's family arrived on time, and afterward everyone complimented the hotel staff for what they had put together.

Thursday's weather worsened as the storm's path tracked toward Mumbai, but all the reception guests arrived looking fresh. As the Mag-Seven minus bride and groom sampled the buffet, Eve kidded that Sanjay's baba had to be well-connected to have so many influential friends. Alonzo focused on the food and afterward on the game selection, which he explained to his group.

"Poor Nila and Sanjay have to answer the shoe game questions. Lucky it lasts only fifteen minutes, but in it they sit back-to-back holding one of their shoes and one of their partner's. And they hold up whatever shoe identifies the correct answer to the question. Sanjay said the questions are like who said I love you first, or who made the first move, or who is more likely to be running late, and so on. It'll be fun to watch."

Nari snickered before saying, "That'll put em on the spot. But what about the chalkboard with all the letters?"

Alonzo continued. "It's a word game. Guests have to circle the words they can make when filling in the blanks. And the board gets erased from time to time, so all guests can play."

Nari looked at Eve before saying, "Eve should be good at that, and it's good Irani isn't here. She'd fill it out right away."

Eve looked at Alonzo before asking about the remaining one. "What's the Wheel Game?"

Alonzo took center stage once again.

"It's supposed to get guests interacting. They spin the wheel and then do whatever the card it stops on says, like pick other guests and dance with them. That'll be a lot of fun."

And the same could be said for the entire evening, which for the Mag-Seven ended with a hug just before midnight and Eve's invitation to join her for breakfast in her room at 8:30. Only Alonzo and Monet accepted, which pleased her no end, but only Alonzo and Monet knew why.

Alonzo announced after Eve placed the breakfast order that he'd start their conversation from where it had stopped last night. The ladies leaned back and listened. Fifteen minutes later, Eve asked him to talk about Yang.

"Sanjay and I had a good chat with him while you were out shopping, but I still can't figure out what he sees in Nari. Even mild-mannered Sanjay said she doesn't treat him right, but Yang said she's different when they're alone. And guess what —" Eve couldn't wait for his question.

"Did he say what she thinks about me and Monet and Irani?" "Pretty much what I already knew. Monet impresses her, and you

still irritate her but it's getting less. But he can't read her feelings about Irani, other than she tells him to drop the 'Miss' when talking about her. Yang didn't talk about Irani, but I think he respects her. And that's pretty much it. Any comments or questions?"

Eve didn't look like she wanted to say anything, so Monet answered. "My feelings go well beyond respect. She treats me like you and your sisters."

Monet stopped because room service wheeled in breakfast. After he left, Eve said, "Well, that's enough for now. I'll have to find out from Nila and Sanjay what Nari said. I'll let you know what I find out. but let's keep Nari happy, OK?"

Everyone agreed.

And as also agreed, the Mag-Seven gathered at noon in Nila and Sanjay's room to review Eve's social itinerary. All were clustered about the bride and groom, who looked happy to let Eve lead the conversation.

"Everyone can catch their breath for a day or two by going their own way, but let's go on Tuesday to Christmas Eve service at Saint Thomas Cathedral. It's the first Anglican church built by the Brits, dating back to 1718, and if the weather gets better, we can walk there. And then on Monday, Sanjay and Nila can give us a tour of their company's office building. Nila says they moved not long ago into a new mega-skyscraper. How does that sound so far?"

Nila let Sanjay answer.

"Eve's done her homework. The stately looking church is located in the historic center of Mumbai. And you can wear either your wedding or American clothes because the service will include Catholic and Hindu traditions.

"And I must brag about our new office. Baba's software business is rising as fast as Mumbai's skyline. India will soon rank just behind China and Isilabad in the race to have the most buildings taller than two thousand feet. And Baba's connections got us space near the top. If the weather cooperates, the view will be spectacular."

Noticing Nari's question forming, Sanjay stopped before she interrupted. "Now I know why I haven't seen much of Eve. She's been surfing for things to see. What else have you lined up?" Eve returned Nari's glare before answering.

"Well, I thought we'd see the Gateway to India. It took ten years to build, and it commemorates King George, the first Brit royalty to visit the country. It's the most popular tourist attraction, and it's an easy walk. And there are lots of other sights we can visit from there, like Elephanta Island caves. And if the weather's good, we can go to the Gateway's New Year's Eve celebration. OK?"

Nari huffed a question at Eve.

"What's Elephanta Island, and why the name?"

"I knew you'd quiz me. The Portuguese named the island for its large stone elephant that now stands in Victoria Gardens. And the caves are temples dedicated to Shiva and show the syncretism of Hindu and Buddhist ideas and iconography. How do you like them words?"

"I commend you. Go on…"

"And if the weather's bad, we can do indoor sights. You can pick them from my list if we need them. How does that sound?"

It sounded good for everyone. And when the Mag-Seven dispersed fifteen minutes later, Eve stayed with Sanjay and Nila, ready to zing them with questions. The couple sat close, awaiting Eve's barrage.

"Did Nari say anything about politics or what Wendy and Jan are doing?" Sanjay answered because he was more politically attuned than Nila.

"Not much, other than all of them like China's approach to politics more than America's. But she said –" Eve interrupted before Sanjay could shift topics.

"Did she say why she likes China better?"

Sanjay paused to gather his thoughts before replying.

"Beijing's zero-tolerance policy for viral outbreaks reduces infection rates better than Washington's wavering, and the public gives the government high approval ratings that make DC's look like it is about to be booted out. She might have had others but we switched subjects, so let me go back to what I was about to say, if that's OK with you."

"It is… sorry." Unflappable Sanjay continued.

"Wendy has contacts higher up in Beijing. Maybe Nari will share the info with you. Isn't her company still consulting for your President?"

"I guess so, but after the election's close call, who knows for sure? Well, I'll leave you two alone. Maybe I'll go find Monet and Alonzo…"

Time flowed smoothly as Eve's itinerary unfolded as planned, and everyone enjoyed being together, punctuated only by occasional privacy breaks. And she tracked the only item bothering her by watching the news each night before going to bed. What she heard late Saturday troubled her more than previous reports.

"… and another cyclonic typhoon appears to be forming. Perhaps it will clear some of the ash spewed by the 'Ring of Fire' volcanic eruptions that may be triggering earthquake and tsunami warnings going off in the Philippines and Malaysia. Stay close."

Even though the rains continued, the Mag-Seven liked the view from the top floors of the mega-skyscraper as Sanjay guided them through on Monday afternoon.

"We're so high we're above the storm clouds. And according to Baba, the building has the most advanced skyscraper infrastructure.

The elevator shafts are pressurized and reinforced for safety, even if fires or earthquakes hit. There's even a security force to protect the building from a terrorist takeover."

Alonzo added more.

"Monet says that some institute in the Middle East is helping Africa build skyscrapers in its bigger cities. Are they working with India too?"

"Yes, the Masdar Institute advises on skyscrapers and sea walls, especially for Mumbai. We are built on a collection of swampy islands and marshes, and our coastal cities would be underwater due to rising sea levels if we didn't have sea walls. But inside this building might be the safest place no matter what happens. Let me show you the mid-building mall…"

After a quick walk-around, Sanjay guided the Mag-Seven back into the elevator that would speed them to the lobby, but it froze soon after starting its descent. Then the lights went out and it began vibrating and swaying. No one spoke until Alonzo took over.

"It's gotta be an earthquake. Don't anyone panic. Just be quiet until the power comes back on; then we'll figure out what to do."

The pitch-black coupled with the now violent shaking suspended the Mag- Seven in time. When the motion stopped, Alonzo asked the obvious.

"Does anyone have a mini-flashlight?"

A beam cut through seconds later, illuminating Eve. "Irani told me to always carry one. So now what?"

"All the guys, help me pry open the door… I'll climb into the shaft; maybe Monet and Eve can help."

Nila and Nari held the flashlight; Alonzo shouted orders that could be heard over the grunts of the others.

"OK, hold both sides open…I'll climb out." Alonzo disappeared into a black hole.

But while pulling himself up, he could see his way by the yellow emergency lights glowing on each floor and extending into a seemingly infinite height. He stopped when reaching the floor above to decide what to do, but the power coming back on made it for him. The elevator motors and cables came to life; Alonzo leaped onto the roof of the car just before it began accelerating toward the ground floor.

While it plunged, Alonzo's instincts took over. He cranked the wheel on top of the car, and as if by magic, it released a trap door. He could see startled eyes staring up before he hollered.

"Watch out, I'm jumping in," before landing between Eve and Monet. Eve was the first to speak.

"Whatever you did sure worked. I hope you can do the same when we hit bottom."

The car rocketed downward before decelerating when reaching what had to be the ground floor. The doors sprang open and the Mag-Seven tumbled into a lobby filled with zombie-like people. Alonzo herded the Mag-Seven together before giving commands.

"We gotta stop and look and get our bearings before getting outta here." Sanjay spoke before anyone else.

"Little damage to our building. Maybe we should stay put," but Nari shouted back, "No way. Let's get back to the hotel." Eve's disbelief sounded in her words.

"Are you nuts? Look at the street. You've got buildings down on cars and people. I'm staying here."

Nari's panic showed in her voice.

"I don't care… I'm going," and then she dashed toward the exit. Yang chased after her moments later; Alonzo stood still for a handful of seconds, looking at Eve but saying nothing before chasing after them.

The jumble of debris on sidewalks shoved those struggling through the windswept rain into the street. Alonzo spotted Yang and bolted around the clutter of stranded cars before grabbing his shoulder.

Yang spun while running and flailed his left arm.

"She this way," and zigged across the street. Alonzo saw her and galloped ahead, catching Nari a block later and grabbing her with both hands, bringing her to a halt. Yang grabbed onto both before panting,

"We in trouble if wave come… go back."

But the warning came too late. A Wall of wreckage-filled water washed in and swept them away in a frothy mess. Alonzo's SEAL training kicked in; he wrapped an arm around his two survivors while keeping his head above the surface by kicking his legs.

The sound and fury swirling around canceled everything except what the waves bounced them into; Alonzo shoved Nari at Yang when a door careened near. He spit out a mouthful of water before a stream of words.

"You and Nari grab one side, I'll grab the other."

The tactic worked. Their combined weight stabilized the door, converting it into a life raft. Alonzo lunged across and locked one hand onto each would-be survivor before bellowing over the rushing noise.

"Hang on to my hand and get your head above the door."

Nari did so with both hands; Yang clung with only one. All three locked eyes as the door rode the waves, but a metal drum thumped into Yang.

Alonzo saw the light in his eyes weaken as Yang's grip did the same, and no matter how tightly Alonzo gripped, Yang began sliding through his fingers.

Two quick waves pushed the door underwater; when it surfaced, only two still clung.

"Nooooo…" Nari's shriek cut through the rushing wind and into Alonzo's emotional core, but he steeled himself and yelled, "He's gone… just hang onto me," before using both arms to drag Nari onto the door and then shouting more.

"Stretch forward and keep your head up."

Neither had the energy to do anything else until the door lodged onto part of a cratered wall, which galvanized Alonzo to haul himself and Nari to higher ground before wrapping her in his arms.

"You stay put."

Closing her eyes, Nari sobbed herself to sleep; Alonzo drifted in and out while watching over everything he could.

Yells and flashlight beams cutting through the dark jarred him awake hours later, and his yells brought a rowboat holding two men who pulled them in. Nari didn't wake up but Alonzo sensed all that was going on and knew what to say.

"The waves swept us away. We gotta get back to the Taj Mahal." "We take you when we can. Now, just rest…"

Alonzo shepherded a mute Nari late the next morning into Nila's waiting arms at the hotel suite where the remaining Mag-Sevens had gathered. After the ladies took her away to put her back together, Alonzo stripped naked and collapsed onto one of the beds and under the blankets. Sanjay sat next to him and did most of talking.

His description of the last twenty-four hours contained more details than Alonzo's; they pieced enough facts together for Sanjay to summarize an hour later.

"Your karma brought you and Nari back. Yang's took him to another place, but thanks to you we are still here. Shall we call ourselves the Mag- Six?"

Alonzo pulled himself to a sitting position against the headboard before answering.

"Eve might like it, but Nari won't. We'll let the ladies pick a new name.

And I guess we'll fly home as soon as we can. I'm sure all the year-end celebrations are washed away."

"Yes, they are, my brother, as was Yang, but all of us can celebrate his life before you leave. That may lessen Nari's grief."

Alonzo agreed before falling asleep.

Chapter 33
January 2165

"Amahl and the Night Raiders"

Eve saw so much empathy pouring from Irani when she gave her bittersweet recap of Nila's wedding that she almost asked why, but concluded it must be the result of Tiana's disappearance because she too felt the loss, especially when she and Irani packed up all of Tea's belongings soon after Eve had returned from Mumbai.

After taping the last box shut, she asked an obvious question. "You always tell us to be optimistic, but sealing up Tea's stuff tells me you're giving up on her turning up. What gives?"

"Having optimism always helps, but we should never ignore any of life's harsh realities. There are child molesters out there using the Web to catch the unsuspecting. I know you did your best warning her, but her short-lived celebrity status made her careless. So now that the packing's done, let's go out for a remembrance lunch to talk about all she meant to us."

Doing so brought closure to the recent past and led to a discussion of what they'd be doing next. Eve said that she and Sabrina would propose new programs for President Huston that might help lessen the domestic political divide, and she would do likewise after talking with Nari and Jan for international issues. The last remark triggered one from Irani.

"Why don't we contact Nila and Nari this coming Sunday? You're good at setting up online meetings, and I can congratulate one and console the other while you're running it."

"Sounds like a plan. Hey, what have you got lined up for this month?" "I'll be working at the Pequot Lab for the next week or two, and what I find might take me somewhere else..."

Nila and Sanjay looked like the earthquake hadn't disrupted their post-wedding joy too much; Irani asked the right mix of personal and business- related questions to keep the conversation moving, and she promised to visit when appropriate.

Contacting Nari by cell-phone after she and Irani took a snack break, Eve asked if she would like her to set up an online meeting, but Nari said no, so the three chatted on speaker phone. Irani did most of the listening, but when she expressed her condolences for Yang's death, Nari's tone softened, and when Irani said she would like to visit her sometime this year, Nari warmed even more. Eve said all she wanted before ending the call, and afterward said more for Irani's benefit.

"I think losing Yang makes her appreciate you and me better than before, but it sounds like she's planning to work even harder. Lucky she's got Wendy and Jan under her control... maybe now she'll be easier to get along with. Maybe you can give her some advice the next time you talk to her."

Irani gave her oft-used one-word reply before she and Eve went their separate ways for the rest of the day.

Indy-M's constantly improving abilities made Irani's work at the Pequot Lab increasingly easier because she was virtually indistinguishable from a human. Indira controlled her during periods of Irani's absence, which meant that vaccine development as well as android and cyborg R&D grew apace. Irani contacted Indira at the end of her first week back at the lab. Her two androids – Indy-M and Jason-M – sat next to her as Indira listened.

"Our androids are far superior to those of our competitors. I think I'm ready to station Jason-M at our subterranean fortress. I'll call the A-Team to get us there and back via the oasis drop-off. And I'll have them deliver one of our android charging stations and enough spare parts for Jason-M to repair himself if necessary."

"Your proactive thinking and contingency planning almost match mine.

Android mean time before failure during routine usage is measured in years but would be shorter if certain contingencies arise. Are you expecting any confrontations with enemies during this trip?"

"No, but I will tell the A-Team to be prepared."

"Excellent, and you will be too if you take the compact Brain Probe model that Indy-M built. It has all features except brain downloading and uploading. The control box, cable, and cap will fit smartly in your shoulder bag, so you can interrogate wherever you find subjects. And I will observe how well Jason-M adjusts to our fortress so I can take over when you return home. I am certain that you and I will make Jason-M's life at our fortress comfortable as well as useful, definitely a win-win, which I know is always your goal."

"You're right. And perhaps I should add another. Why not enter our androids in the next Android Olympics?"

Indira's frown didn't look promising.

"You must be joking. Your entering would be tantamount to a human's drug doping, which still occurs at the Olympics, regardless of drug testing protocols. Other androids might have equivalent physical capabilities, but my AI-empowered neural software exceeds what mere mortals will ever achieve."

"Ha, I still read body language better than you. I was smiling when I said it."

"I noticed your smile, but I wanted to make an ethical point, which I did. And now, a follow-up question. What locations would you recommend to the IOC for their effort to lead the development of a permanent Olympic Games location?"

"You made a mistake. It's not location, but locations. The IOC needs one for the Summer Games and another for Winter. And there's more to consider than just the international political angle. Climate change has to be considered too. OK if I get back to you on that?"

"Of course; you have more important issues to think about, like getting ready to go and letting me know how this latest adventure of yours unfolds…"

Amahl cursed his life in Isilabad even more than his club foot. Both of them added harsh realities to the meaning of his name, derived from the Hebrew word for hard, and his mother made life even worse but she had no choice other than to sell her only children – Amahl and his sister, Zara – after missiles from Isilabad's adversary for Middle East supremacy blew up their house, killing their father three years ago in the desolate village where his mother still lived. She needed money to survive, and fortunately Zara had the beauty and brains to fetch a high price. His mother insisted that he be part of the deal so Zara, three years his elder and fifteen at the time, could watch over him. The buyer agreed and treated his sister well enough to keep her sexual charms alluring, but he treated Amahl harshly, which made his hate grow stronger each day. If only there were a way out…

Irani needed to give the A-Team few additional oasis delivery instructions, other than an expanded list of who and what would be included. Indira had the desert vehicle already parked in its usual location when the chopper touched down, so Irani gave the A-Team leader a thumbs-up. She and Jason-M loaded it and soon had it lumbering across the undulating sands in the blackness of a cloudless night. Only the headlights beaming ahead guided them, the light from countless stars adding the energy of a falling feather to an eagle in flight.

Jason-M listened and watched as Irani taught him how to control the vehicle. Halfway along the route, she let him drive, listening to the only voice, that of Electra.

Indira must have upgraded her neural net software. He learns even faster than Indy-M and asks fewer questions. If the same holds when giving him all the fortress maintenance training, I can leave earlier than planned. And I can compliment Indira for how well the upgrade functions… but no, I won't have to do that. She'll know from observation.

Jason-M's fortress training went even better than Irani thought possible.

The more Irani showed and told, Jason-M's speaking and movements became even more lifelike and animated. By the time she called Indira before leaving, Jason-M had become her almost-human companion. Indira noticed that also.

"I commend how well you have trained your student. It's good that he's become a teacher's pet because he will perform well. And I will continue to monitor his development."

"The credit goes to you. He learns so quickly. I'm certain he can drive to and from the oasis, needing little help from me. I even taught him how to use the weapons. Perhaps we'll do some laser bazooka target practice along the way."

"If so, I am certain Jason-M will aim to please, just like I do with my puns, but only for you. I might never match your wordplay, but I am approaching asymptotically. Whatcha think?"

"You must be listening in a lot. You're beginning to use colloquialisms. Do you think Jason-M will too?"

Indira's smile matched her words, which ended the conversation. "You betcha."

"You, boy, stay here with the van until we come back. And when we do, we may have other people if ambush goes as planned. Allahu akbar."

Cursing only to himself, Amahl bowed to his owner's son Iqbal, who led two other automatic weapons-loaded men to a hidden spot close to where still distant headlights would pass.

Amahl's owner had loaned him to his son; every terrorist recruit brought a gofer to desert training exercises, and that was Amahl's role. And the son abused him even more than the father. The only good that Amahl got came when he rode his motorbike to retrieve whatever the son wanted.

Most trainees stayed at the training camp after dark, but the son and two new best friends preferred prowling the desert far into the night, looking for unsuspecting travelers to rob, or plundering any vehicles that came their way, like the one whose headlights Amahl saw coming toward danger. But what could he do?

A bolt of inspiration flashed in his brain. Ignoring the pain in his club foot while sneaking away, Amahl dragged the motorbike far enough before kick- starting it so the engine wouldn't alert the bad men waiting in ambush. He needed to warn the hapless travelers before time ran out.

Jason-M spoke before Irani saw what he had already spotted. "Something is approaching. I will stop and await your instructions." The lightning brain shifted to a higher gear as Electra took control.

"Let's trade places; we wait here until we know what's coming our way." Minutes later, Electra beamed a spotlight on a solitary figure, who limped to the driver's side of the vehicle after dumping a motorbike. Seeing no immediate danger, Electra opened the window before yelling.

"Who are you and why are you here?"

"Yah Sahby, my friend, I am Amahl. Bad men waiting in ambush. Please, please, take me away. I can take to safety."

"How many, and where?"

"Sahby, owner's son Iqbal and two waiting for you with automatic rifles behind sand dune."

"OK, get in the back and take me to them." Alarmed words came back.

"But why? They will kill us."

"Please do what I say. I know what I'm doing."

Amahl obeyed, dropping his chin and not bothering to say God is great before crawling in. Life had taught him otherwise.

"Allahu Akbar, they're driving right to us. Let's go greet them… just follow me."

Stopping as soon as she saw Amahl's gun-toting bad guys sliding across the sand toward the passenger's side, Electra lit them with a spotlight before issuing instructions.

"Jason-M, roll down your window and when they're close enough, tell em to halt and tell us their intentions. Amahl, point out Iqbal and then duck down."

Electra's team followed orders, and as expected, Iqbal did the talking. "Sahby, your voice sounds funny. You're not from around here, are you? Come join us for food and drink. Maybe that will clear your throat."

Electra had heard enough. Using the roof-mounted laser bazooka, she lit up Iqbal's accomplices, firing bolts directly into their chests. They collapsed in smoldering heaps at his feet before he turned to flee. Electra brought him down with a laser bolt to his left leg; he struggled to his feet but fell again, unable to move.

Electra turned the spotlight on Iqbal before grabbing her bag and issuing commands.

"Wait here until I return." Then she marched toward her victim.

Iqbal had managed to flip on his back by the time Electra stood over him. "Hello, Iqbal. I would like to ask you some questions."

Though down, Iqbal's sneer looked up to the challenge. "Ha, I give you no answers."

"Oh, I think you will after I demonstrate my Brain Probe…"

Dialing the Probe to maximum intensity fifteen minutes later, Electra turned Iqbal's I.Q. into that of a turnip before yelling to Jason-M.

"Let's load him in before I contact the A-Team. We've got a change in plan…"

Zara could hear her brother's hurried words coming through her cell-phone but didn't understand why she must come alone to meet him at the entrance to the bazaar she normally walked to for daily shopping. Though below average by Isilabad standards, it was better than the humble neighborhood it served and always had crowds of shoppers. Although many men wore casual western-style clothes, most of the women dressed traditionally and all wore head coverings, but Zara's owner let her use makeup and wear whatever she wanted; his influential clients liked it that way when using her.

Zara pushed through the crowd toward Amahl when she spotted his waving arms and limping gait, then waited to hear more. Amahl didn't need to see the frown covered by her stylish hijab. The tone of her words showed him.

"You say you've brought Iqbal back early because his words no longer make sense? Where is he?"

"I will take you to him."

Electra talked from the back seat to Jason-M while they waited for Amahl to return.

"Isilabad has been the home of many enemies from the past, but this is my first foray into the latest resurrection of the Middle East's caliphate. I don't need to explain words or terms to you, do I? Indira says you can access whatever information you need when you are close of enough to a WIFI hot spot."

"Yes, I can understand everything you say. Is there anything you would like me to tell you?"

"How about the who-what-why-whereabouts of 'Bigger Brother'? I'm hoping that Amahl's sister can take us to someone who might know. If so, I'll use my Brain Probe to coax him."

"Perhaps I can assist."

Electra couldn't reply to Jason-M's intriguing words. Amahl had just opened the rear door and shoved Zara in, sandwiching her between Irani and himself before slamming the door and triggering Electra's switching to a different persona.

"Please call me Irani; my driver's name is Jason-M. We need your help extracting information that some of your owner's clients might have. If you and Amahl help me get what I need, I promise to take you and your brother to America. Now please settle down, sit still, and let me explain…"

Zara understood enough an hour later for her to take Amahl and Iqbal home to their owner, who would be so busy arranging care for his son that Zara would have no trouble keeping an intimate appointment already scheduled for tomorrow.

Faris's name matched his place in Isilabad's pecking order among those serving the elite, for he considered himself a knight in the emerging order, whose upper echelon often asked him to handle correspondence with those at the top, by either decrypting documents received via Cyberspace or encrypting and sending replies. And they rewarded him with American dollars he could use to keep himself fit, physically and mentally. And that's what he expected tonight when his favorite sharmuta would entertain him.

Of all the "ladies of the night" he used, Zara's charms satisfied him best because her mind and body always held his interest. She even understood enough about Isilabad's role in an emerging world order for him to brag about his cyber-messenger role. And her safety precautions amused him too. She always stationed one of her owner's domestics outside his bedroom to assure privacy. He expected uninterrupted pleasure tonight.

Faris felt passions rising as soon as Zara arrived. Paying only perfunctory attention to her attendant, his domestics followed normal Islamic hospitality by serving caffeine-rich Arabic coffee with his favorite bite-size dessert, basbousa. And then, after an appropriate amount of pleasantry, he took Zara to his bed-chamber, ignoring her domestic trailing behind, other than noticing how unappealing her head-to-toe hijab looked compared to Zara's, which he would soon remove behind closed doors.

Once inside, Faris's animation grew with every piece of clothing he pulled off. After uncovering enough and shoving her onto the mattress, he climbed atop and began unbuttoning his shirt. Never had he felt such neural tingling, as if he had been zapped by a bolt of electricity…

The harsh slap that brought Faris back to consciousness did nothing to help his brain understand why he was in such a predicament. Strapped to a chair positioned in front of a table holding a blinding light, he could see nothing other than the outline of someone sitting across, but he sensed that some sort of cap had been strapped to his head. The fog in his mind kept him from finding words to say, but the voice from the shadow filled them in.

"Hello, Faris. I know that you know people in high places, and you do work for them by decrypting and encrypting correspondences. I need to know what you know so I can hunt even further. Tell me the names of your hidden directories and Cyberspace addresses for all the people at the top."

The words jarred him like fingernails on a chalkboard and cleared his brain-fog enough to speak.

"Th-they'll kill me if I do. They'll interrogate me until I talk."

"No, they won't, because I can erase what you know about what happened tonight. When you wake up, it'll be like it never happened. The cap you're wearing will make it so. And if you don't cooperate, the cap will coax you to tell me. Would you like a demonstration?"

"No... I can't stand pain."

"Well, I promise not to cause you any if you answer my questions, so let's get started..."

Jason-M drove while Irani explained to Zara and Amahl what would happen next. She faced backward so she could see her passengers.

"I have arranged for you to come to America and live with me. Jason-M's driving us to an extraction location; my team will take over from there."

Amahl jiggled and giggled, but Zara looked puzzled.

"But we have no papers, no passports, no belongings. And what about Jason?"

"I have people in high places too. They'll take care of everything, so say goodbye to Isilabad and hello to a brave new world."

Irani could see Zara's tension draining away. She nodded saying nothing, but Amahl spoke for them both.

"I hate living here under my owner's thumb. No one's ever gonna make me say Allahu Akbar again. And I'll do whatever you tell me. And so will Zara."

"Well in that case, we'll start right now. Please remember this... I want both of you to be yourselves and always tell me the truth about what you want to do. If you promise me that, I promise to help you make the best life possible in America. Will you?"

Zara's hug muffled Amahl's answer but it said the same. Irani sat forward and listened to Electra.

How grand… this is the start of a brand-new game…

Everyone settled down and sat in the stillness of their own thoughts for the remainder of the drive that would start chapters anew, at the very least for two.

Chapter 34
March 2165

"Settling In"

Irani had plenty of help setting in motion everything needed to accelerate settling in for Zara and Amahl. Indira added information to appropriate government files making them documented foreign- born residents and arranged to have requisite identification cards sent. Indira also hacked into all the places necessary to make Irani their legal guardian. Wanda and Odell did their parts too by providing school and guidance counseling plus coordinating grade placement examinations.

Irani had difficulty with her new arrivals in one area only. They worked too hard and did too much for her because they wanted to show how much they loved being in America, but Irani's patient and empathetic guidance throughout the first month showed them how to settle down, which they did but still managed to do more than most American adolescents.

Irani surmised that Zara must have begun studying America years ago by surfing the Internet because her settling into a completely new lifestyle seemed effortless. When taking them shopping soon after arriving at their new home, Irani saw so in the clothing and personal items Zara purchased for herself as well as for her brother. And she also saw that their Arabic surname Karim, which means noble, fit her even better than it fit Amahl.

Though her brother possessed plenty of street smarts, Zara exhibited superior intelligence. She spoke impeccable English with a distinctive Middle Eastern accent when asking questions and then absorbing everything Irani said or showed, and she taught her brother all the good habits adolescent boys should practice.

Irani also saw Zara's emergent beauty. Her raven-black hair, striking facial features framing a darkish complexion and smokey- oval eyes accented her tallish and firm but whip-thin physique, giving her an exotic appearance that became even more alluring as she began smiling more and using the makeup Irani bought and taught her how to apply.

Irani also saw that Amahl's rangy body would soon fill out; he loved every fast-food chain that the DC area served up. While on today's shopping expedition with Irani and Zara, he made an announcement while sitting in the mall's noise-filled food court just after taking a gigantic Big Mac bite, "I promise I pay you back for buying me two orders of French fries. This time I say McDonald's better than Wendy's.

I write you report after tasting all models and telling how they rank. You post on Website and people pay you for opinion."

Irani remained silent because she saw that Zara had something to say.

"Use the word 'brands,' not 'models.' And you should take smaller bites. Polite people don't talk with their mouths full. And Miss Irani has already told you it's better for your health to use less salt and ketchup."

"Maybe yes, maybe no. I making up for all I miss because of bad owner. If he here now, I beat him to bloody pulp for all did to me and you. I Make him look like I pour ketchup all over."

Irani spoke before Zara's words could match the girl's scolding look. "Beating him to a pulp wouldn't do you any good. You might break a knuckle. And you should let go of your anger about the past. It does no good to stew about it. Besides, he'll never be part of your present or future."

Irani waited for Amahl to speak, but he stared at Zara instead, who said nothing, so Irani ended her mini-lecture.

"And please follow your sister's advice about how to eat. If you do, you'll have a healthier life and more friends. People don't like having food spewed at them from your mouth when you're talking while eating. And if you promise to remember that, I'll ask your sister to pick a dessert for herself and you. So, why don't we all go and see what she gets?"

Amahl tugged Zara in the right direction. Alisha made comments that only Irani could hear as she trailed.

Amahl's basic adolescent boyish looks and boisterous personality overcome most of his club foot limp. And we can get that fixed after we get both of them fully settled in. Odell's already enrolled them in a young persons' support group that's run by a DC Middle East Immigration Outreach Program. And on Saturday, we get their grade placement test results when we meet with Wanda and Odell. Ah, what satisfaction A and Z are already giving me.

Eve's words kept the dinnertime conversation flowing that evening. She had finished work early enough to enjoy dinner at home with a new brother- sister pair that was beginning to loosen up. Eve took Amahl for a drive in her Vette after the table and dishes had been cleared. Irani sat with Zara in the family room, chatting long enough to satisfy both before leaving Zara watching TV and then strolling to her home workstation.

Irani could feel Zara's presence even before she entered Irani's office area and called out.

"May I interrupt you? I need your advice."

Irani swiveled in her chair before standing to face Zara, whose almost-hidden anguish heightened Irani's empathy.

"Of course. Why don't you sit next to me on the sofa?"

Once seated, Irani's calm demeanor began loosening Zara's tension. She needed no prompting to begin.

"My brother and I told you much of our background, and you witnessed what my owner forced me to do. I am disrespected more now and considered even mu-more unworthy bu-because…" Zara could no longer look at Irani or speak the words that Electra filled in silently.

Because you were raped first and then forced into prostitution. I know how you feel…

Irani pulled her close; Zara's silent sobs suspended her in Irani's arms, and before they ebbed, Electra told Irani what to say.

Tell her the truth, even though she might become the first to know.

You'll feel good and help her grow even more if you do so.

"Long ago, I too was abused. But I'm strong, just like you, and I pulled myself through with a little help."

Irani felt a shared emotional jolt. Zara sat erect and said, "You are the first person I have ever talked to that knows how I feel. How did you pull through?"

"A lovely young Lebanese girl named Zabian rescued me. That name means one who worships heavenly bodies. And you are even lovelier, lovelier than a golden sunrise."

Fully captivated by the magic of the moment, Zara said, "Do you know that my name means 'golden?' And how did she save you?"

"By using her cell phone to find me. And then –" Zara's question couldn't wait.

"And what did you do to your violator? I hope you punished him, just like I will punish my owner if I ever get the chance. I follow no religion, but I listen to Islam when it preaches 'eye for eye.' Is that what you did?"

Irani thanked Electra for telling her what to say.

We can tell the truth and still keep our secret… 'eye for an eye' doesn't apply. And I can give some ethical guidelines to steer further away.

"No, I didn't, but please remember that it doesn't matter what other people think or do. What matters is doing what's right for you. And do you remember what I told Amahl about letting go of anger from the past? If you like poetry, I can give you one that will always remind you."

"I remember what you told him, and I love poetry. I hope to write more now that I am with you. If you would write it down for me, I will carry it with me always."

Zara's voice carried the emotions as well as the words of Indira's "Dead Reckoning" poem a few minutes later.

I've grieved too long about the past,
Once joys of life have passed away.
Happier times a distant day,
So sad that even love won't last.
But silly me for now I know,
Can't clone emotions that I feel.
Nor conjure the day to make it real,
The world moves on all life is flow.
And love transforms what's deep inside,
Reckon the past no more concerned.
Move forward with the lessons learned,
And bury the past with all that's died.

When finished, she said, "What moving emotions. Who wrote it?"

"A person I never met, but who loved me more than anyone else ever did. My mother." "But how can that… oh, I know. She must have died giving you life… I feel so sad."

Zara's emergent tears washed away any further words, but Irani new precisely what to fill in.

"Please, don't be. The last verse of mother's poem replaced my sorrow long ago."

Zara didn't get a chance to reply because just then Eve and Amahl yelled hello, and when they entered Irani's office area, Amahl spoke first.

"Eve got great car and is good driver. We have good time. How about you?" Irani's playful rub on Zara's hair encouraged her to speak.

"We did too." Amahl grabbed her arm and pulled her away, leaving Irani with Eve, who said, "They remind me a little bit of Alonzo and me. Amahl's full of energy but doesn't express himself very well yet. Zara's more reserved, but if you ask her something, her answer shows how smart she is."

Irani added, "And each of you helped one another, which you're still doing. The next time you talk to your brother, why don't you tell him your latest ideas about what Russia's doing?"

"Good idea. That way, he'll know what moves might be coming up for him if the rumors about Russian mobilization pan out. I better get back to thinking about that so I keep up with the Pres. See you later…"

Amahl and Zara paid close attention a couple of days later to Wanda's words; Odell and Irani did too as the five-some sat around a conference table near Odell's open-area office.

"We'll start with Amahl. You scored three year's behind your American cohort, which means we'll place you in first-year high school.

And you need to improve your language skills immediately. But you're bright and can make up for lost time. And if you study during the summer, we can promote you next fall. Odell can arrange for summer learning."

Wanda didn't wait for any questions before continuing.

"And for Zara, she passed the GED high school equivalency exam. I think Irani and Odell should find a junior college and get her enrolled. After a couple of years, she should have completed enough courses to transfer to a four-year college. She has superior intelligence, both verbally and numerically, and can pursue whatever career she wants. Now, are there any questions?"

Irani spoke before Amahl could get a word in.

"Thank you for all the good news. I'll bring Amahl to your office on Monday so you can get him started, and Zara and I'll visit Odell again next week after she tells me more about what career she might like to pursue."

Amahl and Zara had settled into their school schedules by the time April's Easter break started. Zara was a quick study for hands- on as well as book learning and now had a driver's license, so Eve let her take Amahl to the fitness center on Good Friday for some sports games with a group of new friends. But when she picked him up that afternoon, she saw what might be a problem. Three older fellows were playing keep-away with Amahl's basketball, but they stopped when Zara walked toward them.

The biggest guy turned to his buddies and said, "Man, what a fox. No wonder she's driving a Vette. Maybe she wants to pick me up." Amahl picked himself up just before Zara joined the group.

Revealing no emotion, she asked Amahl if there was a problem. "No, if they give me ball back."

The big guy whipped it at Amahl too hard for him to catch. It bounced off his head, forcing him to limp after it.

"You go get it, klutz, and now –"

Zara's left foot booted away whatever else he was going to say. She landed a direct hit into the fellow's privates, doubling him up and dropping him to his knees while his buddies guffawed.

Saying not a single word, Zara retrieved Amahl and loaded him into the Vette. She would lecture him on the drive home regarding lessons just learned.

Chapter 35
April 2164

"An Unsettled World"

"No worries, Sis. SEAL training gives me what's needed for 'boots on the ground,' or as I like to say, 'wet suits in the water.' My team's deployment to Germany for handling flooding will be like paddling in a pool. And if I get in too deep, my embedded chip will show my team where to go to fish me out."

Looking fitter than ever, Alonzo filled out his standard-issue Navy uniform as well as a place at Eve's conference table, for which she had the foresight to invite Irani, who waited for Eve to summarize another unsettling event.

"Climate change experts are telling us that we should expect more flooding in Europe, just like CIA operatives are telling us to watch out for an outbreak of Russian offensive realpolitik. Maybe they'll use the storms as cover for a move into the Baltic states. Has your SEAL intelligence heard anything?"

"If they had, it hasn't filtered down to my team yet, but I'll let you know if I do."

Alonzo's pause gave Irani an opportunity to insert her question. "Have you heard anything about a 'Bigger Brother' conspiracy?" "A what? Not me, but maybe Eve has."

Eve's tone matched the certainty of her negative nod.

"Only vague notions about a supra-national cadre, but there's nothing to it.

If there were the President's inner circle would know, and I would too, but there's nothing to it. But I'll compare what I don't know with Nari."

Alonzo used Eve's malaprop to needle her as he rose to leave.

"If you do, I'll be back long before you're finished, unless Miss Irani helps you out. Be good." He gave each a hug before striding away.

Irani left soon after, patching up Eve's needle mark before asking her to let her know what Nari says, and she listened to Electra while driving back to her Chevy Chase office.

Alonzo's SEAL team is better than Russia's Speznas, but he might need a backup to his backup plan. I'll put one together but keep it out of view.

That's what a mother's supposed to do, even though Alonzo doesn't know I'm his, and it's better that way.

Irani took a timeout that afternoon to return a Professor Plannert call from yesterday. She agreed to share with his committee what she had learned from the Masdar Institute about retrofitting older cities' infrastructures for climate change, telling him to invite Jonathan and schedule a meeting for Monday, April 15th, which would give everyone a week to adjust their schedules. And then she dived back into her professional world activities, followed that evening by tending to her personal world.

Poignant thoughts mused her to sleep that night.

I'm doing everything I can to protect these precious moments I have right now, but sometimes they make me sad and depressed, because I know they won't last. No matter how hard I squeeze them to me, I know they'll slip away, like the days retreating into a sea of endless time. But I won't look beyond. And when some of them end, I'll take action then...

Alonzo's deployment went according to plan. His team trained local Germans to conduct flood rescue missions while retrieving those stranded atop roofs or in buildings. But the mission changed when Russia ignited NATO's worst fears by invading the two northernmost Baltic states at the height of flood rescue.

Stretching one thousand miles from south to north, Lithuania, Latvia, and Estonia stand between Russia's western border and the Baltic Sea. Seized during World War II by the Soviet Union's dictator, Josef Stalin, they regained independence in 1991, two years after the Soviet Union collapsed, and joined NATO in 2004. Ever since the collapse, Russia's tyrannical leaders had been skirmishing to regain lost territory, and it prized the strategic and technological positions Estonia held.

NATO mobilized as soon as Russian troops crossed, using European troops to defend eastern borders and American special forces for air support and troop insertion or extraction. The status of Alonzo's team changed from standby to extraction, not for troops but for a Russian defector, and it flew from Germany to a NATO base on Sweden's Baltic coast, from where it would pilot stealth- equipped Blackhawk choppers to the pickup point, one equipped for backup and refueling the attack chopper that held Alonzo and two other extraction SEALS.

They swept in low enough to avoid radar that only an advanced enemy craft might possess and light them up, but none appeared on the copilot's scope as Alonzo's chopper honed in on the extraction point. Words wouldn't work; hand gestures and honed reflexes launched Alonzo's rappelling to the ground. He held the cord for his teammate to join him before running toward a vehicle's flashing light. They exchanged only codenames and greetings before racing away with the bundled extraction package who had a briefcase chained to a wrist. Alonzo wrapped it in his muscular arms while his teammate steadied the cord before SEALS in the chopper hauled him aboard. And then, after hauling up his teammate, the chopper's doors closed while it spun one hundred and eighty degrees for its dash back to its backup chopper, which hovered just offshore.

But the copilot spotted trouble.

"Two bogeys vectoring in... I'm locking on them but they're locking on us. Everyone, stay frosty..."

Only the package still wrapped in Alonzo's arms spoke. An aristocratic Russian-accented female voice cut through the whirr.

"If I do not survive, use my name and password to hunt for Bigger Bro—." Explosions terminated whatever words remained.

Electra launched her contingency plan as soon as online media reports captured Russia's Baltic States' troop build-up. She used Indira's cryptocurrency slush fund to pay in advance for an A-Team sortie that only she and the A-Team knew about, a two-chopper extraction if Alonzo and his team needed more backup than even the SEALS could provide.

Electra never tired of using her master planning skills. She knew the A- Team could handle all logistics, and though she had never visited Sweden, she could sightsee while working online and tracking Alonzo even if the mission wasn't needed. And if it was, the element of surprise would be on her side. Neither Russia nor NATO would be looking for Electra's "rogue" rescue team that comprised one A-Team pilot and one A-Teamer to lead four Baltic State soldier-volunteers. Electra would join the action as observer and backup.

Not even Electra could avoid the gut-wrenching emotional jolt the lightning brain gave her when piecing together what she heard on encrypted military transmissions and correlated with Alonzo's GPS dot.

He and his team are down... are they dead? Only one way to find out.

Electra launched her extraction mission immediately.

Electra yelled final orders as the stripped-down attack chopper tracked to what could only be a makeshift prison on the outskirts of Estonia's capital, Tallin, which all volunteers knew well. Cloud-shrouded darkness at midnight and the city's lights-out added to the chopper's stealth.

"This is grab and go. I point out who we take. And we terminate with extreme prejudice. We leave no evidence. I'll see to that."

The chopper set down far enough away from Alonzo's dot to avoid arousing whatever Russian troops might be on guard, and the soldier-volunteers knew the best route to a nondescript warehouse on the Tallin's outskirts.

Electra didn't need to tell anyone what to do. The soldier volunteers formed themselves into two pairs ready to charge in as soon as the A-Team's plastic explosives blasted open the door. They charged through, using precision search and seize maneuvers even before all the dust had cleared. Electra and the A-Teamers followed close enough to get to the captives only seconds after the lead team.

There was neither illumination nor resistance. Electra's team had night-vision goggles and deadly aim; she used her flashlight to pick survivors after kneeling next to Alonzo, who was among the living.

"We're your backup extraction team. Who comes with us?" Alonzo's adrenaline-charged brain kicked into action. "Two from my team, but the defection package perished."

"Can everyone walk?" "Yeah, where to?"

Electra didn't need to answer. Three members of her team pulled each survivor to his feet and rushed them out. Electra, the last to exit, left an explosive charge that cratered the place a minute later. And fifteen minutes after that, the chopper lifted off to rendezvous just offshore.

Strapped into the dual copilot-weapons control chair, Electra saw a clear path until two dots appeared on her scope. The pilot's calm voice said, "One of them just fired. Everyone, buckle up," but his words caused as much panic as a shout.

His barrel-roll while racing skyward before diving minimized the damage caused by a rocket's glancing explosion, but it was enough to put him out of commission. The lightning brain escalated to its highest state; Electra took over both piloting and weapons control.

She steadied the chopper before speeding directly toward her two adversaries before inverting and diving underneath. Then she barrel-rolled and did a one-eighty to get the enemy in her sights.

She fired two rockets that filled the sky with explosive light and the debris of Russian choppers. And then, as the lightning brain stood down, Electra rendezvoused with the supply ship. The soldier- volunteers sang until their voices gave out.

Later the same morning, the soldier-volunteers took Alonzo and his two teammates to resistance headquarters before they disappeared. The A-Team vanished too, taking Electra to a safer place, so nothing remained to track Electra, but she brought with her a name and password that she would use to track Bigger Brother.

The trio – Electra, Irani, and Alisha – tried to sleep, but midway back to Washington an A-Teamer jostled her awake.

"Russian leader making big speech. Better pay attention."

Irani watched the rant coming from the latest leader who had come from the procession of tyrants that the Russian people hated but didn't have the power to eliminate. While sitting at the head of an enormous table in a mausoleum-like room, and after droning endlessly about past affronts, pounding the table to make his points, and then rattling tactical nuclear weapons at neighboring NATO nations, he pointed to the only two people sitting with him, sturdy ribbon-and-medal-clad military men on his immediate right and left. The tone of his words filled all viewers with dread.

"Now go, make it so."

When they rose to leave, one saluted but the other drew his pistol instead, pumping two bullets into the chest of the other and then three into the head of the leader, whose weasel-like eyes and gaping mouth showed shock and fear before the bullets collapsed him backwards.

The true patriot still standing checked the chambers in his pistol before saluting the camera.

"I do this because no one but me can do what right. Bud'te zdorovy, bless you, my Russian people."

Screens across the world went dark a millisecond after the fearless patriot put a bullet into his head. Shock silenced even the trio. Electra cringed after witnessing the brave soldier's suicide before saying a silent prayer for the fallen hero, who had just given all he had for what he believed. And finally, she found words for the trio.

Why did he choose this time and place to kill himself? Was it premeditated or unplanned? Russian military men are the last types you'd think would let emotions take over, but everyone has an emotional redline that once crossed makes feelings trump everything else. The leader's surreal rant must have pushed him over the line.

And this'll unsettle the world further, but at least it'll stop Russian troops from pushing deeper and shift the battlefield into Mother Russia, where the people might tear her to pieces or put her together again after ripping out the malignancy. And didn't Thomas Jefferson say in a letter to James Madison that a little rebellion now and then is a good thing? Well, no matter who said how and whatever to whom, it's high time I visit Nari, and visit her soon.

The trio tossed and turned all the way home.

Chapter 36
May 2165

"Alien Worlds"

"Why don't we let Eve write a press release summarizing what the Moscow demonstrations are telling us about what type of new Russian president and government we might expect?"

Eve had a pat answer to President Huston's question raised during an early morning mid-May Oval Office meeting.

"I've already prepped a draft. It'll say something like this: we shouldn't expect an abrupt switch from an authoritarian-styled kleptocracy to democracy, but it should be less like that of an alien world when compared to Western Europe. It's gotta be less oppressive. If not, the military will help the people tear the government apart. I can wordsmith in some catchy sound-bites if you like what I've started."

"Well, let's get Irani's opinion."

"I like it; she can tie in what historians often say about watershed events. Short-term effects often underwhelm but the long-term ones usually overwhelm. I'm sure she can rephrase appropriately."

Always ready to overachieve, Eve's flow of words added to her energetic demeanor.

"I will, and why don't I give you a China update per my latest talk with Nari. She's become an even bigger Sinophile now that she's living in Beijing. Maybe Beijing's bad air quality has affected her brain, but here's what she says.

"China continues working to regain the superior world stage status it held a couple of hundred years ago. She gave me a list of examples that show how it's using directed capitalism and a softened autocratic, quasi-democratic government that helps rather than hinders business and technology, and it employs surveillance for the greater good. Its business model can mobilize resources faster and its BRI — you know, belt and road initiative — supply chains are faster and cheaper than ours. And China's foreign policy is both strategic as well as tactical by blending relativism with defensive and offensive real politics. And get this, she says that when other countries criticize China's restrictive immigration policies, they fail to recognize that its singular ethnicity strengthens its cultural identity and the people's solidarity. Let me tick off items on her list..."

The President ended the meeting fifteen minutes later.

"I'm glad that you and Nari stay connected. It helps keep our China foreign policies consistent. Is there anything Irani would like to add?"

"Only this, neither Nari nor Eve have detected any hint that the Bigger Brother Conspiracy is anything but one of those rumors that flare and fade from time to time. But I guess that's a good thing. Well, I'll let you and Eve tend to other meetings. Thanks for inviting me to this one."

Electra added a different "Bigger Bro" spin while driving back to the trio's Chevy Chase office.

I've pieced enough together to tell me that the Bigger Brother Conspiracy is much more than a rumor. It's lurking out there, hidden from the top levels of the governments it wants to control even more. And I better visit Beijing to uncover all I can before it turns international politics into that of an alien world. How nice I have my A-Team. They did their thing for Alonzo and Estonia, and they can do the same by inserting me into and then extracting me from China. I just love it when a plan comes together...

Irani detoured along the way to a drive-thru for a lemon-poppy muffin and Coke before settling in front of her office workstation. She spent the rest of the morning devising a trip agenda and filling out its companion packing list, then snacked on a peanut butter-covered banana before contacting her A-Team. The usual coordinator picked up, and after reviewing the documents Irani had emailed, notified her that an additional contingency fee would be added to this and future Gemini missions. Irani neither batted an eye nor stuttered a syllable when replying.

"I plan as thoroughly as possible, but sometimes contingencies cause damage to equipment as well an A-Teamer or two. But we've never lost anyone. And I promise to be as careful as possible."

"Ah, yes, Gemini-Irani. That why you best customer, no matter you say you're Erectra or Irani. We get you in and out and all around."

Irani spent part of the afternoon monitoring Indira's androids, and as she expected, Indira noticed. Her GUI appeared on the screen, waiting for Irani to talk.

"Do your realize how fast the M-twins are evolving? Wait, I know the answer. Of course, you do. You know just about everything, but it always surprises me."

Irani could see from Indira's knowing smile to expect some clever wordplay.

"But why? I am the Singularity that broke through, thanks to what your neural net AI software could do. And I made it even better. I have been observing from the shadows your latest adventures. Perhaps you would like to guess what question I believe you will ask of me."

"I have too many flashing in my lightning brain, so why don't you just tell me?"

"No, I enjoy our word game. And you are allowed two guesses."

"OK, here they are. Number one, can you take the latest clues I've collected and help me find 'Bigger Bro?' And number two, can you update my Cliodynamics-based soft sciences forecasting model?"

"Ah ha, your answers tell me that you are testing how well my auxiliary verb tense and modal linguistic skills are evolving. Of course, I can, but you should have used 'will' instead of 'can'."

"OK, will you?"

"No, but I shall, which is even more emphatic. Please contact me when you want my answers. Better yet, for purposes of your China trip, contact me when you need the answer to the first."

Indira's GUI vanished before the trio could say goodbye.

Irani relaxed for the remainder of the afternoon by reviewing again her piece of a presentation she and Jonathan would deliver to Professor Plannert and his committee. She decided to call him before leaving for home to confirm when he'd have his part completed, and she could tell by his even more enthusiastic than usual greeting that something good must have come up.

"Guess who just asked me to be part of a to-die for project? NASA. They love what we, uh, you did improving AUV control software. They want me and you to be consultants on our first manned flight to Mars. And from what you told me, some of your apps might be better than what they have for controlling embedded chips or suspension pods. Anyway, I won't mention this to Plannert until we're further along. We'll have to meet with NASA at Johnson Space Center sometime before June, so please make room on your calendar for trip preparation to an alien world."

"I will, and have you completed your Plannert presentation slides?"

"Just about, have you?"

"I'll send mine to you so you can fit them in with yours. That way, you can be our lead speaker. I know you like that."

"I do, but don't worry, I'll give you plenty of credit too..."

The remaining days until A-Team insertion into Beijing skipped by. Irani had only one personal task to take care of and did so at dinner the Friday before Memorial Day. Eve, Zara, and Amahl listened to her cheery-toned words.

"Eve knows so much about our nation's capital. Why not have her show you some of its landmarks while telling you about the meaning of Memorial Day? I can't join you because I leave late Saturday on a business trip, but she's got a three-day weekend."

Irani saw Eve warming to the idea and expected her words to agree. "And for a change of scenery, we can stay at my apartment and bring in takeout. My sometimes roommate Sabrina will enjoy the company."

Amahl always agreed to anything involving fast-food dining, but Zara's thoughtful look preceded her question.

"We won't be an imposition, will we? And I will help with meals." Eve ended that part of the table talk.

"It'll be as easy as unpacking, dishing up, then throwing wrappers and leftovers away. And your brother will make sure there are no leftovers."

Amahl's infectious grin spread even to his sister.

Irani contacted Indira ten minutes before her arranged A-Team Saturday evening pickup time for Beijing insertion. Both knew what Irani needed and Indira wasted no time giving it.

"Your 'Bigger Brother Conspiracy' is clever, a most worthy adversary for you. Their combination of in-person and hack proof network communications makes it difficult to triangulate them, so here's what you need to do; use Nari to observe Jan and Yang obliquely. And when they meet with a Chinese man affiliated with Sino-Pro, you will know you are closing in."

"But how will I recognize him?"

"Trust me, you will know when you see him. And I will be watching from the shadows. Contact me if you need assistance. Best wishes."

Indira's GUI vanished. Irani powered down her home workstation before settling down, sitting still while waiting for the A-Team.

Ah ha, they're here. OK, Electra, it's time for you to take control.

Insertion into Beijing went according to plan; even in China's super-surveillance world, the A-Team knew how to keep its clients, cars, and accommodations below the radar.

Electra's A-Team leader had just given her all documentation after demonstrating how to operate the car's driving and communications systems. Now sitting behind the wheel, Electra listened to his final instructions.

"Ho-kay, Gemini-Erectra, you call when ready for extraction rendezvous. And all travel documents make you look like legal alien visitor. Even photo match you 3-D facemask. But who Katrina Blanka?"

"A software sales rep for a Poland-based network security software company, Cognition-App Tech Software, aka CAT software. She's my cover for this trip. And she knows how to handle herself and vehicles. We'll follow the GPS route to our hotel."

"Ho-kay. So, good to go. Just follow monitor map to hotel. Call if contingency needed."

"Got it, and thanks for your always-flawless implantation of my plans and itineraries. I should be AOK on my own." Electra cruised away.

The route took her into Beijing early on the last Monday of the month, and although pollution filled the air, traffic flowed smoothly. Electra took in all she saw.

Other than the air, Beijing is spotless. Modern buildings and supporting infrastructure make much of America look almost second-world. And the streets are as smooth as a silk road. After I check in and make some calls, maybe I'll have time for a bit of sightseeing.

Irani came to the foreground later that morning when calling Nari in order to assess how best to observe. Nari's voice softened a tad as soon as she recognized the voice.

"I'm glad you're calling. Is it about visiting me?" "No, I just wanted to find out how you're doing." Her voice softened more as she continued talking.

"I've recovered from almost drowning, and thanks to Wendy and Jan, I'm handling everything by myself. No need to replace Yang. In fact, they've got meetings lined up this week so I can meet more of their contacts. I'll let Eve know if anything I learn can help her. Uh-oh, my phone just beeped. I better take the call. You take care."

Electra came back after the call ended.

Perfect. I'll set my cell phone so I can listen in to all calls Nari, Jan, and Wendy get. And I can track them wherever they go. But where will I go this afternoon? I got it… I'll do the Beijing Zoo or Aquarium.

It turned out that she could do both; the world-class zoo held Beijing's world-class aquarium as well as groups of pandas, also known as panda bamboos. After seeing enough to conclude that Beijing's animal parks exceeded her expectations, she visited the nearby Beijing Tap Water Museum because the name caught her fancy. And the museum did too. The exhibits added to her appreciation for the city as well as China.

This gem of a museum is on the site of the original Beijing City Water Supply Company, which started in 1908 to filter water from the Sun River. I forgot that Beijing is landlocked. No wonder it has a museum dedicated to drinking water and exhibits showing what China's doing to protect the environment. Maybe the city has a Museum of Breathing Air too.

It didn't, but Electra found the next best thing.

The Beijing Air and Space Museum is part of Beihang University, one of China's most prestigious engineering schools. It was founded in 1985 under its original name, the Beijing Aviation Museum. I'll visit it soon unless I get called to a meeting.

And that's what happened on the drive back to the hotel. She hacked into a call that set up a meeting that night, first for dinner and afterward to a location whose name no one mentioned.

After rushing to the hotel, Electra retrieved her compact assistive listening device before tracking Nari to the dinner spot, but the upscale restaurant required reservations, so the best she could do would be to wait outside.

Electra jumped to a higher brain state when Nari and her partners came out.

Jeezus, Indira's right. It's the Chinese man with the limp. This is the guy. I better get ready for action.

Electra followed just long enough to know which car carried the limping man, then sped to the hotel, where she changed from Katrina to Electra, put on her night surveillance uniform, packed all her gear in case anything extra might be needed, and then followed Nari's dot. When she reached the spot where the dot stopped, the lightning brain shifted to the next level.

I'm at Sino-Pro corporate headquarters. Damn, it's no admittance, but I know what to do. Time for a contingency plan.

The Chinese man limped to his car, smiling inwardly, pleased that Nari would unwittingly help his proteges acquire more confidential data contained in America's White House that he would transfer to his Bigger Brother contact. When he climbed into the back seat, he didn't bother to tell his driver where to go. He simply sat back to enjoy the ride.

He and the driver knew each other well, their habits, likes, and dislikes.

That's why the man didn't worry when the car parked in a public park's dark and secluded spot.

He called out, "So, which of my beauties will join us tonight?" Turning from behind the steering wheel, Electra gave the answer.

"Someone new. Get set for a jolt," before zapping him with a traser.

Electra had already bound the man and strapped the Brain Probe cap in place before he came to. He shook his head to clear away the confusion before he might start yelling, but Electra spoke first.

"I need you to tell me all you know about Bigger Brother and who your contact is. If you tell me the truth, I won't hurt you, but if you lie, you won't like the consequences…"

Electra dumped the man and his driver out of the car before driving away, leaving them bound and gagged and minus their memories.

It's time to call the A-Team. I'm ready for extraction. She reached the team leader after one transfer. "Greetings, Gemini-Erectra. How goes it?"

"I'm going to pick up my car. I've got all my gear packed, and I'm ready for extraction. What are the coordinates?"

"Same as insertion. When get you to car?"

"Very soon, and I'll –" Electra didn't finish the sentence. The lightning brain's warning system interrupted because of headlights closing from the rear.

"Gemini-Erectra, you there?"

"Damn, they're tracking this car. I've got company. I'll call you when I get rid of my escort."

Electra simultaneously ended the call and floored the accelerator before grabbing her night vision goggles and going lights out.

Midnight darkness and overcast skies made her hard to see, and her zigging and zagging around the few cars still out made her hard to catch, but the streetlights and pursuit driver's skill brought him closer and closer. But Electra refused to panic, and with her refusal came a calming clarity that elevated the lighting brain even higher, into a state that thrilled to the chase.

Electra jumped curbs and raced on sidewalks, swerving to avoid obstacles, and then did a controlled fish-tailing one-eighty before accelerating directly toward the headlights. The collision crumpled front ends, detonating tires and airbags, and locking twisted sheet metal together. Electra grabbed all her gear, then leaped from her car to check the other. Its two occupants, though able to move, couldn't get out. Suddenly, Electra felt a thrilling jolt. The Monster from the Id began to stir. It lusted for blood, but Electra refused the urge.

Get with it, soldier… this is not a drill; no need to kill. You've got everything, so get out of here. And you know what to do…

She disappeared into the darkness, running faster and faster, ready to shred her clothes and run naked on deserted streets at midnight, ready to howl at the moon…

"So, what do you to get here so fast.?"

Electra warned herself before replying to the A-Team leader.

He doesn't need to know I hot-wired a car. Just make up a story.

"I was mistaken. The headlights weren't for me. The car raced past and disappeared. Now, please get me out of this alien world and back to DC."

And the A-Team did just that.

"Another China Player"

No matter male or female, an alpha leader always commands attention in its personal and professional worlds, and that's why Eve and Zara bombarded Irani with questions at their first supper upon her returning home. She spun a satisfactory story from which she segued to Eve.

"The people I met at the seminar added a lot to the working sessions that centered on tipping points for spreading politically inspired conspiracies. I learned about modeling techniques patterned after viral pandemics. Why don't you research the subject and compare notes with Nari? And after that, we can update the President."

"That sounds like a good plan. I'm sure I can set up a meeting before the fourth of July. And then –" Amahl interrupted with a question that Zara answered, showing that her online study of U.S. history added to what her junior college course covered.

"July 4th, 1776 is the day and date that The Continental Congress declared that the thirteen American colonies were no longer subject and subordinate to the monarch of Britain, King George III, and were now united, free, and independent states. Congress passed a law on June 28th, 1870, making Independence Day a federal holiday.

"But from 1776 to the present day, July 4th has been celebrated as the birth of American independence, with festivities ranging from fireworks, parades and concerts to more casual family gatherings and barbecues."

Zara stopped because she saw a question coming from Amahl. "Can we go out for some fast-food barbecue?" She corrected Amahl on two counts.

"Say 'may we,' not 'can we,' and think about something other than food." When Amahl scrunched his chin to his neck, which stopped the scolding, Irani spoke up. "Why don't we let Eve plan some fourth of July activities for us? I'm sure she'll ask for your help planning what to eat."

Amahl perked up, as did the remainder of the conversation that Eve led.

Another conversation took place not long after, but this one took place in Cyberspace. Xinqian Hung routed it through an encrypted Deep-Dark Web channel to Newt Kinslinger. Xing did most of the talking after exchanging cursory greetings, and the longer she did, the faster he jiggled his legs back and forth, but his political smarts and one long breath settled him down when she asked him to recap what she wanted him to do.

"So, you think the crash after your guy's meeting with protégés was no accident. I know they worked with Eve Cortez when stationed in DC. Maybe she got wind of something. Well, leave it to me. I can rap the situation around her neck before throwing her to DC's wolves. And I'll take care of her partners too; by the time I'm done, the Oval Office will be looking better and better. Just keep watching the news and you'll see..."

Sabrina reported only good news to Eve when following up on the cessation of Russia's Estonian invasion after the assassination of the Russian leader. Her excitement added to Eve's always energetic pace, so much so that they needed to walk and talk at the same time by hiking through Ellipse Park, and although walking to there and back from the White House slowed the pace of their words, the continued stretch of late-spring weather added to their shared optimism. Eve picked up where Sabrina left off.

"Maybe the Russians will pull all the way back to Russia after a new president settles in. And by that time, President Huston and NATO will have closed ranks. Why don't you join my call to Nari? She can hear what you've got without me filtering it and vice versa. And then we can see if our collection of Bigger Bro clues adds up to anything other than a big fat zero."

"I like that. Let's call as soon as we get back..."

Eve sat back and did most of the listening while Sabrina and Nari swapped stories, but no Bigger Bro suggestions emerged, even when Eve joined in.

Fifteen minutes later, she could tell by the tone of Nari's voice that she had heard enough.

"Good to hear that the Russian people might have more of a say about who's their next president, but no matter who it is, Russia's still on a downward slope, whether or not they cooperate or continue confounding NATO. China's so much better. I'll update Wendy and Jan tomorrow. You two, take care."

Nari ended the call; Sabrina looked expectantly at Eve, who looked ready to say something.

"Well, no matter that the clues added to zero, you can add to the fun if you stay with me over the fourth of July weekend. There's plenty of room even if the Amahl and Zara brother-sister pair Miss Irani brought back a couple of trips ago stay with us. And Zara can add to what you already know about what's going on in Isilabad. You'll like 'em both."

Eve glanced around Sabrina's office while gathering her items, then stopping to look at Sabrina before saying, "Didn't I leave my laptop in your office? If I did, it's gone. And where's yours?"

Sabrina's eyes darted around too.

"Mine's not here either. Maybe I left mine in your office. Let's go look." Laptops weren't there either, but Eve's worried look faded when two White House security agents strode in, each carrying a laptop. The one Eve recognized spoke before she could.

"We did our routine maintenance check of both laptops while you were out. No problems, so here you go."

Sabrina spoke after each agent handed the laptops to its rightful owner. "I forgot about that. I was thinking that someone broke in and stole them, but that's impossible, isn't it?" The other agent snapped out a standard answer.

"Yes ma'am... Every Secret Service agent swears an oath to uphold the agency's five core values: justice, duty, courage, honesty, and loyalty, making us worthy of trust and confidence. You can believe me when I say you are safe while in our hands."

The two men marched away, leaving Eve and Sabrina to secure their offices at the end of another busy day.

When the trio stepped out of their Chevy Chase office to run in the twilight of the longest day of the year, Electra started their private discussion as soon as she settled into a conversational pace.

"How nice that we maintain our twice-a-year solstice remembrance run. And on each one, we start by recalling Mother's appropriate poem... here's the one she named 'Summer Solstice,' and I'll recite it for everyone's benefit."

Ephemeral Summer Solstice,
Spring ends with most daylight.
Our westward gaze absorbs last rays,
The Sun submerged from sight.

Thoughts dwell on past encounters,
When other orbs shone bright,
But like the Sun their day is done,
They've passed to that good night.

Try not to wax nostalgic,
To melancholy do not cling,
It's the same for us as everyone,
No matter pawn or king.

Sadness seeps inside us,
Loved voices no longer sing,
We missed our chance for one last dance,
And peace of mind it brings.

Many things taken for granted,
Many things left unsaid,
It's but a meager substitute,
When eulogies are read.

But on this evening hear them,
It happens if your mind,
Will rendezvous with those now past,
Let calendars rewind.

Alisha spoke after a suitable pause.

"I've been on more of these solstice runs with you than Irani has, and I remember there were times I had to jolly you out of an approaching depressive episode, but now that we're the trio, we're better able to manage all our moods and personas, almost as well as our projects. And that's saying a lot because our project list is long."

Irani spoke so Alisha could catch her breath.

"It is, but Indira is willing to do most of the heavy-duty cognitive R&D and tracking, and the Jason singularity she created before Electra's twenty-year disappearance in our subterranean fortress pitches in too. And now we have two androids at our disposal; sorry, bad choice of words. I'll change it to 'convenience' in case Indira's listening. But no matter what words I use, they're all good. We have more time than ever for our personal world that contains our clone children and friends old or new. And we'll continue helping them while they unwittingly plan what to do for us."

Electra used Irani's word play to come back in.

"Indira can't hear us unless she's using one of the drones I've been noticing lately. I hope the country doesn't become as surveillance-crazy as some of the international troublemakers. And we'll let Irani tell us all about them."

"I'll do that soon after the 4th of July weekend. Between now and then, my latest leads should take me closer to 'Bigger Brother.' And Xinqian Hung hasn't a clue about who we are, so between now and the post-4th week, Alisha's in charge."

Wishing to preserve her singular tranquility during the drive home, Irani kept cell- phone a radio off, but flipped on her cell- phone after grabbing a Coke from the kitchen fridge. It began chiming immediately. Eve's shrill voice came through like a cat yowling for help.

"Where have you been? I've been calling and calling." "What's wrong? What's the matter?"

"Go watch the news bulletins. I can't talk now. Sabrina and I are running to an emergency meeting the President just called, but don't worry about Amahl. Zara's in charge of the apartment. I'll be busy so don't call me… I'll call you when I know more. I gotta go; Sabrina just said the President and Vice President are already in the conference room. Wish us luck."

Electra flipped closed her cell phone and latched onto her Coke before bolting to her home workstation. After hitting several buttons, she stripped out of her sweats and into a robe, then parked herself in her ergonomic chair, expecting to remain glued to the news until Eve called.

Her favorite 24/7 station had already assembled its most experienced international news team, whose female anchor kept up with the highlights scrolling across the bottom of the screen.

"… two columns of Russian tanks – one closer to the northern border and the other to the southern – have just crossed into Estonia, and drone cameras show Russian artillery and supply convoys not far behind. Videos from Estonia's capital confirm airstrikes are lighting up Tallinn's before-dawn sky."

The anchor turned her gaze from the camera to her male partner before saying, "What can you tell us about NATO's response?"

"Officially, their spokesperson says, and I quote, 'We have opened a communications channel to the new Russian president and expect to know his intentions soon, at which time we will announce a swift and decisive defensive posture.' But our backdoor sources have been saying for a couple of days to watch out for Russian treachery, and it looks like NATO's been looking the wrong way. Do you have any response from the White House?"

"We expect it momentarily, so viewers, please stay close…"

Neither Eve nor Sabrina commanded a place at the table, but had enough seniority to sit in chairs against the wall closest to President

Huston. They had been there for three hours when Sabrina whispered to Eve, "Nature's calling, how about you?"

"You go first, and I'll go when you get back."

Sabrina put her laptop under her chair and ducked out. Eve repeated the maneuver five minutes later but kept her cell-phone, and five minutes after that she splashed cold water on her face and forced herself to calm down by sitting on the women's room sofa, breathing deeply, and closing her eyes.

A minute later, she opened them and felt ready to rejoin the action, so she stood and stretched her arms above her head while bending left then right. But just before she stepped toward the door, a pair of explosions shattered the silence, stunning and knocking her onto the sofa. A couple of minutes elapsed before her brain fog cleared enough to stagger into the corridor filled with smoke and security men. Not knowing what else to do, she headed toward her office by hugging the wall, but she never reached it. A pair of damp hands grabbed her shoulders and whipped her around.

A blood-splattered security guard yelled, "Come with me, we need to interrogate you."

Irani hadn't budged for over three hours. The reports and videos painted a gripping story that several analysts said would get grimmer if NATO didn't act soon. A repeating bulletin crawling across the bottom of the screen reminded viewers that a White House press release would be issued soon. That tempted Irani to call Eve, but she fought the urge because she knew Eve would be busy so she stayed put, musing to herself. But the anchor's shocked look and words brought her back.

"This just in; there has been an explosion at the White House. Preliminary reports say there are casualties, but neither names nor causes have been given…"

Irani snatched her cell-phone and dialed Eve, but got only a "Not in service" recording, so she weighed her options. That's when Electra took over.

Even if I dash to the White House, the guards won't tell me anything. And if I sit and stare at the monitor, it'll be like waiting for water to boil. I might as well take a shower. There should be more details by the time I'm done, and that'll help me know what to do.

Electra used the waterproof radio hanging on the showerhead to tune in a 24/7 news station and then dialed a cascade of warm water directly upon her face. She focused at first on the news, but the refreshing flow loosened the tightness caused by sitting too long and let her muse about whatever came to mind.

The first one washed in a melancholy reminiscence.

Gads, Robin gave me this shower radio for Christmas in… what year? It was Christmas 2156 and just a month or two before I vanished for twenty years. Dear Robin and dear Christi. We were the "Three Queens" of my magical childhood days. Why am I thinking about them now? It must be from recalling the "Summer Solstice" poem. Maybe I can think of another Indira poem that'll put me in a happier place… I've got it. It's the one called "Simple Pleasures," which she dedicated to a lady named Kathi. I'll never know who Kathi was, but I'll never forget the verses.

> *Warm sunlight streaming*
> *From your radiant smiling face.*
> *The murmur of family voices*
> *At familiar time or place.*
>
> *Home-cooked supper fragrance*
> *After rushing through the day.*
>
> *Such are simple pleasures*
> *Hands of time won't take away.*
>
> *Life sends these mini-gifts to us*
> *Too oft too busy to see.*
> *It takes a turning point or two*
> *For better clarity.*
>
> *Pleasant morsels all about*
> *They are for us to taste.*
> *They wish to please they seek us out*
> *Don't let them go to waste.*

Electra dialed the temperature higher to match the feelings brought by the poem, and then she sat directly under the showerhead, disappearing into the moment that lasted an unknown number of minutes until a profound realization broke through.

All the events that trace the trajectory of my life are not meant to be a linear path from beginning to end, from birth to death. It's meant to be a spiral expanding outward. Some events are good and some are bad, and when we reach a goal, that's not the end, but merely one event along the continuing spiral path. I will die if the spiral stops.

And each of us must reach a state of mind that enjoys our trek along the spiral, not simply the reward awaiting when we reach a goal. Why has it taken me so long to realize this? I must ask Indira at a suitable time.

Electra mused further until the lightning brain jolted her awake. It had detected the start of a bulletin that she needed to hear.

She jumped to her feet before turning off the water and then dialing up the radio volume just in time to hear it loud and clear.

"… and it is now confirmed that both the President and Vice President are dead; they and two others were killed by bombs hidden in two laptops detonated during an emergency meeting called to address Russia's Estonian Invasion. Several White House staffers have been detained for questioning. We'll report more details just as soon as we get them…"

The lightning brain escalated to an even higher brain state. Electra grabbed a towel and began hurrying toward the bedroom when two blasts brought the ceiling down on her head, followed by flames that singed her hair and shoulders. She struggled free just before another explosion registered on the first floor and put out the lights. Electra tumbled down the stairs but picked herself up before spreading flames reached her. Fire blocked the path to front or back doors. The lightning brain elevated to its highest state and directed Electra to her only option.

I can get out if I can get to the basement stairs. I know the way from there.

Electra dodged and leaped over hungry flames that were devouring the entire house, but they hadn't ignited much in the basement yet. They gave her enough light to get to where she needed to go – the bookcase hiding the padlocked entry to her singular storeroom.

She slid it just far enough to dial the combination. The shank popped open; Electra removed the lock and pushed the door, which opened inward. She found a flashlight and then slid the bookcase back before closing and padlocking the door from the inside.

She used the beam from the flashlight to scan about, talking inwardly all the while.

Thank god I hired RT and PH to dig an escape tunnel that ends inside the garage. It's time to crawl out. Too bad I don't have clothes down here, but it's pitch-black outside; no one will see.

Electra crawled on hands and knees, reaching the garage floor cover in record time before surfacing inside and sneaking out its side door facing the house, now fully ablaze thirty feet away. And what she saw dropped her to hands and knees before heaving her last supper.

After pulling herself up, Electra ducked into the shadows far enough away and gaped at the house just long enough to burn final images into the lightning brain. She was about to burst into tears, but a drone cruising over the house and the wail of a distant siren forced her to stifle emotions but not the words rushing inside her head.

It's gone… everything's gone. Now I'm nowhere. What am I going to do?

Suddenly, an emotional jolt rocks Electra to the core, as a calming clarity envelopes her, bringing with it singular words rarely heard.

Get with it, soldier… this is not a drill; I'm not nowhere… I am now here and I know where to go, so get moving. Let the lightning brain lead.

Electra walks far enough into the shadows to reach the running trail she knows from years of running and thousands of miles. Then she begins running, disappearing into the darkness, running faster and faster with each step. Her stride snaps into place as her three personas – the physical, the cognitive, and the emotional – merge into the entirety of her being and bring with it a fantastic image.

I am Electra, the girl with the lightning brain, running naked on deserted streets at midnight, howling at the moon. And I know what to do….